HEAT
LIGHTNING

HEAT LIGHTNING

A Tinhorn Western

WILLIAM W. JOHNSTONE

and J.A. Johnstone

PINNACLE BOOKS
Kensington Publishing Corp.
www.kensingtonbooks.com

CHAPTER 1

Leonard Pope, secretary for Judge Franklyn Grant, looked up when he heard footsteps echoing in the back hall of the judge's law office in Wichita, Kansas. "Mr. Dunellen," he greeted the grim-looking Irishman. "Is Judge Grant expecting you?" If that was the case, Pope's boss had not mentioned it to him.

"No, I don't suppose that he is," Dunellen replied. "But I'm sure he'll want to hear what I've come to tell him. Is he in?"

"Yes, the judge is in, but he is working on a very busy schedule," Pope answered. "Is it important? Could it wait until tomorrow?" He knew for a fact that Grant did not like to be surprised by one of his agents.

"It's best I tell him today," Dunellen replied in his usual unemotional manner. "I'm leaving Wichita today, and I don't intend to come back."

"Oh," Pope responded, as he was taken quite by surprise. "Does the judge know you're planning to leave?"

"Damnit, man," Dunellen responded. "I told you I've come to tell him today, right now. I suggest you tell him I need to talk to him and let him decide if he wants to see me. But I'll not wait around here all day. I have to get started on a long trip."

"Wait here," Pope said at once. "I'll go and tell the judge you're here to see him." He got up from his desk and walked halfway back down the hall to enter the door to Grant's office.

Inside, he found the judge sitting at his desk, drinking a cup of coffee. "What is it, Leonard?" Grant asked patiently.

"Hate to bother you when you're having your coffee, sir, but that sinister Irish agent of yours is at my desk, and he's insisting that he has to tell you something. I told him you were very busy this morning, but he said he was leaving Wichita sometime today."

Grant was obviously not in a mood to discuss Dunellen's personal problems. Dunellen was well paid for his services, and it was one of the conditions of his employ, that his personal problems remain personal. It was risky enough that he came to this office when he was sent for. There was not much chance that anyone around Grant's office would recognize the Irish assassin, but Grant wasn't comfortable having him show up uninvited. The best thing to do, he decided, was to see what he wanted and get him out of his office. "Send him on back, Leonard. I'll see what's on his mind."

Pope left his office, and in a couple of minutes, Dunellen showed up in his doorway. "Ira," the judge greeted him. "Leonard tells me you need to see me about something. What's on your mind?"

"I came to let you know that I'm leaving Wichita today, and I didn't want to do it without telling you," Dunellen said.

"Where are you going?" Grant asked. "And how long are you going to be gone?"

"I'm going to Texas, down near Houston, and I'm not coming back," Dunellen stated frankly. "It's time I got into another business."

His declaration came as a complete surprise to the judge and was not welcome news at all. Dunellen was perfect in his role as an assassin. Tidy and efficient, most of his work passed for an accident. He was not an especially large man, but he was strong, with powerful hands. He would be hard to replace. "What are you going to do in Houston?" Grant asked. "Did someone offer you more money? Maybe I could afford to increase your pay, if that's your reason for leaving."

"No, that's not it a-tall," Dunellen replied. "I'm going into the cattle business."

"You what?" Grant couldn't believe what he heard. "You don't know anything about raising cattle."

"That's a fact, but I can learn. I have a cousin who has a cattle ranch north of Houston. I'm going into partnership with him. I'm buying into it with the money I've saved over the years working for you. I'm getting too old for the work I do for you. You need younger men. I'm going to be forty-two in a couple of months, and I can feel my body slowing down. I want to build something with the years I have left. I came to this country to make something I could be proud of. I'm not proud of being an assassin."

Judge Grant found it hard to argue with Dunellen's decision. Being honest with himself, he never suspected the cold, emotionless killer of having any thoughts about his future. But he had to agree with him. Had he waited a few years longer, he might not have been as efficient as he now was. "Very well, Ira," Grant said. "I think that you are the only person who knows when it is actually time to retire from your current line of work, and I respect your judgment on the matter. I'll tell you what," he went on, "to show my appreciation for the service you have performed for me, I am going to give you a hundred and fifty dollars to help pay for your trip. And I'll wish you the best of luck with your new adventure." He didn't confess it to Dunellen, but he hoped that parting gesture would inspire him to remain loyal to his vow of secrecy in the future. Maybe there was no need to worry, since he said he was going all the way down to Houston, Texas. At any rate, one hundred fifty was cheaper than what it would cost him to send someone that far to silence him in the event it became necessary. He got up from his desk and walked to his office door with him and shook his hand. And Dunellen walked out of his life, holding the hundred and fifty in his hand. He would add it to the small fortune he had amassed over the years he worked for Judge Grant, killing and robbing. Living like a monk in a monastery, saving every cent he could in preparation for this day, he was ready to build the empire he envisioned.

That was a little over two years ago, and yet Ira Dunellen remembered that morning in the town of Wichita as if it had happened only two days ago. He had no ambitions to establish himself as the head of a hardworking Irish family, so he had been easily swayed to the easy money on the wrong side of the law. At first, he was content to get by with a share of the money from a train robbery, or a stage holdup, and the occasional bank robbery. Because he was strong and tough and had no conscience, he was soon recommended to Judge Franklyn Grant to handle the elimination of roadblocks in the judge's plan of conquests. The first year he filled the role of assassin, he was contacted by someone who was nameless, and he didn't even know who he was working for. In time, he was so dependable that he was eventually allowed to report directly to the judge for his assignments.

As he had told Grant on that morning when he notified

him that he was leaving his service, he was growing tired as he grew older. What he had not told Grant, however, was that he was tired of playing the role of assassin *for him*. He wanted to control the money from a position of power, and have some underlings play the role of peon to him. He saw only one possible path to gaining a position of power. It was the only one open to him, and that was through his cousin, Conan Daugherty, who had come to this country on the same boat as he. But Conan chose a different path to travel, opposite the one that Ira was drawn to. Conan was drawn to the cattle country of Texas. And during the years that Ira was rising to the top of the world of robbery and death, Conan was working to settle his own piece of land and become one of the many small ranchers in that part of Texas. In the process, Conan had also married and started a family. Thinking about it now, Dunellen had to laugh when he thought of Conan's reaction when he showed up on his doorstep one spring day. He let his mind replay the scene.

He pulled his horse to a stop at the edge of the creek and let the black Morgan gelding drink while he studied the small house on the other side with two small children playing in the front yard. "Not very grand," he muttered as he took in the barn and outbuildings behind the house. "Not very grand indeed," he pronounced, disappointed to find that Conan had not done better for himself. He rode on across the creek, leading his packhorse behind him.

When he rode up and stopped in front of the steps, Arleen Daugherty stepped out on the porch. "Can I help you, sir?"

"Yes, maybe you can," Dunellen answered. "I've been looking for the home of Conan Daugherty. Some farmers I passed back on the road told me it was the house by the creek with the pretty lady and the two little tykes."

"Well, I doubt that," Arleen replied, "but this is the Daugherty ranch. Why are you looking for my husband?"

"Because I'm his cousin, Ira, and I haven't seen him since we got off the boat here in this country."

She smiled then, although she was not overjoyed to have a grown man show up unannounced, and uninvited. "Oh, well," she managed, "then you'll wanna ride straight out behind the barn. That path will lead you to the pasture where Conan's haying. He'll be excited to see you."

"I'll leave my packhorse in your corral there, then I'll see if I can find Conan." He tipped his hat and wheeled the Morgan around to head for the barn while she hurried back into the house to see if she could find enough to cook. Ira unloaded his packhorse and turned it out into the small corral. He put his packs in the barn, then climbed back on his horse and followed the path behind the barn. *It's a damn good thing I got here*, he thought, *because it looks like Conan isn't doing very well*. He rode only a little farther before he saw his cousin cutting hay and piling it in a wagon. "If that ain't the damnedest . . ." he uttered when he saw him. He didn't come all the way to Texas to work in a field like that. He planned to have a crew of men to do those jobs. It was obvious that Conan was going to need a dose of ambition.

He rode his horse right up behind him before Conan was aware he was there. "I swear, Cousin, can't you hire anybody to do that?"

Conan jumped, startled. When he managed to turn around, he stood lost for a moment before he realized who it was. "Ira!" Conan exclaimed. "You gave me a start. If you ain't a sight for sore eyes! Whaddaya doin' here?"

"I came down here to see how bad you're doin', and I have to believe you're doin' pretty damn bad."

"Whaddaya talkin' about?" Conan responded. "I'm doin' pretty doggoned good. I've got three hundred and fifty acres, with a house and a barn, and right now I've got three hundred head of cattle. Did you meet Arleen?"

"Yeah, she told me where you were. You've got three hundred head of cattle? Three hundred ain't enough to fool with. Whaddaya gonna do with 'em?"

"Come spring, I'll drive 'em to the railhead up in Kansas," Conan answered.

"You're gonna drive three hundred cows all the way to Wichita or Abilene?"

"Well, not by myself," Conan replied. "There's several of us small ranchers that'll drive our cows in with the Rocking-C Ranch. They'll have over two thousand cows, and we'll help them drive the whole herd. I did that last spring when I didn't have but two hundred head."

"Well, all that small thinking is over," Ira told him. "I came down here to put you in the cattle business. In the first place, we need cattle, so this winter we're gonna build a herd. And we need a crew to do that."

"Wait a minute, Ira. What are you talkin' about? I don't have the money to do what you're talkin' about." He was surprised by Dunellen's sudden arrival and baffled by his cousin's remarks about what he needed and what they were going to do to increase his production.

"Do you think I'd come all the way down here to partner up with you without some money to pay my way in?" Dunellen insisted. "I brought a little money to get us started, and it's the best time of the year to hire a crew. There'll be a lot of cowhands ridin' the grub line this winter. We can pick up all we need just by giving them three meals a day, plus enough money for tobacco and a drink of likker."

"I don't know, Ira." Conan hesitated, not at all sure that his cousin knew what he was talking about. "I'm pretty satisfied with the progress I've made here on this place. I'm supportin' my family and steadily growin'. I ain't got enough work for any extra men."

"Don't worry about that. There'll be plenty of work for them to do. I'll take care of that." *This is going to be harder than I thought,* Dunellen told himself. *He has no vision beyond what's for supper.* He considered calling it off and going someplace else to build his cattle empire. But he decided it was best to stick with his original plan because Conan already had a nucleus of three hundred cows, and it would be easier to build a herd around them. He had hoped that Conan had more than three hundred, but he was not surprised, now that he had seen the progress that his cousin seemed satisfied with.

And that was the start of the Cloverleaf Cattle Company. Dunellen had to smile when he thought about it now. The look of astonishment on Arleen's face when Conan told her that his cousin was a permanent guest was enough to cause a chuckle when looking back on it. He could still sometimes hear them arguing about it in their bedroom at night, especially about the kind of men he had hired. But the fact they could not deny was the sudden growth of the cattle herd after a midnight raid in Mexico. The herd continued to grow over that first winter, while most of the smaller ranches lost cattle. It finally became too much for Conan to handle when Dunellen insisted they had to leave his little ranch and move their cattle north to more open pasture. Conan was obviously reluctant to think about pulling up stakes and moving. And that was the status of the partnership at the present, which found Dunellen waiting at the chuckwagon for his cousin to join him. Instead of eating with the crew, they planned to ride back to the house for supper.

"I thought for a minute you mighta rode back to the house without me," Dunellen said when Conan finally showed up.

Conan said, though, "I had some trouble getting a little bunch of cows out of a gully on the other side of the creek. You ready to go?"

"Yep, I'm ready." He got on his horse and followed Conan out of the camp. When they were out of sight of the camp, Conan pulled his horse to a stop and waited for Dunellen to catch up. "What's the matter?" Ira asked.

"I need to talk to you before we go home," Conan said. "And I'd just as soon Arleen didn't hear the conversation."

"All right," Dunellen said, "let's talk." He climbed down from his horse, expecting to hear more bellyaching about the way they were going about building a herd. "What is it that's bothering you? The stolen Mexican cattle, the ones we cut out from some of the other ranches? What is it?" He dropped his horse's reins on the ground and walked over to sit down on a large tree that had evidently been struck by lightning.

Conan stepped down from the saddle and walked over to sit down beside him. "Ira," he began, "you're my cousin and I want you to be successful in anything you wanna do. And it's been all your money that's made it possible to hire cowhands to build our herd. I'm pleased with our foreman, but I've gotta be honest with you. I'm not comfortable with most of the other men you've hired. They seem better suited to rustlin' cattle than tendin' 'em."

"We need men like that sometimes," Ira insisted. "And let me remind you, I went along with your recommendations, and we hired Lucas Sawyer as our foreman because of his knowledge of tendin' cattle and movin' the herd.

So far, he hasn't done a bad job teachin' some of my rustlers to take care of the cattle they steal. Right?"

"Rustlin' cattle in Mexico doesn't bother me much," Conan said. "Although I wish we didn't have to do that. But some of the men are pickin' up strays from some of my neighbors' herds."

"That's because I told them to," Ira replied. "Now that we're fixing to move our herd north to better grazing, they're not your neighbors anymore, and they can recover."

"There's another thing that ain't settin' right with me, givin' up my homestead and movin' north of here. This is where my family is bein' raised." He saw the impatient look on Ira's face, so he made himself say what he wanted to say. "I think it would be best if we split our partnership, and you take your half of the herd and go north with it. And I'll stay here."

And make sure you return every brand that ain't yours, Ira thought, disgusted. He was long past his gentle patience with his cousin, but he decided he'd make one more try. "Conan, we've just got a good start on building a herd that can make us some money before long. And you and Arleen and the little ones wouldn't have to live in that shack any longer. We're heading where the big operators work."

"All the same to you, Ira, I'll just stay with the small ranchers, but I wish you luck with your plans to be one of the big operators."

"Sorry you feel that way," Dunellen said. "Are you absolutely sure?"

"I am," Conan answered.

"I guess that's the difference between you and me," Ira said. "I make my own luck." He got up from the tree trunk and extended his hand. Conan grasped it, prepared to shake, but was startled when Ira clamped down on his hand and jerked him up from the trunk to be caught by the throat by Ira's other hand. With hands still powerful, Ira clamped down on Conan's throat, crushing it while meeting his cousin's panic-stricken stare with the cool steel of his own, ignoring the dying man's frantic struggling. Finally, Conan's body went limp, and Ira released him, letting his body drop back across the tree trunk. "I've really had no place for you in my plans, but I need all the cattle, not just half. It was just a question of when." He picked up Conan's body and lay it across his saddle, then stepped up onto the big Morgan and started for the house, leading his cousin's horse.

CHAPTER 2

Arleen saw them when Dunellen passed the kitchen window on his way around to the front of the house. She screamed when she saw her husband lying across his saddle, and she ran to the front door to meet them. "Conan, Conan," she repeated over and over as she ran to him.

"He's dead," Dunellen said.

"No! No!" She sobbed uncontrollably while she tried to lift up his head to kiss his face. "He can't be dead! God, please!"

"I'm afraid he's dead," Dunellen said. "There's nothing you can do about it. His horse stumbled over a gully, and he took a fall. Looks like he broke his neck, so I brought him home to bury him." She collapsed to sit down on the ground, sobbing. "These things happen when we don't expect 'em," he continued. "Only thing you can do is get up and keep on going. I'll go bury him behind the barn, and then we'll go eat supper." If she heard him, she made no response as he turned the Morgan and led Conan's horse toward the barn.

After he took care of the horses, he got a shovel and went back to the spot where he had dumped the body, a spot where the ground looked soft. Then he dug a grave just deep enough to fully cover the body and dragged Conan into it, then filled it with dirt. When he was finished, he went back to the house to find Arleen sitting in the middle of the front-room floor. She was holding Angus and Brendan close to her. He looked at her for a few seconds before he said, "I put him in a nice grave. Here are some things he was carryin' in his pockets I thought you might want—a pocketknife, some matches, and a watch. I didn't figure you'd want his gun and holster, so I left it with his saddle." She made no response, so he placed them on the side table. "We were heading home for supper when he took that fall. Don't reckon you threw the food out, did you?" When there was still no response from her, he said, "I'll just go take a look in the kitchen to see if you started anything. The living have to go on eating."

He went into the kitchen and found that she had anticipated their arrival for supper, and there were some beans and potatoes warming on the edge of the stove. There were biscuits in the oven that were on the verge of burning up, so he pulled them out. The coffeepot was sitting on the table, so he looked in it and found there was water and coffee in it, ready to be put on the stove. So he put it on to boil. "No meat," he said, "but enough other stuff to get by on." He dished up a plate and sat down at the table to eat. Shortly after the coffeepot started bubbling, she came into the kitchen, her two youngsters, Angus and Brendan, in tow.

"Where did you bury Conan?" she asked.

"Put him in a nice spot back of the barn," he answered. "Were you gonna cook some kind of meat for supper?"

She ignored his question. "My sons and I are goin' to go say goodbye to their daddy," she said, and started crying again.

"I know things are lookin' kinda bad right now," he told her as he put some molasses on a biscuit, "but you ain't necessarily at the end of the road. You ain't a bad-lookin' woman, and I might need a woman myself. I'm gonna be movin' the cattle a ways north tomorrow or the next day. You can go with me."

His suggestion stopped her cold, and she couldn't speak for several long seconds, scarcely able to believe this was happening. "Are you insane?" she demanded. "My husband just buried not fifteen minutes ago and you're asking me to marry you? If you hadn't shown up here uninvited, my husband would still be alive. And you think I'd marry you?"

"Well, I never said anything about marryin' you. I just said I could use a woman to cook and keep my bed warm at night. It's too bad about Conan, but that ain't no call for a woman your age to dry up and die."

"Your answer is no!" she cried out. "And I expect you to be out of my house when I come back from my husband's grave. Come, boys," she said. "You must say goodbye to your father." She picked up a shotgun that was standing in a corner by the kitchen door.

"Best not come back too soon then, 'cause I'm gonna finish eatin' supper before I go anywhere. It ain't fair to blame Conan's death on me anyway. Hell, blame it on the horse that threw him. I know he was your husband, but he was my cousin, and I've known him a lot longer than you have. I'm a little older than Conan, but we used to play together back in Ireland when he was a little fellow, like Brendan there. I think he would want me to take care of you, now that he's gone."

"Out! By the time I get back!" she insisted and went out the back door, carrying the shotgun and ushering Angus and Brendan ahead of her.

* * *

Conan's grave was not hard to find. The "nice" spot that Ira said he picked was the closest spot to the barn that wasn't packed hard by the horses and cows. The shovel was on the ground beside the grave, a sign of Ira's careless concern about the burial. The mound over the grave was not very big, giving her the impression that Conan wasn't buried very deep, and might therefore be subject to violation by an animal. So she decided to disinter his body and give him a proper burial. She had been given no time to say goodbye, and she wanted very much to do so. With that thought in mind, she took the shovel and started shoveling the dirt away. As she suspected, she did not have to go very far before she saw his clothes through the loose dirt. She carefully uncovered his body as the tears began again, but she was determined to make a better grave for him. When all the dirt was away, she found him lying in a grave that held his body only inches below the sides of the excavation.

It was a struggle, but she was determined to pull his body out of the shallow grave, and with six-year-old Angus trying to help, she finally accomplished it. Then she posted Angus at a corner of the barn with instructions to alert her if Ira came out of the house and came toward the barn. After carefully cleaning the dirt away from Conan's face, she held him and kissed his cold cheeks. She noticed the odd bruising around his neck and realized there were no other marks of injury. It occurred to her later that there were a couple of fresh scratches on Ira's face, while there were none on Conan's. It seemed to her that there would be other signs of a broken neck, as well as cuts and scrapes, if Conan had been thrown from his horse. At this critical moment, however, she was too emotional over the loss of her husband to think straight. Most important to her now was the matter of digging a deeper grave to give Conan a safer resting place. And as soon as she accomplished that, she must be concerned with the safety of her children.

She worked with the shovel for the best part of an hour before she finally decided the grave was deep enough. Then she pulled Conan over to the edge of the grave and tried to roll him slowly over the side in an attempt to land his body faceup. The body, stiff with rigor mortis by then, rolled more like a log, however, and ended up on its side. There was nothing she could do to move it, so she gave him a tearful apology, professed her undying love for him, then covered him up. The decision to be made next was what to do about the insane man in her house.

She had ordered him out, and she suspected that he planned to defy her. To this point, it appeared she was right. For Angus had watched the house while she was working on the grave, and there had been no sign of Ira Dunellen outside it. In her time of crisis, it hadn't even occurred to her that his horses were in the barn, and he would have come to get them if he was going to leave. What to do? She didn't know. And she was very much afraid of him at this point, for her and her children. Her closest neighbors were Jim and Dinah Nash and their three children. Their house was two miles down the road, so she decided to go there. While Angus still watched the house, Arleen put the bridle on her mare but didn't bother with the saddle. She climbed on the little mare she had named Sweet Pea. Then she reached down, and Angus lifted Brendan up to her. Angus scrambled up behind his mother, and they rode out of the barnyard and onto the road. It was quite late by then, but Arleen knew Jim and Dinah would welcome them.

Back at the house, Ira was beginning to wonder why Arleen had not returned. She had made the mistake of ordering him out of her house, and he was eager to demonstrate what happened to anyone who gave him ultimatums. To further intimidate her, he had stretched out on her bed to let her know he did whatever pleased him. He had begun to get impatient, however, wondering how long she needed to say goodbye to Cousin Conan. Then it occurred to him that she might have decided to sleep in the barn that night. He let that thought simmer in his brain for a while until he had to go and find out. So he got up from the bed and walked out the front door. Very much aware of the shotgun she took with her, he decided to go out the front and walk around the house to approach the barn from the side. That way it would be harder for her to spot him coming until he was right at the barn door.

It was a dark, moonless night, which was in his favor. With no sign of anyone around the barn door, or the corral, he slipped up to the door and paused there to listen for sounds from the children. But there were no sounds. Asleep already? It didn't seem likely. He decided they were not in the barn, so he walked on inside. Remembering there was a lantern hanging on a nail near the front door, he went back and found it. When he lit it, he could see almost all of the small barn, but he walked to all the corners anyway. Either they knew a real good place to hide, or they weren't there. It was pretty obvious that they were not there. Surely they hadn't left the place.

To be certain, he kept the lantern and went to check the smokehouse and the outhouse. Then he wondered if they had sneaked back inside the house while he was looking in every nook and cranny outside. *Maybe she's in the house and gone to bed*, he thought. *And she thinks I'm sleeping in the barn, like I always have. Ain't she gonna be surprised when I jump in the bed with her?* Then he remembered the shotgun she was carrying and decided a bit more caution might be best. With that in mind, he drew his six-gun from his holster, then, moving as quietly as he could manage, stepped up to the back door and tried the knob. It opened easily, which caused him to become even more wary. He tiptoed through the kitchen to the bedroom, only to find the door open and no one there. *She took off*, he thought.

Just as well, he thought. *I don't feel like wrestling with a young woman tonight anyway.* To be sure, however, he went into the front room to make sure she was not there. Then he slid the bolts on the front and back doors and crawled into the bed. In no time at all, he was asleep, and he didn't awaken until sunup the next morning. There was still no sign of Arleen and the children, which was just as well with him. He built a fire in the kitchen stove and filled the coffeepot with fresh water. For breakfast, he ate a couple of cold biscuits from the night before. Satisfied then with the way the prior day and evening had gone, he went to the barn and saddled the Morgan gelding and loaded the packhorse. It was time he moved his herd to new pastures, unhindered now by his reluctant partner and cousin.

She watched the house from a low ridge approximately one hundred yards from her front yard, waiting to see if he had left early or not. She decided that surely he would have gone to be with his crew before now. So she got up from the bush she was watching from, then immediately knelt down again when he walked out the back door. She remained there until after he went into the barn and came out again a little later, riding the Morgan and leading the packhorse. Still, she did not move until he disappeared from her sight following the path behind the barn. With her shotgun in hand, she went back to the other side of the ridge and got on the mare. She had left Angus and Brendan with Dinah Nash, so she knew that her children were safe. She rode Sweet Pea up to her front porch and hopped down. When she tried her front door, she found that it was locked. Not sure if that was good or bad, she went around to the back door and was relieved to find it was not locked. Going inside, she held her shotgun ready to fire, even though she had seen him ride out of sight.

When she went into her kitchen, she could see where he had made himself some coffee and eaten the cold biscuits. Then she went into the bedroom and was sickened by the obvious signs that he had slept there. The dirt on the quilt was evidence that he hadn't bothered to take off his boots. She had an overpowering urge to thoroughly clean her house, but she wasn't going to touch it until she was positive that he was gone for good. With that thought, she went back out the back door and marched to the barn. Inside the barn, she went to the small tack room where Ira had slept since he had arrived. She was gratified to see that he had taken his bedroll and all his other things with him this morning. "Good," she uttered, "he's not coming back." Even so, she was not going to bring her children back until she was sure. She knew she could not stay there, now that Conan was gone. She could not support them. The only option she had was to return home to live with her father. After her mother succumbed to a bout of pneumonia and passed away, her father was left a widower with a young son, Arleen's younger brother. In the last letter she received from her father, he said that he had taken the job as postmaster in a little town called Tinhorn. So he and Jimmy were leaving the old home and starting out somewhere new. Arleen had no idea where Tinhorn was, but she thought that her father and Jimmy could use a woman's touch in their new home. And maybe Angus and Brendan could benefit by having an Uncle Jimmy. She decided it best to write her father and tell him of Conan's death and her intention to bring her sons to Tinhorn to live with him, if he agreed. Jim and Dinah welcomed her and the children to stay with them, if it was necessary, until she made arrangements with her father to make the trip to Tinhorn.

CHAPTER 3

Had Arleen known what was on Ira Dunellen's mind, she would have had no fear at all of staying in her home. Dunellen had no reason, nor desire, to return to her simple little house beside the creek. He was ready to move his entire herd north to more ample pastures, and he planned to increase the number of cows he owned as he drove his herd over several counties. The cowhands he had hired were well-suited to his methods of increasing his stock and he wasted no time in getting underway. None in his crew of riders openly questioned the sudden death of Conan Daugherty.

He drove his cattle northeast in search of the ultimate location for the headquarters he planned to build, where there were greater areas of grazing potential and no opposition from small farms or ranches. With the intention to abandon his lawless activity in the building of his herd, he began to hire more cowhands who knew how to raise cattle and rid his payroll of some of those who were little more than outlaws. He had a very capable foreman in Lucas Sawyer, who was experienced in construction as well as managing a cattle ranch. He was well-qualified to oversee the building of Dunellen's new headquarters, as well as tending a herd of cattle the size of the one he now owned.

He scouted the land that was Anderson and Cherokee counties with one of the older hands he had hired. Jack Spade said he had hunted in that area before and was somewhat familiar with it. There was good water from a couple of rivers, and the homesteaders had not ventured into it as yet. "This is the spot, right here," Dunellen exclaimed when they reached a healthy, flowing creek running through a natural pasture.

"Yes, sir," Jack replied. "This'ud be a good'un all right. It's been a while since I rode through here, but if I recollect, it ain't very far down this creek to the Neches River. You might wanna take a look and see if you druther build it on the river."

"We'll take a look," Dunellen said, although he was satisfied the location by the creek was what he wanted. They followed the creek for three miles before they reached the river. Dunellen didn't have to take a close look. He made his decision at once. "No, the first place by the creek is better. That's where I want the ranch built. There's no need to look any farther. We'll build it back up the creek."

And so construction was started on Dunellen's ranch house. Wagonloads of lumber were brought in from Tyler, thirty miles away, and half of the crew of cowhands were put to work as carpenters. It was then that an unforeseen roadblock appeared in Dunellen's trail to establishing his empire. He was only aware of it after construction of his ranch house and barn was well underway.

Lucas Sawyer, his foreman, made the discovery that caused Dunellen to go into a rage. Lucas, being a conscientious foreman, took it upon himself to scout out the river to see where best to control most of the big herd. Like Dunellen and Spade, he followed the creek to the river. But then he followed the river north for a few miles. When he returned, he reported to Dunellen. "Did you know there's a town on this side of the river about three miles north of the point where the creek joins it?"

Dunellen was astonished. "No, hell no. A town? What are you talking about?"

"Yes, sir," Lucas answered. "There's a good-sized little town there. I came to a sawmill and asked a fellow there what town it was, and he said it was Tinhorn." Dunellen appeared to be speechless for a few moments, so Lucas continued. "It was a pretty busy sawmill. It's too bad we didn't know it was there. We ordered all that lumber from Tyler, and we've got a sawmill about six miles away from here."

Dunellen didn't care about the lumber; he was seething inside to find there was a town on his range. "On this side of the river, did you say?"

"Yes, sir, on this side," Lucas answered. "I didn't ride on up into the town, but I could see the buildings, a couple of 'em two stories."

"They'll have to go," Dunellen muttered to himself, obviously enraged. "They'll have to go," he repeated, this time loud enough to make sure Lucas heard him. To Lucas, the statement was a bit ridiculous. Surely he didn't think the town would move. He knew, however, that his employer was often unrealistic in what he expected of others.

"It's fortunate that we have plenty of range to work with here," Lucas suggested. "Plenty of river access, too. I expect if we keep the main herd south of the creek, those folks in town won't even know we're here."

"To the contrary," Dunellen responded vehemently, "I want them to know I'm here! And I want them to respect the name of Cloverleaf."

"I'm sure they'll learn to pretty soon," Lucas said, not wishing to linger when it looked like Dunellen was about to rant on about the town. "I'll get back to the barn now. It looks about ready to nail a roof on the hayloft." He left Dunellen sitting on the newly finished front steps of the house and led his horse to the barn. He pulled his saddle off his horse and turned him out to graze with the other horses, then he heard a voice behind him.

"How's it going, Lucas?" Lucas turned to see Gabby Skelton coming toward him. "I saw you talkin' to the boss up there on the steps. Did he say anything about when he'll get my cookhouse built?" Gabby was signed on as the chuckwagon cook by Lucas's recommendation, since he had done that job for the last ranch Lucas had worked as foreman. "Does he ever complain to you about the cookin'?"

"He said it was fit to choke a hog," Lucas said while trying to keep a straight face.

"The hell he did," Gabby snarfed. "If he thought that, he wouldn't say nothin' about it. He'd just draw that Army Colt he wears sometimes and blow my brains out."

Lucas looked serious for just a second before he answered. "There's more truth in that than you know." Then he shrugged and said, "He's never complained about your cookin', but you don't have to worry about that but a few days longer."

"You found him a cook?" Gabby showed some excitement over the prospect. "Where'd you find one?"

"She came to him, lookin' for the job. An older lady: She was the cook for a little dinin' room in Tyler till it closed down." He looked around to be sure none of the other men were within earshot before continuing. "She musta heard Mr. Dunellen braggin' to somebody about the place he was gonna build. And she walked up to him and asked for the job. Her name's Atha Cheney. She and her husband, Henry, are comin' to take care of the house for him."

"Well, I'll be . . ." Gabby started. "I sure hope they didn't shut it down because the cookin' was bad."

"He asked her the same thing and she said that wasn't the reason they went outta business. She's willin' to take the gamble of comin' out here and fixin' a few sample meals for him to see how he likes her cookin'," Lucas said. "Mr. Dunellen told her if he didn't like it, she'd be in her wagon headin' back home." He looked at him and chuckled. "That oughta make you feel better, since you're still here."

"I reckon," Gabby said, then hesitated, as if there was something else he wasn't sure about.

"What's on your mind, Gabby?" Lucas asked. "You act like something's eatin' at you."

"I don't know, nothin', I guess." Then he said, "Oh, hell, I trust you, Lucas, but that man scares me. You reckon we've signed up with the devil? Whaddaya think about his cousin Conan? Mr. Dunellen says he got throwed off his horse on the way home, and now Dunellen ain't got no partner anymore. It's all his. You ever think about that?"

Lucas could well understand how Gabby could concern himself with thoughts of that nature. Dunellen was beginning to take on a godlike demeanor. "I don't know what to tell you, except maybe we're judgin' him too quickly. There's no doubt that he believes laws that apply to average men don't apply to him. Maybe after we're set up here and raisin' cattle, like he hired us to do, we'll see that he's just tryin' to be the biggest cattleman in Texas. As for poor Mr. Daugherty, maybe his horse did throw him, and he broke his neck. I was sorry to hear about that. Conan Daugherty was a decent man, and a fair cowman. As far as whether or not we made a mistake signin' on with the Cloverleaf brand, I reckon we'll just have to wait and see."

"It looked like to me that whatever you told Mr. Dunellen over there on the front steps a few minutes ago got him a little up in the air. What was that about? Unless you ain't supposed to tell the hired help," he joked.

"Oh, that. That was because I told him there's a town we didn't know about. And it ain't but six miles from the ranch headquarters we're buildin' here."

"What's wrong with that?" Gabby asked.

"It's on this side of the river, and Mr. Dunellen don't want no town on his range."

"What's he gonna do about it?" Gabby wondered.

Lucas shrugged. "What can he do? The town is already there. He'll just have to learn to live with it."

"Seems to me it oughta be right handy to have a town that close," Gabby offered. "Beats the hell outta havin' to go all the way to Tyler every time you want a drink of likker."

"I suggested that," Lucas said, "told him they had a busy sawmill, too. But all he could say was that he didn't want a town on his range, so they'd have to go."

Gabby chuckled at that. "Wonder how he figures to accomplish that?"

They first showed up as an occasional stray once in a while, close to the river. But gradually the cattle increased to several at a time near the south end of town. Hannah Green, whose boardinghouse was located south of the main business district, had more than a few occasions when she chased stray cattle out of her yard. At first it was a mystery, because there were only a couple of small ranches within a few miles of Tinhorn, and the town had never seen strays from them before.

Before long, it was not uncommon to see two or three cows lumbering down the middle of the main street. And soon after, Sheriff Flint Moran and his special assistant, Buck Jackson, began to get requests from the merchants to remove the cattle from around their stores. To Flint and Buck, it was obvious that the appearance of the strays was not the result of a large herd being driven through the county. If that had been the case, the strays would have been a onetime occurrence, and not a lingering problem. The nuisance of the stray cattle became of concern to Mayor Harvey Baxter, owner of the Bank of Tinhorn, and he called a meeting with Flint and Buck to discuss the issue.

"Maybe I'm concerned about something that's not going to amount to a problem at all," Baxter confessed. "But I don't recall ever having so many stray cows show up on the streets of our town before. And it seems to me like it's getting worse. I can't believe that all of a sudden, all the small ranches in the county have just opened their gates and let their stock wander."

"I ain't got no idea," Buck replied, "but you're right, Mr. Mayor. We ain't had so many strays hangin' around town in all the years I've been here."

"Only reason I can think of," Flint offered, "is maybe a really big cattle outfit has moved their headquarters into the county, and we're just now feeling the effects of it. If that was the case, however, I woulda thought we would have seen some new cowhands in town. And I haven't seen more than one or two strangers in our saloon. How 'bout you, Buck? You notice any new faces?"

"Can't say as I have," Buck replied. "I'll ask Jake Rudolph if his business is pickin' up. If there is a new outfit movin' into the county, we'll find out pretty soon."

"I expect you're right," Baxter said. "And if that's the case, I'm sure we can talk to the owner and let him know his strays are hanging around our streets."

* * *

"Look yonder, Drew," Charley Tate called out. "There's three of 'em standin' in that creek." He pointed to three cows drinking in a small creek between them and a farmhouse and barn on the other side of the river. Drew Price turned his horse in that direction and Charley followed him. When they reached the creek, they drove the three strays out of it and headed them back toward Cloverleaf range.

Something more caught Price's interest, however, and he commented on it. "There's a helluva lot of tracks on the other side of this creek, and a lot of 'em are horses or mules. I don't think Mr. Dunellen's got any cows wearin' horseshoes," he joked. "And there's a lotta tracks leadin' toward that house over there. I got a feelin' we've been feedin' some sodbusters free Cloverleaf beef. I expect we'd best make a neighborly call and explain to those folks that we ain't here to feed 'em."

"I reckon you're right," Charley said, gave his horse a kick with his heels, and followed his partner, who had already started following the tracks leading to the barn behind the farmhouse. Charley always found it entertaining to watch Price deal with anyone butchering one of the Cloverleaf's cows.

Standing near the back of his barn, Lonnie Stevens looked up in startled surprise when the two riders suddenly appeared in the front of the barn. He didn't have to guess that their unannounced visit was directly connected to the longhorn steer tied to the open barn door. "Howdy," Drew Price greeted him. "I see you're in the cattle business. We're in the cattle business, too. Me and Charley work for Mr. Ira Dunellen. He owns the Cloverleaf Ranch, and his cows all wear the Cloverleaf brand. What brand is on your cows?" When Lonnie just stood there speechless, unable to come up with any explanation at the moment, Price continued. "Take a look at the rump of that cow, Charley, so we can make sure we don't get any of his cows mixed up in our herd. I don't want this fine feller, here, to think we're low-down, sneakin' cattle thieves."

"Cow's wearin' a Cloverleaf brand, Drew," Charley said with a grin, anticipating the entertainment to follow.

"Cloverleaf?" Price asked, pretending to be shocked. He climbed down from his horse, so Lonnie could get the full intimidation of his large size. "Did you know that, sodbuster? Were you fixin' to butcher a steer with our brand on it?"

Lonnie finally found his voice. "No!" he squeaked, "No, sir, it was in my garden, and I had to chase it outta there. I wasn't gonna butcher it."

"I don't know, sodbuster. Don't look like to me you was chasin' that cow. You got a rope on that cow, and you tied it to the barn door. What did you do, ride the damn cow outta the garden?"

"Yessir, I mean, no, sir, I didn't ride the cow outta the garden." Lonnie, finding himself in a desperate situation, was not sure what to claim.

"Looks like to me you was either gonna butcher that cow or ride it. And range law says if you catch a man butcherin' your cattle, you can shoot him. Ain't that right, Charley?"

"That's right, Drew," Charley said. "We can shoot him, if he ain't just been ridin' that cow."

"I was just gonna ride the cow," Lonnie pleaded. "I was gonna ride it back to the other cows at the creek."

"I'd like to believe you, sodbuster," Price said. "But I don't think you can ride a steer, so you're gonna have to ride that cow back to the creek right now to show me."

"Can't you just take the rope and lead your cow back off my land?" Lonnie pleaded.

Price drew his .44. "I knew he was lyin'. He can't ride that cow."

"Wait, wait!" Lonnie cried out when he saw the drawn pistol. "I'll ride the cow!" He hurried to the barn door and untied the steer, then he crawled on its back. The cow, now confused as much as Lonnie, didn't make a move. When Lonnie started kicking his heels and yelling, "Giddyup," the cow went crazy. At first, it ran sideways in one direction, then back in the opposite direction while Lonnie tried to steer it by holding on to its horns. Finally, the crazed cow took off toward the creek, bucking for all it was worth until it deposited Lonnie on his backside, awaiting execution.

Price climbed back on his horse and rode after him. When he came up to the spot where the cow had deposited Lonnie, he gave him a warning. "You ever think about stealin' a Cloverleaf cow again, I'll string your guts up on your barn door." Then he rode on after Charley, who was chasing the cow back with the other strays to the sound of his cackling laughter.

Lonnie picked himself up and walked back to the barn, mortified to find his wife waiting there, holding his shotgun. "I know what you're thinkin'," Marge said before he had a chance to speak. "I'm glad you ain't a big enough fool to try to take on two armed bullies when you ain't got a weapon yourself. I brought your shotgun in case they came back. We'd see how big they were then."

"I 'preciate what you're sayin', hon," Lonnie said, "but I feel lower'n an egg-suckin' dog. I couldn't do nothin'. I didn't even have the pitchfork in my hand."

"Thank goodness for that, is what I say," Marge replied. "You better not do some stupid thing like that and leave me with two boys, ten and twelve."

"Doggone it, this is our land," Lonnie complained. "We homesteaded this piece of land because there was other farms, just like us. Them damn cattle ranches ain't got the right to threaten a man on his own land. I reckon I'm gonna have to start wearin' my gun."

"Tomorrow's Saturday," Marge said. "We've got to go into town, so we'll ask some of the other folks if they're havin' trouble with stray cattle. If they are, maybe we can talk to Sheriff Moran, and he might be able to do something about it."

"I doubt it," Lonnie replied. "And when we come home, if I find another damn cow in our garden, I'm gonna shoot it on the spot. And we'll eat the damn cow, if that's the only way we can eat the food we raise in our garden."

Saturday, the one day of the week that brought the sleepy town out of the near desertion of the rest of the week, came this time on the heels of a heavy rain. The rain had stopped by the time Flint walked into Clara Rakestraw's Kitchen for breakfast. "Good morning, Sheriff," Clara greeted him cheerfully. "How are you this fine morning? Does the weather suit you?"

"'Mornin', Clara," Flint returned. "I reckon it'll have to. There ain't much I can do about it." Seeing Bonnie standing next to the kitchen door, he nodded to her, and she answered him with a smile. A second later, Mindy came out of the kitchen, carrying a cup of coffee. She started toward his usual table, then paused to make sure he was heading to that table. He nodded, so she continued toward the table, placed the coffee cup on it, and stood waiting for him to sit down.

"'Mornin', Mindy," Flint said. "How are you today?"

"I'm fine," she answered. "You know, I keep thinking

you might pick a different table, but you always come to this one by the kitchen door."

"This is Buck's favorite table," he replied. "Since we eat together most of the time, I'm afraid he might get indigestion if we switched to another table."

She laughed. "He might at that. It's been two years since you became the sheriff. Bonnie and I thought you might wanna pick a favorite table, over by the window or in the back corner."

"I can't take a chance on Buck gettin' indigestion," Flint joked. "Besides, I believe he's right. We sit here and you can see if our cups need fillin' every time you go in or out of the kitchen. Buck might be smarter than we think." He paused then, when the door opened. "Here he is now."

"I'll get his coffee," Mindy said. "It's Saturday. Margaret always makes pancakes on Saturday. Are you going to have them, or do you want your usual?"

"I'll take the pancakes," Flint replied. "That'll help me remember what day of the week it is."

"Lotta folks go to church tomorrow," Mindy joked. "Maybe that would help you remember what day of the week it is, too, if you went there every week."

"That's what the Reverend Morehead has been tellin' me. I might go to church one Sunday to hear Lance Morehead wrestle with old Satan one of these weeks. Hannah Green says he gives the devil a real fight."

"Take Buck with you when you go," Mindy said, and left to get Buck's coffee.

"Take me where?" Buck asked, having heard her last remark as he approached the table. "Where you goin'?" He pulled a chair back and settled his frame on it.

"Church," Flint answered. "Mindy suggested I oughta take you to church tomorrow, but I was just gonna send you in my place."

"I went to church one Sunday," Buck said. "That was back before you was hired as my deputy. I'd never been to church before, and I wanted to see what they had to talk about every week. 'Course, that was the little log church on the bank of the river, and Abner Cruise was the preacher. It's gone now, and so is Abner, but he went on so hard about all the evil out here in the world, he had me worried for a week. That was enough church for me. . . . Damn! They look good," he exclaimed when Mindy placed a stack of pancakes on the table before Flint. "I'll try some of those flapjacks, too."

They were finishing up their coffee when the young cowhand staggered in the front door of the dining room and stood gaping drunkenly at the few people at the tables. "I swear," Buck commented, "this early in the mornin'?" It was obvious he belonged to one of the horses left tied at the hitching rail at Jake's Place all night. "I reckon he didn't sleep it off, and I expect he's needin' some coffee pretty bad." Neither one of the two lawmen made a move to intercept the drunken young man, preferring to give him the chance to conduct himself in a civilized manner. Buck, especially, having fought his battles with an addiction to alcohol for nearly half his life now, could sympathize with the young cowhand's battle to regain his senses. They watched as Bonnie approached him, since Clara was in the kitchen at the moment.

Bonnie sized him up pretty quickly. It wasn't difficult, since he was having difficulty standing up without holding on to the open door. He was fairly large in size, but his smooth cheeks and chin were obvious clues to his youth. "You lookin' for some coffee and solid food?" Bonnie asked.

"I sure am, sweetheart," the cowhand slurred, "the sooner the better."

"All right," she replied. "I'll sit you down at a table. Give me your gun first."

"Give you my gun? The hell I will. Whaddaya want my gun for?"

"Everybody leaves their gun on the table over there when they come into Clara's Kitchen. It's the rule. It ain't just you."

"You think I'm drunk," he said.

"I'm pretty sure of that," Bonnie answered. "And you don't need to have a gun on you when you're drunk. So, give me the gun, and I'll put it on the table for you, and then I'll get you some coffee, all right?"

"I may be drunk, but I ain't stupid," the young man replied. "And I ain't never too drunk to handle my six-shooter, if anybody wants to find out." He reached down and pulled the weapon out of his holster.

"Uh-oh," Flint said, and he and Buck got up quickly. Aware of the trouble then as well, Clara came rushing out of the kitchen. Flint motioned for her to stop, so she did, and she stood in the kitchen doorway watching anxiously. "I'll distract him, if you'll take him from behind," he said to Buck. Buck nodded and walked over to the other side of the room while Flint walked up to confront the drunken young man. "What's the trouble, neighbor?" Flint said. "Is Bonnie givin' you a hard time?" The young man was at once wary of the man wearing a badge. "You can put that gun away. That's just one of the rules of this dinin' room, if you wanna eat here."

"I don't know what kinda game you folks are tryin' to pull here," the cowhand said. "I'm just tryin' to get some breakfast, and I ain't givin' nobody my gun."

"All right," Flint said, and held his hands out in front of him, palms up to show they were empty. He nodded to Buck, who had walked up behind the young man. The stranger grunted helplessly when Buck suddenly grabbed both his arms and pulled them behind his back. With a vise-like grip, he shook the drunken man's hand until his pistol fell on the floor. While Buck still held his arms, Flint handcuffed him. The drunk almost fell down when Buck released him, causing the big lawman to grab his arm again to support him. Flint picked up the dropped weapon and stuck it in his belt. "Now," he said to him, "you need to sleep that drunk off. We've got a good cot waitin' for you and a pot of coffee. And we'll have the ladies here fix you something to eat for breakfast. Now, you can't beat that, can you?" He told Mindy to have Margaret fix a meal for the cowhand, and he'd come back to get it, and Ralph's breakfast, too. He and Buck walked him out the door, practically carrying him between them as they transported him down to the jail.

When they got to the jail, they were met by a curious Ralph Cox, whose first question was, "Did you bring my breakfast?"

"No, we brought you a guest instead," Buck answered him. When he saw the look of panic on Ralph's face, he explained. "Me and Flint had to carry this drunk cowhand down here. We didn't have enough hands to hold him and two plates of food, too. Why don't you walk up to the front door of the dinin' room and Clara will give it to you?"

"I reckon I could," Ralph replied. Since his first days in the Tinhorn jail were spent as a prisoner, Ralph had never gotten used to being a free man. Basically an innocent soul, he had been given an unofficial pardon by Flint and Buck, and instead of transferring him to prison, they let him remain in Tinhorn to assume the duties of jail caretaker. He had stayed on in that capacity for two years now, with his only compensation free food and an occasional allowance whenever he needed something. He was accustomed to either Buck or Flint bringing him his meal when they went to the dining room. For that reason, he was uncomfortable going to Clara's and asking for his food. And that was why he was delighted in the next few seconds when Mindy appeared at the office door.

Flint went to the door to meet her while Buck took the cowhand back to one of the two cells. "Mindy, you didn't have to bring those plates down here," he said. "I was gonna send Ralph up to get 'em."

"They might have gotten cold by the time Ralph came to get them," she insisted. "Besides, I wasn't very busy, and it gave me an excuse to get outside for a few minutes."

"Well, that was mighty nice of you," Flint said. He took the plates from her, turned around, and handed them to Ralph, who was standing, grinning, right behind him. "There you go," he told him. "Take your pick, then take the other one back for that young fellow." Back to Mindy then, he said, "I'll walk you back to the hotel."

"There's no need for you to do that," she replied, "unless you're doin' it just to be sweet."

He chuckled in response. "I reckon I'll do it just to be sweet." He held the door for her, and they stepped outside.

"How long will that young man be arrested?" Mindy asked as they took a leisurely walk up toward the hotel and Clara's Kitchen.

"Oh, he's not really under arrest," Flint replied. "We'll just keep him in a cell till he sleeps it off, give him some coffee and something to eat and let him go. I haven't had a chance to find out yet, but I hope he doesn't have enough money to get drunk again." He shook his head slowly before adding, "I oughta arrest him, though, for leavin' that horse tied to the rail at Jake's all night." He thought about that for a moment. "If he does have any money left, I think

I'll make him go pay Lon Blake for takin' care of that horse and feedin' it a portion of oats."

When they got to Clara's, he thanked Mindy again for bringing the plates and told her he'd see her at dinnertime. She insisted it was no trouble, gave him a sweet smile, then went inside thinking, *He cares more for that drunk's horse than he does for me.*

CHAPTER 4

It was almost dinnertime when young Tim Walker woke up to find himself on a cot in a jail cell. Only vaguely aware of how he got there, he sat up and swung his feet over on the floor, almost hitting a slop bucket that had been pulled up beside the cot. The motion caused his head to spin slightly and prompted a queasy feeling in his stomach. For a moment, he thought he was going to need the bucket again. But after a few minutes, his stomach settled somewhat and his head stopped spinning, leaving only a dull ache. When he felt stable enough to look around him, he realized he was the only one in the cells. When he turned his head back to the front, he was startled to find a man outside the cells, watching him. "I've got a pot of coffee on the stove," Ralph said. "You want a cup?" Tim nodded at once, though he said nothing. "You hungry?" Tim nodded again. "The sheriff got a plate of breakfast for you, but it's pretty cold now," Ralph said. "But you can eat the pancakes and bacon and put somethin' in your stomach. I'll get it for you."

"Thank you, sir," Tim finally spoke. He remained sitting there on the cot, and in a few minutes, Ralph returned with a cup of coffee and a plate of food. Tim was astonished when Ralph set the coffee down on the floor to free one hand so he could swing the cell door open. "It wasn't even locked?" Tim asked.

"Nah," Ralph answered. "You ain't under arrest. The sheriff just thought you needed a place to sleep off that drunk." He chuckled then and commented, "You sure as hell tied on a big one."

"I reckon I did," Tim said. "I ain't ever been that drunk before." He took a few quick sips of the hot coffee, then wrapped a cold pancake around a couple of strips of bacon and ate that with it. "Mister, I sure do appreciate it. I reckon I musta showed my butt at that eatin' place up by the hotel. I reckon I just can't handle my whiskey like I thought I could."

"Not many people can," Ralph remarked. "Like I said, though, you ain't under arrest. You can go anytime you're ready."

"Can I lay down on this cot a little while longer?"

"Sure, we ain't got no prisoners right now," Ralph said. "Maybe you can catch up on your sleep."

"Sheriff Moran?"

Flint looked up from his desk to see a tall, rawboned man standing in the front doorway. "Yes, sir, I'm Sheriff Moran. Can I help you?"

The stranger came on into the office and Flint stood up to talk to him. "My name's Lucas Sawyer. I'm the foreman at the Cloverleaf Ranch. I understand you've got one of my men locked up. Tim Walker's his name. I've come to see what I can do about getting him out of jail."

"Tim Walker," Flint repeated. "He hadn't even told us his name. Cloverleaf Ranch," he repeated. "We suspected we might have a new outfit movin' into the county, but you're the first person who's been into town to tell us about it." He paused then and nodded toward the cell room. "Except Tim Walker, but we were gettin' plenty of signs from the stray cattle we've started seein' in our streets." He was about to say more, but Buck walked in the front door then, so Flint introduced him. "Buck, this is Mr. Lucas Sawyer. He's the foreman for Cloverleaf Ranch." Back to Sawyer then, he said, "This is Buck Jackson, special adviser to the sheriff's office. Mr. Sawyer's come to get his man outta jail, Buck."

Sawyer looked a little impatient with the introductions, and he felt a slight suspicion that he was going to have to pay a heavy fine to get Walker out of jail. "All right, Sheriff, you've got my attention. What's it gonna take to drop the charges on Tim Walker? My boss ain't one to stand for much when it comes to a shakedown from a small-town sheriff."

Flint looked at Buck and chuckled before replying to Sawyer. "Sounds to me like you folks at Cloverleaf have had some bad experience with small towns. Tim Walker's not under arrest. He slept off a drunk that was too powerful for a young man of his drinkin' experience to handle. He still ain't lookin' too good, but I never had the opportunity to see him sober, so I can't judge for certain. There aren't any charges against him. He's free to go whenever he feels like he can make it. Come over here and I'll let you ask him if he's ready to go." He walked over and opened the door to the cell room.

Still a little uncertain, Sawyer walked over to the door, and he saw Walker stretched out on a cot. "Tim," he called out. "You ready to get outta here?"

Recognizing the voice, Tim sat up on the cot. "Boss, is that you?"

"Yeah, it's me," Sawyer answered. "You ready to go?"

"Yes, sir, I reckon." He got up, then to Sawyer's surprise,

he opened the cell door and walked out. When he walked by Ralph, he said, "Thanks, Ralph."

"You bet. Take care of yourself, Tim," Ralph replied.

When they came back in the office, Tim made it a point to thank Flint and Buck, again to Lucas Sawyer's amazement. Still, there was one more order of business on Sawyer's agenda. "I appreciate your cooperation and understandin' for a young man's foolish affair with alcohol, but there was one more thing. Tim rode into your town on a horse and saddle that belongs to Cloverleaf Ranch." He got no farther than that before Buck interrupted him.

"That dun he left at the saloon is at the stable at the end of the street. Lon Blake's the owner. If there's any charge for takin' care of the horse, you'll have to work that out with him."

"He might charge you for a portion of oats," Flint said. "I doubt he'll charge anything else." Sawyer just nodded in response, still finding the whole incident hard to believe. "There is something you might give me a little help on," Flint said.

"If I can," Sawyer replied. "What is it you need to know?"

"We never heard of Cloverleaf Ranch until this mornin'. Where is your ranch headquarters located? If I had to guess, I'd say the trouble we're havin' here in Tinhorn for the last couple of weeks with stray cattle might have something to do with Cloverleaf."

"It might have," Sawyer admitted. "For the last several weeks we have been movin' our cattle to a new range. The ranch headquarters is being built now. It's about six miles from Tinhorn. The owner is Mr. Ira Dunellen and we've doubled the size of our herd, and we needed grazin' land near the rivers."

"I was afraid somethin' like that was happenin'," Buck

saw fit to comment. "We're already gettin' strays wanderin' down the middle of the town. Maybe Mr. Dunellen can concentrate most of his herd a little farther south of Tinhorn."

"Maybe so," Sawyer said. "He's a reasonable man." Even as he said it, he had an urge to bite his tongue, knowing how Dunellen had reacted when he had suggested the same thing the sheriff just recommended. He was well aware of Dunellen's plans to overrun the little town of Tinhorn. The town stood between his range and the river on that end of it. "In the meantime, your town council should consider the increase in business a ranch the size of Cloverleaf can bring to your town. It might even be worthwhile to think about moving your town to the other side of the Neches River." As ridiculous as that sounded, he said it anyway, as a small support of his employer's logic.

"That would be quite a costly move," Flint said. "I doubt many of these small shops could afford to build across the river. The land on the other side of the river is owned by farmers and small ranchers. They ain't likely gonna wanna sell their land to the shop owners. Hell, they don't wanna move anyway. Better tell your boss the town owns four hundred acres right along the river, bought by a tinhorn gambler named Jacob Trehorn to build a town. So he'll need to do whatever he has to do to control his strays. The town has an ordinance that says it's against the law for animals to run loose in the town limits."

"I'll give him the message," Sawyer said. He looked at his young cowhand then. "Let's go pick up your horse, Tim." They left to go to the stable.

"I see trouble ahead," Buck said. "I can't believe there's any cattleman, no matter how big an outfit he owns, who thinks an established town will move just to accommodate his blame cows. And, hell, the town owns the land it's settin' on. I see trouble ahead," he repeated.

"I'm afraid you're right," Flint agreed.

"I swear, though, I didn't know there was an ordinance against stray cows inside the town limits."

"There ain't," Flint said, "but I expect there will be as soon as the council meets to discuss the problem. I expect I'd best go talk to Harvey Baxter and give him a little warnin' about the problems we can expect from an outfit that big on our doorstep. I'll go up to the bank now to see if I can catch him. Then I'll meet you at Clara's, unless you wanna go with me to see Baxter." As he expected, Buck said he'd just wait and meet him at Clara's. Flint always tried to include Buck in any important meetings, strictly out of respect for the years that Buck served as sheriff. And like today, Buck usually opted out.

Listening to the discussion, as he always did, Ralph saw the necessity to remind them that, if they got to talking such serious talk, sometimes it was easy to forget other important things, like bringing his dinner plate when they came back from Clara's.

As Flint expected, the news of the Cloverleaf Ranch headquarters being built only six miles away from town was quite troubling to Harvey Baxter. It could be good news for the merchants of Tinhorn, or it could be bad news. It all depended upon the ranch owner's desire to be a good neighbor or not. Maybe, Baxter thought, he wasn't even aware of the town's existence, but that seemed unlikely. It would be reason enough to call for an emergency meeting of the town council. "We'll have an ordinance on the books," Baxter said, "for whatever good we can get out of it."

When he walked out of the bank, it was time for Clara

to open her door for dinner, so Flint went directly to the dining room. He was surprised to find Tim Walker waiting at the door for the "Open sign" to appear. "I thought you were on your way back to the Cloverleaf," Flint said when he walked up behind him. "You decide to eat dinner first?"

"No, sir," Tim exclaimed at once. "I got my horse and I'm goin' back right away. I just wanted to stop here first and apologize to the ladies for this mornin'. I wasn't taught to act like that. I spent every last dime I had in that saloon last night. I don't even know what I thought I was gonna pay for my breakfast with. I reckon I found out I ain't no drinker. I still feel pretty rough. I think I'll crawl into my blankets as soon as I get back. We ain't even built the bunkhouse yet."

"Where's Sawyer?" Flint asked. "Is he still here?"

"No, sir, he went on ahead, 'cause he was in a hurry to get back, and he said maybe he'd get back before Gabby threw the rest of the chuck out."

Flint was amazed by the young man's sense of responsibility, so much so that he had to ask, "How old are you, Tim?"

"I'll be fifteen in a couple of months," he replied.

Flint was surprised. He was big for his age. Flint knew he was young, but he figured him to be a couple of years older than fifteen. "You picked a hard way to learn how to drink whiskey. I think you'll feel a little bit better when you get some solid food in your belly. Why don't you eat some dinner before you ride back?"

"Like I said, I'm broke," Tim reminded him.

"I'll stake you for a meal," Flint said. "You can be my guest."

"Oh, I couldn't do that," Tim replied at once, already astonished by his experience with the sheriff's department of Tinhorn so far.

"Sure you can," Flint said, just as Clara came to the door

to open it. "Here's one of the ladies you wanna apologize to." He stepped aside and motioned Tim in before him, eager to see Clara's reaction upon seeing her first customer for dinner. He wasn't disappointed. Upon seeing the young man standing in her door again, she was at once speechless. Then she noticed Flint standing behind him, wearing a grin of amusement. She looked back at Tim, still at a loss for words.

"Ma'am," Tim started, "I ain't here to cause no trouble. I just wanted to tell you I'm powerful sorry for how I acted this mornin'. I especially wanna apologize to that lady yonder." He pointed to Bonnie, who had caught sight of him by then and, like Clara, was stopped dead in her tracks to stare at him. "I was drunk," he confessed needlessly.

Clara suddenly recovered. She smiled then and said, "Yes, you were, and I accept your apology. Bonnie, come over here." She looked back at Tim and asked, "What's your name?"

"Tim Walker, ma'am."

"Right," Clara said, enjoying the incident now. "Bonnie, come here. Tim's got something to tell you."

"I'm coming," Bonnie said. Mindy followed her to the front door, but stepped over to stand beside Flint, who had moved out of the way.

"Did you tell him he had to do that?" Mindy whispered to Flint.

"No, ma'am, I did not," he stated. "I didn't even know he was here till I got here."

They listened while Tim apologized for his behavior earlier that day and confessed that he had never, ever gotten that drunk before in his young life. His apparent sincerity was enough to melt even Bonnie's sarcastic nature. It was an experience the women of Clara's Kitchen were not accustomed to. And when he had finished saying what he felt obligated to say, Clara asked if he was going to eat dinner with them. "I hadn't planned to," Tim said, and confessed that he was broke. "But Sheriff Moran told me I should eat some solid food, and I could be his guest."

"He did, did he?" Clara asked. "Well, I'm afraid I can't allow that. You'll eat today as a guest of the women who work at Clara's Kitchen."

Buck came in the door in time to hear the cheer that went up from the three women standing near the entrance. "That's more like the reception I deserve every time I come in here," he joked. Then he, too, was taken aback upon seeing young Tim Walker in the group near the door. He was immediately informed of what had just taken place, which he found especially humorous. "Well, come on then, let's sit down and start eatin'," he said, "before they change their minds. You know how fickle women are."

"Just follow them," Clara said to Tim, "and the girls will take care of you."

"Yes, ma'am," Tim replied, "but I have to put my gun on the table first. I remember that much from this mornin'." Clara had to chuckle while she watched the young man dutifully place his gun on the table. She would have forgotten to remind him.

While a friendly and considerate gesture on the part of the sheriff's department and Clara's Kitchen, Tim Walker's complimentary dinner provided Flint and Buck with a great deal of information about Cloverleaf as well. According to what Tim told them, the owner, Ira Dunellen, was seldom seen by the men who worked his cattle, now that the ranch house was built. As far as the cowhands were concerned, Lucas Sawyer was the boss. They worked for him, although they knew that the supreme orders came

down from Dunellen through Sawyer. Tim told them that
the crew had driven three thousand cows into that corner of
their range specifically to graze them closer to the river. He
also said there had been no concern about the strays unless
they had reports of people stealing them or butchering
them. In that case, Sawyer usually sent Drew Price and a
few of the others out to investigate. "Last night was the first
night Lucas let any of the crew come into Tinhorn, and that
was only three of us," Tim said. "We drew straws for it. Me
and Jack Spade and Andy Hatcher were the lucky ones. We
started drinkin' till I passed out. When I woke up again,
Jack and Andy were both gone. But they left me with a full
bottle of whiskey, so I decided I might as well have some
of the dog that bit me. I don't remember much after that
until I came here this mornin'." He looked at them apolo-
getically and shrugged. "There'll be more of the boys
comin' into town today. It bein' Saturday, Lucas said anybody who ain't got night watch is free to go to town." That
wasn't very good news for Flint and Buck, knowing it a
good possibility they would have to earn their salaries
that night.

"I hate to say this, but I've got a feelin' that's the last
friendly conversation we'll have with a cowhand from the
Cloverleaf," Buck said as they were walking back to the
jail. Tim Walker rode back to the ranch content that he had
made some friendly acquaintances in the town of Tinhorn.
And the women at Clara's had a positive image of the
Cloverleaf crew, based on their visit with one innocent
young man. As they approached the sheriff's office, Flint
was thinking the town looked like any typical Saturday in
Tinhorn, with one exception. The hitching rail in front of

the saloon was filled with saddled horses. "Looks like Jake oughta be happy," Buck commented.

"Yep, I was just thinkin' the same thing," Flint said as he went up the steps to the front door of his office. When they went inside, they found Ralph talking to a man Flint recognized as a farmer he had seen before.

"Here they are now," Ralph announced and took the plate of food from Flint's hand. "Sheriff," he said to Flint, "this here's Lonnie Stevens. He's got a farm across the river, and he's wantin' to talk to you about some trouble he's havin' with that new outfit that's moved their cows in."

"Yes, sir, Sheriff," Lonnie took over. "Just like a lotta folks on that side of the river, I've been havin' a lotta trouble from this new cattle company that's moved into the valley. Stray cows! Every day, I'm runnin' stray cows outta my garden, and that ain't the worst of it. I've been threatened by two of their men that came onto my land and made me ride a steer that I put a rope on so I could lead it outta my garden. Held their guns on me and made me get on the fool cow and try to ride it." He paused to look at Buck, then back at Flint to make sure they got the picture. "I didn't have my gun or it'da been another story. We ain't never had any trouble with stray cows before this crowd moved thousands of 'em into the valley. And they ain't even tryin' to keep 'em rounded up to stay with the rest of the herd." He paused again to see Flint's reaction to what he had just told him.

It was an uncomfortable situation for Flint. Buck knew what was going through his young friend's mind because he had been faced with it so many times in the past. "Mr. Stevens, I can surely see why you're reportin' this to me, but I'm wonderin' what you expect me to do about it."

"Go out to that ranch and arrest them two that came onto my farm and threatened me," Lonnie said. "Catch 'em when they come to town. I've got a wife and two young'uns that are gonna be left alone if somethin' happens to me."

"I sympathize with you completely," Flint said. "But I've got no authority to arrest anybody outside the town limits of Tinhorn. As for catching 'em when they come to town, I can't arrest 'em just on your word that it happened, even if I believe you, and I do. If I leave Tinhorn to go after somebody, then I'm breakin' my word to protect the people in Tinhorn, and I'll be kicked outta my job. I hate to have to tell you this. I'm just as sorry as I can be, but I just can't go out arrestin' folks outside Tinhorn." He didn't bother to mention that the town of Tinhorn didn't want the added expense of feeding and housing prisoners caught out in the county. "The best I can do is forward your complaint to the U.S. Marshals Service, but I don't know what kind of response we'd get."

Buck made no comments as he sat there and listened to the conversation between Flint and Lonnie. But he knew how badly Flint felt when he could offer no help with Lonnie's problem. Buck had been in the same spot many times when he was sheriff. It was tough to tell people they were on their own when they decided to settle on a piece of land supposedly policed by the rangers or marshals, but usually by no one. He felt sure Flint could now appreciate the frustration he had with him when he was a deputy and insisted on riding off to hell and back after someone.

Lonnie just stood there for a few moments to let Flint's words sink in. "So, I'm just on my own, right? I reckon I'da saved my time if I'd just gone to Harper's store and bought some extra shotgun shells." He shook his head in frustration. "Lemme ask you this, what if I kill one of their cows and eat it? Will you arrest me for it?"

"No," Flint said, "what happens outside of town ain't any of my business." He knew when he said it that Buck was staring at him, wanting to catch his eye, but he didn't meet his gaze. He was going to have to hear about it when Lonnie left, about the number of times Buck had stated that he didn't concern himself with anything outside the town limits.

"Well, I reckon I'll be goin'," Lonnie said and walked out of the office.

"I don't reckon I need to say anything," Buck said.

"No, you don't," Flint replied. "What happens outside of town ain't none of my business, right?"

"It's liable to be harder on you than it was on me," Buck said. "You kinda built yourself a reputation while you were my deputy, ridin' all over the county to go after people. Folks didn't think anything stopped you from goin' to get some outlaw that needed to be stopped."

"Mayor Baxter wanted you to stop by the bank after you ate dinner," Ralph remembered then. "I told him I'd tell you to go see him as soon as you got back."

"I just had a meetin' with him before I went to eat," Flint said. "Did he say what he wants?"

"Nope, just that it was important," Ralph said.

"Hell, every meetin' with Baxter is important," Buck said, "to him, anyway."

Chapter 5

Mindy Moore glanced out the window on the side wall of the dining room as she collected dirty dishes off some of the tables. She stopped then and concentrated her gaze on a familiar figure walking up the street toward the hotel. It was a walk that always caught her attention. *Flint*, she thought, *what's he carrying?* Then she realized he was carrying a plate. *He's returning Ralph's dinner plate.* Without a word to Bonnie or Clara, she placed the stack of dishes she was carrying on a table and hurried to the door to meet him. She stood there for only a few moments, long enough to get a puzzled look from Bonnie, until she heard his boots on the steps outside. She opened the door then. "Flint!" she gushed, pretending surprise. "Did you forget something? Oh, is that Ralph's plate?"

"Yep," Flint replied. "I've gotta go see Harvey Baxter at the bank, so I thought I might as well drop it off on my way. Thought I'd get here before you locked the door."

"We're getting ready to lock it in just a little while. But there's still some coffee in the pot, if you wanna come in and have a cup."

"Oh, no, thank you just the same," Flint said. "I thought I musta drunk up all you had a little while ago at dinner."

"You sure? It wouldn't be any trouble," she coaxed.

"I expect I'd best go on over to the bank and see what Mr. Baxter has on his mind. Ralph said it was important." He handed her the plate. "I'll see you at supper."

"Bye," she said and watched him when he turned and walked away. She closed the door then and turned to find Bonnie grinning at her.

"'Bye,'" Bonnie imitated and giggled.

"Kiss my foot, Bonnie," Mindy said and pushed by her to go back for the stack of dirty dishes she had left on the table. She stopped halfway when she realized they were gone.

"I picked 'em up while you were in dreamland," Bonnie told her. "When are you gonna pin that man down and ask him his intentions?"

"When I think he actually has some," Mindy answered. "I'll be sure to let you know."

Flint walked into the bank and, seeing Harvey Baxter's office door open, walked on across the lobby to find Baxter standing beside a file cabinet. "Yeah, Flint, come on in," he said when he saw him in the doorway. He went back to his desk and sat down. "Sit down," he invited, and Flint sat opposite the desk. "I had dinner with John Harper," Baxter began. "We talked about this problem we're facing with the Cloverleaf Ranch. We decided it might be worthwhile to appeal to this man's sense of neighborly cooperation. Since I own the one bank in town, and John owns the biggest feed and supply store. The only feed and supply store, I should say. We might officially welcome him to our community. At the same time, we could encourage him to do his business with us. We thought it would be proper to have you go along with us, kinda like an official escort."

Flint raised a skeptical eyebrow. "Whatever you say, Mr.

Mayor. If you want me to ride along with you, I'll be happy to go. But when I was talkin' to Dunellen's foreman, Lucas Sawyer, I got the impression that Dunellen is figurin' on forcin' the town of Tinhorn to close down, or move out, cross over to the other side of the river, so his cows can get to the water."

"I know there was talk of that," Baxter said. "But I can't believe the man is insane enough to even consider such a possibility, to close down an entire town. At any rate, I think it important to meet Ira Dunellen and hear from him, firsthand, what his intentions are."

"I reckon I couldn't argue with that," Flint said. "When are you figurin' on goin' out to his ranch?"

"We decided to go Monday morning," Baxter said. "Any problem with that?"

"No problem," Flint replied, "since we've got a good man to take care of the town while I'm gone. I know I don't have to tell you that. What time do you wanna leave?"

"Right after breakfast. Their new ranch house is supposed to be six miles from here, so we should have plenty of time to ride out there and be back in the afternoon."

"In the meantime," Flint pointed out, "we'll get a chance to see what kind of men are riding for the Cloverleaf brand, since this is their first Saturday night in town. And while I'm at it, I'll try to find out how to get there. I know it's only six miles from here, but I don't know in what direction to go six miles."

"All right, then," Baxter said, "Monday morning we're set to go. I'll just meet you at the stable at seven thirty."

"I'll be there," Flint told him, and got up to leave. He was thinking seven thirty certainly gave them time to have breakfast, as he went out the front door. Walking back toward the jail, he again noticed that Jake's Place was busier than usual. *I think I'll go have a look*, he thought.

"Flint," Rudy acknowledged when Flint walked in and came over to the bar. "You drinkin'?"

"I reckon not," Flint replied. "I just thought I'd stop in to see if anything was goin' on in here." He glanced at the four men sitting at a table, working on a bottle of whiskey. "Cloverleaf?"

"Yep," Rudy answered, "they're from Cloverleaf. Rode in about half an hour ago. They've been workin' on that one bottle. Probably about ready to buy another one."

"No trouble, though?" Flint asked.

"No," Rudy replied, "no trouble a-tall. At least, not so far. They just ain't had a drink of likker in a long spell, is what they said, and they need to catch up."

Flint took a few moments to study the four new faces and decided they must be some of the older cowhands. He decided to go over and get directions to their headquarters while they might still be able to remember them. "Afternoon," he said when he walked up to the table. "You boys ride for the Cloverleaf Ranch?"

One of the four, who looked to be older than the other three, answered him. "That's right, we ride for the Cloverleaf." He eyed the badge on Flint's vest. "Are you the sheriff?"

"Yep, I'm Flint Moran. I'm the sheriff. I just wanted to ask you a question. Where is your ranch headquarters located? We here in Tinhorn didn't even know there was a new ranch nearby till about a week or two ago, when a lot of stray cows started showin' up. If I was wantin' to go out to see the ranch, how would I find it?"

"That's easy," the man said. "There's a creek that empties into the river about three miles south of here. Follow that creek back west about three more miles and you'll be there. It ain't all built yet, but the ranch house is done, and the barn is almost done."

"Much obliged," Flint said and started to turn away.

"This is our first time in Tinhorn," the man said. "Looks like you've got a nice little town here."

"Glad you appreciate that," Flint responded. "We're tryin' to keep it that way. Nice, quiet little town where fellows like you can come in and have a peaceful drink without bein' bothered. We ain't like Dodge City or Wichita. To save a little trouble, you might tell your friends that it's against the law to set off firearms inside the town limits of Tinhorn. And if they eat in Clara's Kitchen, next to the hotel, they'll have to take off their guns while they're eatin'." He smiled and added, "That's so the peaceful citizens can eat without being scared to death."

One of the other men at the table leaned over toward the one who was doing the talking and said, "I reckon all that'll change when Drew and Charley and the rest of that bunch hit town later on tonight."

Flint pretended he didn't hear him, but the names Drew and Charley, he figured he'd remember. "Enjoy your time in Tinhorn," he said and headed for the door. "See ya later, Rudy," he said when he passed by the bar.

When he got back to the office, he found Buck sitting at the desk he had sat at for years before Flint became sheriff. Buck jumped up immediately. "Oh, sit back down, Buck," Flint said, and sat down on a stool next to Ralph's bench. "I think we'd better expect a little trouble later on today." He went on to recount his visit with the four cowhands. "These four fellows were just having a quiet drink of likker. I figure they were part of the older fellows that work for Cloverleaf, at least old enough to have gotten over their wild younger years. Any crew the size of the one Dunellen must have is bound to have a wild bunch mixed in with the peaceful ones. And they're liable to bust loose tonight 'cause, accordin' to what Tim Walker told us, they ain't had a night in town for a long time."

"I hope they don't get here before we can eat supper," Buck commented. "We'd best go first thing."

"Yeah, we will," Flint said. He was hoping Buck would be all right after supper. He had worked on his drinking problem, and he had seen improvement. But he was still pretty much useless after supper every night. *Well*, he thought, *it won't be any different than when I was the deputy. The town was my responsibility at night.* "Anyway, we'd better expect to have some guests tonight. So, Ralph, you might as well get fresh water buckets in both cells, and empty your slop buckets."

"Already ahead of you, Boss," Ralph responded. "Ever since Tim Walker was in here this mornin', I've had a feelin' we was gonna see some more of that crew."

"Good," Flint told him. "I knew you were ready to handle it." He looked at Buck and winked. "All we can do now is wait and see if maybe I was completely wrong."

As the afternoon wore on, both Flint and Buck took a walk about the town, but as suppertime at Clara's Kitchen approached, there was no sign of any additional visitors from the Cloverleaf Cattle Ranch. Flint and Buck were at Clara's door when she opened up. "You boys must be extra hungry tonight," she commented when she unlocked the door to let them in.

"We're kinda in a hurry tonight," Flint told her. "So, we'll eat and go pretty quick."

His comment brought a little frown of disappointment to Mindy's face as she poured two cups of coffee. "What's your hurry?" she asked. "Is something wrong?"

"No, nothing like that," Flint answered. "We're just

expecting to see some cowhands in town who ain't ever been here before. And we wanna be sure to let 'em know they need to behave."

"They might show up here, looking for supper," Clara said, "after they get good and liquored up down at Jake's."

"That's a possibility," Flint said. "But we'll try to be handy if you need us."

"Maybe it's a good idea he showed up," Clara said. She nodded toward a heavyset man sitting at a table by himself. "Maybe I'll ask him to stick around a while." Buck nodded in agreement.

Flint looked at the man but couldn't place him. He looked slightly familiar, so he figured he'd seen him around town somewhere. "Who is he?"

Clara jerked her head back to do a double-take. She said, . "He's my husband, Jim."

"Well, I'll be . . ." Flint started, astonished. "I forgot you were married. I know I ain't ever seen him in here before. Has he ever been in here durin' open hours?"

"Of course he has," she replied. "He just doesn't hang around much."

"Well, tell him to hang around tonight," Flint said. "He's a husky-lookin' fellow. Damn near as big as Buck."

"He's a good man," Buck said. "It was him and John Harper that talked Harvey Baxter into hirin' you as a deputy."

"Well, I reckon that makes me the dumbest one in the room," Flint said.

They managed to get through their supper uninterrupted and remembered to carry a plate of food back to the office for Ralph. On the way back, Flint felt he had to ask Buck if he was going to be all right. It was nearly the time of night when Buck usually bade him good night and retired to his room to deal with his demons. "Damn right I'm gonna be all right!" Buck responded. "I might need to take one good drink to settle my blood, but that's all I'll need. I ain't about to let you have all the fun with those boys from Cloverleaf."

"I knew I could count on you," Flint said. "Looks like most of the stores are closin' up for the day. I think I'll walk the street one more time. Make sure everybody locks up tight."

"Good idea," Buck said. "I'll walk with you." He was fighting an urge to stop in his room and take a couple of drinks, but he hoped if he stayed with Flint, he had a better chance of abstaining. So, the two lawmen went back out to walk the street, fully expecting trouble.

Trouble was not far away. Four riders approached the main street of Tinhorn from the south. When they came to Lon Blake's stable, they reined their horses to a stop to take a look at the town. "It ain't much of a town," Drew Price stated. "I don't see but one place that looks like a saloon."

"It looks like they're closin' the whole damn town up for the night, and we just got here," Lem Dixon said.

"Well, let's wake 'em up again," Price said. "Come on, Charley, I'll race you up to that hotel and back to that saloon."

"You're on," Charley Tate replied. Price drew his six-gun and fired it in the air. Charley pulled his and did the same, and the horses jumped to a full gallop. Their two other companions started to race with them, whooping and yelling, but decided to stop at the saloon and let Drew and Charley finish the race.

Up the street, Flint and Buck had stopped at Harper's Feed & Supply to talk to John Harper as he was moving some items inside his store in preparation for closing. They were discussing the planned trip Flint and John were going to take with the mayor Monday morning when they heard the sudden gunfire that announced the arrival of the visitors. In a few seconds, the two cowhands from Cloverleaf galloped past them, yelling and firing their pistols, chasing the few people left on the street to run for cover. Whooping and laughing, they continued up the street to the hotel. They circled their horses around and around while they reloaded, obviously intending to race back down the street. "I reckon we'd best have a talk with 'em," Flint said. He picked an axe handle out of a barrel full of them that John was about to wheel inside the store. "Mind if I try one of these out?" Buck knew what he had in mind, so he pulled one out as well. "You particular about which side?" Flint asked. When Buck said one was as good as the other, Flint said, "I'll go across the street then." And he walked over to the other side to await the cowhands' return trip.

With pistols reloaded, the two hell-raisers kicked their horses into a gallop again, paying no attention to the two men standing beside the street. In a blatant display of daring, Price let his reins drop and raised both arms up in the air, firing his pistol and yelling his brains out. It inspired Charley to do the same, offering targets too good to pass up. Buck and Flint swung their axe handles as hard as they could to make up for the absence of weight, since there were no blades on the handles. With the horses at full gallop, it was enough force to unseat both riders to land on their fannies in the middle of the street.

Dazed and disoriented, the wind knocked out of them, both victims of the Tinhorn welcome committee struggled to get on their hands and knees. Thinking that possibly the sharp pain in their chests and bellies was caused by a bullet, they felt their shirts for blood. Confused when they didn't find any, they suddenly became aware of the two men standing on either side of them.

"Welcome to Tinhorn," Flint greeted them. "It's against the law to discharge a firearm in the city limits of Tinhorn, punishable by a ten-day jail sentence. It's obvious to us that you weren't aware of that law, so we're willin' to cut you a little slack this one time. I'll be frank with you fellows, though, we don't stand for no rowdy behavior in Tinhorn. So the second time you come down the middle of our streets raising hell like that, you'll be knocked outta the saddle with a .44 slug. In case you're wonderin', this is the sheriff's office you're dealin' with. Now get up from there, pick up your pistols, and holster 'em." He nodded toward their two horses, which were now standing in the middle of the street in front of the saloon. "You need to get your horses tied up at the rail, so they ain't standin' around loose. Enjoy the rest of your evenin'."

He had no sooner said that when Lem Dixon and Alvin Jeeter, the other two in the cowhand foursome, walked out to get the two loose horses. They led them back to the rail at Jake's Place and tied them with their horses. "I swear . . ." Alvin was inspired to ask, "you reckon that was enough to raise ol' Drew's temperature?"

"I expect we'll be listenin' to what happened for the rest of this evenin', and what he's gonna do to that feller," Lem said. "Let's go on in and get us a drink." They walked through the small crowd that had gathered at the door of the saloon when they heard the shooting. When they were inside, they paused briefly to look the room over. Drew liked to be in the center of the room, so everybody in the saloon could benefit from whatever he had on his mind to talk about. So they picked a table next to one where a card game had evidently been in progress.

Alvin walked to the bar and smacked his hand down

hard several times. "Bartender!" He yelled it out, causing Rudy, who was at the door with everyone else, to look around.

"I'll be with you in a minute," Rudy called back, still straining to see out into the street.

"I want a drink now," Alvin said and reached over the bar to find a bottle. He grabbed a couple of glasses off the bar and took the bottle over to the table. "I don't know what the hell is in this bottle," he said to Lem. "It ain't got no label. I hope it's the good stuff." They poured a drink and tossed it back. "It don't taste too bad at that." He poured another just as Rudy came back inside.

"Couple of hell-raisin' cowhands met up with Sheriff Moran and Buck Jackson," he said to the two at the table. "Sorry to make you wait. What's your pleasure?"

"Our pleasure was to get a drink of likker," Lem said. "And I wanted it when I walked in, not after a while sometime."

"Well, again, I'm sorry to make you wait, what would you like?" Rudy asked.

"This'll do," Alvin said.

Pretending he had not noticed the bottle on the table until then, Rudy said, "Oh my goodness! How did that get out here?" He hurried over and picked the bottle up. "You didn't drink any outta this bottle, did ya?"

"Why?" Alvin asked, at once alarmed. "What is it?"

"Bottle acid," Rudy said. "I use this to clean the spittoons and take off some of the crud that cakes up on the shot glasses. That's the reason there ain't no label on it."

The faces of both men turned pale.

"What will it do to you if you drink some of it? Will it kill you?" Lem asked.

"I don't know," Rudy answered. "I ain't never had nobody drink any of it before. Corn whiskey might be good to water it down a little. You wanna try a shot of that? It'll dilute this acid, most likely."

"Yeah, bring us a bottle of corn whiskey," Alvin said. "You oughta be more careful where you leave that other stuff around."

"I expect you're right," Rudy said. "I reckon I never thought anybody would drink out of a bottle with no label on it." He put the bottle back under the bar, where he always kept it. There was no label on it because it was Jake Rudolph's private bottle of expensive scotch whiskey. And Rudy didn't like it when anybody reached behind his bar and took something, so he decided to give these two saddle tramps something to think about while they sat around in the saloon. He picked up a bottle of corn whiskey and took it to the table.

When he walked back to the bar, he heard one of them confess to the other, "I swear, I've got a right peculiar feelin' in the pit of my stomach. Are you feelin' all right?"

CHAPTER 6

Drew Price and Charley Tate walked through the little gathering of spectators at the saloon door, and they promptly followed them inside. "What the hell are you lookin' at?" Drew demanded of Tom Dawkins, a young man who worked at the sawmill south of town. Tom didn't answer, but he met Drew's stare with one of his own. Seeing their companions seated at a table, Drew and Charley went directly to them and sat down.

Rudy didn't wait for them to come to the bar; he picked up a couple of glasses and took them to the table. "Your friends are drinkin' corn whiskey," he said. "You wantin' anything different?"

"Might as well finish this bottle first," Drew said, still plenty hot from his rude welcome to Tinhorn. He gritted his teeth as he felt his ribs, thinking one or two of them might be broken. With his other hand, he poured himself a drink before handing the bottle to Charley. "It's a wonder somebody ain't called that blowhard out," he stated.

Rudy couldn't resist. "I see you met our sheriff," he commented.

Drew cocked his head to give Rudy a hard stare. "Yeah, I met him. The younger one, I reckon he's the sheriff, since he did all the talkin'."

"That's right," Rudy said. "The younger one's the sheriff. The other one used to be the sheriff. You mighta heard of him. Name's Buck Jackson."

"Nah," Drew said. "I ain't ever heard of him. What's the sheriff's name? Flint Moran, huh?" he responded when Rudy told him. "I'll remember that name. Feller like that don't usually last a long time before he meets up with somebody who don't wanna put up with him." Rudy decided it a good idea not to annoy Drew any further. There was evidence enough of a real troublemaker in the man's scowl.

"I bet I'm gonna have a helluva bruise across my belly," Charley complained to Lem Dixon, "even if there ain't nothin' broke inside me. My behind is hurtin' about as much as my belly, though. I sat down hard on that dirt. How 'bout you, Drew? Your tail hurtin' like mine?"

"Nah," Drew lied. "Take more'n that to make my tail hurt." Most of his pain was centered in his pride, and the fact he had been made to look the clown in front of the three men he rode in with, plus the crowd of spectators. It wasn't something he took lightly, and it didn't help when he became aware that the four men at the table next to his had resumed their card game. However, they seemed more interested in listening to the talk at his table, especially Charley's buffoonlike complaints about his aches and pains. Finally, he let his annoyance be known when he caught Tom Dawkins staring at him. Recognizing Tom as the man he had exchanged glares with when he walked in, he demanded, "Is there some business you think you've got at this table?" When Tom wasn't sure how to answer, Drew said, "I advise you to keep your nose outta what's goin' on at this table, else I'm liable to teach you how to mind your own business."

Surprised by Drew's strong reaction and obvious challenge, Tom had no desire to get into it with the hotheaded stranger. But there was also the principle of a man's pride. So he tried to carefully word his response. "I ain't really been payin' much attention to what you and your friends are talkin' about. I'm a lot more interested in what's in my hand after the deal."

"I catch you eyeballin' me again and you better get ready to have a gun in your hand," Drew responded. "I see you're wearin' one. I reckon that's just for show, ain't it, you yellow-bellied sodbuster?" There was an immediate pause in the general noise of the saloon after Drew's response.

Acutely aware of it, Tom Dawkins found himself in a dangerous situation, one he had had no intention of being a part of. He looked at Drew Price, glaring at him now with a crooked smile gradually forming, and he was at once afraid that this would not be the first gun duel the man had fought. He did not want to back down, but he was not willing to bet against a man so eager to fight him. Seeing his hesitation, Drew issued his final threat. "If you don't get on your feet and face me man-to-man, I'm gonna shoot your cowardly butt where you sit."

For Tom, there was no longer any choice. He was dead either way. "There ain't no reason for this," he muttered weakly as he got up from his chair.

Drew, who had already gotten up and taken a position in the center of the room, stood waiting. At the moment, Tom represented Flint Moran in Drew's mind. And shooting Tom down would be a preview of what he would do to the sheriff. "All right, sodbuster, whenever you're ready."

"We don't have to do this," Tom pleaded, no longer concerned about his reputation as a man.

Enjoying himself now in the face of what he read as out-and-out cowardice, Drew said, "All right, Dead Man, he'll count to three, and we'll draw on the number. Count to three, Charley."

Grinning with delight at the entertainment, Charley started the count. He got as far as two before he felt the cold nose of a Colt .44 pressed against the back of his neck. "You say 'three' and this gun is gonna knock a hole in the back of your head."

When the count stopped at two, Drew took his eyes off Tom for a second, long enough to see Flint behind Charley. At the same time, he felt his gun being lifted from his holster. He automatically reached for it, only to have his wrist captured in the iron grip of a powerful hand. Before he had time to react, his left arm was snatched back behind him and handcuffed to his right. He tried to struggle, but it was a useless endeavor against the power of Buck Jackson. Flint drew Charley's gun from the holster and stuck it in his belt. "You two are just bound and determined to get in trouble, aren't you?" Flint cuffed Charley's hands behind his back. "We let it slide when you came into town raisin' hell, and here you are, breakin' another law in our town. I'm afraid you've earned yourselves a little jail time and an appointment to see the judge. We don't stand for gunplay in our town." Even though he threatened it, he didn't really think he would turn them over to be tried by Judge Graham Dodge. He figured a couple of days in jail might send a message to the rest of the Cloverleaf Cattle Company that they should behave whenever they came to Tinhorn.

Fuming, Drew Price was not willing to go peacefully. With his hands cuffed behind his back, however, there was not a great deal he could do to avoid going to jail. Still, he threatened to resist. "Maybe I don't feel like walkin' to your damned ol' jail. If you want me in that jail, you're gonna have to carry me."

"That ain't a problem," Flint told him. "Buck, if you'll guard these two, I'll get the rope off one of those horses out front and we'll drag these boys to jail."

"I'll walk," Charley said at once.

"Okay, then we don't need but one rope," Flint said and started toward the front door.

"I'll walk," Drew said reluctantly.

"Good decision," Flint said and motioned toward the door with his pistol. "Start walkin'."

The crowd of spectators parted once again, this time for the sheriff and his prisoners. They walked them across the street to the jail, where Ralph met them at the door. After relieving the prisoners of their weapons and all other possessions that might be used as a weapon, they locked them away in the smaller of the two cells.

As soon as Flint turned the key that locked up the two Cloverleaf men, Drew started with his warnings about making an enemy of Ira Dunellen. "You're gittin' ready to make the biggest mistake a sheriff can make," he started. "When you make Ira Dunellen your enemy, you're gonna find out what trouble is." He looked over at his companion and said, "That's a good name for this town, ain't it, Charley? Tinhorn, and they've got 'em a genuine tinhorn sheriff."

"I'm not making an enemy of Ira Dunellen," Flint informed him, ignoring the personal insult. "I'm only locking up people who don't think they have to obey our laws. I hope Dunellen becomes a good neighbor for the town of Tinhorn. If he's the right kind of man, I don't think he'll approve of your behavior in our town."

"I reckon you'll find out what kind of man Ira Dunellen is," Drew replied.

"I reckon so," Flint agreed.

Back at Jake's Place, the two Cloverleaf cowhands sat at their table with their bottle of corn whiskey. "Ain't that a helluva note?" Lem Dixon asked Alvin Jeeter. "We shoulda known Drew would get into some kinda trouble. You think we shoulda jumped in there and helped him and Charley? Them two couldn'ta whupped the four of us."

"Maybe not," Alvin allowed, "but who knows how this crowd in here woulda acted if we'd jumped on their sheriff and his deputy? All four of us mighta ended up in jail, or maybe doin' a little dance at the end of a rope."

"I expect it'd be a good idea for us to ride on back and warn the rest of the boys about shootin' up the town when they ride in," Lem suggested.

"Yeah, we better warn 'em, but there ain't no hurry. There ain't but six more that ain't been into town yet. And Lucas said they couldn't go till tomorrow mornin'. So we might as well finish this bottle of whiskey. And I've been thinkin' I might wanna have a little visit with that gal talkin' to the bartender. There's a couple of fellers come down them steps since we've been settin' here, and they looked pretty happy." Concern for the contents of the bottle with no label were already forgotten.

"Well, if you'll take my advice, you'll go ahead and talk to her before we finish this bottle of whiskey," Lem suggested. "You're more likely to know what the hell you went up there for."

"You talked me into it," Alvin said. "I'll go talk to her now, before somebody else gets the itch. What about you? You wanna talk to her?"

"Nope, not tonight anyway. I'll wait for you, and when you're done, let's get on back to the ranch. You can tell her I love her, too."

"I'll tell her," Alvin said and got up to approach Lucy. After only a few minutes, she led him up the stairs. Lem had a couple more snorts out of their bottle, then went to talk to the bartender until Alvin came back downstairs with a foolish grin on his face and his pocket three dollars lighter.

"Too bad about your friends," Rudy said as they were leaving. "Reckon there'll be any more of your crew in town tonight?"

"Not tonight," Lem said. "Some of the other boys will be here tomorrow, though."

"Right," Rudy said as they walked out the door. He passed that information on to Flint when he came in to check the saloon again later that evening.

Good, Flint thought, because Buck had decided to knock off for the night after they got Drew and Charley locked up. Flint had told Buck he thought there was not much danger of any more of their crew showing up this late. He was glad to hear Rudy say the same. Buck had done well to stay steady as late as he did. Maybe there was a chance he would beat his demons in the long run. He untied the two horses that belonged to Drew and Charley and led them down to the stable. Lon Blake had already locked up and gone home, so Flint unsaddled the horses and turned them loose in the corral. When Lon came in the next morning, he would know where they came from, and he would take care of them. One more look around town to satisfy himself that all was peaceful, then he retired to the sheriff's office, where he found Ralph still awake and awaiting his return.

"I was hopin' you was comin' back here tonight," Ralph said when Flint walked in. He was never comfortable without Flint or Buck in the office overnight when there were prisoners in the cells.

"Yeah," Flint said. "I figured I'd sleep here tonight to make sure our prisoners don't cause any trouble."

* * *

The next morning found the little town of Tinhorn in its typical peaceful Sunday atmosphere. Buck surprised them when he showed up at the office bright and early, well before the time Clara usually opened the dining room for breakfast. "You musta had a good night's sleep," Flint commented when he walked in. "Did you smell the coffee Ralph just made?"

"Didn't see no sense in stayin' around in bed," Buck replied cheerfully, obviously feeling good first thing in the morning for a change. It was a good sign as far as Flint was concerned. Buck had too many good years left in him to surrender to alcohol. "Have any trouble outta those two last night?" Buck asked.

"Not any more than usual," Flint said. "The one that wanted to shoot it out with Tom Dawkins complained about his rights to defend himself. And he told me about all the trouble I was gonna find myself in when Ira Dunellen found out I'd put him in jail."

"He must be a real important man," Buck joked.

"They went to sleep after that," Flint continued. "So Ralph went in and slept in the other cell. I think they're just wakin' up. Is that right, Ralph?"

"Yep," Ralph answered. "I think they smelled the coffee."

"You make a full pot?" Flint asked. Ralph said he did, so Flint said, "Ask them if they want a cup."

"They already said they wanted a cup," Ralph said. "I told 'em it was up to you whether they got one or not."

"I reckon they could use a cup," Flint said. "Fill a couple and I'll go in with you."

Ralph started to fill two cups but paused after filling the first one. "That's cuttin' it pretty close on this pot. Are you gonna want another cup?"

"No, Buck and I are goin' to breakfast in about twenty

minutes. I'll wait till then." Ralph filled the other cup with the last of the pot, then picked up the two cups and followed Flint into the cell room. Upon seeing the coffee come in, both prisoners rushed to the cell door. "Stick your hand through the bars and Ralph will put a cup in it."

They did that, then stepped back far enough to get enough room to sip it. After a few sips of the hot liquid, Drew, still brash, spoke out. "All right, we spent the night in your damned old jail. How 'bout lettin' us out now?"

"You're gonna be with us a little longer than one night," Flint told him. "Threatening to kill a man is a little more serious offense than drunk and disorderly conduct. You weren't even drunk when you threatened to kill a man if he didn't stand up and face you. So you'll be here a while. I've gotta find out when we can get a judge to schedule you for a trial."

"What about me?" Charley asked before Drew had time to protest. "I didn't threaten to shoot nobody."

"No, but you're guilty as an accomplice in the planned murder of the man," Flint told him, hoping that was the right word for it.

"You're gonna be in more trouble than you ever thought of before when Ira Dunellen finds out you arrested me," Drew repeated his warning of the day before. "You'll be lucky if you still have a job as sheriff when he gets through with this two-bit town. They named it right when they called it Tinhorn," he informed Flint again.

"'Preciate the warnin'," Flint said. "In the meantime, we'll try to make your stay with us as comfortable as we can. We'll bring you breakfast in about an hour or less. Enjoy your coffee."

"You're a dead man," Drew charged.

"That's one more death threat, Ralph," Flint said. "We'll have to remember to tell Judge Dodge about that one, too."

After talking it over with Buck, he had already decided not to send the two of them up before the judge. But he and Buck both thought it would be a good idea to hold them in jail until after the planned meeting with Dunellen on Monday. It might serve to notify Dunellen that Tinhorn would not hesitate to punish wrongdoers in the town.

They waited a few moments longer before leaving to walk up to the hotel and the dining room, so as to give Clara time to open her door for breakfast. They were still a few minutes early, enough to draw a couple of comments for their eagerness to eat. "Good morning," Bonnie greeted them. "Have a seat and I'll get you some coffee. I suppose you're in a hurry to get your breakfast, so you can get to church early and get seats in the front row."

"That's right, Bonnie," Buck replied. "The sermon this mornin' is about you, and we wanna get there on time, so we don't miss any of it, especially all the bad parts."

"Well, you better prepare to stay late 'cause it's bound to be a long sermon," Bonnie fired back at him.

"Good mornin', Bonnie," Flint said. "We'll be needin' three plates of breakfast to take back with us this mornin'."

"Did you arrest two of those Cloverleaf riders?" she asked, knowing one of the plates would be for Ralph.

"That's right. Buck and I arrested two of 'em in Jake's Place last night."

Mindy rushed in from the kitchen at that moment with two cups of coffee, which she placed on Buck's preferred table. Bonnie, never passing up an opportunity to tease the young girl, pretended to whisper to Flint. "Don't worry, I won't tell Mindy what we were talking about."

Knowing Bonnie well, Mindy paid her no mind. "Mornin', Flint," she said sweetly. "Mornin', Buck," she added then. Clara came from the front to join the other two women at the table. All three were anxious to know if the lawmen had any notions about whether or not they might be visited by men from the Cloverleaf Ranch.

"We don't have any idea whether you will or not," Flint told them. "But I don't know why they would cause you any problems if they did come in. We told those fellows in Jake's last night to let the other riders know they would have to take off their guns if they ate here. Buck and I will keep an eye on 'em while they're in town. So far, we've just met up with a couple of troublemakers from that ranch, and they're in jail right now."

"You ladies act like we're in some kinda war with that crew from the Cloverleaf brand," Buck commented. "It ain't no different from any other times when we've had some troublemakers hit town. Rudy Price told Flint last night that there were some other hands who were plannin' on comin' to Tinhorn today. Evidently, their foreman, Lucas Sawyer, didn't want the whole crew leavin' the ranch at the same time, if they're raisin' as many cows as they claim. So he split 'em up. It would be my guess that the men who are supposed to show up today ain't the real hell-raisers who can't wait to hit the saloon. So, maybe some of them will want a fine Sunday dinner. I'm sure they'll be tickled with the food they get here."

That seemed to put things in the proper perspective for the three women. "I guess we were puttin' the cart before the horse," Clara said. "It'll probably be a Sunday like every other Sunday."

It turned out that Buck was pretty accurate when he summed up the situation. The six remaining men to visit Tinhorn split up when they came to town. There was no firing of guns on arrival. Two of the men did go to Clara's Kitchen for Sunday dinner and were not reluctant to leave their guns on the table while they ate. The other four men spent their time in Jake's Place, joined later by the two who ate at Clara's. There was no trouble from the Cloverleaf brand. There was, however, a couple of stray cows that had to be chased out of the churchyard.

Tying up loose ends and making arrangements to leave her small ranch took a while, so it was months before Arleen Daugherty got her first look at Tinhorn, Texas. Entering the town at the south end, she looked at the shops and businesses on both sides of the one main street as Paul Roper drove her wagon along the main street. He pointed to Harper's Feed & Supply as they drove past and told her that was where he worked. Pointing to another building, he said, "There's the post office where your pa works. It's closed on Sunday."

Turning at the side street beside the hotel, Paul drove the wagon to a small frame house and pulled up in the yard. He stepped down and turned to assist Arleen down, while Angus jumped off the back of the wagon. "Wait!" Arleen warned the four-year-old when he attempted to follow his brother down as well. Paul hurried to the back to lift Brendan out.

"Arleen!" Jimmy Wheeler yelled as he ran out the door of the house to greet his sister. He was followed shortly by their father, who took his daughter in his arms, and they both cried. Seeing the confusion that caused for Angus and Brendan, Jimmy told them, "I'm your Uncle Jimmy. They're all right, they're just glad to see each other."

After their embrace and Louis Wheeler had a chance to welcome his two grandsons, he took time to thank Paul Roper for going after Arleen. He had gotten permission from John Harper to let Paul go down and move his daughter to Tinhorn, and he had given Paul ten dollars to do it. "I can take care of it from here," Wheeler told Paul. "You've done a fine job and I appreciate it."

"Don't you want me to take the wagon down to Lon Blake's and take care of the horses?" Paul asked.

"No, thanks, anyway," Wheeler replied. "You got 'em here safe and sound. I can take care of the rest. Jimmy and I'll do the unloadin'."

Arleen and her boys said goodbye to Paul, and she thanked him again for seeing her family safely there. "I know it doesn't look like much more than a shack," her father apologized for the size of the house. "But this was all Jimmy and I needed. He's moved his stuff out of the pantry he was using for his bedroom, and your two boys can sleep there. I figured I'd put you in the one bedroom, and Jimmy and I can bunk in the front room. We ain't got no use for a parlor anyway. We'll get you unloaded, and I'll take the horses and the wagon to Lon Blake's stable. Then tonight, we'll eat supper at the hotel dining room."

"Oh, Papa," Arleen said, "we don't have to do that. Maybe I can rustle up something simple. Do you have anything to cook?"

"Not much," he answered. "No fussin' over that tonight. We'll eat at Clara's Kitchen tonight, and you can go to the store and get your kitchen set up tomorrow." She nodded and smiled, happy to be here and far away from her home and memories of Ira Dunellen.

CHAPTER 7

It was not difficult to find the new headquarters of the Cloverleaf Cattle Ranch. Flint started out by following the instructions he had been given by one of their cowhands. He soon found, however, that there was already the beginning of a permanent trail to the ranch just from the activity of the last few days. He found that, even had there been no trail, the ranch would be easy to find by riding downriver until striking the creek, then following the creek to the ranch. On Buster, riding along beside Harvey Baxter and John Harper in Baxter's buggy, Flint had the feeling of a guardian of a peace committee. He couldn't help feeling like he was accompanying a commission on its way to negotiate a peace contract with an invading army. Soon after leaving Lon Blake's stable on the south end of Tinhorn, they encountered small groups of stray cattle that caused some concern to the two businessmen. "For as big a cattle baron as they say he is, he's mighty careless about keeping his cattle together," John Harper commented.

"I'd have to agree with you," Baxter said. Flint made no comment, but it was his opinion that it was not carelessness at all. It was more like a plan of attack on the town, and the stray cows were the first of his invaders. It seemed a ridiculous thing to think, but he still thought about the casual suggestion Lucas Sawyer made that it might be a good idea for the town to move across the river. Consequently, he was anxious to meet Ira Dunellen, so he could judge the man for himself. Was he a man who thought entire towns should move out of his way?

After a ride of almost an hour and a half because of the buggy's pace, they saw the barn and a great two-story ranch house in the distance. They could see that there was still minor work to be done before the house would be completely finished. The barn appeared to be completed and the framework was up for the bunkhouse, and several of the men were nailing on siding. As they drew closer, the men working on the bunkhouse spotted them, and one of them walked away from the group, evidently coming to meet them. Flint recognized him as the foreman, Lucas Sawyer.

"Mornin'," Sawyer greeted them when they pulled up beside him. Recognizing Flint, he acknowledged him. "What can I do for you, Sheriff?"

"Mornin'," Flint returned. "This is Mayor Harvey Baxter and Mr. John Harper. They rode out here this mornin' to meet your boss, Mr. Dunellen." Turning to look at Baxter then, he said, "This is Mr. Sawyer. He's the foreman."

Baxter took over then. "Good to meet you, Mr. Sawyer. As Flint just said, I'm the mayor of Tinhorn, but I'm also owner of the Bank of Tinhorn. Mr. Harper, here, owns Harper Feed and Supply. We came to welcome Mr. Dunellen to the county and, specifically, to the town of Tinhorn. We have a strong sense of cooperation with all the ranches and farms that have been drawn to the services that the town offers. And we feel that it's important that we establish the same cooperation between the town and Cloverleaf Ranch."

Lucas Sawyer nodded, as if he understood Baxter's intent to be neighborly, but it was Flint's opinion that the foreman thought his boss was probably not the slightest bit interested in wasting time talking to the mayor. "Well, that's mighty neighborly of you folks to come all the way out here to tell Mr. Dunellen that," Lucas said. "I know he wouldn't want to miss your visit, but I'm not sure he's here right now. He likes to take his mornin' ride to make sure the cattle are being cared for properly, and I'm not sure if he's out right now or not. I've been workin' with the men building the bunkhouse, so I'll go to the house right quick to see if he's here or not. Wait right here, and I'll be right back." He paused only a moment to witness the helpless expressions on the faces of Baxter and Harper before turning and walking briskly toward the house.

"Well, wouldn't you know we picked a bad time to show up here?" Harper asked. "Most likely the only time of day he ain't home."

"He's here," Flint said. "I think it's safe to say Dunellen's foreman always knows when his boss has left the headquarters. He's goin' to the house to see if Dunellen wants to be bothered with a visit from the town of Tinhorn." He shrugged, then added, "I think he'll see us because he'll wanna know why we've got two of his men in jail." He didn't express it, but he was also of the opinion that a man like Ira Dunellen would want to size up his competition. And Flint wasn't sure that Baxter and Harper could cause him much concern. "We might as well pull on up to the front steps, so His Majesty doesn't have to walk far." He nudged Buster and moved up closer to the porch. Baxter looked as if he wasn't sure they should ignore the foreman's instructions to wait where he had said.

"What is it, Lucas?" Ira Dunellen asked. "Atha said you wanted to see me." He sat back in his big leather desk chair and took a sip from the cup of coffee that Atha Cheney, his cook and housekeeper, brought him.

"Sorry to bother you, Boss," Lucas apologized for disturbing him. "Three fellows from Tinhorn just rode in. The mayor, Harper from Harper's Feed and Supply, and the sheriff, they say they wanted to come welcome you to the county."

Dunellen looked irritated. "Oh, they do, do they? Well, I've got better things to do with my time than talk to them."

"I told them I didn't know if you had rode out to check the stock this mornin', and I wasn't sure if you were here or not," Lucas said. "Want me to tell 'em you ain't here?"

"Yeah, tell 'em I'm not here. . . . No, wait, tell 'em I'll be happy to meet them and I'll be out in a few minutes. Then leave 'em to wait by the front steps. Tell 'em I'm workin' on something important, which is no lie." He held up the cup of hot coffee Atha just brought him. "I've got to finish this before it gets cold. But you don't have to tell them that."

"Yes, sir, I understand," Lucas answered. "I'll tell 'em you'll be a few minutes." He left him to enjoy his coffee and went out the front door and down the steps from the porch where the Tinhorn delegation was waiting. "Mr. Dunellen said he'd be happy to meet you. He's workin' on something he's right in the middle of, but he shouldn't be longer than a couple of minutes."

Baxter thanked him, and he and Harper stepped down from the buggy to wait for their audience with Dunellen. Lucas left then and returned to the construction of the bunkhouse. Flint dropped Buster's reins to the ground and walked over beside them. They made small conversation for a while until they became aware of the time they had been waiting. Finally, Flint thought the game had gone on long enough. "That son of a gun is playin' a game with us," he declared. "Wants to see how long we'll stand out here and wait for him. Whaddaya say I go up on the porch and knock on his front door till he comes out?"

"No, Flint," Baxter responded. "Let's not start off bad with the man. This is a peace mission, after all. He didn't have any warning that we'd be here. Maybe it was a bad time to fall in on him."

It just happened at that moment that Buster saw fit to drop a couple of calling cards in the dusty yard in front of the steps. It inspired Flint to comment, "Buster speaks for both of us." Harper laughed, and Baxter tried not to but was forced to emit a chortle. Dunellen came out the door then, curious as to why they were laughing.

"Sorry to keep you waiting, gentlemen. What can I do for you?"

After introducing his party, Baxter went right into the little speech he had been practicing, the main theme of which was how important it was to have cooperation between the Cloverleaf and the Tinhorn people. He suggested how convenient the town could be for all the needs a big cattle outfit had, while stressing how important it was to obey the town's laws. "There are actually nuisance laws in place as well," Baxter said, "like laws against unattended livestock on the streets of the town, for example."

"If you're talkin' about stray cattle," Dunellen responded, "there's not much you can do about that. Cows will stray. You can't build a fence around three thousand cows."

"But you can determine where you graze your cattle," Flint responded. "With the size of the range you've taken over, you could move the bulk of your herd somewhere other than right on top of a town that's been there for years."

"You might see that as unfortunate for you," Dunellen responded. "But it is my range, and the section closest to Tinhorn has some of the best grazing spots. I'd be a fool to give them up." He concentrated his gaze on Flint then. "Tell me, Sheriff Moran, why do you have two of my men locked up in your jail?"

"That's where we put folks who break the law," Flint answered.

Plainly irritated now, Dunellen asked, "Just what law did they break?"

"To be more specific, we have to say 'laws,'" Flint said, "because they broke more than just one. They broke the law against shooting firearms within the town limits and the one against horse racing on the main street. They broke the one about disturbin' the peace with their yellin' and whoopin' and shootin' their guns. The more serious law they broke was attempted murder when they tried to make an innocent bystander stand up and be shot. I reckon we could add resistin' arrest, too, because they didn't come peacefully. Now, I should point out to you that both men were given a warning with no charges against them after they broke the first law. But they saw fit to challenge the rest of our laws. So, they gave me no choice but to put them in jail. If you'll promise me you'll talk to them about the seriousness of their lawbreakin', I'll release them from jail this afternoon. The town of Tinhorn is willin' to meet you halfway. If you respect our laws, we'll cooperate with you to make life easier for both of us. But I will continue to enforce our laws."

Judging by the fire in Ira Dunellen's eyes, it was obvious that he was not thrilled by the young lawman's lack of respect for him. Harvey Baxter's face registered mild shock for Flint's frank declaration of his intent to punish lawbreakers. Only John Harper grinned in reaction and looked ready to give Flint an "attaboy."

"Was there anything else you people wanted to discuss

with me?" Dunellen finally asked. "Because I have more important things to turn my attention to."

"As mayor of Tinhorn, I want to stress that we came here today hoping we could find a way to cooperate with each other, so that no one's life is interfered with. And all we're really asking is that you control your stray cattle, and your men act civilized when they come into our town. Is that really asking a lot?"

Dunellen cast a cold eye in the mayor's direction. "I can't really be bothered by what a few stray cows do," he said. "And the fact is, I don't need your town. I can send my own supply wagons to Tyler and buy my supplies for the same price you pay for the stock you'd turn around and sell me. Now, I'll say good day to you and good luck with your pitiful little town." He turned to leave as Baxter and Harper climbed back into the buggy, but stopped again for a final word for Flint. "And Sheriff, you might pick up your horse turds off my walkway." He turned and went up the steps.

"Right, Mr. Dunellen," Flint called after him. "I'm sorry about that." He reached in his saddlebag for his right-hand glove, since the droppings were quite fresh. Then he picked them up and placed them on the porch steps. "There," he said, "that'll make it easier for your housekeeper to take care of 'em."

Baxter cringed and almost got back out of the buggy to remove Buster's tokens of respect. He wondered if it had been a mistake to bring Flint with him. He said as much to John Harper, but Harper was convinced that Dunellen's lack of cooperation would be the same with or without Flint's presence. "Hell, Harvey, Dunellen ain't the least bit interested in gettin' along with us. I think Flint's right, Dunellen's figurin' on chasin' us across the river, so he can water his cows there. He's likely thinkin' about changing the name from Tinhorn to Dunellen. We're gonna have to stand up to that man, and we ain't likely to do it without Flint Moran." He shook his head and uttered half a chuckle. "I reckon we're gonna have to learn to live with a town full of cows."

They drove back to Tinhorn with nothing positive to show for their efforts. It didn't help the mood of the mayor when they encountered a stray steer standing in the street at the south end of town. "I'll take care of it," Flint said, and told Baxter to go on to the stable. The cow showed no fear of Flint when he dismounted beside it and didn't move while he tied a rope around his neck. He had considered throwing the rope, but he wasn't that good a roper, and it was a little more difficult roping a longhorn cow. Still thinking about Dunellen's attitude about the stray cows, Flint decided to make better use of the situation. So, he rode straight through town and out the road to Tyler, leading the cow. He continued on for a quarter of a mile until reaching a small wagon track leading off the road that led him to a small house and barn.

"Howdy, Flint," Richard Burnett called out when he saw him approaching the barnyard. "Whatcha got there?"

"How ya doin', Richard?" Flint returned. "I got a proposition for ya."

"Looks more like a cow," Richard came back, always one to crack a joke. He knew Flint mostly from what his sister told him about the young sheriff. Margaret, who did the cooking for Clara's Kitchen, talked a great deal about Flint and what a crush Mindy had on him.

"I know Clara buys a lot of pork from you for the dinin' room," Flint explained. "I thought you might want some beef for a change. So, I'm hopin' we can make a trade. You butcher this steer and take enough steak to Margaret to cook for two prisoners I've got locked up in the jail, and you can keep the rest of the cow for yourself to do with as you please. Whaddaya say?"

"That's a right good deal for me," Richard replied. "I ain't had any beef for quite a spell."

"I need to get it to Margaret for supper tonight," Flint said. "Is that any problem?"

"Nope," Richard said. "I'll butcher him this afternoon and take the meat to Margaret in plenty of time for supper. She'll be tickled to get some fresh beef. I'm sure you, Buck, and Ralph would enjoy a steak, too."

"Good enough," Flint declared. "We'll all enjoy it. Thank you, Richard."

"Thank you," Richard insisted. "I don't get much beef."

Flint rode back to the stable, where he unsaddled Buster and left him in the corral. He couldn't help feeling that it was only proper justice that Dunellen should bear the expense of feeding his own men. From the stable, he went directly to the office, where Buck was keenly interested in what had resulted from the visit to Cloverleaf. "It was about what you would expect when you're tryin' to negotiate with a man like Ira Dunellen," Flint said and went on to tell him how cold the cattle baron was toward them.

"Well, you got back in time for dinner, so whaddaya say we walk on up to Clara's?" Buck suggested.

"Good idea," Flint responded. "I know I'm ready to eat. I think I'm in the mood for a good steak later on tonight for supper, and we oughta treat our prisoners to one, too." He told Buck about the deal he made with Margaret's brother. "It was too late to ask him to cut us out some steaks for dinner, but he can get some to her in time for supper tonight."

Buck was tickled to hear about the deal and thought it the perfect use for Dunellen's stray cows. "Those two in the cell mighta known that cow personally," he commented. By the time they reached Clara's Kitchen, he had heard a full report on Dunellen's reaction to the meeting. "I coulda told Harvey Baxter he was wastin' his time tryin' to talk to a fellow like Dunellen. He don't think the rules apply to him. I'm afraid we're gonna have some real trouble with him before we're done."

"I'm afraid you're right," Flint replied as they walked in the door.

Hearing Flint's reply, Bonnie, who was standing at the door talking to Clara, asked, "Right about what? I'd like to know what Buck was right about."

"Everything, so far," Buck answered her. "I even know what you're gonna serve for supper tonight."

"Is that so?" Bonnie responded. "What's it gonna be?"

"Some fresh steaks from a prime steer," Buck answered.

Listening to their nonsense, Clara had to comment. "That may sound good, but it's not what Margaret's planning. I know that because I know we ain't got any fresh beefsteaks."

"Richard Burnett is butcherin' today," Buck said. "And he's gonna deliver some fresh steaks to your establishment this afternoon. Me and Flint are sure plannin' on eatin' a big steak, and we expect one for each of our prisoners, and one for Ralph, too. It's kind of a celebration."

Clara and Bonnie both looked at him as if he was talking total foolishness. "Margaret hasn't said anything to me about her brother bringing us fresh beef."

"That's because Margaret don't know it yet," Buck told her. "Flint just worked the deal out with Richard a little while ago."

Clara still wasn't sure that Buck was not in one of his silly moods, so she looked to Flint to make some sense of what Buck was claiming. "What is he talking about?"

"Like he said," Flint told her. "Dunellen refuses to make

any effort to control his strays, so I thought if he wants to keep supplyin' stray cows, we might as well put 'em to good use. He shouldn't complain as long as we're feedin' his men with 'em."

"Are you two going to eat, or just stand there talking?" Mindy was standing at the table near the kitchen door, holding two cups of coffee.

"Henry said Mr. Dunellen wants to see me," Lucas Sawyer said to Atha Cheney when she answered his knock at the kitchen door.

"Yes, Lucas," she replied. "He's in his study. You can go right on in. Did Henry go back to the washhouse?" Her husband, Henry, served as a general handyman around the ranch house, and his job that morning was to fix the pump in the washhouse.

"I don't know, Atha, but I think he already fixed the pump. I don't think there was much wrong with it. Heck, it's a brand-new pump."

"I swear," Atha declared, "you woulda thought he mighta told me. He knows I've gotta do a load of wash for Mr. Dunellen."

"I noticed that Mr. Dunellen's visit with the delegation from Tinhorn didn't last very long," Lucas commented. "He didn't even invite them in the house, did he?"

"No, he didn't," she replied. "And he wasn't very happy with them, especially that sheriff."

Lucas nodded his head thoughtfully when he thought of the young sheriff. He could see that Flint Moran was going to cause trouble for Dunellen's plan to eventually move that town out of his way. He left the kitchen then and went up the hall to Dunellen's study, where he found his boss studying a plat of the ranch headquarters. He looked up when Lucas walked into the room. "When are they going to finish the bunkhouse?"

"They'll get all the sidin' on it today," Lucas told him. "I'd say they'll have the floor in in two days. The rest should go pretty fast—hang some doors, set a couple of windows. But the men can move in while that's bein' finished."

"Good, good," Dunellen replied, then abruptly changed the subject. "I want you to ride into town and get those two men out of jail."

"Drew and Charley," Lucas replied. "Right, I'll saddle a horse and ride to town right away." He couldn't help thinking that Dunellen always ordered him to do things and never told him to *try* to do something.

"I'm tempted to send half a dozen of the boys in and break them out of that two-bit jailhouse," Dunellen said. "But you seemed to do a pretty good job of getting young Tim Walker out of jail when Moran had him locked up."

"This might be a little different," Lucas was quick to remind him. "Tim wasn't actually under arrest. The sheriff just let him sleep off a drunk."

Dunellen paused to consider that. "I'd forgotten that, but you're still likely to get some cooperation outta that clod."

"The town council seems to think he's a pretty effective sheriff," Lucas said, willing to give the devil his due.

"Nonsense." Dunellen snorted. "He's a hired gun, no more, no less. We'll prove that in the long run. You might let him know he's in for a rough time of it if he continues to fight me."

"Yes, sir, I'll let him know," Lucas replied dutifully, although it was obvious to him that Dunellen had not judged the man, Moran, the same as he had.

CHAPTER 8

Just as Flint had assured them, Richard Burnett delivered a load of freshly butchered beef to the back door of Clara's Kitchen. Ralph spotted Richard's wagon when he drove past the sheriff's office, and he alerted Flint. So, Flint walked back up to the dining room to see how much meat was actually delivered. He found that Margaret's brother had kept only a small portion for his personal use. When he walked around to the back door of the dining room, he found Margaret standing at the back of the wagon, her hands on her hips as she looked at the raw meat on her brother's wagon. Seeing Flint walk up, she said, "Well, Sheriff, there appears to be more than enough beef to take care of supper. Looks like good beef."

"That it does," Flint replied. "I'm lookin' forward to supper, and I know my two prisoners will be delighted, not to mention Ralph. So I'll see you at suppertime." He started back toward the sheriff's office, pleased that Clara had not come out yet to inspect the beef. He figured he had already answered enough questions from her on the visit to the Cloverleaf Ranch.

A Monday that started off quietly in the town of Tinhorn looked to be continuing as the day grew older. Motivated mostly by boredom, Flint walked around town, stopping in to talk to some of the merchants along the way. He looked in on his horse at the stable and passed some time talking to Lon Blake. When he left the stable, he noticed a dun horse tied at the rail in front of the sheriff's office, so he went to find out who it belonged to. "Here he is now," he heard Buck say as he was opening the door. He recognized the tall, rawboned man standing in the office.

"Well, Mr. Sawyer," Flint greeted him. "I didn't expect to see you again today. What can we do for you?"

Buck answered before Lucas had a chance to speak. "Mr. Sawyer is wantin' us to let his two men outta jail. I told him if it was up to me, he's welcome to 'em, but it ain't up to me."

When Buck paused, Lucas spoke. "I won't beat around the bush with you, Sheriff. What's it gonna take to get those two released?"

"I'm surprised you have to ask me that," Flint answered. "I told Mr. Dunellen this mornin' that if he would promise me he'd tell those two men to behave themselves when they come to town, I'd turn 'em loose this afternoon. I was disappointed when he wasn't interested. But I figured he liked it better when they weren't around. I know we'd like it a whole lot better if they were gone from here." He gave Lucas a friendly smile and said, "They'd have already been gone, and you wouldn'ta had to ride to town today. I reckon they'll have to serve some more time in jail, and maybe they'll learn to act like civilized human beings."

"What if I promise to make them behave themselves?" Lucas asked. "Mr. Dunellen is the owner, but I'm the one those men work for. I'm the one they call Boss. They damn sure better do what I tell 'em or they're gone from Cloverleaf."

"Well, that is something to consider," Flint said, stroking his chin as he thought about it. "I'll tell you the truth,

Lucas—you mind if I call you that? You can call me Flint—
I trust you a little more than I trust the man you ride for. If
you give me your word you'll control those two jaspers in
there, I'll let 'em go tonight."

"I give you my word," Lucas said at once.

Flint pretended to be thinking further on the subject,
then he continued. "I'll tell you what I'll do. In the name of
cooperation between Cloverleaf Cattle Company and the
town of Tinhorn, I'll release your men after supper tonight.
It's suppertime right now, so I think it wouldn't be neighborly for me to cut 'em loose and send 'em home without
any supper. Buck and I are fixin' to go to Clara's Kitchen
for supper. Why don't you come along with us? Because it
wouldn't be polite to make you miss supper, too. Clara will
fix up two nice suppers for your men and we'll bring 'em
back here for them. Then everybody can go home with full
bellies. Whaddaya say?"

Lucas didn't know what to say. He found it hard to believe Flint was really serious. On the other hand, it was a
way to gain Drew and Charley's release—and they were
going to get a free meal out of it, so if the sheriff was that
crazy, why not? "That's a right fine idea," he said. "It's
mighty neighborly of you and the town."

"Good," Flint said. "Buck, you ready? Ralph, lock the
door after us. We're goin' to supper." As they filed out
the door, Buck caught Ralph's eye and winked. Ralph
didn't understand why, but he winked back.

When they got to Clara's, Flint introduced Lucas to
Clara and told her he was the foreman at Cloverleaf Ranch.
Flint was very apologetic when he had to remind Lucas that
it would be necessary for him to leave his gun on the table
near the door. Lucas hesitated for only a moment before
mumbling, "What the hell . . ." and placed it on the table.
Clara was so astonished by Flint and Buck's supper guest,

she hadn't even thought about reminding Lucas of the rule. She was even more confused, since she now knew how Margaret's brother had come in possession of the cow she was serving up for supper. Both Mindy and Bonnie were standing by the lawmen's usual table. Mindy was already holding two cups of coffee, so Bonnie asked Lucas if he wanted coffee or water. He picked coffee. She went at once to get him a cup.

Always the curious one, Bonnie placed the cup of coffee on the table, then went directly to the front door to question Clara. She had noticed when they came in with the stranger that Clara appeared to have lost her composure for a moment. "Who is he?" she asked Clara.

"He's the foreman at the Cloverleaf Ranch," Clara answered.

"Oh, my stars . . ." Bonnie dragged out softly. Then a mischievous grin slowly began to form on her face when she was struck by the irony of his visit on the first day of the new item on the menu. "Well, let's make sure he enjoys his supper," she said cheerfully then and went back to help Mindy. When she got back to the table, she asked Mindy if she had taken their orders yet. When Mindy said she was about to, Bonnie didn't hesitate. "Well, gents, Margaret's cookin' steaks tonight. How do you like 'em? Rare? Burnt? Somewhere in the middle? We won't guarantee it, but we'll try to cook 'em the way you want 'em."

The meat was pretty good, not as tough as Flint had thought it might be. The conversation was sparse, as he had expected it to be. "To be the biggest cattle ranch in Texas," was his simple answer when Lucas was asked what Dunellen's goal was.

"Do you think he'll make it?" Buck asked.

"I don't know," Lucas answered honestly. "He's already come a long way toward it in the time that I've been working for him. So I wouldn't bet against him." Flint took the opportunity to study the tall, slim foreman carefully, and he decided that Dunellen had made a wise choice. He could imagine that Lucas was a strong, serious foreman who had little time for nonsense and probably expected 100 percent out of his men. Finally, Lucas asked the question. "That was a good steak. Where does Clara's Kitchen get their beef?"

"Oh, here and there," Flint answered him. "A good portion of the meat for the dinin' room comes from the cook's brother's farm. But he raises pigs mostly, so he supplies just about all of the bacon, ham, chops, and such. As far as beef, though, that usually comes from a cow that's broke a leg or had some other kind of accident. There's been a little more of that within the last few weeks." He paused, as if something just occurred to him. "This might notta been the best night to invite you to supper, when Clara's havin' beef. That's probably about all you get at the ranch. Too bad Margaret ain't servin' pork chops tonight."

Flint felt pretty sure Lucas was well aware that they were feeding him and his men in the jail Cloverleaf beef. But he had to admire the coolness of the solemn foreman as he dined on what he undoubtedly knew to be one of his stray cattle. He confirmed it when he responded to Flint's comments. "Not at all," he said. "I like some pork occasionally. Usually have bacon every mornin'. But I always enjoy good beef, and I know this tonight came from good stock."

When they had finished supper, Bonnie and Mindy brought out the three steaks for the jail. Lucas thanked Flint for the meal, then followed Buck outside while Flint waited to pay Clara for Lucas's supper. "What's this?" Clara asked when Flint held out the money.

"It's for his supper," Flint answered. "I invited him to

supper. I didn't expect you to give it to him just because Buck and I don't pay for ours. The town council pays for ours, but it sure doesn't pay for Cloverleaf hands."

"Keep your money, Flint," Clara insisted, pushing his hand away. "I know you were just showin' that fellow what was going to be happening to his cattle if he didn't keep 'em away from town. So I wanna do my little part, too."

"I 'preciate it," Flint said, put his money back in his pocket, then took the plate of food Mindy was holding for him.

"Will you be here for breakfast in the mornin'?" Mindy asked.

"I sure will," Flint replied with a smile.

"Well, good night, then, I'll see you in the mornin'. I hope you have a good night."

"Good night," Flint returned and went out the door.

Mindy watched him as he walked to catch up with Buck and Lucas. Then she turned around to confront her two grinning coworkers. "What?" she demanded.

"'Good night. I hope you have a good night,'" Bonnie teased. "'I hope you dream about me all night long.'"

"Kiss my foot, Bonnie. You're just jealous. Isn't she, Clara?"

Clara shook her head slowly, a smile on her face. "If she isn't, she oughta be."

When they got back to the jail, they found that Ralph had made a big pot of coffee in preparation for his enjoyment of a steak supper. "I know you're anxious to get back to the ranch," Flint told Lucas. "But I'm gonna have to hold your men till they finish their supper because the plates and the knives and forks belong to Clara's Kitchen." Lucas gave a little chuckle, even though he was not positive that

Flint wouldn't pull some stunt to back out of the deal he made to let them go. He felt better when Buck sent Ralph to the stable to get Drew and Charley's horses.

Lucas didn't have to wait long, however, for the two prisoners ate the supper Margaret prepared for them in short order, anxious to get out of their cell. When they were ready to leave, and both Charley and Drew were in the saddle, Lucas turned to Flint and said, "You're a fair man, Sheriff. I appreciate that."

"Glad you think so," Flint replied. "I think you're a sensible man. I figure Dunellen's lucky to have you. I want you to convince him that we'd be happy to be a good neighbor to him. But this town is strong, and it will not surrender to his cattle empire."

"I understand what you're tryin' to say," Lucas said. "And I'll try to explain your position to Mr. Dunellen, but we might be tryin' to stop a tornado."

Drew Price sat on his horse, impatient to get started. He couldn't hear the conversation between Lucas and Flint, but his mind was boiling with thoughts of revenge for his arrest. A crooked smile broke out on his face as he stared at the sheriff. And he thought, *We'll meet again, and next time it'll be on my terms. You're a dead man, Flint Moran.*

Standing beside Flint, Buck saw the way Drew was staring at him, so he felt the need to warn his young friend. "Partner, don't ever turn your back on that feller. I think you made a real enemy outta that jasper."

"I expect you're right, but I'll give you the same advice," Flint said. "I don't think he enjoyed his stay with us."

A similar conversation was taking place on the trail leading to Cloverleaf Ranch. "I advise you to quit steppin' on Flint Moran's toes," Lucas Sawyer said to Drew Price.

"I have an idea there was a good reason to hire that young man to replace Buck Jackson as sheriff. I'd never heard of Flint Moran before we moved onto this range. But I had heard of Buck Jackson, and he had a helluva reputation."

"Ah, you know me, Boss," Drew responded. "I just like to have a little fun once in a while. That dead little town needs somethin' to liven it up, and what me and Charley was doin' wasn't hurtin' nobody. Ain't that right, Charley?"

"That's right, Boss," Charley said. "We was just makin' a little noise."

When they got back to the ranch, they found that most of the crew who weren't riding night herd were sitting around the unfinished bunkhouse. Drew and Charley received welcomes that were more of a sarcastic nature, and they replied in kind. As was his usual habit, Lucas spread his bedroll a little apart from the rest of them. When the bunkhouse was finished, he would have a private room partitioned off from the main room, where the men's bunks would be. He decided to wait until morning to report to Ira Dunellen that he had been successful in getting the two men released. As a rule, Dunellen did not like to be bothered after he ate his supper, unless it was a matter of life or death. And Lucas didn't think it was. He doubted that Dunellen knew which of his men were Drew Price and Charley Tate. It was the fact that the sheriff had the audacity to arrest any of his men. So, when morning came, Lucas ate with the men as usual, then took his time to arrive at the back door of the huge ranch house.

"Good mornin', Lucas," Atha greeted him. "The master has been askin' about you. He's in the dinin' room."

"Mornin', Atha. Is he still eatin' breakfast?" He didn't want to interrupt Dunellen's breakfast.

"Yes, he's finished, but he's still sittin' at the table, drinkin' coffee and waitin' for you to report."

"I'da been here sooner if I'd known he was that anxious to hear what happened," Lucas said and started toward the dining room at once. Atha went along behind him. They walked into the large dining room, where Dunellen was seated at the head of a long table. Atha went straight to the coffeepot on the small stove to see if it was empty. "Mornin', sir," Lucas said. "I'da been here sooner, but I didn't wanna interrupt your breakfast."

"Well, did you get my men outta that damn jail?" Dunellen asked bluntly.

"Yes, sir, I brought 'em back here after supper last night."

"Good," Dunellen responded. "I knew you could get them out if anybody could. Sit down and have some coffee. Atha, is there still some coffee left in that pot?" Atha said that there was. "Well, pour Lucas a cup." There didn't seem to be any question as to whether he wanted it or not, so Lucas sat down and thanked Atha when she served it. Dunellen continued then, his mood much improved since Lucas was successful in freeing the men. "Did you have to pay that sheriff any money to let them go?"

"No, no money," Lucas answered. "As a matter of fact, I was treated to a free meal at the hotel dinin' room. And Price and Tate were given their supper before they were released. That was the reason they paid for my supper."

"Treated you pretty nice, eh?" Dunellen said with a chuckle. "Sounds like that little crock of sodbusters is finally starting to realize they can't stand in the way of progress."

"I don't know, Boss." Lucas hesitated. "I found it a little odd that the hotel dinin' room was serving beefsteaks. Price and Tate got a nice steak for supper, too. There was an occasional remark or two about how they were having more beef lately. They never came out and said it, but I believe they wanted me to know they were feedin' me and my two men meat from a stray cow. I'm assumin' that was the message they wanted to give me, that if we didn't control our strays, they'd eat them. They never came right out with it, but that was my impression."

Dunellen's smile remained in place for a few moments after he realized what Lucas was insinuating. Then it seemed frozen on his face until his foreman finished speaking. "So they want to call my bluff, do they?" he said softly. "Well, they might think they've got problems with stray cows. I'll give them real problems. I'll show them what it's like to fight me. Here's what I want you to do." He then gave Lucas specific instructions on how he wanted to make his point with the people of Tinhorn, that they were foolish to keep their town between his cattle and water. "Today, Lucas, this morning," he emphasized, "start moving more of the cattle in that direction. And I want to make it clear, the men are to shoot anyone who tries to steal one of my cows."

Lucas had not expected Dunellen's reaction to be so drastic, and he wondered now if he had been wise in reporting his suspicions about the steak supper. It was too late to worry about it now, however. He had been given his instructions, and he would do as he was told, just as he was paid to do. But he wasn't sure it was a good idea, especially the order to shoot anyone who stole one of the cows. When he went back to the bunkhouse, he told the men who had been doing the carpentry work on the building to put away their tools and saddle up. When Lem Dixon asked why, Lucas answered, "You're supposed to be cowhands, ain'tcha? Well, today you're gonna move some cows."

"I thought we already moved 'em to where they were gonna stay till roundup," Alvin Jeeter said.

"That's true for the most part," Lucas replied. "We're

just gonna drive about two hundred of 'em a little over six miles north."

"Six miles?" Lem questioned. "What are we gonna do, take 'em to Tinhorn?" He chuckled in appreciation of his humor.

"As a matter of fact," Lucas answered. "Now, get saddled up."

Overhearing the conversation, Drew Price sang out, "Hey, Boss, I wanna go with you."

"Me, too," Charley Tate spoke up, to no one's surprise.

"All right," Lucas said. "I ain't takin' but six of ya." He saw Tim Walker standing there, so he said, "You come along, too, Tim. You need all the practice you can get."

"Remuda?" Tim asked, since that was always where the youngest and the most inexperienced rode on a cattle drive.

"No," Lucas replied. "There won't be any remuda. We're not goin' but six miles. Just pick a strong horse. You won't need but one."

"You already got your six?" Moon Murphy asked, thinking there might be the possibility to go into town for dinner and maybe a drink.

"You make number six," Lucas said. "Now, let's get saddled up and get goin'."

CHAPTER 9

"What tha hell . . . ?" Lon Blake murmured softly to himself when he saw the first few cows wander past his stable. He walked out to the street to get a better look and discovered a group of a dozen or more following behind the first few. "I swear," he uttered when he looked back beyond that group and saw what looked like a whole herd of cattle. But there were no riders driving the herd, and the cows seemed intent upon following the leaders. And the leaders continued right up the middle of the street. Lon moved back to stand inside his barn door to watch the whole herd fill the street. Still, he saw no one herding the mob of cattle, wandering seemingly aimless, confused by the people on the street, now running to get out of their way.

A short distance south of Lon's stable, Demrie Mullen saw the cattle go past his sawmill. Had he been curious enough to ride back to see if there were more cows behind those he saw, he might have seen the seven Cloverleaf cowhands who had driven the cattle to this point. "You think they'll make it to the river, Boss?" Moon Murphy asked.

"Maybe, maybe not," Lucas replied. "They'll most likely wander around town, now that we ain't drivin' 'em no more. If some of 'em wander on between the stores, lookin' for grass, they might find the river. It ain't that far from the stores. The main thing is they're gonna fill up the main street for a while."

"Ain't we goin' into town?" Drew Price asked.

"No, not for a while anyway," Lucas answered. "Mr. Dunellen wants the people in town to think that's just a big bunch of strays. We go in right after 'em, they'll know we drove 'em here on purpose. They need to know they can have a helluva lot more trouble from stray cows than the few they've seen so far. Then maybe they'll stop their belly-achin' about a few strays. So right now, we'll go back to that creek we crossed about a quarter of a mile behind us and take it easy for a while. Then we'll go into town, lookin' for our stray cattle."

"It's gittin' late into the afternoon," Alvin Jeeter complained. "We shoulda brought a packhorse with some chuck. We ain't et nothin' since breakfast, and it looks like we ain't gonna be back in time for supper."

"After we go in and drive our strays out of town, we'll leave 'em by the river, and we'll go to that saloon, Jake's Place, and buy some supper. He's got a cook there that ain't that bad, accordin' to what some of you told me." He read the complaints on their faces, so he quickly reassured them. "Mr. Dunellen gave me three dollars to give each one of you fifty cents to buy you some supper. If I heard right, she don't charge but a quarter for a bowl of stew. So you'd have enough for a shot of whiskey, if you wanted one." He looked at Tim Walker and said, "Tim, you'd best just buy another bowl of stew." His suggestion was followed by a chorus of joking remarks for the young boy. In high spirits now, with the news that there was going to be an opportunity to go to the saloon, they turned back their horses and headed for the creek.

* * *

"Flint, come take a look at this," Ralph yelled from the front window of the office.

"What is it?" Flint called back. He and Buck were preparing to walk up the street to Clara's for supper.

"Just come look," Ralph replied.

Flint got up from his chair and went to the window. Buck got up as well and followed him. Both stopped dead still when they saw the cows gathering in the street. "Why, that miserable old coot," Flint declared. "I reckon he's darin' us to kill all those cows." They walked outside to see just how many there were.

"Son of a . . ." Buck started to blurt out but was stopped when he saw the street between the jail and the stable filled with cattle, bawling and bellowing their confusion. He turned to Flint and japed, "What about it, Sheriff? Do we arrest 'em and put 'em in the jail? I ain't sure Clara will wanna feed that many prisoners."

Flint laughed, but for only a minute, before he saw a cow stumble up upon the boardwalk and knock down several display racks that were in front of Harper's Feed & Supply. "We'd best see if we can't drive 'em on outta town before they start tearin' things up. I'm goin to get Buster. I think I'll do better on a horse."

Buck said, "I think you're right," and went with him.

"Figured you might want him," Lon said when Flint made his way, pushing and shoving through the herd to get to the stable.

"'Preciate it, Lon," Flint said as Lon handed him the reins, then went to get Buck's horse when he saw him behind Flint. "I'm goin' out the back door," Flint said to Buck. "I'll go around behind 'em and see if I can get 'em started again. If you can drive that first little bunch on out the north end of town, maybe the main herd will follow them." Buck thought that as good a plan as any, so he threw his saddle on his horse as soon as Lon led him out.

Flint rode Buster out the back door of Lon's barn and rode around behind the corral, heading south. He was almost to the sawmill when he got to the rear of the herd, where he pulled the buckskin around and fired a couple of shots in the air. It was enough to cause the cattle to move, and as he had hoped, they saw Buck leading the smaller group of cows up the street. So they followed. When he heard the shots, Raymond Chadwick, the blacksmith, grabbed his rifle, not sure if he needed to defend his life or not. When Flint came into view, driving the cattle, Chadwick fired a couple of shots in the air, too, to keep them moving. Since there was not a blade of grass anywhere on the main street of Tinhorn, the cattle showed no desire to remain there. Consequently, the town was spared any real damage.

"You'd best step up here on the porch, ma'am," Fred Johnson called out to a young woman with two small boys in tow. He had come to the door when he heard the shots.

Arleen turned to see who had spoken and saw Fred standing near the front door of the hotel. She turned her head to take another look at the cattle approaching in the street, actually filling the entire street. She and the boys had just come from visiting her father in the post office, and she wasn't aware of the approaching cattle until she was crossing the street and heard the shots. "I think you're right, sir. Come Angus, Brendan," she called to her sons, and they climbed the steps to the hotel porch.

Fred walked out on the porch as well. "It's best to give a bunch of steers a little room. You can never tell which way they're gonna turn."

"I know that for a fact," Arleen replied. "My late husband raised cattle."

"Fred Johnson's my name. I'm the front-desk clerk. You're Louis Wheeler's daughter, aren't you?"

"Why, yes, I am," she answered. "Arleen Daugherty, and this is Angus and Brendan," she said, patting each one on his head. "We're glad to meet you, Mr. Johnson."

"Welcome to Tinhorn," Fred said. "I hope you learn to like it as much as most of us do." The lead cows were passing in front of the hotel now, and Fred waved to Buck as he rode by. They stood and watched as the herd of cows charged through town. "Here comes the sheriff, driving them out of town."

"My, my," Arleen asked, "does something like this happen very often?"

"No, not really," Fred answered. "It never happened before some fellow named Dunellen brought a big herd of cattle right to our doorstep."

She was still facing the street, so he was not aware that the color was suddenly drained from her entire face when she grabbed the back of the chair she had been standing beside to keep from falling. The shock upon hearing his name was almost enough to cause her to faint. It was too much to believe that she had come to the same place that monster had moved his herd. Why, she wondered, had her father not told her that devil was right outside the town? But then she realized that her father had no way of knowing who Conan had gone into business with. *I can't stay here*, she thought at once. *What if he finds out I'm here?* She sat down in the chair, and when Flint had ridden by, driving the last of the cows, she got up and immediately went back to the post office.

* * *

Flint and Buck managed to keep the cows moving until they were all a good way beyond the town limits. They were discussing what best to do with them when Lucas Sawyer and his six cowhands appeared. "Well, I'll be . . ." Buck uttered. "Here comes the cavalry to save the town."

"Looks like we got here a little too late," Lucas said as he and his six men pulled up around the two lawmen. "We've been lookin' for this little bunch of cattle. They broke off from some of the herd we had south of here. We were hopin' to catch up with 'em before they got anywhere near Tinhorn. But I reckon a cow wants to go to town just as bad as a cowhand does."

"It sure looks that way," Flint replied, "lately, anyway." He and Lucas exchanged knowing smiles.

"Just the two of you drive these cows out of town?" Lucas asked. Buck said that was a fact. "Not bad for a couple of lawmen," Lucas said. "When you get tired of lockin' up drunks and hell-raisers, maybe you oughta come lookin' for a job at the Cloverleaf Ranch."

"We'll keep it in mind," Flint replied. "In the meantime, Mr. Dunellen might be interested to know the city council is considering an ordinance to fine the owner of any stock left unattended in the town. So what it'll amount to is we'll build some stock pens to keep your cows off the streets. And you can buy 'em back at four dollars apiece is what I understand."

"I'll be sure to tell him," Lucas said. "And right now, we'll move the cows over by the river and let 'em graze while my men and I ride back into town to get some supper. I'm afraid they'll mutiny on me if we don't. Would that be all right with the gentle folk of Tinhorn?"

"Why, sure," Flint replied. "We're glad to have our friends from Cloverleaf come in anytime, as long as you leave the cows on the range, where they're supposed to be."

"Thank you, Sheriff. Stop by the saloon and I'll buy you a drink."

"I might do that, Lucas," Flint responded.

"It'd be my pleasure," Lucas said, then told his men to get the cattle moving.

They all turned to do his bidding, all except one. Drew Price made it a point to ride by Flint's horse before following the others. "You and your sidekick are workin' outside the town limits now, ain'tcha, Sheriff? You're out here in our country now, where that badge don't mean nothin'."

"That's right, Price, except this ain't your country," Flint answered him. "You're ridin' on government-owned property. Get a little farther up this road and you'll be on a settler's private property. He filed a claim on it. Maybe Ira Dunellen has filed on the rest of the state of Texas, but I ain't heard anything about it yet."

"Come on, Drew," Charley Tate yelled at him. "We gotta move these cows."

"See ya later, Sheriff." Drew smirked, and loped off after the other men.

Buck pulled his horse up beside Flint's. "Like I said before, we'd best keep an eye out for that one. He's thinkin' about callin' you out."

"You think so?" Flint japed. "Maybe I better stay back in town. Gunfights are against the law in Tinhorn."

"You can joke about it all you want, but that fool's got it in his head he can take you down, Flint, and it might be when you least expect it. He must think he's pretty doggoned fast. In all the time we been workin' together, I ain't ever seen you go up against anybody. Are you fast with that Colt you're wearin'?"

Since Buck paused and waited for an answer, Flint shrugged and said, "Not especially. I've always been able to draw it quick enough to pop a rattlesnake or something like that. I don't think I was ever as fast as my brother, Joe. Now Joe, he used to practice drawin' his six-gun. I remember one time when I was about fourteen . . ." That was as far as he got before he realized Buck was staring, openmouthed, at him as if he was witnessing the ranting of a crazy man.

"Your brother Joe ain't the sheriff of Tinhorn, and he ain't the one a no-account saddle tramp is thinkin' about challengin' to a shoot-out," Buck declared. "We don't know nothin' about Drew Price, how fast he is or anything else. Him and that halfwit that follows him around tried to get Tom Dawkins to face him. They musta had some reason to think Price could beat Tom. That tells me he's done it before."

Flint could see that Buck was truly upset about his apparently lackadaisical attitude about the possibility of his falling victim to a fast-gun's challenge. "I appreciate your concern, partner, but let me assure you that I don't have any intention of accepting any challenge from Drew Price or anybody else." He grinned then and added, "Like I said, it's against the law in Tinhorn."

"You just remember that," Buck told him. "It ain't been that long since you took the job of sheriff away from me. And I don't want it back." He gave Flint a firm nod of his head. "Hell, let's go eat supper." They wheeled their horses and headed back to town.

"What did you do with them cows?" Lon Blake asked when they rode back to the stable.

"Some of the Cloverleaf hands showed up after we drove 'em outta town," Flint said. "They said they'd take care of 'em. We'll go ahead and put the horses away. I don't reckon we'll need 'em anymore tonight."

After leaving the stable, they stopped in at the jail to let Ralph know everything was all right and promise him that they would not forget to bring his supper back with them. Then they walked on up the street to Clara's, stopping several times along the way to answer questions about the cattle. They could not assure them that it wouldn't happen again. They didn't say so, but they both felt sure it would happen again and again until the town gave up, or they found a way to stop it.

Flint should have anticipated a cowboy welcome when they walked into Clara's, but they didn't expect all three women in the dining room to give him a rousing cheer. "There he is!" Bonnie sang out. "Our own ride-'em-cowboy sheriff. We were a little worried when we heard the gunshots, but then we saw Flint drivin' a herd of cattle right past the door."

"I wasn't drivin' 'em by myself," Flint was quick to inform her. "Buck was ridin' point. It was him that led 'em out of town. Matter of fact, we're thinkin' about gettin' into the cattle business and give ol' Ira Dunellen some competition. Ain't that right, Buck?"

"Hell no," Buck answered and led the way back to his usual table.

Mindy walked along beside Flint. "That was really something, wasn't it? What did you do with them?"

"Buck and I drove them about a quarter of a mile out the Tyler road and turned them over to a crew of men from Cloverleaf who said they were looking for them."

"Maybe after this they'll keep their cows out of Tinhorn, do you think?"

"I have to be honest with you, Mindy, I expect we'll still see the strays from time to time, like we have been seein'. And I'd be surprised if they don't drive another big bunch of 'em through town again." As soon as he said it, he regretted putting worrisome thoughts into her pretty head.

"Nothin' for you to worry about, though. Just make sure you get out of the street if you see cows coming."

"You don't have to tell me that," she said cheerfully. "I'll go get your coffee." And she was off to the kitchen.

He sat down at the table, and they made small talk with the women until their supper was served and they were left to eat it. Only then did Flint broach the subject that he thought might be working on Buck's mind. "I know Lucas said they were coming to Jake's to get some supper. I expect it'll be a little while before they get here, since they're probably settling down that herd of cows. So, I'll go over to Jake's tonight and make sure nothing gets out of hand. It appears to me that Lucas runs that crew with a pretty firm hand. I doubt he'd let any of 'em go wild. So, you might as well go on to your room, and I'll keep an eye on our Cloverleaf friends."

"I 'preciate what you're tryin' to do, Flint, but I'll be okay. I don't trust that pack of coyotes to have a peaceful supper and a quiet drink, then climb on their horses and ride back to that herd of cattle. Not for a minute do I trust 'em. And they're a little much for one man to handle. You know that. I ain't sure two of us can handle the seven of 'em, but we've got a better chance with two of us than you'd have by yourself."

"Pretty much between a rock and a hard place, ain't we?" Flint said.

The evening started quietly enough for a weeknight, and when Flint decided to take his customary walk around at closing time for most of the stores, he noticed the horses tied at the rail at Jake's Place. So he decided to take a look inside to see if Lucas was keeping his men under control. He stepped inside the door and stood there for a minute while he looked over the room. It was noisy as usual, but not raucous by any means. Lucas and his six men were occupying two tables on the far side of the room. At the moment, they appeared to be enjoying some of Rena's stew. Jake was talking to Rudy at the far end of the bar, so Flint walked on in and went down to join them. "Evenin', Flint," Jake greeted him. "I'd offer you a drink, but I know you don't usually drink when you're workin'. Maybe you ain't workin' now. How 'bout it? Want a little snort of my scotch?"

"Thanks just the same, Jake," Flint replied. "But I'm afraid if I take a drink of that high-priced likker, I might want it all the time. And I can't afford it." Across the room, Lucas caught sight of him then and signaled for him to join them. "Besides, I just remembered, I told Lucas Sawyer I'd have a drink with him tonight." He gave Rudy a wink and said, "So, that'll be the cheap whiskey, right?"

"That's kinda like sleepin' with the enemy, ain't it?" Jake joked.

"I reckon you could call it that," Flint replied. "Right now, though, I'd do almost anything to keep the peace between Cloverleaf and Tinhorn." He pushed away from the bar and went over to Lucas's table.

"I thought maybe you weren't gonna show up for that drink I offered you," Lucas said when Flint walked up. "There's some clean glasses there in the middle of the other table. Grab you one and I'll pour you a drink." He picked up a bottle and held it ready.

"I don't normally drink when I'm supposed to be workin', but I think I'll take you up on it on this occasion," Flint said and started to reach for one of a couple of glasses resting upside down in the middle of the table.

The glass he started to reach for suddenly shattered and threw shards of glass across the room, followed by the sharp crack of a Colt .44. The suddenness of the shot right in their midst caused those seated at the table to recoil, a couple of them going over backward in their chairs. Only one remained seated, his six-gun in hand, still aimed at the glasses. "I'll be damned if I'll drink with no low-down, yellow-belly lawman," Drew Price declared. Just like everyone else around the two tables, Flint was stunned for a few moments, but he rapidly recovered and dropped his hand on his Colt. Price swung his arm around to aim his pistol at him. "What have you got to say now, Sheriff? Are you fast enough to draw it and fire before I pull the trigger? Or are you gonna arrest me for disturbin' the peace? Maybe I oughta have mercy on you and give you a chance to settle it with me man-to-man."

"Yeah, Drew," Charley Tate babbled like a monkey on a chain, "settle it with him man-to-man. Let him stand up and face you man-to-man."

"Shut up, Charley," Drew blurted out. "How 'bout it, Sheriff? Have you got the guts to face me man-to-man? 'Cause if you don't, I'm gonna shoot you down just like I'd do a dog that won't hunt. Make up your mind. I ain't gonna wait around here till you work up your nerve."

"I'm gonna remind you again that it's against the law to duel in Tinhorn," Flint stated calmly. "If you put that gun back in the holster, I'll hold you in jail until you can have a day in court. Right now, you've only shot a whiskey glass. If you're smart, you'll holster that weapon, and you might get off with drunk and disorderly."

He heard Rudy call out then from the bar. "He killed a man," Rudy blurted out. Flint risked a quick glance toward him in time to see a stranger, who had been standing at the bar, finally lose his grip on the edge of the bar and slump to the floor, Drew's bullet in his spine.

"I reckon this just ain't your day, Sheriff," Drew spat and

cocked the pistol, still aimed at Flint. The report of the pistol seemed louder because it was so sudden. The look of surprise on Drew's face seemed even more bizarre with the small black hole in his forehead, exactly in the center. Drew remained sitting upright in the chair for what seemed long seconds, until Flint reached over and eased the hammer back down before taking the .44 from his dead hand. Drew slumped forward then with his head on the table.

Flint looked around then to see Buck replace the spent cartridge in his six-gun. "Much obliged, partner," he said, and Buck acknowledged it with a nod of his head. Flint turned toward Lucas and suggested, "Some other time for that drink. Might be a good idea to finish up your supper and head on out of town, in case he's got any friends that don't like the way this ended up." He had his eye on Charley Tate, who was still in total shock upon seeing his hero slain.

"Flint, I was just as surprised as you were," Lucas insisted. "I didn't have any idea he was apt to do something that crazy. I knew he hated your guts, but I never thought he'd try anything like that. I think we were about ready to head back to the ranch anyway, so we might as well get started."

"What about Drew?" Charley blurted out. "We just gonna leave him here?"

When Lucas didn't answer right away, obviously not concerned with any particular feelings of loss for the troublemaker, Flint offered to take care of the body. "We'll have the undertaker come get the body of the fellow Price killed. If you want, we can let him dig a hole for Price, too."

"I appreciate it," Lucas said, then looked around and asked, "Anybody rather take Drew back to the ranch with us to bury him?" Nobody cared enough to want to dig a grave, not even Charley, who asked if he could search the body for any keepsakes. "Go ahead," Lucas said. "See if he's got enough money to pay the undertaker." Then he asked Flint how much the undertaker would charge.

"About a dollar," Flint told him, "maybe a little bit more, since you ain't leavin' anything on the body that's worth anything." Flint looked at Buck, who was still watching with his gun in hand, an incredulous expression on his face over the discussion about what to do with the body. He scanned the faces of the Cloverleaf cowhands and saw none that indicated a need for vengeance for the death of their fellow cowhand. He concluded that Charley Tate was the only true friend who mourned Drew Price's death. He was a half-wit, but half-wits could pull the trigger on a Colt handgun, so he kept his gun out.

"I heard the shots," Walt Doolin announced from the front door of the saloon.

"Yeah, come on in, Walt," Jake Rudolph yelled back at him. "We were just gonna send somebody to get you. We've got two bodies you need to take care of."

Walt came in and looked at the two bodies. "Who are they?" he asked. "Anybody know?" He was told the man in front of the bar was a stranger, and no one knew anything about him. The poor, unlucky drifter was just standing at the wrong spot at the bar. And the one slumped over on the table was a victim of the sheriff's office. "So there ain't no funeral for either one of 'em. I'll go get my handcart."

After Walt hauled the bodies away on his handcart, and Lucas and his men rode out of town, Flint and Buck walked back to the office. "I need to thank you for savin' my life tonight," Flint said as they crossed the street. "I didn't antic-ipate that move by Drew Price, caught me completely by sur-prise. And I didn't even know you had come in behind me."

"I told you I would be here tonight," Buck said, knowing

that Flint hadn't been convinced when he told him earlier. He had wanted to drown himself with the half bottle of whiskey he had in his quarters but knew it wouldn't be enough. "I told you I would be here to back you," he repeated, knowing he could never admit that he had come back to Jake's with his only purpose to get a full bottle of whiskey to take him through the night.

"Hell, I never doubted it," Flint lied.

There was still the matter of a small herd of about two hundred cows grazing by the river just north of town. Lucas maintained that they intended to drive the cattle back south of Tinhorn, but he and his men would return to their headquarters that night, since they had no camping supplies with them. He said they would eat breakfast in the morning and come back for the cattle. He insisted that he was trying to cooperate with him and the town of Tinhorn. But Lucas Sawyer was becoming quite an enigma to Flint and Buck. He seemed to be a straight-talking, fair-dealing individual, yet there was no doubt in Flint's mind that he would carry out every order from Ira Dunellen, no matter how barbaric or uncaring. "I know what he said," Buck advised, "but I expect it'd be a good idea to ride up the river in the mornin' to see where those cattle are."

"I agree," Flint replied. "I was thinkin' I'd go saddle Buster up as soon as Lon gets to the stable in the mornin'. I'll see where those cows are and make sure they ain't wanderin' back toward town."

CHAPTER 10

Lucas and his five men rode into the Cloverleaf Ranch about an hour and a half after leaving Tinhorn. Contrary to what he had told Flint Moran, he didn't bother to go back up the river to check on the cows. He assumed it unnecessary because at that time of night, the cattle were settled down right where they were. So as soon as they rode out the north end of town, they had circled back and headed straight for Cloverleaf. When Gabby Skelton, the bunkhouse cook, heard them ride in, he went to the barn to find Lucas. "Henry Cheney said to tell you that Mr. Dunellen wants to see you as soon as you got back."

"Is that so?" Lucas replied. "Did he say anything about how late to come see him?"

"Long as it ain't after nine o'clock," Gabby said.

"Well, it ain't anywhere near that, so I reckon I'll take care of my horse before I go up to the house."

"Did you boys get any supper?" Gabby asked.

"I reckon you could call it that," Lucas said. "It was some kind of stew, but it wasn't beef, so I don't think we were eatin' Cloverleaf meat."

"I weren't sure when you boys would be back, so I didn't try to save nothin'. But I baked an extra batch of biscuits, just in case you didn't get anything to eat. And I'll make you some coffee." He paused, then looked around the barnyard. "Who's missin'? You took six with you, didn't you?"

"You can't guess who's missin'?"

Gabby took another look. "Drew," he said. "I shoulda knowed that right off. What happened? He get hisself arrested again?"

"Nope, this time he got himself killed. He pulled his six-shooter on the sheriff, and the sheriff's deputy, or whatever he is, shot him. Drilled him right between the eyes."

"That sheriff was most likely givin' you a hard time," Gabby assumed.

"No, as a matter of fact, he wasn't," Lucas said. "He stopped in the saloon to have a drink of whiskey with me. I invited him to."

"What about the cows?" Gabby asked. "Was they still in the street?"

"No, they were about a quarter of a mile upriver. The sheriff and his deputy drove the whole bunch out of town."

"Well, I'll be. . . . Mr. Dunellen ain't gonna like that," Gabby responded.

"No, he ain't," Lucas said, "and I expect I'd better go tell him right now." He turned his horse loose to graze with the others and started toward the back door of the house.

"Well, I'll be . . ." Gabby mumbled to himself again as Lucas walked away. "Ol' Drew Price finally got hisself a third eye, right in the middle of his forehead. Ain't that somethin'? Reckon somebody's gonna have to rock Charley Tate to sleep tonight." He shook his head slowly, trying to imagine what it must have looked like. "Lem," he called out when he saw Lem Dixon carrying his saddle into the barn. "Lucas said Drew got shot." He hustled after him to hear more details about the shooting.

* * *

Lucas rapped on the kitchen door and waited. In a few seconds, Atha opened the door. "Come in, Lucas," she said.

"I hope I ain't too late," he said, actually hoping that he was. At that moment, he decided he would rather have waited until morning to go over it with Dunellen. "Henry," he said, just then noticing Atha's husband sitting at the kitchen table. He and Atha were having a cup of coffee when he knocked on the door.

"Lucas," Henry acknowledged.

"You're not too late," Atha said. "He wanted to talk to you as soon as you got back. He won't go to bed for another hour yet." She walked over and opened the kitchen door. "I'll tell him you're here." He waited there while she walked up the hall and knocked on the door to the study. In a few moments, she was back. "You can go on in. You know which door."

"Right," he said and went to the study.

"Come in, Lucas," Dunellen greeted him, "and tell me how the people of Tinhorn liked the latest strays in their precious town." When Lucas hesitated slightly, Dunellen asked, "You did drive those cows right up the main street, didn't you?"

"Yes, sir. When we broke off from the drive, the lead cows were already in the street, and the rest were following behind. They were moving peacefully right up main street. I backed the men off then, so nobody would know the cows were being driven."

"Did they bring the town to a complete standstill?" Dunellen asked, a grin of satisfaction on his face.

"Well, sir, they filled that street up, just like we figured they would, but I can't truthfully say it brought the town to a standstill."

A dark frown immediately appeared on Dunellen's face. "What do you mean? What happened?"

"Well, sir, apparently Sheriff Moran got behind the herd and kept them moving." Dunellen's teeth clenched with the mention of Flint's name. "His partner, Buck Jackson, got behind the first dozen or so cows and drove them out the north end of town. The rest of the herd followed the leaders and they moved right on through town. Moran and Jackson didn't stop till they drove the whole herd about a quarter of a mile north of town."

"You must not have cut out enough cows to drive in there," Dunellen said, "if Moran could move them out by himself." He had anticipated complete chaos, with the people running for their lives, unable to do anything with the cows.

"We drove a little better than two hundred cows into that little town. I promise you, that street was choked plum full, from one end to the other. If the sheriff hadn't got in behind them before they started breakin' off and runnin' up alleys and tryin' to get into the doors, they woulda made a mess of the town."

Fully angry now, Dunellen threw his empty whiskey glass at the fireplace, only to become even more angry and frustrated when the glass bounced off the wall and failed to smash. "Flint Moran!" He forced the name through clenched teeth. "He's like a thorn in my toe. I want him plucked out. Go back to the bunkhouse and send Drew Price in here. I want to talk to him."

Lucas was hoping to avoid that issue, and he was surprised that Dunellen knew one of his hands from another. "That's another thing I was fixin' to report to you. Drew can't come talk to you because he's dead." Dunellen jerked back his head as if he'd been punched, but he waited for Lucas to explain. "Drew's been threatenin' to settle up with

Moran for throwin' him in jail. Tonight, he made a move to take Flint Moran out when we went into town to get something to eat. He drew on him and was fixin' to shoot, but Buck Jackson shot him in the head before he could pull the trigger."

It seemed to be almost too much for Dunellen, for he suddenly calmed down and asked a question. "Which one of the men is fast with a six-gun and not afraid to test his skill against another man with the intent to kill him?"

"I'm afraid I don't know of any of the other men that are like the one you describe," Lucas answered. "I have to be totally honest with you, Mr. Dunellen. You've got a good crew workin' your cattle. But that's all they are, cowhands, not gunslingers. That's not to say they ain't got the guts to fight, because they'll shoot if they're shot at. And they'll risk their necks to protect your cattle. But they ain't fast-draw killers. Drew Price was the only one that thought he could take any man with a gun in his hand. Last night, I reckon he found out how good he really was."

Dunellen listened to his foreman's evaluation of the men riding for the Cloverleaf brand, remaining calm in spite of the flames raging inside his veins. It was a feeling of helplessness he had never experienced. He didn't like to admit it when he was wrong, but he thought now that he had made a mistake when he let most of the back-shooters and dry-gulchers go in favor of cattlemen. He was accustomed to giving Lucas an order, and the order would be carried out, whether it was the purposeful destruction of fences or stampeding a herd of cattle through a farmer's crops. It didn't matter what, he gave the order and Lucas saw that it was done. Now this insignificant little town called Tinhorn dared to impede his progress. After a long pause when Dunellen made no comment at all, Lucas asked, "You want me to drive that herd back into town again tomorrow?"

"Yes," Dunellen said, then paused, still deciding what might work best. "No." He changed his mind. "I want you to move those two hundred head back just south of the town and leave them there. They'll still wander into town, but I think it will be more effective if they show up in smaller numbers, four or eight at a time. Put a couple of the men on the herd to make sure they keep wandering." He was thinking if it was just three, or four, or eight, it would seem natural, and the town would have to think they were fighting the dumb beasts and not Ira Dunellen. "Do you understand?" he asked Lucas.

"Yes, sir, I think I see what you want," Lucas answered. "I'll take a crew up there right after breakfast in the mornin', and we'll move those somewhere where the town will be the natural place to wander." He started for the door then, anxious to leave. But Dunellen stopped him.

"One more thing, Lucas. I want you to gather all the men together in the morning at breakfast. I have something I want to say to them."

"Right, sir, I'll make sure nobody goes to work before you get there." He left then, wondering what that was all about. In the past, Dunellen seemed to keep a stone wall between himself and the lowly cowhands who maintained his empire. When he returned to the bunkhouse, he passed the word to Gabby Skelton that Mr. Dunellen wanted to address the crew before anybody left the headquarters in the morning. He knew Gabby would see every one of them.

"What's that all about?" Gabby asked. "He ain't ever wanted to talk directly to the men before. I thought you was his speechmaker. I wish to hell he was comin' down from his throne to announce he was gonna order the construction of my cook shack so I could quit feeding you fellers outta my chuckwagon."

"Maybe that's exactly what he wants to talk to us about," Lucas joked. "He's tired of you being hampered in your cookin'."

"Could be he's wantin' to say a few words over Drew Price's untimely death," Gabby suggested, continuing the japing, "wantin' everybody to remember what a great man Drew was." He glanced around then to make sure Charley Tate wasn't close enough to hear them joking. "He might ask Charley to say a prayer."

Lucas chuckled with him after his comment, but it struck him as a sad thing that not one of the crew, other than Charley, gave a damn if Drew was killed. It also struck him as odd that Dunellen had asked to see Drew. He shrugged it off and said, "Maybe he's gonna fire the whole damn bunch of us because those cows didn't know he wanted them to stay in town till they tore it down." He left the chuckwagon then, to tell some of the men down at the other end of the bunkhouse not to wander off in the morning before Dunellen addressed them. Just as it had with Gabby, the news that Mr. Dunellen was going to come down to the bunkhouse in the morning to talk directly to the men caused considerable speculation. There was immediate concern that he might be sending some of them to the grub line, now that they had moved his cattle halfway up the state of Texas to his new headquarters. But Lucas assured them that they were all still needed to maintain over three thousand cattle. There was some thought that he might be unhappy with the time it was taking to complete all the buildings at the ranch headquarters. Of all the suggestions, however, none came close to touching the reason behind Dunellen's visit to the bunkhouse.

* * *

Dunellen made his appearance right after the night herders came in for breakfast. He opened with a question to Lucas Sawyer. "Are they all here?"

"Yes, sir," Lucas answered. "They're all here."

"Good," Dunellen said. "I'll make this short because we've all got plenty of work that needs to be done. I don't know how much Lucas has told you men about what you're a part of here. But I think it's time you appreciated the part you're all playing in the history of our state. When we're through, Cloverleaf will be the largest cattle producer in the entire country. We're destined to become that producer, no matter what man or what town might stand in our way. We have no choice but to push them out of our way. Right now, the unimportant little town of Tinhorn is hogging our water rights. I have no desire to destroy the town. We will simply push it across the river, where it will be more prosperous in the long run. There is one man, however, one thorn, who is standing in the way of destiny: Sheriff Flint Moran. He doesn't have the intelligence to know he should step aside. There's only one cure for a man like that, just as there's only one cure for a dog with rabies. So for that reason, I'm offering a two hundred dollar reward for any man who kills Flint Moran, no matter the circumstances. If nobody sees you, bring me his badge to prove you shot him. You might keep that in mind when you go into Tinhorn for a drink." He turned to face Lucas, who was struck speechless, like everyone else. "That's all I have to say. You can get the men back to work now." He turned on his heel and marched back to the ranch house, leaving Lucas to answer questions he had no answers for.

The first one came from Lem Dixon. "I ain't sure I heard what I just heard," Lem blurted. "Lucas, is that on the level? Does he really mean that?"

"You heard the man," Lucas answered. "Sounded to me like he meant it. I'm just as blown away as the rest of you.

Speakin' for myself, I'm not goin' after Moran. I'll shoot him if he shoots at me, but I'm not an assassin. I'll leave that part to each one of you and your own conscience. Two hundred dollars is a lot of money, but you might have to spend it pretty damn fast before you go to the gallows."

"That's right," Lem said. "You'd have to pick a fight with him, then beat him to the draw. Then it wouldn't be no crime."

"You could get you a good spot and pick him off with a rifle," Moon Murphy suggested.

"But you'd have to prove it was your shot that got him," Alvin Jeeter said. "And there'd be half a dozen of us that claimed we done it."

"Forget about it for now," Lucas said, knowing that was going to be pretty hard to do. He still found it hard to believe that Dunellen had made such an offer. He wondered if his obsession with Flint Moran had been so great that it caused his brain to warp. "We've still got our jobs to do," he reminded them. "I'll take the same crew I had yesterday. Let's go move that bunch of cattle back below the town."

"We're one short," Charley Tate said.

"We'll be all right," Lucas told him.

"Drew weren't worth a damn herdin' cattle anyway," Alvin said, no longer afraid to speak his true feelings, now that Drew wasn't there to make him pay for it.

"He was better'n the rest of us, herdin' cows or anythin' else," Charley declared.

"He was better at talkin' hisself up," Alvin claimed, "mostly about how fast he was with his gun. But he weren't fast enough to keep Buck Jackson from puttin' a hole in his head, and him with his gun in his hand."

"That big deputy of Moran's slipped in the door when nobody was lookin'," Charley insisted. "Drew didn't even know he was there. It weren't a fair fight."

"Shoot," Alvin declared, "that's the only kind of fight Drew Price would be in, one that ain't fair."

"You two, knock it off," Lucas interrupted. "The man's dead, so it doesn't make any difference now anyway. We're gettin' paid to work the cattle and we're already gettin' a late start."

Lucas and his crew started out again for Tinhorn. This time, Lucas didn't plan to avoid the town, as they had when they drove the herd of cattle to the edge of the main street. There was no need to avoid being seen, since he had told Flint he would be back to drive the cattle back to the main herd. Since it would be a shorter distance to ride straight through town than to go around it, he figured he might let Flint know they had come to get the cattle. "I reckon you all have better sense than to take a shot at the sheriff, if we see him," he couldn't help saying to his men. As soon as he said it, he still found it hard to believe that Ira Dunellen could have made such an incredibly stupid statement to a crew of men. It offered more proof that Dunellen didn't know his men at all. He thought about what he was supposed to do this morning. Dunellen's instructions were to move all two hundred cows back south of the town, then cut out several head in small groups and leave them to wander into town on their own.

It was the middle of the morning when the Cloverleaf riders walked their horses down the main street of Tinhorn. Lucas pulled up to a stop in front of the sheriff's office. Both Flint and Buck were in the office, but it was Ralph who spotted the riders. All three came outside to talk to Lucas. "Just thought I'd let you know we're on our way to pick up those cows," Lucas said. "Havin' any more trouble with strays?"

"Not so far this mornin'," Flint answered him. "I thought I might ride up the river to see if they were still where you left them last night."

"You're welcome to ride on up there with us," Lucas said. "We could probably use some help from a fellow who drove 'em all the way up the river by himself."

Flint laughed. "I can't take all the credit for that. Buck was ridin' point. I don't expect you need any help from me. You're on your way to get 'em. That's all I needed to know."

To the Cloverleaf men sitting there on their horses, listening to their boss exchanging small talk with the sheriff, it was a strange scene. It was no secret that several of the Cloverleaf cowhands had lawless activities in their past, but how many had killed? Alvin Jeeter stared openly at the young sheriff and thought, *Flint Moran, two hundred dollars, cash on the hoof. I don't know if I could pass that up if I had the right opportunity.*

Moon Murphy pulled up beside Jeeter and gave him a knowing grin. "Whatcha thinkin' about, Alvin?"

"I'm thinkin', if it weren't so early, I'd like to go across the street and get a drink of likker," Alvin answered.

Moon laughed and replied, "Right. How much would two hundred dollars buy?"

CHAPTER 11

Lucas found the small herd of cattle within a hundred yards of the place they had left them. He had the men round them up and start them out to the west of Tinhorn, planning to turn them in a more southerly direction once he was clear of the town. Since neither Flint nor Buck showed up to watch them, he had the men cut out a little group of half a dozen cows when they drove the herd across the road out of Tinhorn that led to Tyler. He left Alvin and young Tim Walker to herd the six cows down the road toward Tinhorn with instructions to keep them heading in that direction until the rest of the herd was out of sight. They were approaching the hotel when Alvin said, "We'd best leave 'em here. We get any closer and somebody's liable to see us."

"This don't make no sense to me," Tim said, "tryin' to get strays to go to town."

"It don't have to make sense, boy," Alvin told him. "Just do what the man tells you and let him worry about what's right and what ain't." They wheeled their horses and hurried to catch up with the others.

The rest of the two-hundred-cow herd was driven only about halfway between Tinhorn and the Cloverleaf headquarters. Lucas had sent two more men to drop another half dozen cows at the south end of town. "Maybe they'll aggravate the folks enough to suit Mr. Dunellen," Moon commented.

"More likely they'll be glad to get some more fresh meat," Alvin returned. "The main thing is we're gonna be back to the ranch in time for dinner, and that beats the hell outta the last time we drove this herd somewhere."

"I'm thinkin' about ridin' into Tinhorn tonight after supper," Moon said. "I think I've got enough money left to escort that little Lucy gal upstairs, with enough left over for a drink of likker. You wanna go with me?"

"That don't sound like a bad idea," Alvin replied, "the likker part, I mean. I ain't got enough left for the other. And payday ain't for another week. Maybe some of the other boys will wanna go. The more the merrier, and sure as hell the safer with that sheriff they got."

"Damn," Flint swore softly when he saw two stray cows grazing peacefully on the narrow grass belt Gilbert Smith had planted on three sides of his hotel. He had wondered how good a job Lucas and his men did in their roundup. Seeing the two strays answered that question. Then he saw three more cows coming from behind the hotel. He decided he'd better try to see if he could drive the five strays somewhere and pen them up. The question was where. He quickly decided he needed to take them to jail, but he would need to drive them somewhere temporarily until he could get a pen built. The only place he could think of was Lon Blake's stable. "And Lon ain't gonna wanna do it," he stated.

With no more time for planning, he circled around behind the three cows coming out from the rear of the hotel and started driving them toward the street. He thought back about the few cows he raised before he became a deputy sheriff. Of the three sons of Ryan Moran, only he, the youngest, was interested in raising cattle. And while Joe and Nate farmed the plot of land their father had filed on, it was Flint who kept the family supplied with beef. His brother Nate's son, Jack, had picked up the cattle interest when Flint left. Thinking about that now as he started the three cows down past the hotel, he wheeled Buster around to the left to flush the two cows off the grass belt. Now he had all five trotting down the street. "Ride 'em, cowboy!" Walt Doolin yelled when he came out of the post office and saw Flint driving the strays. When he passed Clara's Kitchen, another cow came from between that building and John Harper's store to join the other five, giving him an even half dozen. He hoped there were no more scattered among the buildings.

"I swear . . ." Ralph started when he stepped out of the office door to see what was causing the hooting and hollering.

Seated at Flint's desk, Buck looked toward the door and asked, "What is it?"

"It's Flint" was all Ralph said, but that was enough to get Buck on his feet and start him toward the door.

"What the hell? . . ." he drew out softly when he saw Flint now approaching at a slow walk. He went out in the street to help if he could.

That was what Flint was hoping for, so he called out to him, "Tell Lon to open his corral!"

Buck understood at once. Flint didn't have any place else to put them. So he trotted down to the stable, puffing like a locomotive to meet Lon, who was coming out of his barn to see what was causing the commotion. "Open the gate to the corral!" Lon hesitated, as if he wanted to discuss it. "Open the damn gate!" Buck ordered.

Lon clearly didn't like the idea, but he went about opening the gate. "I don't keep cows in there with the horses," he insisted. "My customers won't like it a bit."

"It's just temporary, Lon, till we get a place ready for 'em." He sincerely hoped that was the case. "Now, hold that gate wide like that, and we'll run 'em right in there." Flint slowed down almost to a stop. The cows reacted accordingly, so when they finally reached Buck at the side of the street, he grabbed the lead steer by the horns and turned it toward the open gate. The other five followed it into the corral, and Lon closed the gate. There were only seven horses in the corral, and they gathered together at one end, seemingly no more hospitable than Lon.

"Flint, what the hell?" Lon pressed. "I can't have no damn . . ." That was as far as he got before Flint interrupted.

"It's only temporary," Flint said. "I know it ain't what you want, but I didn't know where else to drive 'em. And I want you to know how much I appreciate your help with this stray problem."

"You got anything in mind, partner?" Buck asked.

"I'm goin' up to Harper's to see if he's got some barbed wire fence," Flint replied. "If he does, and I can afford it, then we'll get some boards for posts from Demrie Mullen down at the sawmill. And we'll build a fence on the back of the jail. As far as I'm concerned, these cows are under arrest. So, jail is where they're supposed to be."

"That's the craziest idea I ever heard of," Buck could not keep from saying. "They're gonna have to have water and feed, and your pen ain't gonna be big enough to hold many. Besides, you're gonna have to hear the damn cows all day long."

Flint could see Buck's point. "All right, what would you do with 'em?"

"Hell, take 'em on back by the river where so many

people have camped before. It's right behind the jail, and there's plenty of grass and water right there. We can string enough wire along the bank to give 'em plenty of room to graze. And if somebody steals 'em, they ain't our cows anyway."

Flint paused to consider his suggestion. The river was about one hundred yards behind the jail and the other buildings on this side of the street. It was an open one hundred yards of mostly shoulder-high weeds and only a couple of trees. It was a better idea than his, he decided. "Now I know why they're payin' you more than a deputy's salary. We need to go back there and see how much wire we need."

"I'll hitch up my wagon," Lon offered. "You're gonna need one, if you're gonna put up wire." He was inspired by his urgent desire to get the cows out of his corral.

"Much obliged," Flint said. "We'll take you up on that." Flint left his horse at the stable, and he and Buck took Lon's wagon to John Harper's store. When John was told what their project was, he was anxious to help with the best price he could offer and gave it to Flint on credit. He said he would make an appeal at the council meeting for the town to pay for the wire. Flint promised to pay for it himself if the council denied it.

"I don't think they'll deny it," John said. "All the merchants want the stray cow business dealt with."

Next, they drove the wagon across the open patch to the spot they had in mind beside the river. They had enough wire to stretch over a distance of about forty yards, so they made an estimate of how few posts they could get by with. "A lot of those bigger bushes are stout enough that we can use 'em as posts," Buck suggested. "This ain't no permanent fence. All we want is a wire the cows can see. They'll stay close to the water anyway."

Demrie Mullen donated the posts and loaned them the tools to dig the postholes. When Ralph saw the wagon return behind the jail, he locked the office door and joined the party. When they had stretched their fence about halfway the planned distance, they were surprised by the arrival of six cows being driven by Raymond Chadwick. "You ain't the only cowboy in Tinhorn!" he yelled. "Is this where you're roundin' 'em up?"

"This is the place," Flint yelled back, and when the cows saw the river, they went down to the water's edge. Flint asked. "You get these cows from Lon?"

"No," Chadwick answered, "they just wandered in the south end of town. And after I saw all the attention you've been gettin', I decided to round 'em up." When he saw what was going on, he went back to his shop to get a heavy sledgehammer to drive the posts in the ground.

Flint looked at Buck and asked, "You reckon that's a coincidence? Six cows from the north end of town and six cows from the south end?"

"If it is, it's a mighty peculiar one," Buck answered.

Word of Flint's cattle holding pen spread through town very quickly, resulting in quite a few visitors, most with suggestions on how to improve the rather crude enclosure. Flint had to explain more than once that it was merely a temporary enclosure, a place to confine the strays that showed up in town. And hopefully the problem would soon be solved. "What if Ira Dunellen doesn't pay to have his cattle back?" someone asked.

"Then I reckon we'll find one of the smaller ranchers on the other side of the river who would like to buy the cattle at a dirt-cheap price," Flint answered. "But first, we'll have the biggest barbecue this town has ever seen." That brought a small cheer from the few people who were standing there at the time.

It was close to suppertime when they nailed the last piece of wire to an oak tree that was leaning out over the water. With Lon's help, Ralph brought the six cows from the stable and introduced them to their temporary home. They appeared to like it just fine. Flint was not sure how long that might last, but he was ready to leave it to them to decide.

"Well, good evening, Flint," Clara greeted him warmly. "I heard you had a hard day on the range, herding your cattle."

"That's surely a fact," Flint answered, "and I'll be honest with you, I don't think I was cut out for it."

"Well, come on in and sit down. I see Mindy waiting at the table for you with a fresh cup of coffee. Where's Buck? Isn't he coming to supper?"

"He oughta be here any minute," Flint said. "I left a little bit early to go by the post office. I had a letter I had to mail."

Bonnie walked up in time to hear his comment. Never one to pass up a chance to tease, she said, "I hope it wasn't a letter to some little honey you ain't been tellin' us about."

He chuckled. "Hardly. It was just some sheriff's business." He had no intention to discuss the letter with any of the girls in the dining room. He had left the office early because he wanted to catch Louis Wheeler, the postmaster. The letter he took to the post office was to Ira Dunellen, and he hoped Wheeler could tell him how he could get it officially delivered to Dunellen. Much to his surprise, Wheeler told him that Dunellen had mail delivered there in Tinhorn. Of course, Tinhorn was the closest post office to him. But Flint had figured that maybe Dunellen had mail delivered to Tyler, since he was set on erasing Tinhorn from the Texas map. "No," Wheeler said, "he gets mail here. He never comes here personally. Lucas Sawyer checks with me every so often."

So, Flint's problem was nonexistent. He posted his letter to Ira Dunellen and then went directly to Clara's for supper. He hoped the letter would appear official enough, and he read it over again in his mind as he walked to Clara's.

> *To Ira Dunellen, owner, Cloverleaf Cattle Company.*
> *Please be advised that twelve cows belonging to*
> *you have been arrested for loitering within the*
> *bounds of the town of Tinhorn and will be held*
> *pending bond of four dollars ($4.00) each for their*
> *return. Signed, Sheriff Flint Moran, Tinhorn, Texas.*

That was about as good as he could do, he supposed. He didn't expect to receive any payment from Dunellen, but he was pretty sure it would start a fire under the would-be conqueror of the meek little town of Tinhorn.

"Evening, Flint," Mindy said as she placed the cup of coffee on the table while he pulled out the chair. "I hear you've had a busy day. I didn't see you when you drove those cows down the street. But I heard you're building a fence behind the jail."

"Not a real fence, just a temporary one," he said. Like Clara, she asked if Buck was coming to join him, and as he had told Clara, he said he expected Buck any minute. "It's a good idea to get a head start on him anyway," he joked. So Mindy went to the kitchen and filled his plate, ignoring Margaret's pretended shocked glances at the portion sizes.

He was almost finished before he stopped to wonder what had happened to Buck. He was about to get up and go to see if anything was wrong when his big partner walked into the dining room. "Well, I'll swear," Buck exclaimed, "so there you are!" He sat down heavily in the chair opposite him. "I've been settin' down there in the office, waitin' for you to come back from the post office. You said you were comin' back to the office."

"I never said that," Flint declared. "I said I'd meet you here."

"You said to wait for you at the office," Buck insisted.

"You're hearin' strange voices," Flint said. "Might be a good idea to go see Doc Beard and let him check that out."

"When we go back to the office, we'll ask Ralph if you said to wait there," Buck said.

Hearing the argument, Bonnie couldn't resist taking advantage of it. "Your attention, ladies and gentlemen," she announced to the customers. "There is a terrible fight goin' on in the Tinhorn sheriff's department. The trouble is, we don't know who to call to break it up."

"Shut your mouth, Bonnie," Mindy said. "You'll have people believing your silly talk."

Flint laughed. "Pay no attention to her, Mindy. Everybody knows you can't believe anything that comes outta her mouth."

Bonnie laughed with him, then declared, "Now you've hurt my feelings. I'm going in the kitchen to cry."

"Bring some more coffee with you when you come back," Buck said.

Flint sat for a while watching Buck eat, but when he decided he would have a slice of pie, Flint declared that he had better go on ahead and take Ralph's supper to him. He looked at Mindy and smiled. "Looks like I've already made enough people wait. That all right with you, Buck?"

"Yeah, go on ahead. I wanna take my time with the pie."

Flint picked up Ralph's plate, which Margaret had already brought out to the table, and started toward the door. Mindy walked with him.

"You and Buck aren't really mad at each other, are you?" Mindy asked, obviously concerned.

"Good gracious, no," he assured her. "We were just japin' each other." It suddenly occurred to him how incredibly innocent the young girl was. In a wild Texas town like Tinhorn, she needed someone to take care of her. "Tell you the truth, Buck might be right. I might have told him I'd come back to the office. I'll have to own up to that when he gets back. Right now, I've got Ralph wonderin' if I've forgotten his supper." He gave her a warm smile. "Good night, Mindy. I'll see you in the mornin'."

"Good night, Flint," she returned and closed the door behind him.

He went down the three steps and started to walk toward the street when he heard the voice behind him. "Sheriff Moran." It came from the corner of the building, catching him completely by surprise. The speaker had to have been hiding around the corner of the dining room, waiting for him. Flint stopped but hesitated to turn around because he was holding a plate of food in his right hand. He decided his best chance was to drop the plate as he turned, to free his hand to reach for his six-gun. He didn't like his odds, but he couldn't see that he had any other option. "Sheriff Moran," it came again, but this time there was a plaintive tone, as if uncertain.

"Can I turn around?" Flint asked.

"Yes, sir," the voice answered, "but I don't want nobody to see me. Can you step around the corner of the buildin'?"

Still a little wary, Flint said, "All right," and walked to the corner of the dining room. "Tim," he exclaimed when he saw Tim Walker, the young boy he had taken in so he could sleep off a drunk. He was standing in the shadow of the building. "Why are you hiding?"

"I don't want nobody to see me talkin' to you," he said, "and I've gotta tell you somethin'."

"What is it? Tell me what?" Flint asked.

"Mr. Dunellen put a two-hundred-dollar price on your head," Tim choked out.

He was stunned momentarily, even though he found it hard to believe the man would go to that extent. "Are you sure, Tim? Why do you think that? Who told you Dunellen put a price on my head? Maybe you mighta heard wrong."

"He told me," Tim answered. "This mornin' before we rode out, Mr. Dunellen came down to the bunkhouse and said he would give anyone of us two hundred dollars if we killed you. I didn't hear anybody say they were gonna take him up on it, but there were a couple who talked a lot about what you'd have to do to get away with it."

"You're kinda takin' a chance comin' to me with this, ain'tcha?"

"Yes, sir. That's why I hid. I don't want any of the men to see me talkin' to you. They'll know I told you. It ain't right, him tellin' us to kill somebody, and I know for a fact that you're a good man. So, you be extra careful, Sheriff."

"I will, Tim, I appreciate what you're doin'. Are there any of the other men in town with you?"

"Yes, sir," Tim replied. "I left Alvin Jeeter and Moon Murphy at the saloon. I told 'em I had just enough money to buy a good supper at this dinin' room, and if I didn't see 'em later, I'd see 'em back at the ranch."

"Good idea," Flint said. "Are you goin' inside now to eat?"

Tim almost blushed. "No, sir. I was lyin' to Moon and Lem. I ain't got no money."

"So you ain't had no supper. Right?"

"No, sir. I coulda got somethin' at the bunkhouse before we left, but I was afraid if I did, they wouldn't believe I wanted to buy supper here."

"Here," Flint said, "take this plate and go sit down on the back steps and eat it." He handed the plate to him. "If you don't wolf it down too fast, I'll be back with a fork for you."

"I can't take your supper," Tim started to protest.

"It ain't my supper. I already ate mine. This was for Ralph, back at the jail. Don't worry, I'll get him another one." He turned around then and went back inside.

"Flint, I thought you were gone," Clara said when he walked back in.

"I need another plate of food to take back with me." Flint said.

"I thought you just walked out of here with a plate for Ralph," Clara said.

"I did. But I dropped it and broke the plate. I'll pay you for the plate and the extra food."

"Nonsense," Clara said. "Accidents happen."

Mindy rushed up, just then having seen him come back inside. "Flint," she exclaimed when Clara went to the kitchen for the plate of food, "is something wrong?"

"No, nothing's wrong, but I could use a favor. Would you pour me a cup of coffee to take with me?" She nodded vigorously. "And if you'd walk me to the door, could you stick a fork in my pocket? If you do, I swear I'll explain the whole thing at breakfast in the mornin'." He glanced at Buck then, gaping at him, waiting for an explanation. So he walked over to the table and said, "Don't ask me now, I'll tell you the whole story back at the jail." He turned around then and walked back closer to the door.

Margaret came out of the kitchen with another plate of food. He took it from her and thanked her. He thanked Clara again while Mindy passed him, heading for the door. She opened it for him. Then, keeping her back turned to Clara, she slipped a fork in his pocket and handed him a fruit jar, half full of coffee. "You'd spill half of it out of a cup before you got to the jail," she whispered. He gave her a wink and went out the door.

Outside, he walked around the building and found Tim sitting on the back steps, eating with his fingers. "Here," Flint said, "this oughta make it easier." He handed him the fork, then the fruit jar. "I brought you some coffee to wash that down with."

Tim eagerly took the coffee from him and began to thank him profusely. "I didn't expect to get no supper tonight, much less this kinda supper. I don't know how to thank you."

"I think you've already done more than enough to make up for it," Flint told him. "Now, I'd better take this plate to Ralph before it gets cold. When you're done, just leave your dishes on the steps. And Tim, I appreciate what you've told me. Thank you." He left the young boy to finish his supper and took the new plate of food to Ralph, who was probably already worrying about it. He couldn't keep himself from eyeing the alleys he passed, what with the startling news he'd just received from Tim Walker. At the same time, he wondered if the young boy had misinterpreted something Dunellen had said. Maybe it was even something said in jest. He decided that sounded like a more reasonable explanation.

Chapter 12

As he expected, Ralph was standing by the office window, watching the street. "I thought you and Buck forgot all about my supper," he said when Flint walked in. "You was gone a long time."

"You know, we've told you this before, you could always walk up to Clara's to get your supper. They would give it to you."

"I don't like to go up there to get it," Ralph explained. "I just feel funny about it. I mean, me startin' out as a prisoner in the jail and all."

"Sometimes you take dirty dishes back to Clara's," Flint countered.

"Yeah, but that's different," Ralph replied.

"Well, just whatever suits you," Flint said when Ralph made no attempt to explain why. "Buck oughta be back here pretty soon now. Tell him I've gone over to Jake's Place." He left Ralph to enjoy his supper.

"Look what's comin' here," Moon Murphy said to Alvin Jeeter when Flint walked in the door of the saloon. "Two hundred dollars, cash on the hoof." They both watched him with new interest as he took the room in before he walked over to the bar to talk to Rudy. "We could both shoot him and split the money," Moon japed.

"Whaddaya reckon these men in here would do, if we did shoot him?" Alvin wondered aloud. He looked around at the few customers, speculating on whether or not they would rise in retaliation. "I expect we wouldn't make it out the door," he decided.

"I think you're right," Moon agreed. "The only way to do it is to go up against him face-to-face. I wonder how fast he is with that Colt he's wearin'. I ain't ever heard anybody talkin' about how fast he is."

"Why don't you call him out? Then when I see how you do, I'll decide if I wanna try him or not."

"Ha," Moon grunted. "That ain't my style. I expect I'm just like you and most of the other boys. If I catch him in the right place, I ain't gonna pass up a chance to collect two hundred dollars. I figure I'd be doin' a lot of people a favor."

"Better make up your mind 'cause he's comin' this way," Alvin said when Flint left the bar and started walking in their direction.

"Evenin'," Flint said as he approached their table. "Did you fellows get that little bunch of cattle moved back to your range this mornin'?"

"We sure did, Sheriff, got 'em all moved away from your town," Moon answered him.

"You sure you got 'em all?" Flint asked. "We had about a dozen more show up on the street today."

"Is that a fact?" Alvin asked. "Well, there ain't no doubt about it, we didn't leave no strays from that bunch this mornin'."

"By the way," Flint said then, "I just came from the post office a little while ago. Mr. Wheeler asked me, if I saw any of you Cloverleaf riders in town, would I tell you he's got some mail for Mr. Dunellen. You might tell your boss that. Might be something important."

"Lucas Sawyer usually takes care of the mail and stuff like that," Moon said. "Mr. Dunellen don't like anybody else messin' with it. We'll tell Lucas."

"Much obliged," Flint said, and when they both looked at the door, he turned to see Buck walk in. "Well, enjoy your evenin'." He went to meet Buck then.

"What's goin' on, Flint?" Buck grinned as he met him at one end of the bar. "Clara said you dropped Ralph's supper and broke the plate. Maybe you need a drink. Is that why you came to the saloon?"

"I had to tell her something," Flint replied. "I didn't drop it and I expect they'll find the plate on the back doorstep."

Buck was really curious then. "What are you talkin' about?"

"I gave Ralph's supper to Tim Walker," Flint started to explain, but Buck interrupted.

"Whadja do that for?"

"Hold your tongue for a minute and I'll tell you," Flint said. He went on then to take Buck through the whole sequence of events from the time he first walked out of the dining room. "He didn't want anyone seein' him talkin' to me, not even the women in the dinin' room. And it wouldn'ta been too good for him if any of the Cloverleaf crew knew he told me what Dunellen offered."

"That old man must not be right in the head," Buck declared. "To make an offer like that, he'd have to have his brains scrambled." Bringing his thoughts back to the moment, he asked, "So what did you come to the saloon for? You thinkin' about tellin' those two at the table you know about the reward? We can't arrest 'em for something the crazy man they work for said." He paused to swear.

"Damn, Flint, you've gotta have eyes in the back of your head from now on."

"I just came in here to see how many Cloverleaf men were in town," Flint said.

"You coulda asked if they was in town to shoot you," Buck japed.

Ignoring the joke, Flint continued. "I found out from Louis Wheeler that Ira Dunellen and the Cloverleaf Ranch are set up to receive mail in Tinhorn. So I just told these two that Dunellen has some important mail in his box."

"Your notice about the cows under arrest?" Buck asked.

"Right. I can't wait to see how he's gonna react to it. Maybe he'll offer a couple of hundred for your life, too."

"Maybe so," Buck replied, then stopped laughing. "Let's take this threat seriously, Flint. I know it's a crazy thing he's proposed, but one or more of that gang ridin' for him might be as crazy as he is."

As Flint and Buck walked out of the saloon, the two Cloverleaf cowhands were approached by Lucy Tucker, who had been previously engaged in another business deal. "Hello, boys, which one of you cowboys was wantin' to visit me?"

"I reckon that would be me, honey," Moon answered her.

She extended her hand, and he took it and got up from his chair. She led him up the stairs to her room. When his visit was over, she didn't rush him because she sensed he was not completely satisfied. When she asked if there was something wrong, he said, "No, honey, ain't nothin' wrong with you. It's me. I think I let that sheriff of yours bother me. He came in and talked to me and Alvin about them stray cows we ain't got nothin' to do with. I reckon I let it get in my head."

"You shouldn't bother yourself about Flint Moran," Lucy told him. "He's just tryin' to do the best for the town that he can. If you had many dealings with him, you'd find out that he's a good man."

"Maybe so," Moon allowed. "I reckon he watches the town most of the night before he goes back to the jail to go to bed."

"Not real late," Lucy said. "The town pretty much shuts down around nine or ten o'clock, and that's when he goes to bed. But he don't sleep at the jail. Buck's got a room next to the jail. Flint has a room at Hannah Green's boardin' house."

"Don't that put him too far away from town, if there's some trouble?" Moon asked, seeming concerned.

"It's not that far," Lucy said. "It's just across from the stables down the street. If anything happens in the middle of the night, Buck's right there in the jail and Flint would be there in five minutes."

"Sounds like you like him pretty much," Moon said. "Does he come see you a lot?"

Lucy laughed. "Flint don't come to see me a-tall, but I still like him pretty much. He's been good for Tinhorn."

"Well, I ain't gonna have no bad feelin's about him next time I come to see you," Moon said. "And next time I'm gonna pay you for the whole night."

"Goodness me," Lucy responded. "You must be rich."

"I'm expectin' a big payday pretty soon," he said with a wink.

She extended her hand and led him out to the hall. "I'm gonna freshen up a little before I come back down." When she was satisfied he was out of earshot, she mumbled, "You better bring a whole damn sack of money if you want me to spend the night with you."

"Well, it musta been pretty good to paint a grin like that

on your face," Alvin said when Moon flopped down in his chair.

"I'll say it was," Moon replied. "It was money well spent."

"You ready to get on back to the ranch now?"

"No, I ain't," Moon responded. "I ain't through yet."

"You got some more money?" Alvin asked. "You said all you had left was enough for your ticket for a ride upstairs."

"I did say that, didn't I? Well, it just so happens my plans have changed. I'm fixin' to do a little job first that'll pay me two hundred dollars."

"What the hell are you talkin' about?" Alvin reacted at once and looked around them at once to make sure no one heard Moon. "Lower your voice! You thinkin' about callin' Flint Moran out?"

"Hell no. I ain't lost my mind. I'm gonna shoot him down when he goes home tonight. I've told you what I'm fixin' to do, but I ain't gonna tell you no more about how I'm gonna do it, if you ain't wantin' to go fifty-fifty with me. I figure it'd be a little bit safer if there was one of us to back the other'n up." Alvin hesitated, not at all sure he was ready to risk going after Flint Moran. So Moon told him a little more. "That little gal up there ain't particular about what she tells about anybody. So, for the price of one little ride, I know when Moran goes home to bed. And I know where he goes. He don't sleep at the jail, or in the hotel. So it'll be him walkin' home in the dark, and me right behind him. And if you wanna go in on it with me, you'll be right behind me, holdin' the horses. Soon as I shoot him, we're on our horses and out the south end of town." He waited for Alvin's decision. "Whaddaya think? We'd be gone before anybody knows what happened. There ain't a chance they could get up a posse quick enough to come after us. I can do it by myself, but I'm willin' to pay you a hundred dollars to be there with the horses as soon as we need 'em."

"You sold me," Alvin said, "I'm in. Fifty-fifty, right? One hundred dollars for my part in it. Right?"

"That's right, partner, that's the deal. It'll be easy. Lucy said Moran will stick around until nine or ten tonight, dependin' on when all the other places are closed for the night. Then he walks to that boardin' house at the south end of town, a little bit farther and across the street from the stable. The main thing we gotta do is make him think we've left town, so we need to find us a place where we can hide the horses and keep an eye on the street, so we'll know when he starts for home. Once he starts down toward the stable, I can stay pretty close to him on foot, and you can stay far enough behind me, so he don't see you and the horses." That sounded pretty simple to Alvin, and pretty safe. And the thought of a hundred dollars for nothing more than holding the horses while Moon did the job was too much to pass up.

The job now was to kill a little time, so they remained there for a while longer. Alvin still had a little bit of money, so he paid for a couple more shots of whiskey to keep the bartender from wondering why they were still sitting there. Finally, they figured it was time to leave. "Better get on back to the ranch, I reckon," Moon said to Rudy on their way out. "Mornin' starts pretty early on the Cloverleaf. Lucy like to wore me out anyway."

"Right, thanks, boys," Rudy responded. "Don't fall off your horses on the way home."

Outside the saloon, they took a few moments to look up and down the street. Everything looked buttoned up for the night, with only Jake's Place still lit up. "Look yonder!" Alvin suddenly whispered when Flint came out of the sheriff's office across the street. He paused when he saw them.

"Get on your horse!" Alvin said. "Let him see us leavin'."
They climbed on their horses and started out at a slow walk
toward the south end of town. Flint only watched for a
moment before making his final round on the street. "He's
headin' up toward the hotel," Alvin said. "We need to find
us a place to hide."

"Over by the river," Moon said, "behind the jail." So as
soon as they felt sure the darkness had swallowed them
up, they left the street and cut across the open field of
weeds and headed toward the trees that lined the river.
Plowing through the high weeds, they suddenly pulled up
short when they heard a cow snort. "What tha . . ." Moon
started when his eyes adjusted enough to identify the
moving objects close to the river. When he saw a white
rag that appeared to be suspended in midair, he realized
it was actually tied to a strand of wire. "There's some cows
penned up here."

"I bet it's them cows we left this mornin'," Alvin said.
"They're plannin' on keepin' 'em for good. We can cut 'em
loose."

"Not tonight, though," Moon replied. "We don't need to
wake everybody up. We can come back with some more of
the boys to take them cows back. We'd best stop right here.
We can see the street from here, but we're far enough back
in this field, so he can't see us. We don't need to start these
cows to bawlin'." So they stood in the weeds, holding their
horses and watching the street.

After saying good night to Ralph, Flint had walked out
of the office to take a final check of the town before calling
it a night. He had just stepped off the bottom step to the
office when he spotted the two Cloverleaf cowhands getting on their horses in front of Jake's Place. He had paused

there a few moments to see if they were leaving town. When they rode on down toward the south end, he was satisfied that they were on their way home. So, with his rifle in hand, he started up the street. Now, he was finishing up his patrol, having walked up to the hotel and passing back by Jake's Place at the present. No need to go inside the saloon, he figured, so he kept walking, feeling more than ready to crawl into his bed. A lot had happened that day. When he passed by Clara's Kitchen, he wondered if any of the women had found the dish and fork on the back step. *I owe Mindy an explanation for that little business*, he thought.

He walked by the stable, the last place to check on, and saw that everything was locked up securely. It served to remind him that it was time to get Buster some new shoes. *I'll tell Raymond in the morning*, he thought. Thinking the town was good for the night, he walked across the street and proceeded down through the trees toward the path to the boardinghouse. He was hopping a little ditch beside the road and the path when it hit him. Like a sudden blow with a hammer, it struck him in the back and knocked him to the ground, facedown. The sound of the shot lagged behind the blow that caused him to fall. He lay flat, unmoving, not sure how bad he was hurt. "You got him!" he heard Alvin exclaim excitedly.

"Bring the horses!" Moon yelled.

"I'm comin'," Alvin yelled back. Then, remembering what Dunellen had said, he yelled, "The proof! Get his badge!"

In the excitement of actually pulling off the assassination, Moon had forgotten that. So he ran to the body and rolled it over, groping for the badge, never noticing the Colt .44 pointing toward his breastbone. "You lookin' for this?" Flint growled and pulled the trigger. Moon was killed almost instantly when the bullet went up under his breast-bone and into his heart. He crumpled over on his back. Shocked motionless for a second, Alvin's only thought was to get away. While he scrambled in panic to climb on his horse, Flint deliberately forced himself to a sitting position. Then he picked up the rifle he had dropped, took careful aim, and fired one shot that slammed into Alvin between his shoulder blades, knocking him from the saddle. Flint lay back on the ground then and tried to determine how badly he had been wounded. He made an attempt to get up, but the pain it caused was so intense that he remained on his back. He heard some sounds like people shouting, but he wasn't sure from where they originated. He found out later that it was probably Ralph banging on Buck's wall and trying to wake him up. It was actually Paul Roper, one of the men who had a room at Hannah Green's boarding-house, who found Flint with Moon Murphy's body beside him. Several other men responded to the gunfire and Ralph directed them toward the stable. Nolan Carson and Raymond Chadwick were two of the first to arrive at the scene. Moments behind them, Buck Jackson arrived with his nightshirt half tucked into his britches.

"Looks like they shot him in the back," Paul said. "But he's still alive, and he got the one that shot him."

"There's another one dead back yonder about twenty yards," Nolan Carson, the carpenter, said. "I saw them both at Jake's tonight. There's two saddled horses standin' in the street."

"We need to get him to Doc's right now," Buck said. The trouble was the doctor's office was up at the other end of town, past the hotel. "Paul, hitch up Hannah's buggy. We can take him in that."

"Buck," Flint said, "never mind the buggy. I can ride up to Doc's. Just help me get on a horse."

"You sure?" Buck asked. Flint said he was, so Buck said, "Grab one of those horses in the street." Chadwick ran back and caught one of the horses and Paul caught the other one. They led both of them back to Flint. Buck picked Flint up and set him in the saddle. "I'll ride the other one and lead him up there. Can you hold on, partner?"

"I can hold on, but I don't feel like I can race you there," Flint said, grasping the saddle horn to remain upright.

His flippant remark was a good sign as far as Buck was concerned, so he climbed up in the saddle on the other horse. Paul handed him the reins for Flint's horse, and Buck walked the horses slowly up the street. When they reached Doc Beard's house, the only lights were from the lamp in the kitchen and one in the bedroom. So Buck went to the kitchen door after making sure Flint could remain upright in the saddle. "Who is it?" Doc demanded from inside the kitchen.

"Buck Jackson," Buck answered. "Open up, Doc, Flint's been shot!"

Doc opened the door immediately, completely skipping his usual complaints about patients knocking on his door after office hours. "Bring him in the front door," he directed. "Birdie!" he yelled then. "I'm gonna need you!"

"I already in my nightgown," the little Cherokee woman called back.

"Well, put on your robe," he yelled at her. "It's Flint Moran, and he's been shot. Hell, I'm in my nightshirt. Go open the front door and let Buck in while I go put on my pants."

Like her husband, Birdie acted at once when she heard it was Flint who was wounded. She picked up the lamp and hurried to the front door to unlock it. When she opened it, she found Buck waiting on the porch with Flint riding piggyback. She held the door open for him, and when he came in, she picked up the lamp again. "Follow me," she said and led him into Doc's surgery. She put her lamp on a table beside Doc's operating table. "I help you," she said. Then she put Flint's arms around her neck and, together, she and Buck transferred Flint from Buck's back to the table. To Flint, she said, "You rest. I go get water hot." She hurried out of the room. Passing Doc on his way in, she said, "Shot in the back. He bleed a lot."

"Sit him up till I get his shirt off," Doc told Buck. He was anxious to see exactly where Flint was shot in his back. Working quickly because of the amount of blood Flint was losing, he removed his vest and shirt. "Okay, okay," he said, more to himself than to Buck. "Maybe it ain't as bad as it coulda been."

Buck had never seen Doc exhibit such concern over a bullet wound before. He had to remind himself that on the numerous occasions he had witnessed Doc's surgery, it had been performed on outlaws. He realized now how much the town needed Flint. Before, he had thought that he was the only one who depended upon him. "He's gonna make it, ain't he, Doc?" He couldn't imagine that he wouldn't.

Doc recovered his typical hard-fact, clinical tendency then, after he was able to get a better idea of the angle the bullet took upon entering Flint's back. "Well, I think he might," he said, answering Buck's question. "He's breathin' good, so the bullet missed his left lung, and I don't see a sign of any broken bones. It looks like the bullet buried itself in the muscle near the collarbone. I'll have to go in and see." Birdie came in at that moment with a pan of hot water. She didn't wait for Doc's instructions but proceeded to clean the blood away from the bullet hole. Doc continued. "After we clean him up, we'll put him to sleep, and

I'll see if I can remove that bullet without causing too much damage. It's gonna take some time, and he's gonna be unconscious. So if you've got business to take care of with the ones who shot him, you might as well go on about it." Buck was reluctant to leave, but he knew he had things to take care of, so he said he'd be back and for Doc to do whatever was necessary to take care of Flint. "Don't worry," Doc reassured him, "Birdie and I will take care of Flint."

Buck left the doctor's office then and took the two horses back to the scene of the shooting. A few more of the townsfolk had responded to the sounds of gunfire, and some had found their way to the path to Hannah Green's boardinghouse. One of them was Lon Blake. When Buck rode up leading an extra horse, Lon said, "I figured you might want to get in the stable. I woke Walt Doolin up and told him to bring his handcart. What about Flint? How bad is he hurt?"

"Well, it looked pretty bad," Buck answered. "But Doc said it might not be as bad as it looks. He's operatin' on him right now."

Jake Rudolph walked over to hear the conversation. "Cloverleaf men," he volunteered. "They were both in the saloon this evening. Paul Roper said they shot Flint in the back, and it looks like he got both of 'em before they got away. You reckon Dunellen sent them in here to kill Flint?"

"I reckon," Buck answered simply. Back to Lon then, he said, "I expect I'm gonna need your wagon when Doc's finished with Flint. I don't know if he'll keep him there a while or send him home to heal." Lon assured him he would make himself available whenever the wagon was needed.

Not satisfied with Buck's simple answer to his question, Jake asked another one. "If you think Dunellen sent them in here to kill Flint, ain't there something we can do about that? I mean, tell the Texas Rangers, or the U.S. Marshals Service?"

"And show 'em what proof we've got that Dunellen sent them to kill Flint? We can't question those two dead men, can we? Maybe they just got drunk enough at your place to try to get even with Flint for shuttin' down all their hell-raisin' here in town. We could question the rest of his hands and ask them if he sent those two to kill Flint. You reckon any of 'em would say he did?" He wasn't inclined to mention the fact that young Tim Walker had told Flint there was a price on his head. He was afraid that if he let that out, Tim would be in danger. And that wouldn't be the right thing to do. Jake nodded slowly, as if he understood the difficulty in pointing a finger at anyone. As for Buck, he didn't know what their reaction should be. Flint took care of the would-be assassins, but it was still an attempted murder, and it was instigated by Ira Dunellen. When he could talk to him again, maybe they could decide what needed to be done.

CHAPTER 13

Buck went back to Doc's after leaving the two Cloverleaf horses with Lon Blake to take to the stable until he decided what he was going to do with them. When he arrived at Doc's, he found that the operation to extract the bullet from Flint's shoulder was completed, and Doc tossed the slug to him. "Put it in your pocket and maybe you might wanna give it to Flint to use as a lucky piece. He did fine, and the only reason I can give for it is this damn bullet took the only route to follow into his body that avoided major organs, bones, and vessels. He did just fine. He's awake now, but he's still fighting the woozy feeling a patient has when he wakes up from the chloroform. I'm gonna keep him here tonight so I can check on him in the morning. Then you can have him. You can go on in to see him now. Just don't stay too long."

Buck went into the surgery, where he found Birdie fanning Flint, vigorously waving a wide, lace-trimmed fan in Flint's face in an effort to give him some fresh air. The fan seemed out of place in a doctor's office, more suited to a dancehall. She got up and left when Buck walked in.

"How ya doin', partner?" Buck asked. "You ready to go back to work?"

Flint answered him with a weak smile. "Maybe not

tonight," he slurred. "Give me until tomorrow, all right?" Then he got serious for a moment. "Did I get the second one?"

"You did," Buck replied, "right between the shoulder blades."

"I wasn't sure. I was sittin' down when I shot at him." He paused to take a breath. "It's hard to get that stuff Doc knocked me out with outta my lungs. I'm sorry about rootin' you outta bed for this business. It's all my fault for bein' so damn careless. I saw those two ride outta town. I mean, I thought I saw 'em ridin' outta town. And they caught me good, didn't they?"

Buck had to snort a chuckle in response. Then he said, "It seems to me like those two boys caught the dirty end of that stick. I don't think you've woke up good from that chloroform yet, else you wouldn't be talkin' so crazy. You get you some sleep tonight, and I'll come get you in the morning, take you to your room. I talked to Hannah Green, and she said she'd take care of you till you felt like you were ready to get up and move around. You know, it was Paul Roper who found you. He thought it was somebody huntin' close to the house."

"I swear," Flint declared, "I bet Hannah had already gone to bed."

"She had, but she was awful glad I came to tell her about you. She said she'da felt real bad if she hadn't been ready to take care of you tomorrow."

"I shoulda had my mind on my business when I started home tonight, especially after what Tim Walker went to the trouble to tell me. What happened to him anyway? Did he hang around town?"

"Nobody saw hide nor hair of him after you talked to him," Buck said. "I reckon he just went back to the Cloverleaf. He told you he didn't have any money, so you know he wasn't plannin' to give drinkin' a try again. I expect he came into town with those two just to warn you." They talked only a short while longer before Doc came back in and told them it was time to let Flint get some rest, so Buck walked to the door. "I'll come get you in the mornin'," he said. "I expect I'll get to Clara's early and get some breakfast. I'll take Ralph's to him, then I'll come get you. Hannah said Myrna would be tickled to death to cook for you."

True to his word, Buck was at the door to Clara's Kitchen before she was scheduled to open it. "You're early," Clara told him. "Where's the sheriff? Isn't he gonna eat breakfast with you this morning?"

At first, Buck thought she was making a rather poor joke. He fixed a grin on her and started to tell her so. Looking at her innocent face then, he asked, "You really don't know, do you?"

Now she was confused. "Know what?" she asked.

"Flint got shot last night. He won't be comin' to breakfast." Her face blanched and her mouth dropped open. "How the hell could you not know?" Buck asked. "A town this size, everybody knows what's going on all the time." When she just continued to stare at him, he said, "It did happen down at the other end of town," he allowed. "But you shoulda heard some shots. There were three shots fired."

"Oh, Buck, we didn't hear any shots. Jim and I live out past Doc Beard's place. Margaret doesn't live close to town either. And Bonnie and Mindy both have rooms in the back of the hotel, and when we close here, they both go straight to their rooms. Even if they heard any shots, they aren't likely to go see who shot 'em." She started wringing her hands, concerned. "What am I gonna tell Mindy?"

"Tell me what?" Mindy asked as she came from the kitchen carrying a stack of dishes.

Clara rushed to her and took the dishes from her. "Flint's been shot," she said and placed the stack of dishes safely on one of the tables.

Buck was dumbfounded when he saw the shock on Mindy's face, and he realized the impression he had caused. "He ain't dead!" He blurted it out. "He's at Doc's right now, and when I'm done eatin', I'm goin' to pick him up and take him to his room at Hannah's. Hannah's gonna take care of him till he gets on his feet again." He looked from one of them to the other. "I didn't go to make you think he was dead," he apologized.

Bonnie, who was supporting Mindy after she almost collapsed, remarked, "We ought not even let you eat after the way you gave us the news."

"But he's gonna be all right?" Clara asked.

"Oh, hell yeah," Buck said at once. "You know it takes a helluva lot to stop Flint."

"Who shot him?" Clara asked.

"It was two Cloverleaf men, sneaked up behind him when he was walkin' home, and shot him in the back." Mindy almost dropped again, so Bonnie pulled a chair over and sat her down on it. Buck went on. "After they shot him down, one of 'em came up and rolled him over, and Flint gave him a belly full of lead. The other'n ran for it then, and Flint sat up and picked him off with his rifle. It musta been a helluva thing to see."

The three women stared at him as he described the assassination attempt and the way Flint responded to it. And when he finished, Bonnie commented, "Well, we're so sorry you weren't there to see it." She looked at Clara then and asked, "Should we feed him?"

"Yes, if we don't, he won't ever get outta here to take

Flint to Hannah's so he can have some breakfast. I assume she's gonna feed him, or are you wanting two plates to take back with you?"

"Hannah said she'd feed him," Buck said, "since she'll be lookin' after him anyway."

"I swear, Buck . . ." Clara started when she saw Mindy's distressed reaction to that statement, but she couldn't think of the right words to explain her impatience with him. So, instead, she said, "Well, let's get you fed, so you can take Ralph's, and maybe you can take Flint to Hannah's, so he can get some breakfast before it's suppertime."

Buck picked Flint up in a wagon he borrowed from Lon Blake and hauled him back to his room behind the boardinghouse. Since Flint's room was actually an addition to the main house, connected by a narrow, covered porch, it sat a little higher off the ground. Because of that, Buck pulled the wagon up at the front of the house, though Flint insisted on walking to his room instead of being carried. Buck figured it would be easier for him to take the two steps up to the porch in front. If he had used his usual entrance at the back porch, he would have to walk up four steps. "Doggone it, Buck," Flint complained, "I ain't as weak as you think. I coulda walked up the back steps."

"Doc said you ain't supposed to put no strain on your body a-tall," Buck replied. "It's best you go in the front."

"Yeah, but this way I have to walk through the whole house and out the back door," Flint complained as Buck helped him off the wagon. "It was bad enough havin' to ride from one end of town all the way to the other sittin' in the back of a wagon."

As Flint had feared, except for the boarders who had already gone to work, the rest of Hannah's renters came out of their rooms to show their support for their wounded sheriff. Hannah met him at the front door and walked with him and Buck through the house and into his room. She took great care in getting him settled on his bed and propped up with pillows and quilts to a sitting position. He said he was ready to eat when she asked if he was hungry, so she left to go to the kitchen. Buck pulled the one chair in the room up close to the bed, and a short time later, Myrna and Hannah came in with a breakfast tray and a coffeepot. Hannah asked Buck if he had eaten breakfast, and he said that he had. "Well, we brought you a cup for some coffee anyway," she said. To Flint, she said, "You eat plenty of that meat. Doc said you lost a lotta blood and you need to build it back up."

"You don't have to tell me to eat plenty of Myrna's cookin'," Flint said. "It's always good." His comment brought the smile to Myrna's face that he sought.

The women left him to eat his breakfast, with instructions to send Buck for the coffee when needed. So, while Flint ate, he and Buck discussed their possible reactions to the attempted assassination. "I don't know what good it would do to notify the U.S. Marshal," Buck speculated. "I don't know if that kid, Tim Walker, has the guts to tell a judge that Dunellen offered a reward for your death. And even if he did, Dunellen's gonna deny it, and you know the rest of that crew are gonna stick with Dunellen. What it boils down to is a couple of cowhands tried to kill you, and you killed them instead. It's the risk you take on when you're the sheriff in a small town. I'm afraid we're right in the same place we were before, a damn war between Cloverleaf and Tinhorn."

"I'm afraid I have to agree with everything you just said," Flint responded. He would have made sure he returned the horses and the bodies of the two would-be killers to the Cloverleaf if he had not gotten shot. He regretted the fact that he was in no condition to follow through with that. He didn't mention it to Buck, however, because he was afraid he might take it upon himself to do it. *And that could be dangerous*, he thought. *Besides, Buck doesn't operate outside the town limits.*

Lucas Sawyer stood looking at the two empty bunks in the recently completed bunkhouse. He went back to Gabby Skelton's chuckwagon, where he was still cleaning up after the breakfast meal. "I told you they never came back last night," Gabby said before Lucas could ask him again. "Tim Walker went into town with 'em, but he came back pretty early. He said Moon and Alvin were at the saloon when he left to come home."

"I'm surprised to hear they had enough money to get too drunk to find their way back home," Lucas said, disgusted. "I'll have to tell Mr. Dunellen to dock 'em one day's pay. I'll give 'em till this afternoon before I report it to him."

When his two missing men failed to show up for the noon meal, Lucas went up to the main house to report it to Dunellen. The news irritated Dunellen, just as Lucas expected, and he told Lucas he could inform them that they would be docked two days for their carelessness. Still in a huff, he walked out to the front porch with his foreman, lecturing him on the evils of being too soft with the men. He paused suddenly in midsentence to exclaim, "Who the hell is that?" Lucas turned to see what had caught Dunellen's eye and spotted a group of three riders. They were leading two horses with bodies lying across the saddles. The rider in the lead was easily recognized as Buck Jackson, so he knew at once that Murphy and Tate were returning to the ranch. He went down the steps to meet them, while Dunellen remained at the edge of the porch.

"Afternoon," Buck called out. "We thought you might be wonderin' what happened to these two Cloverleaf hands, so we brought 'em back for ya. We figured the horses might be worth something, and you'd want them back."

Lucas glanced at his boss to see if he was going to respond, but when he just stood there, obviously smoldering in his fury, Lucas replied, "I can't help but notice that those two men appear to be dead."

"Oh, that!" Buck responded. "I figured you might wanna know why they ended up missin' this mornin'." Although his speech was casual, he held his rifle in one hand, the butt resting on his thigh and the barrel pointing toward the sky. The two riders with him were on either side, spaced an equal distance from his horse. Like him, they held their rifles at the ready. "These two fellows musta forgot that it's against the law to murder someone in the town of Tinhorn, especially when it's the sheriff you're tryin' to murder. So they hid in the bushes last night till it was time for Sheriff Moran to go home. Then they sneaked up behind him and shot him in the back. I don't know which one did the actual shootin'. There wasn't but one shot fired at Sheriff Moran, so I can't really say which one earned the two hundred dollars." Both Lucas and Dunellen blinked at the mention of the reward, but both kept a tight lip.

Silent until that moment, Dunellen could not resist asking the question burning his tongue. "Is Sheriff Moran dead?"

"Oh no, sir, Flint ain't dead. It'd take a helluva lot more than that saddle trash to kill Flint Moran. As a matter of fact, Flint took the bullet in his back, then turned around and killed both of these two-bit assassins." He let that sink in while he watched Dunellen clenching his teeth in frustration. "The sheriff woulda come out here to bring your boys home, but he had a meetin' scheduled that was a lot more important." Then, after fashioning a wide, friendly smile for their benefit, he said, "Good day to you. Sorry we couldn'ta brought you more cheerful news."

Chadwick and Carson both dropped the reins of the horses they had been leading, and all three riders backed their horses away from the steps. The two Cloverleaf horses started to follow them until Lucas caught their reins and held them. When Buck deemed it safe enough, he wheeled his horse and went back through the front gate at a lope.

At a loss for what to say, Lucas stood there, holding the two horses with the bodies of Alvin Jeeter and Moon Murphy in full rigor mortis across their saddles. He turned to look at Dunellen, still standing at the edge of the porch, and waited for instructions. "Get them out of my sight!" he finally commanded, turned around, and went back into the house.

Lucas led the horses to the barn, where he found Jack Spade and Andy Hatcher working in the hayloft. "Grab a couple of shovels and a pick," Lucas said, "and come with me. We've got a couple of graves to dig."

"Who died?" Andy asked.

"Alvin and Moon," Lucas answered. Then, before they could ask how, he said, "Tryin' to collect two hundred dollars." Not particularly happy about being the unlucky ones to catch the chore, they grumbled openly. "I'm gonna help you," Lucas said. "Come on, let's get 'em in the ground before they start to smell."

"Hell," Jack snarled, "Alvin smelled pretty bad when he was alive."

"Did they really try to collect that two hundred dollars?" Andy asked.

"I reckon so," Lucas said, "because accordin' to what that sheriff's deputy, or whatever he is, said, they shot

Moran in the back, and he killed both of 'em. You'd best take my advice and forget about that reward. That sheriff is bad news. Even if you were lucky enough to kill him, all that two hundred dollars would buy you is a reputation as the man who killed Flint Moran. Then you could spend the rest of your days tryin' to keep it. But that wouldn't be a long time because there's always some jasper out there who's faster than you." Both men denied having any thoughts about collecting the reward money.

They dug the grave for Alvin and Moon across the creek from the barn, where the ground was fairly soft. After they pushed the bodies off their horses, they found them so stiff with rigor mortis that they couldn't straighten them out. So Lucas decided to bury them both in the same grave. "We'll dig it good and deep and make it a square hole. With their bodies locked in that L-shape, we can face 'em, and they oughta fit in a square hole just right."

At about the same time the callous burial was completed at the Cloverleaf Cattle Company, a young lady was knocking at Hannah Green's front door. Unaccustomed to having people knock on her door, it took a few minutes before Hannah realized there was someone there. "Why, Mindy Moore!" Hannah exclaimed. "I'm sorry it took me so long to answer the door. I'm so used to havin' my boarders coming and going all the time that I don't pay attention when it's someone else. "What can I do for you, honey?"

"I heard about Flint gettin' shot and was wonderin' if maybe it would be all right with you if I was to visit him to see how he's doing."

"Why, how sweet of you!" Hannah replied. "Of course it would be all right with me. I'm pretty sure he's awake right now. At least he was when I checked on him about fifteen minutes ago. Come on in and I'll walk you back to see him." Mindy followed her through the house, then out the kitchen door. When she found herself being led through the washroom and then to the back porch, she had a moment of fright, thinking that Hannah was marching her out of the house, and she was not welcome at all. She breathed a sigh of relief, however, when Hannah marched across the narrow bridge to the attached structure. She tapped on the door and called out, "Flint, are you decent? You have a visitor."

"Yes, ma'am, at least I've got clothes on, if that's what you mean."

Hannah opened the door and stepped aside so Mindy could pass by her. She smiled warmly to the young girl, as well as to herself, while thinking she might have discovered something that she would never have guessed. She took a quick look at Flint, but he showed nothing more than surprise. "You want the door open or closed?" Hannah asked him.

"Don't matter," Flint answered. "Maybe leave it open, so there'll be more air."

Hannah hesitated a moment longer to watch, just in case there might be something she could report to Myrna. But when both Flint and Mindy were slow in reacting, she finally said, "If you need anything, just give me a yell." She pulled the door shut behind her, then opened it again. "I forgot. You said open."

"Mindy," Flint finally spoke after Hannah had gone, "what are you doin' here? Is anything wrong?"

"Is anything wrong?" she repeated his question. "Yes, something's wrong! You've been shot. That's what's wrong." She shook her head in frustration. "Buck said Doc told him you were lucky you weren't killed. I had to come see if you're all right. I hope you don't mind."

"Of course I don't mind," he replied, still surprised that she had come. "It's mighty nice of you to care how I'm doin'. I reckon I just didn't expect to have any visitors. So I wanna thank you for comin' to see me." Then it occurred to him that she was probably there on behalf of the women at Clara's Kitchen. So he asked, "Did Clara send you to see me?"

Instantly impatient with his apparent ignorance, she reacted at once. "Hell no, Clara didn't send me. She doesn't even know I'm here. I wanted to see if you're okay." Realizing she might be exposing her feelings too soon, she added, "That's what real friends do."

He was touched to think she had come on her own and he wanted to express it. But he knew he wasn't good with words, and he was afraid he might say something stupid. Still, he had to say something. "I count myself lucky to have you as a friend," he finally forced out. "I reckon if anybody asked me to name my best friends, I'd start with you, and then I couldn't think of anybody else." As soon as he heard what he had just said, he cringed inside, and wished he could take it back.

"Am I your best friend?" Mindy asked.

He nodded. "I reckon so."

"You're my best friend, too," she said. "That's why I worry when I hear you've been hurt." *Best friends*, she thought, *well, that's a start*. They talked a while about the problems with Ira Dunellen and the town's cow problem. Then she reminded him that he had promised to explain the reason for a second plate and a fork to take with him on the night he was shot. He told her all about Tim Walker, swearing her to secrecy, and the fact that he was evidently an honest young man. By that time she said she had to get back to Clara's. It was time to start preparing for the evening meal.

He thanked her for coming to visit him and said that he planned to be back to work the next day. He said he could sit around the sheriff's office as well as he could in his room. And she lectured him about giving his wound the proper time to heal. He insisted on getting up off the bed to see her to the door, where she paused to offer her hand. He took it as if to shake it but held on to it for a few moments longer. *It's a start*, she thought.

CHAPTER 14

"Where in the world are you going?" Hannah asked when Flint walked into the dining room, dressed for work the next day.

"Good mornin', Hannah," he said. "I'm goin' to sit down at the table so I can enjoy one of Myrna's fine breakfasts. It's something I don't get to do as often as I'd like."

"You didn't have to get all dressed up to come to breakfast," Hannah declared. "I would have brought it to you, just like I did supper."

"I know, and I appreciate that, but I'll be goin' on into the office this mornin', so I might as well be dressed for work. I told Buck I'd be in this mornin' when he was here last night." As he anticipated, she protested, but he told her he felt good enough to walk to the jail. And he promised that he would have Buck bring him home if he didn't feel up to it that evening. "I wanna thank you again for takin' care of me, you and Myrna, too. It's temptin' to take advantage of your generosity, but I really think I can make myself useful at the office." He was concerned about whether or not Buck could hold his whiskey demons at bay, now that he was responsible for keeping the peace at night, as well as in the daytime. He really didn't know how long he could go before his wound became too painful to ignore. But he felt he owed it to Buck to find out.

Buck had come to check on him right after he ate supper last night. He told him about his ride out to the Cloverleaf ranch to return Dunellen's two would-be assassins. "I wanted to give him something to think about, that he might notta thought about before. So I got Nolan Carson and Raymond Chadwick to ride out there with me. Flint, I ain't never seen a man as mad as Ira Dunellen was. He was so mad he couldn't hardly talk. I'll bet if I coulda jammed a pine limb up his backside, it woulda caught on fire."

Thinking back on that conversation this morning, Flint tried to imagine what effect that failed attempt on his life would have on Dunellen's plans. He hoped it would serve to discourage any further attempts on his life, but he didn't know how many men were of like mind with the two he had just killed. "What?" he blurted out, just then realizing someone had asked him a question.

"I didn't go to wake you up there," Ben Arthur, Hannah's oldest boarder, cackled. "I said, would you pass that jar of honey down this way, if you ain't fixin' to finish it?"

"Sorry, Mr. Arthur, I reckon I had my mind on something too big for a brain my size to handle." He picked up the jar of honey and passed it down to him. It was enough to remind him of what Buck had told him, that he would need to develop eyes in the back of his head. *Short of that*, he thought, *at least be aware of what's going on at the breakfast table*.

When he finished breakfast, he stopped in the kitchen long enough to tell Myrna how much he had enjoyed it. Then Hannah followed him out the door to the back porch, where he had left his rifle propped against the wall. She remained there to watch him as he walked out of the yard, toward the road. Aware of her eyes upon him, he figured if he staggered at all, maybe she would run after him and lasso him, then drag him back to his bed. Although his arm was not in a sling, his shoulder was heavily bandaged under his extra shirt. Hannah said she would try to wash the blood out of the shirt he had been wearing, but she could only patch the bullet hole. He imagined he felt a little stab of pain when he stepped over the little ditch between Hannah's path and the road, the spot where he felt Moon's bullet slam into his back. His wound was uncomfortable, it felt as if he was carrying a dead weight in his shoulder, but he could walk, even though the short walk to the jail seemed a bit longer today.

He received a similar reception at the jail to the one he had gotten at the breakfast table. Both Buck and Ralph questioned his decision to come to the office. Buck understood his reluctance to sit on his bed all day to be waited on by Hannah and Myrna. Ralph, however, couldn't understand that attitude at all. "Nothin's happened since I talked to you last night," Buck said, "except our herd of cattle has grown by four more cows. They were brought in by Demrie Mullen. He said he found 'em standin' around the sawmill. I told him they weren't officially within the city limits, but I let him put 'em in with the dozen we've already got."

"Tell him about the post office," Ralph prompted.

"I was fixin' to," Buck replied. "He's talkin' about Lucas Sawyer. Comin' back from breakfast, I saw Lucas comin' out of the post office. He was carryin' something that looked like a letter, so I figure they finally got around to pickin' up that letter you wrote."

This was news that Flint was very interested to hear. He had no idea how Dunellen would react to the letter. He was sure, however, that he was not going to pay for the release of his cattle. After his offering of a reward for an assassination, Flint believed the man was capable of going to any extreme to have his way. Maybe it was a mistake to have baited a lunatic like Dunellen was proving to be. Had Flint decided not to fight him, then Tinhorn would have rapidly become a wild Texas town where the streets were filled with stray cattle. Dunellen was probably accurate in that regard. The major merchants would have eventually closed down and moved out, leaving the town dying in the Texas sun. "Well," he sighed and looked at Buck, "we may have to fight to protect our herd." Before Buck could answer, the office door opened and Lucy Tucker stuck her head inside.

"Sheriff Moran, I need to talk to you," she said.

"Is there some trouble at Jake's?" Flint asked.

"No," she answered hesitantly, like a bashful child. "I need to talk to you."

"All right," he said. "Well, come on in, Lucy. What can I do for you?"

"I need to talk to you alone, in private," she said, now looking more frightened than bashful. Flint and Buck were amazed, having never known Lucy to be anything less than brash and bold while dealing with her customers in the saloon.

"Uh-oh, Flint." Buck couldn't resist. "Wonder if it's a boy or a girl?"

Flint ignored the insinuation. "All right, Lucy. I'm sorry we don't have a private room to talk in, but if you don't mind, we can go back in the cell room and we can talk there. Is that all right with you? There's nobody in the cells." She nodded. He got up from his chair, flinching when it caused a sharp pain in his shoulder.

She reacted at once, reaching out to help him up. "I'm so sorry, I shouldn't have come here botherin' you."

"No, it's no bother, just a little healin' that needs gettin' done with," he assured her. He pointed her toward the cell room and followed painfully along behind her. They went into the cell room and he closed the door behind him, leaving Buck and Ralph looking at each other in curiosity. They were no less curious than Flint, however, so as soon as they were inside the room, he asked if she would like to sit down on one of the cots.

"No, I'll just stand here. I need to tell you something, and I'm ashamed to have anybody else know it. I wasn't gonna tell you, but I feel so bad that I had to."

"Why don't you just go ahead and tell me, and I'll see if we can't work it out to make it right." He thought he was getting a clue now. She had likely stolen some money from Jake, and she was afraid he was going to fire her.

"I want you to know I feel so bad about it," she started. "I just wasn't thinkin'." She paused to get her strength up before she finally released it in one short burst. "I'm the one who told Moon Murphy where you live and about what time you walk home." She hung her head as tears started to streak down her cheeks. "I'm the one that caused you to get shot. You mighta been killed. And I'm so sorry. I wasn't even wonderin' why he was so interested in what you did. I'm so stupid."

Flint couldn't believe it. She was so sincere in her admission of guilt, he immediately felt sorry for her. "Lucy, don't cry. I appreciate you tellin' me, but you're not the reason I got shot. If you hadn't told Moon anything, they just would have hid somewhere and kept watch for me to start for home and they woulda shot me. You're not the reason I got shot. I got shot because they were determined to follow me and shoot me. Anything you told Moon didn't make any difference. They woulda still shot me. So you just forget about that business with Moon. It wasn't your fault, and I don't want you worryin' about it anymore. All right?"

"All right," she said, her face alive with the relief she felt. "I'm glad I told you anyway."

"I'm glad you did, too."

"Like I told Moon, you're a good man, Flint Moran. And if you ever want a free ride, all you have to do is let me know."

"I appreciate that," he responded, "but I'd rather keep you as a good friend instead of me bein' just another customer."

"Well, anytime you need anything from me as a friend, you just let me know," she said as he opened the door for her. She swept through the office with a lighter step, now minus the load of guilt she had carried in. "See ya later, Buck," she said casually and went out the front door.

"Whatever you told her sure musta been the right medicine for what was ailin' her," Buck commented, anxious to hear what her problem was.

"Wasn't anything at all," Flint told him. "She said a customer threatened to report her to the sheriff for overchargin' him."

Buck thought it was strange for her to come to the sheriff for something like that, but he bought it. "Hell, it's her fanny. She can charge what she wants."

"My thoughts exactly," Flint said.

Later that afternoon, Buck walked into Jake's to have a little drink before supper. He passed Lucy on the way in and thought to give her a little support. "It's your fanny, Lucy, you can charge what you want," he said as he walked on past her on his way to the bar. Puzzled by his remark, she turned to look at him, but he didn't look back.

Maybe he's already had a couple of drinks, she thought.

"There was a letter at the post office for you," Lucas said when he reported to Ira Dunellen, and he handed him the envelope.

"Did you mail my letter without any trouble?" Dunellen asked as he took the envelope.

"Yes, sir, he said it would go out on the train this afternoon."

"Good," Dunellen said and turned his attention to the envelope. When he saw it was from the office of the sheriff of Tinhorn, his nostrils flared and a deep frown appeared on his face. He ripped the envelope apart and unfolded the letter. Lucas commented to Gabby Skelton later that day that Dunellen had turned so red in the face as he read that letter, he thought he was going to explode. "It was from the sheriff of Tinhorn, and I was able to tell what the letter was about just by the words Dunellen was sayin' out loud. It was like he was arguing with the letter while he was readin' it. I didn't get it word for word, but I'm pretty sure it was tellin' him that the town was holdin' his stray cattle under arrest. And he was gonna have to pay for 'em, if he wants 'em back."

"I swear," Gabby responded. "I bet he was fit to be tied. How much do they want for 'em?"

"I don't know," Lucas replied. "I couldn't make that out. I don't know if he said the cost out loud. Least, I didn't hear a number. It don't make much difference what the number is anyway. He ain't gonna pay it. What I'm concerned about is what he's gonna do. And I'm afraid it's gonna be to tell me to mount up all our men and raid the town. If that happens, there's gonna be a permanent war between Tinhorn and Cloverleaf."

"I swear," Gabby said again. "You don't reckon he'll mount all the boys up and send 'em chargin' into that town to take those strays back, do ya?"

Lucas inhaled a deep breath and replied, "I don't know, Gabby. I reckon we'll find out. He's called for another meetin' with all the men in the mornin'. This'll be just the second one he's called since I've been workin' for him. So he's got some kind of announcement he thinks is important to make. I just hope it ain't a declaration of war. I didn't sign on for that."

"Just between you and me, there's a few of the other boys that didn't sign up to be cavalry soldiers either," Gabby said. They sat there on the bench by the bunkhouse, silently considering what they had just discussed for a few minutes while sipping the coffee Gabby had made. Then Gabby thought to ask, "What was the letter he had you take to the post office this mornin'?"

"I haven't got any idea," Lucas said. "He didn't say anything about that, except to ask me if I mailed it. Just some of his financial business, I reckon, or maybe legal. It was addressed to Judge Franklyn Grant in Wichita, Kansas. Maybe he's goin' after the sheriff in court for holding his cattle." He took a quick swallow of his coffee before pouring the last of it on the ground and dropped the cup in a tub filled with water and some other dirty cups. "I expect I'd best get my bones into the saddle and trot out to tell the boys ridin' herd about the meetin' in the mornin'."

Ira Dunellen came down to the now-completed bunkhouse the next morning while the men were eating the breakfast Gabby had prepared for them. In contrast to the fire-and-brimstone reaction to Flint Moran's letter concerning the strays that Lucas expected, he seemed to be in a calm mood as he addressed them. "First thing I want to say is this: I made a mistake when I offered a reward for the killing of Sheriff Moran. As you all know, it resulted in the deaths of two of our men at the hand of Sheriff Moran. So as not to tempt any more of you to go after this obvious gunman the town has hired to act as sheriff, I'm withdrawing that offer of a reward. The battle to determine who rules over the grazing lands of Texas continues, however. But we will fight a more clever battle, one in which we have the superior army in the form of our cattle. I am instructing your foreman to send a couple of men into town to find out where they have penned up the stray cattle they have captured. Or should I use their term, 'arrested'? Actually, they are being held for ransom. Well, two can play that game. We have enough cows to overrun the town. Not in one stampede, mind you, but in a constant stream of strays until they reach the point where there are too many for them to handle. The town will start helping us drive the cattle out, once they get a bellyful of their streets and alleys filled with cattle. And their women and children won't be able to cross the street without being afraid of being run over by the cows."

Lucas was surprised by Dunellen's announcement, and he studied the faces of his crew during the address. What he thought he saw was a general look of relief among most of the men sitting wide-eyed while Dunellen took back his offer of two hundred dollars. Lucas knew his men, and he was certain that, for the most part, they were simple cowhands. Drew Price had been the only would-be gunslinger, but there were a couple of men left who would not hesitate to take a man's life if there was a profit in it. Lem Dixon and Charlie Tate came to mind right away. As for himself, Lucas was not certain at what point in Dunellen's planned conquest of Tinhorn would be too much for him to continue. It would be hard to walk away from a job where he had complete authority over the actual operation of the cattle business, as well as the salary he was being paid. He was glad to hear Dunellen's decision not to assassinate the sheriff, however. Possibly his plan to continue aggravating the people of Tinhorn with stray cattle would eventually be discarded as well. For Lucas was convinced that the merchants and the post office were not going to move across the river as Dunellen thought.

When the meeting was over, Lucas sent the men out to their work, with the exception of two. Dunellen had instructed him to send a couple of men into town to find out where they were keeping the strays they had captured, and how many they had. So he picked Tim Walker and Andy Hatcher, two men he knew would be less likely to cause any trouble in town. "Whadda we do if we find where they've got 'em?" Andy asked.

"Nothing," Lucas answered. "We just wanna know where they're keepin' 'em. Count 'em so we'll know how many they've stolen. Try not to look too conspicuous while you're lookin' for 'em."

Andy looked at Tim, but he looked as puzzled as he was. "Try not to look too what?" Andy asked.

"Obvious," Lucas answered. "In other words, don't let 'em know you're lookin' for the cows."

"Whadda we gonna do when we find out where they are?" Andy asked. "We gonna try to take 'em back?"

"Damnit, I told you, don't do anything," Lucas snapped. "We'll do whatever the boss says to do after we find out where they are. Right now, all he wants to know is where they are and how many they've got so far. So get goin'!" They hustled out of the bunkhouse, and Lucas stood there watching them talking back and forth on their way to the barn. *That's a helluva team to send to scout the enemy*, he thought, *the young and the stupid*.

* * *

Another thing Lucas wasn't aware of was that the *young* half of his spy team was a double agent. Having warned Flint Moran that there was a price on his head—information that proved to be of no use in preventing the sheriff from being shot—Tim was now intent upon informing Flint that the reward had been canceled. Tim's problem was how to tell Flint without Andy finding out. "I ain't so sure we're welcome in town after Moon and Alvin tried to kill the sheriff," Andy speculated as he and Tim walked their horses past Lon Blake's stable. They halfway expected to be shot at as soon as they were recognized as Cloverleaf cowhands. But no one paid any attention to them, so they continued on up the street. Whenever they passed an alley, they peered down between the buildings on the chance of spotting their cattle penned up. Then it occurred to Andy that, if they had to hold some cows, they would most likely pen them up by the river.

"Well, that sure as shootin' makes more sense, don't it?" Tim agreed. So, when they rode past the hotel and the post office across the street from it, they cut over to strike the river. Then they followed it back to the south, paralleling the street. They soon came to the little bunch of cows inside the barbed wire enclosure.

"Look yonder," Andy said and pointed. "It's right behind the jailhouse." He chuckled when he remembered a comment Dunellen had dropped. "We shoulda looked here first thing. Didn't Mr. Dunellen say those cows were arrested?"

"We're supposed to count 'em," Tim reminded him.

So they both started counting, and both came up with a total of twenty-two. "Well, we found 'em, and we counted 'em," Andy declared, "so, our job here is finished. It was mighty hard work," he japed, "and I think it calls for a drink of likker before we ride back to Cloverleaf. How 'bout it, Tim? You about ready for a drink?"

"I reckon not," Tim replied. "I quit drinkin' a little while back on account of a problem I have with likker."

"What kinda problem?" Andy asked. He had not been in town that night to witness Tim's first real drunk, which resulted in his sleeping it off in the Tinhorn jail.

"I just don't seem to get along too good with likker. I ain't got no money anyway, so it don't matter. You go ahead and have a drink, I'll just walk around a little bit, then I'll come look for you in the saloon. Is that all right with you?"

Andy shrugged. "Sure, that's all right with me. Damn shame, though, as young as you are, to have to give up likker. Hell, you ain't even growed up yet."

"I don't miss it none," Tim said. "I don't even think about it anymore."

"I swear, that's terrible," Andy commented. "Maybe you was meant to be a preacher instead of herdin' cattle. But even the preacher takes a little drink when he thinks there ain't nobody lookin'." He gave him a helpless shrug of his shoulders. "Where you gonna walk to?"

"Nowhere," Tim said, "just gonna stretch my legs a little bit, then I'll come get you in the saloon." Andy gave him another shrug, and they rode out through the high weeds between the cow pen and the street. "I'll just take a little walk," Tim repeated as they tied their horses to the hitching post in front of Jake's Place. "Then I'll come get you."

"Fine by me," Andy replied. "I won't be hard to find. I'll be the feller with a drink in his hand and a smile on his face." He headed for the door.

Tim stood there at the rail until Andy disappeared inside the saloon. He waited a couple of minutes before walking up to the batwing doors of the saloon and peering inside to make sure Andy was going to be in there a while. When he saw him engaging in a conversation with Lucy Tucker at the end of the bar, he turned and headed across the street to the sheriff's office.

Flint looked up from his desk when he heard the door open. "Howdy, Tim, what can I do for you?"

Tim took a cautious look in Buck Jackson's direction and hesitated. Buck was in the process of pouring himself a cup of coffee, and he nodded to Tim. Flint saw the young boy's uncertainty when he looked at Buck, so he tried to put him at ease. "You don't have to worry about Buck, if you've got something you wanna talk to me about. Buck and I don't have any secrets between us. He knows you told me about the reward. I believed you, too. But I wasn't as careful as I thought I was, and I got shot anyway. I still wanna thank you for tryin' to help me."

"I'm glad you're gonna be all right." Tim finally spoke. "I came into town with another fellow. He's in the saloon, and I've gotta hurry back before he sees me here. I just wanted to tell you that Mr. Dunellen ain't offerin' a reward for your death anymore. He said it cost him two men, and he ain't offerin' it no more. I figured you'd like to know that."

"You're right," Flint said. "I'm glad to hear that. Thank you again, Tim."

"You're welcome," Tim replied. "I gotta go now before Andy sees me comin' outta here."

"Right," Flint said. "If he does see you come out, tell him I saw you on the street and took you in here for questionin'."

"Yes, sir," Tim replied and hurried out the door. He went across the street, instead of angling straight for the saloon. He felt he had done nothing wrong when he warned Flint before the shooting. And he felt it the right thing to do to tell him there was no longer a price on his head. Out of loyalty to the man who paid his salary, however, he felt no obligation to tell the sheriff why he and Andy were sent into town.

Back in the sheriff's office, Buck walked over to the window with his cup of coffee and watched the young boy take his zigzag route back to the saloon. "He didn't say anything about the cow pen or how many there were in it."

"That's because he's an honest young man," Flint said. "He still rides for the Cloverleaf brand."

Buck walked to the cell-room door, opened it, and yelled, "Ralph!" In a few seconds, Ralph came to the office. "You sure it was Tim?"

"Tim and some other feller," Ralph answered. "I just finished emptyin' the slop buckets when they rode up beside the cows. They counted 'em, then rode across the field to the street."

"So, now we know that Dunellen will have the location and the number of cows he's missin'. I reckon we'll just have to keep a sharp eye on our herd back there and try to catch 'em if they try to steal 'em back."

CHAPTER 15

In the lawless little town of Delano, Kansas, across the Arkansas River from Wichita, it would be impossible to find one person who had ever heard of Tinhorn, Texas. Close to six hundred miles away, that was hardly surprising. It was two weeks' ride on a good horse. So, it was ironic that on the same day Tim Walker and Andy Hatcher were scouting for their captured cattle, one person who did know Tinhorn, Texas, walked into Bloodworth's Dance Hall in Delano. A young man, dressed in black, with long, dark hair that almost reached his shoulders, he stood in the doorway, looking over the crowded room. He was looking for someone, and when he didn't see her on the dance floor, he shifted his gaze to search the tables along the sides of the room.

It was a night of irony, for when the young woman sitting in the lap of cowhand Ben Fry happened to look in the direction of the door, it was to lock eyes with the young man in black. "Oh, hell!" she blurted out. "It's Cash! And I think he sees me. I gotta get up from here!" She tried to get out of Ben Fry's lap, but he wasn't ready to let her go, having already spent quite a bit of money to buy her drinks. It was an investment that he figured should guarantee him the satisfaction of seeing her bedroom. "Lemme go, Ben! If I don't go to him, he may kill us both."

"To hell with him!" Ben said, clamping down even harder on her arms. "I ain't bought all the likker you drank just to saddle-break you so he can take a ride. There's other women in here to take his money."

"Damn you!" she swore. "Let me go or you're gonna be sorry."

He gave her a big grin as she struggled helplessly to get out of his lap. "I didn't see no sign on you that said you was private property. What's he gonna do? Smack you around a little?"

"I reckon he will," she warned, "but what he's gonna do to you is worse. Let me up from here and I'll try to go stop him."

"Nah, let him come on over here. I'd like to see what he's gonna do. He don't look big enough to make a whole lotta noise."

Finding it totally useless to struggle against the powerful hands that held her in his lap, she finally gave up and sat quietly awaiting the wrath of Cash Kelly. He walked across the floor between the couples dancing to a slow number that reduced the actual dancing to a squeezing and groping exercise. When he got to the table, he didn't meet the outright stare coming his way from Ben Fry. Instead, he focused his gaze on the woman, as if she was alone at the table. "Lola," he said softly, "why didn't you come when you saw me at the door?"

"I tried to, Cash, but he wouldn't let me go," she answered.

"What the hell business is it of yours?" Ben spat. "She didn't go to you because she's with me. And if you don't get your slick behind outta my sight, I might have to teach you some lessons your mama shoulda taught you last year when you was in grade school."

Cash shifted his gaze from Lola to fix it on Ben and said calmly, "I'm not talking to you, so you keep your mouth shut. Do you understand me?"

"Why, you foul son of a . . ." was as far as he got before Cash slapped him hard across his face with his leather gloves. Stunned, Ben released his grip on Lola's arms, and she immediately jumped off his lap and moved to stand beside Cash. Furious, Ben reached down for his gun, but Cash already had his in hand.

"Pull that weapon and you're a dead man," Cash told him, still deadly calm. "Lola and I are leavin' now, so you just go back to your drinkin', and maybe one of the other women will put up with you. You almost made a dumb mistake tonight. One a night is enough. Don't make another one." He said to Lola then, "Come on. We'll get outta here and go to my room." She nodded obediently, turned with him, and started toward the door. "Don't walk too close to me," he warned as the people on the dance floor opened up a clear path to the door. Halfway there, they heard a sound like someone taking a sudden breath. Cash spun around immediately, drawing his pistol again as he did. His shot slammed Ben in the chest before the startled man had time to raise his weapon to aim. "I warned him," Cash announced to the shocked witnesses, then turned to speak directly to the bartender. "I warned him, Corky."

"You sure did, Cash," Corky Jones answered. "There ain't no question about it. He drew on you when your back was turned."

With that fact firmly established, Cash took a quick, precautionary look over the crowd of spectators for any signs of retaliation. There was no indication that Ben Fry had any friends with him, at least none who were willing to test the lightninglike reactions of the young man in black. There were plenty of witnesses who saw that Fry had drawn first, and it was a case of pure self-defense, so Cash holstered his six-shooter and said, "Come on, Lola," and started toward the door again, but Corky asked him to wait a minute because he had a message for him. So he walked over to the bar. "What is it, Corky?"

"I didn't wanna yell it out while you were walkin' out the door," Corky said. "Judge Grant was in here a couple of nights ago, and he told me to tell you that he wants to see you, just as soon as you were back in town. He said it's important."

"Right. Much obliged," Cash said. "Better give me a bottle to take up to the room with me. Put it on my bill." He paused. "On second thought, I'll just pay my bill right now."

"You musta had a pretty good trip outta town this week," Corky said as he pulled a ledger from under the counter.

"You could say that," Cash replied. It had been a big score, thanks to the tip-off that the Atchison, Topeka was carrying a big payroll. He pulled out a healthy roll of money and brought his bar bill up to date. He picked up the bottle Corky had placed on the bar and walked out the door with Lola Sanchez proudly holding on to his arm. Outside, they went around to the side of the building and used the outside stairs that led up to the private rooms. There was no access to these rooms from inside the dance hall. The stairway inside led only to the rooms occupied by the dance hall women. Lola shared one of these rooms with a woman named Peggy, but she stayed with Cash, in his room, when he was in town.

"You want me to pour you a drink?" Lola asked when they went into the room.

"Yeah," he answered as he looked in the saddlebags he had carried up to the room before going in search of Lola.

He found what he was looking for in the saddlebags, a fat, sealed envelope, which he dropped into his inside coat pocket. "I've gotta go over the bridge and see the judge in the mornin'," he said, referring to the bridge across the Arkansas River, to Wichita.

"You want me to go with you?" Lola asked.

"No," he answered, "you can't go with me to see the judge."

"Why not?" she protested. "I've seen him in here before."

"That may be so, but you ain't ever seen him in Wichita, where he's particular about the class of people he's seen with," Cash told her. "I won't be gone long, and I want you here when I get back. You understand?"

"I understand," she replied, like a child told that she had to go to bed, "but I don't see why I can't go with you."

"Because you're a whore," he told her frankly, having lost his patience with her. "And if you don't stop complainin', I'll find another one who'll be happy to take the job for a lot less than what I'm payin' you."

"Cash, honey, you don't mean that. I stay with you because I love you. You know that."

"Yeah, I know that," he said sarcastically. "You'll love me till money do us part, right? You just be here when I get back." He finished his drink and poured himself another. Then he poured another one for her. "That oughta be enough for you tonight. This ain't that watered-down stuff Corky gives you women to drink."

She was still asleep when he woke up the next morning. So he didn't disturb her until after he checked his coat to make sure the envelope he had put in the pocket had not been tampered with while he was asleep. He also checked his pants pocket and his saddlebags. Only then did he wake her to tell her to wait in the room for him. "I don't wanna have to go lookin' for you when I come back." She promised she would be there.

He went to the stable to get his horse for the short trip over to Wichita. Out of consideration for Judge Franklyn Grant's reputation, Cash rode around to the back of the large, two-story house that served as the judge's law office. He went in the back entrance and walked up the long hallway to the reception desk at the back of the parlor. Judge Grant's secretary, Leonard Pope, heard Cash coming up the hall, and when he saw who it was, he got up from his desk to meet him. "Mr. Kelly, have a seat and I'll tell the judge you're here." Cash sat down on a straight-backed chair in the corner of the room while Leonard went down the hall Cash had just come up. He opened a door halfway down the hall and went inside. In a few seconds, he was walking back to the parlor. "You can go right in, Mr. Kelly. The door's open." Cash went back then to the open door and entered the room.

"Cash Kelly," Judge Grant announced as Cash walked in. "I trust you had a good trip."

"Yessir," Cash replied. "Everything went pretty much like we expected." He reached into his inside jacket pocket, pulled out the envelope, and handed it to the judge. Grant slit the envelope with a letter opener, reached in with his thumb, and ruffled the currency. Then he opened a desk drawer and dropped it inside. That was typically the entire procedure, so Cash prepared to withdraw.

He was surprised when the judge said, "Have a seat, Mr. Kelly. I've got something I want to discuss with you." He sat down in one of the two chairs at either end of Grant's huge desk. "First, I want to tell you that I've been more than satisfied with the work you've done for me." He paused to hear Cash's "thank you," then continued. "I just received a letter from an old colleague of mine who needs a man of special ability to help him solve a problem he's having with a small-town sheriff in Texas. He asked if I could recommend a man skillful enough to eliminate this particular sheriff in an open, fast-draw contest. Since I have never heard of a shooter faster than you, I naturally thought you might want the job. What are your thoughts on the matter?"

"I can't help wonderin', if there's a problem with the sheriff, why doesn't your friend just send somebody to shoot him in the back and be done with it?" Cash naturally asked.

"Those were my thoughts as well, when I read my friend's letter," Grant replied. "However, part of his letter said this pathetic little town was blocking his range and his access to the river. It would be my guess that my friend wants a dramatic destruction of the law authority of the town, so the people would believe their little town was destined to become a fast-draw arena. And it would be difficult to entice anyone to take on the job of sheriff." He shrugged. "As I said, it's my guess that's his reasoning, and maybe it won't matter to you after you hear what he's willing to pay for your service."

"You might be right," Cash remarked, definitely interested.

"He said in his letter that he's willing to pay as much as eight hundred dollars to the right man." He smiled when he saw Cash's reaction. "That's right, eight hundred."

"Where is this town?" Cash asked.

"It's in Texas. I doubt you've ever heard of it. I know I never have. Its name is Tinhorn, and the sheriff's name is Flint Moran." Grant paused then, when he saw Cash's face blanch. "Have you heard of it?"

Cash didn't answer immediately as he took a moment to

recover his emotions. "Yes, sir, I've heard of it. It's about twenty-five miles south of Tyler, a good two-week ride from here." He didn't tell the judge, but he had just offered him a job that he had planned to do on his own for some time. Now there was an opportunity to gun down Flint Moran and be paid eight hundred dollars to do it. It was like an outright gift. "I'll take the job," Cash said, "and I'll start out for Texas tomorrow, if you say I can trust this man's word to pay the price he offered."

"I don't blame you for questioning," the judge said. "You can trust Ira Dunellen to do what he says he will do. You take care of his problem and he'll pay you. I'll wire him and let him know you're on the way."

A man with a reputation for having no emotions at all, Cash Kelly walked out of Judge Franklyn Grant's office with his thoughts turning over and over in his head. Fate had become the messenger telling him it was time to settle the score with Flint Moran. It was time for Billy Crowe to rise from the dead and seek the vengeance he was destined to take against the man responsible for the deaths of his father, Abel Crowe, and his brothers, Frank and Jasper. On his way back across the river to Delano, his mind took him back to the little town of Tinhorn, Texas. Flint Moran was the deputy then, and having already killed Billy's brother, Jasper, Flint had put two bullets in Billy as well, and arrested Billy, his father, and his other brother. Even then, at that early age, Billy Crowe was the fastest hand in the territory with a six-gun. Moran had taken him to the doctor for his wounds. And, unknown to the deputy, the doctor had given young Billy Crowe a whole bottle of laudanum for his pain. The doctor warned him not to take more than a teaspoon a couple of times a day. He told him that more than that could kill him. Cash now remembered Billy Crowe's dread of the hangman's noose, and the decision he made to avoid it. He didn't even tell his father and brother that he had the laudanum. When they were asleep one night, he had downed the whole bottle before he went to sleep. He remembered nothing after that until he woke up alone to find himself lying on a table in the undertaker's mortuary.

The details of that time came rushing back to him as he crossed the river bridge to Delano. He thought of the undertaker, who was also the barber, shaving a customer in his shop while Billy Crowe came back from the dead and slipped out the back door of the barbershop. He went to the stable and stole a horse and saddle and put Tinhorn as far behind him as he could ride before resting the horse. His father, Abel, and brother, Frank, were tried and hanged. He felt no responsibility for not having tried to break them out of jail. He had a wounded shoulder, but he promised himself that he would avenge their deaths when it was time. In the time since then, he had aged a couple of years. He had taken the name of Cash Kelly and established himself as a fast gun. He had no concerns about being recognized as Billy Crowe, with his long hair, his mustache and beard. And he had no fear when it came to facing Flint Moran, or any other man for that matter, for he had already died once. He was totally convinced that this was fate telling him it was time to avenge his father's and his brothers' deaths. With someone coming to him with an offer of eight hundred dollars to do the job, how could it be anything else?

He rode back to the stable to leave his horse. He told Leroy Atkins, the owner, that he would be needing the horse again in the morning, as well as his packhorse. "You just got back in town," Leroy said, "and you're headin' out again tomorrow? You ain't takin' much time for restin', are you?"

Cash smiled at him. "They don't pay much for restin'," he said.

His comment was good for a chuckle out of Leroy. "I reckon that's right," he said as Cash walked out of the stable.

He went to his room for Lola, but she was not there, so he went back downstairs and into the dance hall. There was nothing much going on this early in the day, for the musicians didn't tune up until after the noon meal. The bar was fairly busy, however, so he went over to ask Corky if he had seen Lola. "She's settin' back there in the corner, jawin' with some of the other ladies," Corky said. But one of the women had seen Cash come in the door, and she alerted Lola. So when Cash turned toward the back corner of the room, it was to see Lola hurrying to meet him.

"Cash, honey," Lola explained, "I just came downstairs to talk to the girls for a minute. I was just fixin' to go back upstairs."

"Let's walk down the street and get somethin' to eat instead," Cash said to her surprise. "I ain't ate anything since I got up."

Surprised by his calm attitude, for she expected to be sworn at for not waiting in his room as he had told her to do, she cheerfully suggested, "We could go to Marvin's."

"That's as good as any," he replied casually, again surprising her, for in the past, he never ate there because he said they charged too much. "Did you eat anything?"

"No," she lied. She wanted to make him think she had waited for him. "Maybe I should run upstairs and freshen up a little, get my shawl. Is it chilly outside this mornin'?"

"That's up to you," he answered. "It didn't seem that chilly to me."

She was amazed. Something had happened to change his personality. "I'll just go without a shawl," she decided and grabbed his arm. She turned to give the other women sitting at the table a cocky smirk as they walked out the door. Marvin's was a small dining room just wide enough to accommodate one long table that would seat twelve and three tables in a row against the wall that sat two. Every customer got the same thing, cooked by Marvin himself, and served by his wife. Cash and Lola chose one of the small tables, and Cora brought them coffee in heavy mugs and asked, "Corn bread or biscuits?"

It was a good, hearty breakfast, more than enough to satisfy their appetites. When they had finished, Lola could not keep herself from asking, "What happened in Wichita this mornin'? How come you're treatin' me so nice?"

He looked surprised by her question. He had not realized he was treating her any differently than usual. He considered her question for a few seconds before answering her. "I reckon I just feel peaceful this mornin'." Thinking deeper, he decided that his mood was more one of contentment because he was going to take care of something that had to be settled before his brothers and father could rest in peace. "I'm goin' outta town again tomorrow mornin', and I want you and me to have a good night. I'll be gone for a good little while."

She immediately looked distressed. "Where are you goin'?"

"Down to Texas on a job," he answered. "It'll take me two weeks to ride down that far, so I might be gone a month." She started making a little whining noise as if she was about to cry. "Don't get all upset," he told her. "I'm gonna pay for my room and I'll leave you some money to get by on."

"Oh, Cash, I kinda thought you mighta been thinkin' about marryin' me," she fretted.

"I have been givin' it some thought," he confessed. "But the timin' just ain't been right. Maybe when I come back, after I get this job done, we'll talk about it."

"You swear?" she asked.

"I swear."

"Maybe you could take me with you," she suggested then.

"No way in hell," he replied. She looked pouty, but not for long because he had sworn he would talk about marrying her when he came back.

They went back to his room over the dance hall for a while after breakfast until he said he had to buy supplies for his trip to Texas the next day. So he picked up his packhorse at the stable and took it to Delano Supply, where he bought everything he thought he would need. When he was satisfied, he took the horse back to the stable and unloaded the packs. "I'll be back in the mornin'," he told Leroy, and returned to his room. He was not surprised to find that Lola was not there. *Most likely in the bar downstairs, bragging to all the women that I said I'd marry her*, he thought. So he went back downstairs and went into the dance hall. As he suspected, Lola was in the middle of a quartet of women, telling them all she wasn't gonna be wrestling around that dance floor with dirty old saddle tramps after about a month from now. He walked over toward the bar, waiting for her to see him.

"That's him," Corky told a rangy individual he was talking to down at the end of the bar. "That's Cash Kelly." Then he called out, "Cash, feller here said he needed to see you about somethin'."

"Is that so?" Cash replied. He looked at the man at the end of the bar and thought he looked kind of familiar, but he couldn't actually place him. "You wanna see me?" he asked the man who was staring at him, a thin smile the only sign on the man's face.

"I'm Simon Fry," the stranger said and waited for Cash's reaction. When there was no sign of recognition coming from Cash, the man said, "You killed a man in here yesterday. His name was Ben Fry."

"Was that his name?" Cash responded with no show of concern.

"You shot him down, killed him, and you didn't even know his name."

"I don't give a damn what his name was," Cash replied. "He pulled a gun on me, and that's what happens to any-body who pulls a gun on me, no matter what their name is."

"Ben Fry was my brother," Simon said, getting more and more aggravated with Cash's total lack of concern.

"I don't care if he was your sister," Cash said. "When I was walkin' out of here, he pulled his gun, fixin' to shoot me in the back. He made a big mistake when he pulled on me. Corky can tell you that." He paused then, waiting for Simon to decide what he was going to do. When Simon made no response, but continued to sneer at him, Cash asked, "So what are you gonna do? Make the same mis-take? Maybe you can catch the same train to hell that your brother is on. Make up your mind. I've got things to do that are more important than you and your brother." The noise in the room suddenly lessened as those drinkers closest to the bar caught wind of what might suddenly happen.

Simon had come looking for Cash with one purpose in mind, and he decided Cash's apparent attempt to bluff him was not going to discourage him. "You killed my brother, so you're gonna pay for it." He stepped clear of the bar to give himself more room.

Cash shrugged, indifferently. "It's your funeral," he said

to Simon. Then, aside to Corky, he said, "You're my witness, Corky."

"I got you covered, Cash," Corky answered at once. "I saw the whole thing. He called you out."

"Right," Cash pronounced quietly, then stepped away from the bar, and the rest of the conversation in the room went quiet. He turned to squarely face Simon and said, "All right, just whenever you think you're . . ." That was as far as he got before Simon reached for his gun, hoping to get the jump on him. Simon froze, however, when he found himself stunned by the sight of Cash's pistol already looking directly at him, while his own weapon had not yet cleared his holster. Time seemed to stand still for a moment as Simon stood staring at the muzzle of Cash's six-gun, knowing he was going to die. Finally, in desperation, he jerked his pistol up to fire, and Cash calmly pulled the trigger, sending a bullet deep into his chest. He cocked his pistol and watched Simon until he dropped his gun and collapsed to the floor. Then, as a matter of habit, he looked around the room to spot any more potential threats. Seeing none, he released the hammer on his six-gun and dropped it back in the holster. When he saw Lola standing there, gaping like everyone else, he signaled her and said, "Come on, let's get outta here."

Chapter 16

The week that followed the attempted assassination of Sheriff Flint Moran passed peacefully, but it was tainted by the realization that he was not indestructible. He had always been a step ahead of the outlaws that chanced to light in Tinhorn. Now there was an awareness that he could be stopped by an assassin's bullet. When the next week began, and Flint began to show a rapid recovery, there was hope again that he would protect their town. Buck made it a point to be seen on the street a lot more often than usual, and that helped the morale of the town. This, even though there were still stray cows showing up in the streets. There had been no attempt by Cloverleaf to raid the town's cow pen and drive the cows out of town. And the total number of cows had continued to increase. Pretty soon they were going to need a bigger pen. When Mayor Harvey Baxter met with Flint and Buck to express his concern for the people of Tinhorn if a raid happened, they tried to ease his worries. "If a gang of Dunellen's men storm into town and strike the cow pen," Flint explained, "it will most likely be late at night. We figure it will be easier for them to drive the cattle straight down the river, a lot easier than tryin' to drive them through town. So it would be unlikely any of the townsfolks would be in any danger."

"How will you stop them?" Baxter asked. "Are you going to try to get volunteers to help you stop them?"

"No, sir," Flint replied. "Buck and I will take care of it. We don't want to get anybody hurt in this thing."

Baxter didn't understand. "How in hell do you expect to keep them from stealing the cows with just the two of you to stop them?"

"We don't," Flint said. "We want them to take the cows." He paused and looked at Buck for his confirmation. Buck nodded in agreement. "We thought you wanted the cows out of Tinhorn, so we'd let Cloverleaf get 'em out of town for us." He paused again, then asked, "Did you want to keep the cows?"

Baxter was still confused, but he was sure of one thing. "Hell no, I don't want to keep a herd of cattle in the town."

"Good, I thought for a minute you'd changed your mind. It could sure get to be a big problem if we keep collectin' strays," Flint advised. "They'll soon have that whole field back of the jail grazed out. Buck and I figure the best way to get rid of those cows is to pretend we don't wanna get rid of 'em. That way, Dunellen is gonna come after 'em for sure, especially after he got that letter that says he has to pay the town for 'em. He's gonna show us we can't keep his cows."

Baxter finally got the picture then, but he still had a question. "After Dunellen raids our cow pen and gets his cows back, he might just start letting strays wander into town again. Won't we be right back where we started?"

"Yes, sir," Flint answered. "At least, at first we will be. So we'll just keep on roundin' 'em up and pennin' 'em up till we've got more of his cattle than he wants us to have. Then maybe he'll raid again. I figure he's gonna get tired of the game after another raid or two. Then maybe we'll see what his next plan is gonna be to destroy Tinhorn."

"It sounds like a wild plan to me," Baxter said. "But maybe it'll work. I sure don't have any better suggestion. I guess I'll just wish us good luck."

"We need all we can get," Flint replied. "We really needed a smarter brain to work this thing out, but Ralph just ain't interested in the job." He paused for a few seconds, then said, "It might help to look at this problem from a different angle."

"Whaddaya mean?" Baxter asked.

"Well, suppose Dunellen wasn't out to ruin the town. Suppose he was a rancher who was friendly and neighborly as he could be, but he had so many cows he couldn't keep some strays from wanderin' into town. He can't have his men watchin' the town night and day to keep the cows outta the street. So we offer to collect his cows for him and keep them in one place out of our streets, so he can come get 'em from time to time. Just townsfolk and cattleman tryin' to cooperate to solve a problem. That ain't much different than what we figure will happen here. And if we're lucky, he's gonna get tired of sendin' his men in here to steal his cattle back. And maybe he'll move his main herd south of Tinhorn and his strays won't wander this far."

Baxter laughed. "Yeah, I guess you could look at it that way. Still sounds like a fairy tale, though. I guess we'll see if this one comes true."

Lucas Sawyer went up to the main house to report the latest number of cows under arrest in Tinhorn. It was the morning after Andy Hatcher went into town again for a recount. "How many did he count?" Ira Dunellen asked. When Lucas said Andy had counted thirty, Dunellen swore. "And none in the streets?" he asked.

"No, sir. Andy said the bartender in Jake's Place told him

that Flint Moran used to pick up any strays that wandered into town. But now there's half a dozen men who take a rope to a stray as soon as it wanders near, and they're keepin' 'em in that pen they rigged up behind the jail."

"Did he see Sheriff Moran?" Dunellen asked.

"Yes, sir, he said he saw Moran and his deputy, Buck Jackson, comin' back from supper. He said they walked from the hotel down to the jail."

"Did he say how Moran looked? Was he limpin' or walkin' real slow, or anything like that?"

"Well," Lucas hesitated, "I didn't ask Andy a lot of questions about how Flint Moran looked. But from what I gathered, he must have looked like he was pretty much recovered."

"Damn," Dunellen swore. "Those two clowns couldn't even shoot a man in the back. I should have known better than to offer that reward to just anybody. You want a job done right, you get a professional." He glared at Lucas, as if it was his fault.

"I reckon these men are cowhands and not professional killers," Lucas couldn't resist saying. Dunellen was so deep in thought that the remark didn't register with him.

"I want you to pick some good riders—four should be enough—and I want you to ride into that trashy little town and get my cattle tonight. Pick four with some sand in their guts, who won't be afraid to shoot if they're shot at." When Lucas looked a little hesitant, Dunellen said, "They're the same as cattle rustlers. They stole my cows and now they want me to pay them four dollars a head to buy my own cattle back."

Lucas found himself once again battling his conscience, once again thinking, *I didn't sign on for this*. He wasn't sure that Dunellen was not within his rights to take back his cattle, using any means he had to. He heard himself saying, "Yes, sir, I'll pick men I think best for the job."

"Excellent," Dunellen expelled. "I knew I could count on you to do the job right. You're a good man, Lucas. I think it's past time I should think about increasing your salary. I look forward to hearing your report tomorrow morning." He turned on his heel and went back inside the house, leaving Lucas to grapple with his conscience.

On the way back to the bunkhouse, Lucas thought about what he had agreed to do. He had no desire to go to war against the people in Tinhorn. And he knew his reluctance to do so would cost him his job. At his age, he was very unlikely to sign on with another cattle outfit at anywhere close to the money he was making with Dunellen. *I'll go after his damn cattle*, he thought, *and maybe we can do it without killing anyone*. He decided, just as Flint had figured, that the best chance of moving into town and driving the cows out without facing much resistance would be late that night. There would also be less chance of hurting innocent bystanders. He thought then of the men he could trust to do the job without turning it into a wild stampede that might alarm the whole town. There was going to be some noise. That couldn't be avoided. The cattle would be sleeping in the middle of the night. So there would have to be enough noise to startle them into motion. The job would be to drive them together in one direction.

Would there be guards on the herd? That was the next question that entered his mind. Surely not, he told himself. He couldn't picture the merchants and tradesmen in town volunteering to stand guard over the captured cattle. More than likely there was no one other than the sheriff and his deputy to guard the cattle. And the sheriff was still recovering from a wound, while his deputy—or assistant, as he was often referred to—was rumored to have a drinking problem. The more Lucas thought about it, the more encouraged he was that he could pull it off with little or no problems. He didn't like pulling the men off the herd to go on these wild parties Ira Dunellen came up with more and more lately. At least it was best they were coming up this time of year when they weren't concerned with roundup and branding. His job at the moment, however, was to notify the men he was picking to ride this raid with him.

Lucas led his war party of four cowhands out through the Cloverleaf entrance gate after supper. His plan was to ride around Tinhorn and camp on the river north of the town. There, he would rest the horses and men until two or three o'clock in the morning before triggering his raid on the cattle. He had chosen his four men based on their older ages and, hopefully, their less immature tendencies. Bob Skinner was an obvious first choice, since he was the oldest at forty-two and had sown all the wild oats he needed years ago. Jack Spade and Andy Hatcher were for the most part hardworking cowhands. Lem Dixon was the only one with no moral compass, but on this operation there would be no one to lead him off the proper path. And he was good at driving cattle.

Close to the same time Lucas left the ranch, Flint and Buck were finishing off their coffee after a supper in Clara's Kitchen. "Gettin' shot in the back didn't hurt your appetite at all, did it?" Buck cracked. "I can't believe you ate that big slice of pie."

"It was hard work," Flint japed. "But I couldn't be rude and say I couldn't eat it, because Mindy said she made it special for me. She said apple pie is the best pie for healin' wounds like mine."

Buck looked at the young man who had become his

closest friend since he hired him off the family farm to be his deputy. He shook his head in amazement when he thought how mentally sharp Flint was, except in one area. Margaret, Clara's cook, didn't bake that apple pie. Mindy baked it herself, especially for Flint. According to Flint, she baked it for him because he got shot, and she'd do the same for Buck. Everybody else knew Mindy baked that pie to show him she could cook. "What else is that little gal gonna have to do to get you to ask her to marry you?" Buck blurted out before he thought to say it only to himself.

Flint seemed stunned by Buck's outburst. He was accustomed to Bonnie's subtle teasing about Mindy, but no one had ever put it so bluntly as this. Of course, he told himself, he shouldn't be surprised, coming from Buck. Since Buck had asked such a direct question, Flint felt he should give him an honest answer. "Of course I'm aware of what a wonderful girl Mindy is," he said solemnly. "But she deserves better than what I can offer her. When I was your deputy, I wasn't paid enough to support myself without a little help, like the room at Hannah's and a lower price here at Clara's. How could I even think about marriage? Now that I'm the sheriff, I make a little more money. Maybe I could support her. But if that bullet had struck me a few inches to the right, she'd be a widow right now, and worse off than before she married me. She deserves somebody with a better chance of hangin' around long enough to have young'uns and a home. I reckon I think too much of her to ask her to marry me."

For once in his life, Buck was struck speechless. It lasted for about thirty or forty-five seconds, while Flint scraped the last bit of filling from the plate onto his fork. When Buck finally found his voice, he said, "Help me get my foot outta my mouth, will ya? It happens a lot when I don't know what I'm talkin' about. I'll keep it shut from now on."

Almost in a panic to change the subject, he said, "While you finish up, I'll see if Margaret's got Ralph's plate ready to go."

Mindy walked over to the table when Buck left. "Was it fit to eat?" she asked.

Flint pushed the empty plate away from him and took a last sip from his coffee cup. "My mama makes the best apple pie I've ever eaten," he said. "Until now. That piece I just finished is the best I've ever tasted. ."

She broke out with a great big smile. "Don't let Margaret hear you say that. She won't let me cook anything in her kitchen again."

"And don't you ever tell my mama I said that either," Flint replied, and they both laughed as he got up to leave.

"What are you two laughin' about?" Bonnie wanted to know as she walked over to join them.

"I just told Flint that if we both start laughin', you'd come straight over here to see what was so funny," Mindy said.

"Kiss my foot," Bonnie told her. "You said no such a-thing."

"Then she said you'd say that," Flint said, joining in.

Bonnie spun around and started back the way she had come. "Margaret musta dropped some silly pills in that stew tonight," she said as she walked back to join Buck and Clara by the front door.

"Flint looks like he's recovering from that bullet in his back pretty fast," Clara said to Buck when they were distracted by the laughter coming from Flint and Mindy at the table.

"Yep, he is at that," Buck said. "Seems like you can see him gettin' better every mornin' when he comes in. I reckon it's because he's still pretty young. If he was my age, we'd most likely still be haulin' him around in Walt's handcart. He's not even sleepin' in his own bed at night. He's been sleepin' at the office."

"What on earth for?" Clara asked.

"Well, don't spread it around, but we wouldn't be surprised if we got a visit from the boys at Cloverleaf Ranch one of these nights, comin' to get those cows we've got penned up behind the jail. And Flint wants to make sure they don't leave any of 'em behind. So he's stayin' at the jail to make sure he don't miss 'em."

"He oughta go home at night and let Hannah take care of him till he gets healed up from that wound," Clara said.

"Ha," Buck snorted. "You tell him."

"Tell me what?" Flint asked as he and Mindy walked up.

"Tell you to stay home until that wound in your back has a chance to heal up proper," Clara answered.

"It's just about healed up," Flint declared. "I'm just wearin' a light bandage on it now. I can hardly tell it's back there."

"Gettin' shot didn't help his lyin' none a-tall," Buck said.

"Well, let's go take Ralph's supper to him." They said good night and went out the door.

It was another quiet night in Tinhorn, with nothing going on that would cause the sheriff to keep an eye on any particular part of town. Flint spent some time at Jake's Place, talking to Jake and Rudy. The attempted murder of the sheriff had greatly reduced the appearance of any Cloverleaf cowhands. Even the older hands like Bob Skinner and Jack Spade had stayed away, though they had never caused any trouble. "We'll see one or two of 'em once in a while, like Andy Hatcher, but they don't stay long, and they don't make much noise."

They're just in town to count the strays in the cow pen, Flint thought, but he didn't express that to Jake and Rudy.

"I figure they're stayin' away because they ain't sure how the town feels about those two tryin' to put you outta business," Jake said. "I know that don't break your heart," he japed, "but I could use the business."

"I wouldn't worry about it if I was you," Flint told him. "They're only gonna go so long without a drink of whiskey. Ain't that right, Rudy?" Rudy just answered with a grin. "Well, I reckon I'll go on back to the jail. Looks to me like you're about ready to shut it down for the night."

When he got back to his office, he found Ralph waiting up for him. Buck had retired to his room some time before, according to Ralph, but he wanted to make sure where Flint was going to be. "I thought I told you I'd be stayin' here again tonight," Flint said.

"You did, but you mighta changed your mind after you walked around town a little bit," Ralph explained.

"You can go ahead and crawl into bed," Flint assured him. "I'll be here all night."

"You ain't gotta twist my arm," Ralph said and headed for the cell room and the cell he had chosen to sleep in that night.

Flint didn't feel like he was ready to go to sleep, so he sat down at his desk and propped his feet on top of it. He was thinking about the big piece of apple pie he had consumed after a sizable supper, and the smile on Mindy's face when he complimented her. The mental picture of it made him smile now. That was the last thing he could remember before he was awakened by the sound of gunfire and bawling cows. He almost turned the chair over when he charged out of it, grabbing his rifle off the desk on his way to the door.

Outside, it was a dark, moonless night. He moved as fast

as he could through the tangles of weed and grass between the jail and the grassy bank where the cows were penned up. As he got closer, the moving shapes near the river turned out to be riders on horses. When he thought he had better not get closer or the riders would see him, he knelt to look the situation over. The riders had cut the wire at the south end of the enclosure, obviously wanting to drive the cattle south. But the cows, suddenly awakened in the middle of the night, were confused and milling about in circles. He could just make out the rider at the south end of the pen. It was Lucas Sawyer, and he was trying to start the cows out in that direction. He had four men with him, and they were trying to position themselves on both sides of the cattle, in flank and swing positions, Flint supposed. That seemed to be a ridiculous waste of time on a herd of cows so small. He would have thought they could just get in behind them and drive them right out of the pen.

When the cows finally started out after Lucas, his men rode on both sides, and they started down the river. "Damn," Flint uttered when several of the cows at the rear of the tiny herd didn't follow the others. Instead, they turned back toward the pen. "No, you don't," Flint mumbled. "I want every last one of you gone." He moved out of the brambles he had been hiding behind and ran to meet the deserting cows, firing his rifle in the air. That was incentive enough for the deserters. They promptly turned around to go after the main body of steers.

Hearing the shots fired behind them, Lucas and his men thought they were fired at them. "Keep 'em movin'!" he shouted out to his men. "They can't see us! They're just firing blind!"

"That's more like it," Flint said to himself when the last cow disappeared into the darkness of the riverbank. He made his way through the weeds and got back to the office in time to meet Buck coming down the office steps, carrying his rifle. "Too late, partner," Flint greeted him. "We've been rustled, and they got away clean."

"Well, I'm sorry I missed it. I heard that Henry rifle of yours, but Ralph said there were shots before that."

"That was the rustlers tryin' to get the cows to move," Flint said. "They got 'em movin' with Lucas Sawyer ridin' point. They had men ridin' swing and flank. Trouble is, they needed somebody to ride drag, so that's what I did, to make sure they didn't leave any cows behind."

"You're lucky you didn't get shot," Buck said.

"That occurred to me," Flint replied.

CHAPTER 17

It had been some time since he had traveled the road leading south out of Tyler, but it was still very familiar to him. His mind was flooded with thoughts of the last time he was on the road. He was heading north instead of south, running for his life, with two wounds in his right shoulder, afraid they would affect his fast-draw ability. Behind him, in the Tinhorn jail, his father and brother, Frank, were awaiting trial, a trial that found them guilty and was followed by their hanging. The one man responsible for all of that was Flint Moran, and Billy Crowe was not coming back to Tinhorn, because he no longer existed. This time, Flint Moran would have to answer to Cash Kelly.

He was tempted to ride straight into town and, when he found Moran, simply put a bullet in his brain and be done with it. But that would rob him of the satisfaction he would get by letting the sheriff know why he was being killed. He also wanted the payday that Ira Dunellen was offering, so he would play by his rules, as long as the game ended with Flint Moran's death. He stopped to rest the big black Morgan gelding he rode at the creek just short of Tinhorn, since he did not want to arrive in town on a tired horse. It was still early in the afternoon, so he took the time to clean his Colt six-gun. He thought about making a cup of coffee, but he was so close to Tinhorn, he decided to wait and get something to eat there, where someone could serve him. He'd been two weeks on the trail and he was sick of his own cooking.

Not much had changed since he had last seen the little town; a new building here and there, nothing to indicate unusual growth or development. He slow-walked the Morgan down the center of the street, past the hotel and the post office. He considered stopping in Clara's Kitchen for supper but decided he'd rather get something to eat where he could also get a drink of whiskey. So he rode on down to Jake's Place, but he couldn't help staring at the door of the sheriff's office when he passed it, his hand tightening on the reins. He wondered what he might have done if the sheriff had picked that moment to walk out the door. With that in mind, he had to warn himself not to react and cheat himself out of eight hundred dollars. *There's plenty of time*, he told himself as he pulled up before the saloon. *Moran is not going anywhere. He has an appointment with the devil and I'm here to deliver the invitation.* The thought had a pleasing effect upon him, leaving him in a good mood as he walked into Jake's Place.

Rudy couldn't help noticing the young stranger dressed in black when he stepped inside the door and paused there for a few moments to judge what he was walking in to. *That's a gunman if I've ever seen one*, he thought. *He looks slick as glass.* He continued to watch him as he walked toward the bar. "Howdy," Rudy greeted him. "What's your pleasure?"

"Howdy," Cash returned. "I think I need a shot of rye whiskey. Have you got any rye?"

"I sure have," Rudy replied and reached for a bottle on the shelf under the bar. He held it up before Cash, so he could see the label. Cash nodded, and Rudy poured his drink. "Don't believe I've ever seen you in here before. What brings you to Tinhorn?"

"I passed through here once, a long time ago," Cash said, "didn't stay long enough to get to know many people. Can I get somethin' to eat here?"

"You sure can," Rudy answered, "if you're in the mood for some beef stew. That's what Rena's cooked up tonight. Would that suit you?"

"That'll do just fine." He tossed his drink back and said, "I'll just take the bottle and set down over there at that table. And I'd be much obliged if you'd tell Rena to dish out a plate of that stew for me."

"Yes, sir," Rudy said. "I'll go tell her right now. You need anything else, just yell for me. My name's Rudy."

"Glad to meet you, Rudy. My name's Cash Kelly."

Rudy walked into the kitchen then to tell Rena, "Young stranger out there wants a plate of your stew. He's as slick as that lard you just threw in the fryin' pan. I'll bet you he's a fast-draw gunslinger. I hope he ain't got no business in our town."

"Does he want coffee and biscuits with the stew?" Rena asked, not really interested in his reason for visiting Tinhorn.

"I don't know," Rudy said, "I didn't think to ask him." He walked back to the door and yelled, "You want coffee and biscuits with that stew, Mr. Kelly?" Cash said that he did. Rudy turned around to tell Rena and found her standing right behind him holding a cup of coffee. "He said he did," Rudy said.

"Here, you can go give it to him when you go back out," she said and handed him the cup. Then she went back to the stove and dished up a plate of beef stew, picked up a couple of biscuits from the pan warming on the edge of the stove, and followed Rudy over to the table.

"What brings you to Tinhorn, Mr. Kelly?" Rudy asked again, since he didn't give him an answer the first time.

"I'm just passin' through, on my way to see a friend who has a place not too far from here," Cash said, unable to resist fanning Rudy's curiosity.

"Is that a fact?" Rudy replied. "Who's your friend? Maybe I know him."

"He has a cattle ranch close to Tinhorn. Ira Dunellen's his name. You know him?"

Rudy was visibly startled. "Why, no, I don't. . . . I mean I know of him, but he ain't never been in here." He paused and stood there for a few moments, nodding his head. "I reckon I'd best get back to the bar," he said then.

Cash took his time eating his supper, but he didn't plan to linger too long in the saloon because he wanted to reach Cloverleaf before dark. He had no desire to camp out another night when there was the possibility of a good bed. So he finished his stew, paid Rudy, and left the saloon. Judge Grant had provided him with detailed directions to the ranch that were enclosed with Dunellen's letter to him. So Cash knew he had only six miles to go and plenty of daylight left. He nudged the big Morgan into an easy lope out past Lon Blake's stable, heading for the creek three miles away, which he would follow to the Cloverleaf Ranch. Behind him, Flint and Buck walked out of Clara's Kitchen with a plate of supper for Ralph.

When they got to the jail, Flint asked Buck if he was going to go to bed right away. Buck couldn't decide if he was ready for bed or not. To Flint, this was a good sign, for he hoped it meant that Buck wasn't craving a drink of whiskey. So he said, "Good, there are some things I was thinkin' about doin' in that cell room that I'd like to have your opinion on. If you'll take Ralph's plate in, I'll take a quick walk around the south end." He wasn't concerned about the north end of town, since he and Buck had just walked down from the dining room.

Buck went inside, and Flint walked down as far as Hannah's boardinghouse, crossed over to the stable, and came back up the street. His last stop was Jake's Place. He just stepped inside the door and stood there for a moment before he concluded there was nothing going on there. He started to leave, but Rudy saw him and started waving frantically for him to come on in. "What's the problem, Rudy?" Flint asked when he walked up to the bar.

"There's somethin' you oughta know about," Rudy told him. "A fellow came in here a little while ago that's got 'gunslinger' written all over him. And I think he might be here to cause you trouble."

"Is that so?" Flint replied. "Why do you think that? Did he give you some trouble?"

"No, he didn't cause no trouble in here," Rudy said. "That's what worries me."

"Whaddaya mean?"

"I mean he was as friendly and polite as a preacher," Rudy insisted. "He bought a bottle of whiskey and ate a bowl of Rena's stew."

Losing his patience at this point, Flint said, "You're right. That sure sounds like a typical gunslinger. I don't blame you for being worried."

Recognizing Flint's sarcasm, Rudy decided to play his wild card. "He said he came to Tinhorn to visit a friend of his. I asked him who his friend was and he said Ira Dunellen." He paused then and waited for Flint's reaction. "Ira Dunellen," he repeated.

Lucy Tucker had drifted over to the bar to eavesdrop by that time. She spoke up then. "He did look like a professional gambler, or a gunman. He was a fairly young fellow, black jacket, black trousers, black hat, black boots, even his hair was black, and it was almost touchin' his shoulders."

"What the hell would Ira Dunellen want with a friend who looks like a gunslinger?" Rudy asked. "You might think we're crazy, but if he comes back to Tinhorn, you best be careful around him. He just left here about twenty minutes ago."

"Did he just come out and tell you he was goin' to see Dunellen? Or did you ask him if he was goin' to see Dunellen and he said he was?" Flint asked.

"He just came right out with it," Rudy insisted. "I wouldn't have no reason to ask him that."

"He's right, Flint," Lucy said. "He was the one who said it first."

"Did he tell you his name?"

"Yes, sir, and I remember it," Rudy exclaimed. "His name's Cash Kelly." He looked at Lucy for verification and she nodded.

"I appreciate you tellin' me this," Flint said. "I'll keep an eye on him if he shows up in town again." He started back across the street toward the sheriff's office, wondering if there could be anything he should worry about. Rudy and Lucy were convinced that Dunellen had called in a gunman to cause trouble. But that was Rudy and Lucy, he reminded himself. *Maybe this Cash Kelly will be back in town*, he thought. *From the way they described him, he might be a tailor Dunellen sent for, to make him a new suit*. He laughed at the thought, but he related their story to Buck when he went back in the office. Buck was not ready to dismiss it as quickly as Flint had, having experienced such a situation when he was sheriff.

* * *

It was not yet dark when Cash rode through the gate that identified Cloverleaf Cattle Company. It was a sure sign of a man who was impressed with himself, Cash thought, to build a fancy big gate where there was no fence. Instead of going to the barn, he rode straight up to the front door of the ranch house and dismounted. No one seemed to notice his arrival, so he walked up the steps to the porch and knocked on the front door. In a short time, the door was opened, and Henry Cheney stared blankly at Cash. After a few moments, when Henry failed to speak, Cash said, "I'm here to see Mr. Dunellen."

"Mr. Dunellen is havin' his supper right now," Henry said. "If it's somethin' to do with the cattle, you need to go down to the bunkhouse and talk to Lucas Sawyer. He's the foreman."

"Who are you?" Cash asked, hoping strongly that he was not Ira Dunellen.

"Henry Cheney," he answered.

"Good!" Cash said. "You go tell Mr. Dunellen that the man he sent for is here."

"Yes, sir," Henry said, closed the door, and went back to the kitchen to tell his wife.

"Where is he?" Atha asked. When Henry replied that he was on the front porch, she said, "For goodness' sakes, Henry!" And she hurried immediately to the front door. She opened it to find Cash looking out at the yard, his back to the door. "Yes, sir," she said. "Please excuse my husband's manners. He's pretty handy around the house, but he doesn't know much about welcoming guests. Won't you come on in and take a seat in the parlor while I go tell Mr. Dunellen you're here? You say he sent for you? Can I tell him your name?"

"Yes, ma'am," he replied. "He sent for me, and I rode two weeks to get here. My name's Cash Kelly."

"All right, Mr. Kelly, I'll be right back." She directed him to the sofa, then hurried down the hall to the dining room, where Dunellen was drinking coffee after a late supper. Within a couple of minutes, she was right back to the parlor. "Mr. Dunellen said for you to come to the dining room to join him in some coffee." He followed her down the hall.

When Cash walked in, Dunellen stood up to welcome him. "Come in, Cash, and have a seat. You want some coffee? Would you like something to eat?"

"No, thanks," Cash replied. "I already ate supper. I'll take some coffee, though." He pulled a chair back from the table and sat down. "Judge Grant tells me you've got a little problem you could use some help with."

"Unfortunately, that's a fact," Dunellen replied, then paused when Atha brought in a cup of coffee and placed it on the table in front of Cash. He waited until she left the room again before continuing. "You come highly recommended, Mr. Kelly, and that's why I'm offering the price I am. I can obviously hire a cheap killer to put a bullet in the back of Flint Moran's head. But that would not send the message to the town that I want them to receive. I need a man with your skill to demonstrate how helpless their sheriff is against a man of real speed and ability with a firearm. So, your job will be to make him stand up to you, face-to-face. That may take a little doing on your part, because Moran is very much against fast-draw face-offs in the town of Tinhorn. And that's the reason I'm offering eight hundred to do the job."

"I think I understand what you want," Cash said. "But I'm going to need some payment to begin with. The trip down here has already cost me some money."

"No problem," Dunellen said at once. "I thought you might require some advance payment. I'm willing to pay you two hundred now, and the rest when Flint Moran is dead from a gunshot fired at close range, in front of witnesses." He paused to let Cash consider those specific conditions for a moment before continuing. "It would certainly be another notch for your reputation, to be able to kill a lawman like Flint Moran, and not be arrested for it."

"I see what you mean," Cash said. "And you say he's dead-set against duels."

"He is, and I suspect it's because he's not fast with a handgun himself, which is another point in your favor."

Cash shrugged. "It doesn't matter to me how fast he is, he's not as fast as I am. And that's just a fact of life that Flint Moran is destined to find out." His comment brought a smile to Dunellen's face, but Cash didn't tell him that he had come all this way from Wichita to kill Flint Moran, with or without a reward. As for whether or not he could cause Flint to draw his weapon, he was pretty confident he could. To Dunellen, he said, "I'll go into town in the mornin' and get myself a room in the hotel. Then I'll make enough noise to attract Moran's attention. Maybe there's an empty bed in your bunkhouse for tonight."

"You can stay right here," Dunellen was quick to offer. "We've got a couple of spare rooms. You can take your pick. I'll have Henry go get one of the boys to come take care of your horses, and they can have them ready for you in the morning. You can have breakfast with me in the morning. I don't want my men questioning you anyway. The less they know about who you are, the better."

"Well, that's mighty generous of you, sir. I appreciate it. I'll just get my saddlebags off my horse." He got up from the table and went to get his things. Behind him, he could hear Dunellen yelling for Atha to send Henry down to the barn to get someone to come get the two horses. He smiled when he thought, *What would old Abel Crowe think if he could see his youngest boy, Billy, getting such royal treatment from a big-shot rancher like Dunellen?*

When he came back inside, he found Atha waiting for him. She led him farther down the hall, past the study, to the two vacant bedrooms. He picked one, and she took the pitcher from the basin and went to the pump to fill it with water. When she came back, she placed a chamber pot under one side of the bed and asked if there was anything else he needed. He told her there was nothing he could think of. "Mr. Dunellen invited you to join him in his study for a cigar, if you like," she told him.

"I don't mind if I do," he replied. *How 'bout now, Pa? I told you I'd be the fastest gun in the territory*, he thought.

Lucas Sawyer walked out of the barn to meet Tim Walker leading Cash's horses to the corral. "Who's the visitor?" Lucas asked Tim.

"I don't know," Tim answered. "Henry couldn't remember what he said his name was. He thinks he said Kelly, but he's gonna stay overnight and wants his horses ready to go in the mornin' after breakfast. Must be somebody important, if he's stayin' in the house."

"Well, let's take good care of his horses for him," Lucas said as he inspected the Morgan gelding. "Fine-lookin' horse, looks just like the one Mr. Dunellen rides. The packhorse looks in pretty good shape, too. He must be an old friend of Mr. Dunellen's." He smiled at Tim and added, "The man, not the packhorse."

CHAPTER 18

The next morning, Lucas made sure Dunellen's guest's horses were fed, saddled, watered, and ready to go after breakfast. Breakfast up at the house was a little later than that served to the men by Gabby Skelton at the cookshack, however. When Dunellen and his guest walked out on the front porch, Lucas made it a point to lead the horses up to the house himself. He was quite surprised to see that his boss's guest was not an old friend at all. Instead, he was a young man, possibly some kin, a grandson or a nephew perhaps. From the way he was dressed, Lucas thought he could be a gambler, a preacher, or maybe even a lawyer. He didn't consider gunslinger, as Rudy Place had, because Lucas thought gunmen came in different sizes and all forms of dress. He decided the stranger wasn't kin. For had he been, Dunellen would have most likely shown him all around the place. When he said "Good morning" and handed the reins to the young man, he got a curt, "Good mornin'," in return.

"Thanks, Lucas," was as much as Dunellen said to him, then wished his guest good luck and stood back to give Cash room to step up in the saddle. Lucas turned and went back to the barn, under the full impression that Dunellen didn't want him to know who the stranger was.

When he got back to the barn, Tim asked if he'd found out who the man was. "No, Mr. Dunellen didn't introduce him to me, and the fellow just climbed on his horse and rode off. Reckon it ain't none of our business who visits the boss anyway, is it?"

"Reckon not," Tim answered.

It was midmorning when Cash rode up the main street of Tinhorn on his way to the hotel. When he left his horses at the rail and went inside, Fred Johnson, the desk clerk, greeted him with a cheerful, "Good morning. Can I help you?"

"Yes, you can," Cash replied, "if you've got a vacant room."

"Well, I can help you with that," Fred declared. "How long will you be with us?"

"I ain't sure," Cash answered, "two or three days, maybe. Depends on how things go, I reckon." He couldn't prevent the slight smile that formed on his face when it was obvious that no one recognized him now. Even the desk clerk was not likely to have seen him close up before. "How 'bout a room up front with a window? You got one of them vacant?"

"Yes, sir, we do," Fred replied. "Second floor with a view of the street."

"Yeah, that's what I want."

"The rate on that room is a dollar a night," Fred said.

"I'll take it," Cash said and reached into his pocket to take out a roll of bills. "Here's two dollars. If I decide to stay longer, I'll pay up then."

"Thank you, sir," Fred said and turned the register around. "If you'll just sign the register, I'll get you a key." He reached behind him in the cabinet and got a key, then spun the register back around after Cash signed. "You'll be in room 202, Mr. Kelly. Up the steps, second door to your right. Do you need any help with your luggage?"

"Nope, I ain't got any luggage, nothin' but my saddle-bags." He took his key and went to his horses to fetch his saddlebags. He took them upstairs to his room and tossed them on the chair beside the window. He looked out the window at the street below and thought back on the morning he awoke to find himself in the morgue. "Things are a little different this time around," he announced. He walked over and sat down hard on the side of the bed, then bounced up and down on it a few times. "Yes, sir, a little different." He went out the door, locked it, and went downstairs to take his horses to the stable. As he passed by the front desk on his way out, Fred asked if his room was satisfactory. "Everything's fine," Cash said.

He rode back down the street with a feeling like he owned it, on his way to the stable at the south end. He stared at the sheriff's office as the Morgan walked casually past. Then he glanced at the saloon on the other side of the street and muttered, "I'll be back to see you in a few minutes, my good friend, Rudy."

Lon Blake was out by his corral when Cash rode up to the stable. "Howdy," he called out and walked to meet him. "What can I do for you?" He watched the stranger as he climbed off the big Morgan and thought, *I bet that's the fellow Rudy was talking about last night.* He sure fit the description. And Rudy told everyone who came in the saloon that this fellow said he was on his way to visit Ira Dunellen.

"Howdy," Cash replied. "I'm stayin' at the hotel and I'd like to leave my horses with you while I'm here. Water 'em good and give both horses a portion of oats. They've been doin' some travelin'."

"You bet," Lon said. "I'll take care of 'em. Where you ridin' in from?"

"I started out from Wichita a couple of weeks ago, and I wound up here yesterday."

"I reckon you're just passin' through," Lon commented. "There ain't many people headed *to* Tinhorn." He was hoping to get him to say he had come to see Ira Dunellen, but Cash didn't mention it.

"I don't see why folks wouldn't wanna come to Tinhorn," Cash remarked. "Seems like a nice little town. I've heard you've got a sheriff who's fast with a six-gun."

"We got a good one, all right," Lon replied. "I don't know how fast he is with a six-gun, though. I ain't never seen him drawin' against anybody. I think Flint prefers a rifle."

"Maybe that's what I heard and I just got it turned around. Don't make much difference, I expect. But if you're the sheriff, you'd better be fast with one of 'em. Ain't that right?"

"I expect so," Lon said, "one or the other." *This has got to be the same fellow Rudy was talking about, talks half crazy,* he thought. "What's your name, young feller? So I know who these horses belong to."

Cash told him, then he helped Lon pull the saddle and packs off his horses. Lon turned them out in the corral with a promise they'd be put in a stall that night and locked up. "Good," Cash said. "I don't wanna take a chance on that Morgan gettin' stole."

"I don't reckon there's much danger of that," Lon said. They both chuckled over that, with Cash maybe a little harder than Lon, because he remembered a day when a horse was stolen out of this very stable the day he woke from the dead.

Cash left the stable then and walked as far up the street

as Jake's Place. When he went inside, there were only a couple of men standing at the bar talking to Rudy. In the back, Jake Rudolph sat at a table, drinking coffee with Lucy Tucker. Cash walked on over to the bar. Rudy interrupted his conversation with the two brothers who farmed a three-hundred-acre piece of land across the river. "Howdy, Cash, you wantin' a drink?"

"Howdy, Rudy," Cash returned. "Yeah, every once in a while, I get a cravin' for a drink of likker before dinnertime. I think one of them cravin's has hit me today. How 'bout a shot of that rye whiskey you gave me yesterday?" When Rudy reached for the bottle and poured a drink, Cash noticed that the two brothers were eyeballing him frankly, so he asked, "How 'bout you two fellers? You want a drink of likker? I'm buyin'."

His offer caught them by surprise, but they both chuckled and nodded their heads. "I don't ever turn down a free shot of whiskey," one of them said. Older than his brother by the look of gray in his sideburns, it was apparent that he did most of the talking for the two of them.

"Well, it's my pleasure to buy you one today, neighbor," Cash went on. "Rudy, pour my two friends here a drink of rye whiskey. Hell, I mighta even bought the sheriff a drink today if he was here. And that's somethin' I ain't ever done before." He paused, looking as if he was considering such a possibility. "I might do that," he said then, looked at Rudy, and asked, "Does the sheriff come in here to eat his dinner?"

Rudy grinned, thinking now that Cash was already half drunk when he came in. "Nah," he said, "Flint usually eats up at the hotel. Him and Buck don't have to pay for their meals at Clara's Kitchen."

That appeared to sober Cash up right away. "Well, that's too bad 'cause he missed a free drink of likker right here.

Maybe another time." He threw his hands up in frustration. "I gotta go anyway. It was nice meetin' you boys," he said to the two brothers, put some money on the bar, and left.

"Hey, Cash," Rudy yelled after him. "You left me too much."

"Give 'em another drink," Cash called out without looking back. He had mistakenly assumed that Flint ate right across the street there at Jake's, that being handy to his office and Rena not a bad cook, judging by the stew he had eaten there. There was plenty of time, he told himself when he got outside. It was just before noon and the dining room at the hotel may not have even opened yet.

Flint and Buck were at the door of Clara's Kitchen right at opening time for the noon meal. They were met by Clara as she was turning the "Open" sign on the door. "I believe I could save myself a few steps every day if I just give you boys this sign and you can put it on the door when you come to eat."

"Flint was talkin' to me this mornin' about some changes he was thinkin' about makin' in the cell room," Buck told her. "Part of his plan is to move our desks here to the dinin' room to save wear and tear on our boots."

"That would work out all right," Clara came back. "We can use a couple of big, strong men to clean the kitchen every night." She walked them back to their usual table, where Mindy was already placing two cups of coffee. "One of your favorites today," Clara said to Buck, "meat loaf."

"I kept hearin' a voice callin' to me all mornin'," Buck responded. "I couldn't figure it out before, but now I remember it sounded like 'meat loaf—meat loaf—meat loaf. . . .'"

"I think I know what Buck wants," Mindy said with a

laugh. "How 'bout you, Flint? If you don't want meat loaf, you can have ham."

"I had ham this mornin' for breakfast," Flint said. "I'll take the meat loaf."

Mindy went to the kitchen to fill their plates, and Buck recalled the last time Margaret had baked meat loaf. "She served it with them Mexican-style fried beans, and damned if I wasn't downright musical all night long. Who the hell is that?" he interrupted himself when he looked toward the door to see Clara talking to a stranger, dressed all in black. "Looks like Clara is tryin' to explain her no-weapons policy to that young fellow."

Flint turned his head to see. "Doesn't look like he's makin' it a problem," he commented. He took another look and then remembered Rudy's story about the stranger he thought was a gunfighter. He turned in his chair then, so he could get a better look. "That's the stranger Rudy was concerned about. I told you about that, didn't I?"

"Yeah," Buck answered, "but he don't look like he's givin' her any trouble."

"Rudy said he acted kinda crazy. I'll just walk over and let him know she ain't pickin' on him and everybody has to leave their firearms," Flint said, and got up from the table.

"You win, lady," Cash Kelly said to Clara after she explained that only lawmen were allowed to wear their weapons in the dining room. "I'll put 'em on the table." He flashed a smile for her. "It's just that I feel so undressed without them. Uh-oh," he said then because he saw Flint get up. "Looks like one of the lawmen is comin' to arrest me," he joked but took a step to the side, so Clara would not be between him and Flint. Then he stood watching him, waiting to see if Flint recognized him after all the time that had passed, and the changes in his appearance. He concentrated on Flint's eyes, watching for that spark that would tell him the instant the sheriff knew who he was. For he knew that if he saw it, it would trigger the response he hoped for. Flint would reach for his gun, and he would shoot him down right there in front of witnesses who had to say that the sheriff drew first. Cash couldn't hope for a better opportunity to get the job done right away, but the sheriff had to recognize him. For him to have complete satisfaction with the killing, it was necessary that Flint Moran know who it really was who shot him down. And it was critical that Moran realized it just before the moment of his death, so there was no time to tell anyone else who he really was. Billy Crowe was still wanted in Texas. So he watched anxiously for that spark in Flint's eye that would signal recall. But it never came.

Instead, Flint favored him with a friendly smile and asked, "Is Clara givin' you a lotta trouble? She's not pickin' on you because you're wearin' that cross-draw gunbelt with two handguns. She's just following a rule the dinin' room has about leavin' any weapons on the table over there, unless you use 'em to eat with. That way, the gentle folk don't get nervous while they're eatin'. You ain't a lawman by any chance, are you? 'Cause if you are, you can leave 'em on."

Cash relaxed and flashed a smile for Flint. "No problem, Sheriff, I just told the lady I'd be happy to leave my guns on the table."

"That's a fact, Flint," Clara said.

"Then I apologize for buttin' in," Flint said. "I was just gonna explain why the dinin' room has a policy like that. I understand it was started after a couple of fellows had a gunfight in here right after it was first opened. Is that true, Clara?"

"Yes, it is," Clara immediately replied, "and I thought we were all gonna get shot before it was over."

"Well, I hope you enjoy your dinner, Mr. . . ." Flint waited for his response.

"Kelly," he said, "Cash Kelly."

"Right, Mr. Kelly. I'm Sheriff Flint Moran. I think you'll find the food pretty good here."

When he got back to the table, he found a napkin covering his plate. "Mindy put that on there," Buck said. "She was afraid your meat loaf was gonna get cold. I told her I wouldn't let it get cold. I'd eat it before I let it get cold."

"That's what friends are for," Flint said sarcastically.

"Well?" Buck prodded.

"Well, what?" Flint replied.

"You know damn well. The jasper dressed like a funeral director—any trouble?"

"No, not here anyway," Flint said as he carved off a bite of meat loaf with his fork. "He'd already told Clara he'd put his guns on the table. I think Rudy was right, fellow's a gunslinger. He's wearin' two six-guns under his coat in a cross-draw holster. And he's got that look about him. He was sizin' me up when I was walkin' toward him, and he was standin' relaxed but ready, like he expected me to make a move."

"Well, damn!" Buck exclaimed. He hadn't expected that complete and detailed a description of the stranger. "Reckon we oughta shoot him while his guns are on the table?"

"No, but I expect it would be a good idea to keep an eye on him while he's in our fair city," Flint replied.

Buck paused to think about that for a few moments before making another comment. "You know, you said that jasper told Rudy he was here to visit a friend. And the friend was Ira Dunellen. You remember that, don't you? Take one look at that fast-gun. Do you think he's a friend of Ira Dunellen's? He's in town to take care of you."

"That doesn't make any sense, Buck. All Dunellen has

to do is pay some saddle tramp to take a shot at my back, like he did the first time. He doesn't have to hire some fast-gun professional to draw me out."

"I don't know, Flint, maybe Dunellen don't want the folks here in Tinhorn to know he's payin' his own men to shoot you. He'd rather have 'em think you and some gunman got into it on your own, and it didn't have nothin' to do with him."

"I understand what you're sayin'," Flint said, "but it's against the law to duel in Tinhorn. So I'll just have to remind him of that. Then if he still insists, I'll arrest him and lock him up."

"I swear," Buck snorted. "Am I gonna have to break in another new sheriff in this town?"

Sitting at a table next to the window, Cash studied the two lawmen seated across the room from him. Disappointed that Flint didn't realize who he really was, he decided he was going to have to attract his attention some other way. And the best way to do that would most likely be in the saloon, where he might be able to force Flint to deal with him. He needed a sucker to use for bait, and that might not be easy in a town as peaceful and under control as Tinhorn appeared to be. *But maybe I'll get lucky later today or tonight*, he thought. *Right now, I'm going to enjoy this dinner. Flint Moran, I'll deal with you later*. So he attacked the slice of meat loaf on his plate with the appetite of one who anticipated the completion of a vow of vengeance that had long troubled him. By the time he had finished his dinner, he had formed a plan for the death of Flint Moran. Since the two lawmen appeared to be lingering over a last cup of coffee, he decided to take step one in his plan.

He got up from the table and ambled over to the table where Flint and Buck were sitting. "Pardon me, Sheriff, but

I thought I'd tell you, you were right about the cookin' here. That was right tasty meat loaf."

"Glad you enjoyed it," Flint replied. "Tell Clara that. I'm sure she'd appreciate it."

"I will," Cash said. "Say, I wanted to check something else with you. I don't wanna start out on the wrong foot since I ain't ever spent much time in Tinhorn. I like to play cards whenever I can find a game, you know, for a little money to make it interestin'. Any law against that here?"

Flint looked at Buck and winked before he answered. "No, there ain't no law against gamblin' in Tinhorn. There's a law against cheatin' at cards, though."

Cash laughed. "I reckon that goes without sayin'. But I don't have to cheat. I'm just naturally lucky, I guess."

"If you're looking to play an honest game of cards, you won't have any trouble from the sheriff's department," Flint said. "You oughta be able to find one tonight, or tomorrow night for sure, since tomorrow's Saturday."

"Good," Cash said. "Just thought I'd check. Always a good idea to check with the sheriff."

He took his leave then, and Buck was prompted to comment. "Well, maybe he ain't no gunman or funeral director after all. We shoulda figured him for a gambler."

"Well, he's wastin' his time here in Tinhorn," Flint said 'cause the gamblin' doesn't amount to much."

CHAPTER 19

Clara was standing at the front door of the dining room, looking out toward the street after Cash left. When she heard Flint and Buck getting up from the table with the dinner plate for Ralph, she turned to face them. "Be careful," she said, "there's somebody waiting for you outside." Her warning didn't sound particularly ominous, but Flint decided to be cautious nevertheless. He went out the door she held open for him to find one Texas longhorn steer standing at the edge of the street, staring at him.

"Well, here it is," he called out to Buck behind him, "the official first stray of the Second Tinhorn Cattle Herd."

"Actually, it's the third," Buck answered. "I forgot to tell you that Lon put two in the pen before you came in this mornin'."

"Damn," Flint swore. "I knew better, but I was kinda hopin' Dunellen would go ahead and move that main herd down the river and forget about his conquest of Tinhorn."

"That man's crazy," Buck said. "It takes a little longer for crazy people to learn their lesson." He turned to face Clara. "You ain't got any rope around here we could borrow, have you?"

Overhearing, Bonnie answered before Clara could. "Nope. We cooked that up for supper last night."

"Come on!" Flint yelled. "We'll have to drive it down to the jail!" He charged straight at the confused cow, which stood there transfixed until Flint almost reached it. Then it bolted down the street. "Come on!" he yelled again. "Let's keep him goin'!" He ran after the hapless stray, much like a kid playing cowboy.

Mindy wedged in between Clara and Bonnie in the doorway. "Ain't he the cutest thing you ever saw?" she declared before she realized she was speaking out loud. She was mortified to have let it drop out of her mouth, and she was to be reminded of it over and over for the rest of the day. They had to laugh at Buck then, who tried to give chase, holding Ralph's dinner with both hands. But he ran out of wind just past Harper's Feed & Supply. Raymond Chadwick saw what was happening and managed to head off the runaway cow before it got as far as Jake's Place and turn it back toward the jail. Attracted to the noise in the street, Ralph stepped outside to see the reason. Seeing the cow, he stepped back inside and grabbed a coil of rope that hung on a peg near the door. He came back outside and stood on the office steps, watching the befuddled beast, now trotting around and around in a circle in the street. When it came by the steps, Ralph dropped his rope over its horns and brought it to a stop.

"Nice work, Ralph," Flint said as he walked up to him. "I'll take him back to the pen. Buck's got your dinner. You better eat it before it gets cold." The cow seemed to be relieved to be captured and followed Flint willingly toward the pen by the river, to the accompaniment of a rousing cheer and round of applause from the spectators in front of the saloon. It occurred to Flint as he led the cow away that it was a natural reaction for Ralph. That was the crime Ralph was originally arrested for, riding in somebody's pasture and dropping a rope on a cow, then riding off with it.

Cash Kelly was one of the spectators in front of the saloon, and he joined in the applause for the Tinhorn "cowhands." When the entertainment was over, he went back inside the saloon and walked back to the end of the bar where Jake Rudolph was talking to Rudy Place. Cash held up his empty glass and said, "I didn't want you to think I was stealin' one of your glasses." He set it down on the bar and slid it over in Rudy's direction. "How 'bout fillin' it up again? I musta spilled it out there watchin' the show."

"Rudy tells me that you're a friend of Ira Dunellen's," Jake said. "Is that true?" His blunt question was met with a patient smile on Cash's face. "'Cause I didn't know Dunellen had any friends," Jake added.

"Since you ain't particularly shy about askin' questions, I'll tell you this. I met the man for the first time yesterday and I checked into the hotel here today, when I coulda had free room and board at the Cloverleaf Ranch. I have definite limits on what I'll do for money. Dunellen wanted me to do something I don't do. A man has to have standards to live by, no matter what his line of work is. That's all I'm gonna say on the matter. I rode down here on the possibility that I might be interested in an investment. I'm not, so I'm just gonna spend a couple of days to rest up a little, drink some whiskey, play some cards. . . ." He paused when Lucy walked by—"and maybe a few other things."

"You might find this little town is a pretty good place to do all those things," Jake said, thinking of the possibility of helping him get rid of the money he must be carrying. "I hope you didn't take offense since I was so blunt in stickin' my nose in your private business. It's just that Ira Dunellen seems to take great pleasure in causin' trouble for Tinhorn."

"Nah, no offense taken," Cash insisted. "I ain't that thin-skinned, not by a whole lot." He told Rudy to pour him another drink. Rudy did, and Jake told him that one was on the house. "Why, thank you kindly, Mr. Rudolph. Say, what about the card games? Are there any regulars that like to gamble a little bit? I like to gamble. Large stakes, small stakes, pennies, I don't give a damn. I just enjoy the chance of winnin' more than I lose."

"I'm afraid you'll be a little disappointed on that score," Jake told him. "I mean, sure, there's a few men in town that like to have a little game, but it's mostly nickel or dime ante. And it's just poker, instead of faro, which is what everybody wants nowadays. But we ain't set up for faro. Sometimes there's some bigger games when the cowhands get paid and come to town to see how fast they can lose it. But lately, the hands from Cloverleaf have quit comin' in because two of their men tried to kill our sheriff. He killed both of 'em, but the rest of that crew has kinda stayed away."

That wasn't very encouraging news for Cash because he was satisfied that he had a perfect plan to set Flint Moran up for a showdown, one he couldn't avoid. But he made a great effort to hide his disappointment. "Well, like I said, it doesn't really matter to me how big the game is. Maybe I'll talk some of your regular boys into a little penny ante."

Rudy spoke up then. "Lon Blake and Louis Wheeler set in here some nights playin' two-hand poker, but they just play for small change."

"That big dinner I just ate up at Clara's Kitchen was more than I needed to eat," Cash declared. "It's makin' me sleepy. I think I'll go up to the hotel and take a little nap. I'll take a bottle of that rye with me. Then I'll check with you boys later to see if things liven up."

"I believe ol' Cash is really disappointed," Rudy commented after Cash left the saloon. "I swear, I had him figured for a gunslinger yesterday when he came in here. Now I believe he makes his money gamblin'. He shoulda stopped ridin' when he got as far as Tyler."

* * *

"Hey, Lem," Charley Tate called out to Lem Dixon when he walked into the bunkhouse. "Some of the boys are talkin' 'bout goin' into Tinhorn tomorrow, it bein' Saturday. Spade and Skinner are goin'. They say them people in Tinhorn can't fault the rest of us for what Moon and Alvin tried."

"Them folks in Tinhorn ain't got enough guts to stop us if we wanna go to town," Lem declared.

"So, you goin' with Spade and them tomorrow?" Charley asked.

"Nope," Lem said. "I'm goin' into town tonight. I need a drink of likker tonight. And we got our pay today, so there ain't no use in waitin' around for it."

"Did Boss say it was all right?" Charley asked.

"I didn't ask Lucas Sawyer if I could go into town tonight. I ain't got night herd or nothin' else I'm supposed to do. So I reckon I'll go when I damn well please."

Charley couldn't help thinking that was what Drew Price would have done, and Drew was Charley's hero. He missed Drew. Lem Dixon was a lot like Drew. "Hey, Lem, can I go to town with you?"

Lem hesitated. With Charley, it was a lot like takin' a kid along. He'd been acting like an orphan ever since Drew got killed. Lem realized at once that he shouldn't have said he was going into town tonight. But if he told him he couldn't go, he might say something to Lucas about it, and Lucas might have some reason to tell him he couldn't go into town yet. "Yeah, I reckon," he finally answered. "But don't go shootin' your mouth off about it. Throw a saddle on your horse 'cause I'm ridin' out right after supper." Charley went straight to the barn to get his saddle, then left his horse around behind the bunkhouse. That didn't escape the notice of Andy Hatcher.

"What are you up to, Charley?" Andy asked him when he sat down beside him in the cookshack. "How come you're hidin' your horse behind the bunkhouse? You goin' somewhere?"

"We don't want Lucas to know it, but me and Lem are gonna ride into Tinhorn right after we eat supper," Charley said. "Don't tell nobody. I told him I wouldn't say nothin' about it."

"I was plannin' to go to town tomorrow with some of the other boys," Andy said. "But hell, I might go tonight with you and Lem." He was thinking there was safety in numbers, and that was the reason he had planned to go the next day with Skinner and the others. When Lem finally climbed on his horse to go to town, he found that he was now in a party of four, since Andy had joined them and brought Jack Spade along as well.

"I swear," Lem said, "if I ever need to make an announcement to the whole state of Texas, I'll just tell it to you, Charley, and tell you to keep it a secret."

Cash Kelly decided he might as well have supper in Clara's Kitchen before he checked the action in the saloon that night. As before, the sheriff and his deputy were there at their table by the kitchen door. Clara greeted him at the door, and before she could ask, he took his two six-guns out of his holsters and placed them on the table. She gave him a smile in appreciation for his thoughtfulness. "Just in case I decide to shoot somebody while I'm in here, am I supposed to ask my waitress to bring me my guns?" He attempted to keep a serious expression on his face.

Clara laughed and replied, "No, you have to submit a request, in writing, to me."

He nodded to Flint and Buck, then said to Clara, "Looks like nobody's watchin' the town again." He went over to the same table he had sat at before by the window. Bonnie saw him and hurried over to meet him at the table. "Well, here's my favorite waitress," he said in greeting.

"Mr. Kelly," Bonnie replied, "you came back. We must not have treated you too badly the last time you were here. What's it gonna be, coffee or water?"

"How about a cup of tea?"

"Tea? We've got some tea," Bonnie said. "We can brew you up a cup of tea. Is that what you want?"

"Hell no," he quickly replied. "I'm just in the mood to aggravate people tonight. Bring me a cup of coffee."

She chuckled and asked, "What's the matter? You havin' a bad day today?"

"You know, I'll be honest with you. I am," he answered truthfully. "I had a day's work all planned out, and the people I need to work with ain't gonna show up." He gave her a grin then. "And that's all I'm gonna say about it. I'm ready to eat. What are you pushin' tonight?"

"Tonight you can have a steak. We just butchered a cow this afternoon, so we've got fresh beef." She didn't see fit to inform him that the official Tinhorn cattle herd had been reduced from three to two cows by coincidence.

"Well, a fresh steak will sure suit my taste tonight," Cash said. "I'm sure that's what the sheriff's department is havin'. Probably just ate theirs raw, though."

"No, it's fried. How bad do you want yours burnt?"

"Just a little on the outside," he said. "I'd like the middle to be warm." She went to the kitchen to give the order to Margaret and was back right away with his coffee. She left him then to get something for another customer, leaving him to study the two men sitting by the kitchen door. It amused him to think, if they knew who he really was, they would try to arrest him. *They might try*, he thought then, *but damned if they could do it. I wonder why they swapped jobs?*

Cash noticed that the town lawmen didn't linger over their coffee as they had at dinner earlier that day. Then he remembered when he, his father, and his brother, Frank, were in jail here, Buck always disappeared after supper every night. So maybe he wouldn't have to worry about dealing with both of them, if an opportunity came about. It was still early, so he took his time finishing his supper. When he was done, he said good night to the women and went to his room upstairs in the hotel. As a matter of habit, he checked his Colt six-guns to make sure they were clean and ready for use. Satisfied that they were, he went over and stood at the window and watched the street below for a few minutes. The street had not been very busy all day long, and now it appeared to be even slower. He shrugged and turned away. *Might as well hang around the saloon for a while, just in case*, he thought as he put his coat back on.

Outside, he took a casual walk down past the sheriff's office to Jake's Place. He paused just before stepping up on the saloon's porch. Something caught his eye down toward the stable. It was four men on horseback. They were walking their horses past the stable now, and as they became closer, he could guess that they were cowhands. They could only be heading for one place, he decided, so he went on inside the saloon and claimed a table near the center of the room, where he was sure to be noticed. "Rudy, bring me a bottle of that rye, will you?"

"It you're drinkin' all the whiskey you're buyin', you must have a helluva thirst," Rudy japed when he brought a bottle to the table. You took one with you when you left here a little while ago."

"It's still in the room at the hotel," Cash said. "That's for use later on tonight, if I can't sleep. I 'preciate you walkin' it over here for me. I wanted to get this table while it was empty 'cause the light's a little better here. I'm gonna play me some poker, even if I have to play myself." He pulled a deck of cards out of his coat pocket and started shuffling them. "You wanna play me for that bottle of whiskey, double or nothin'?"

"Shoot, no," Rudy replied. "You'd have to play Jake for that bet."

"What's the matter? Don't you feel lucky?" Cash asked, laughing.

"I don't feel stupid either," Rudy came back. He turned then, when he heard the four Cloverleaf cowhands come in the door. "You can settle up before you go," he said and went back to the bar.

"Haven't seen you boys in a while," Rudy said when the Cloverleaf riders walked up to the bar.

"We figured you folks might not wanna see any hands from Cloverleaf for a while, after that business with Moon Murphy and Alvin Jeeter," Jack Spade said. "That was pretty bad business there, and none of us knew they was gonna pull a deal like that."

Impatient with Jack's attempt to smooth over the attack on the sheriff, Lem said, "That ain't got nothin' to do with us. And I got way behind in my drinkin', so how's about pourin' some drinks right quick?"

Rudy figured it must have been payday out at the Cloverleaf, so he got busy pouring drinks, and it didn't take long before the alcohol began to take effect. Pretty soon, the noise increased to the point of bringing Lucy downstairs to see what had happened to the quiet evening. She soon had a couple of engagements upstairs, and the cow-hands became more and more rowdy. Through it all, one man sat at a table in the middle of the saloon, seemingly unmindful of the noise, playing two-hand poker with himself. He finally caught Lem Dixon's interest. "Ain't that the jasper that spent the night at the ranch house last night?" Lem asked Jack Spade.

"I believe you're right," Jack answered. "I didn't get a close look at him, but he's sure dressed the same as that feller."

"What the hell's wrong with him?" Lem asked Rudy and pointed to Cash.

"Ain't nothin' wrong with him," Rudy answered. "He's just hooked on gamblin', and there ain't nobody to play cards with, so he's playin' himself in two-handed poker."

"He's crazy," Lem said, "or drunk as hell. Has he got any money left in his pockets?"

"He ain't drunk," Rudy said.

"Then I reckon he's crazy," Lem said. He pushed away from the bar and walked over to stand in front of Cash. "Whaddaya doin'?"

Cash looked up at him. "I'm playin' poker with myself."

"Is that a fact?" Lem replied. "Who's winnin'?"

"He is," Cash answered with a smile. *Caught one*, he thought. He could tell by Lem's swagger and his half sneer that he figured he could relieve him of his cash. Never having seen the man before, he didn't realize he was one of Ira Dunellen's cowhands. He looked to be the perfect sacrifice to bait Sheriff Flint Moran with.

"Lemme play his hand for him," Lem said and picked up the hand lying facedown on the table and looked at it without waiting for Cash to respond. "How much you playin' for?" Cash told him he was playing nickel limit, so Lem said, "Okay, I'm callin' you. Whaddaya got?" Cash laid his cards down. He had four cards of a ten-high straight. Lem beat him with a pair of jacks.

"I almost had it that time," Cash said. "I just ain't had much luck with straights. That's the third time I've come up one card short on a straight."

Lem sensed that the man didn't know how to play winning poker. Trying to draw one card to fill a five-card straight was evidence enough. "Trouble is, you ain't playin' for any money. I'd play some poker with you if you was playin' for enough to make it worthwhile."

"How much would be worthwhile?" Cash asked.

"Oh, I reckon a little game of three-dollar limit," Lem answered. "I'm not a big poker player, myself, but I'd try a few hands of three-dollar limit. But I need another drink."

Cash noticed he was eyeing the bottle on the table, so he said, "Help yourself to a drink outta my bottle and I'll try a few hands at three dollars."

"That's mighty neighborly of you," Lem said and poured himself a stiff one. "Now let's play some poker. Deal 'em."

That was the beginning of a game that lasted for almost an hour. At first, Cash did not seem able to win a hand, throwing in several winning hands without showing Lem the cards. Lem didn't care to see them anyway. He was winning. Halfway through the hour, he was almost fifty dollars ahead, and the other men became interested in the game. And then Lady Luck seemed to lose her interest in Lem Dixon, and he started losing all that he had won, until he was down to the last of his own money. It could only be because of cheating, and he realized he had been suckered into playing. Finally, he made the accusation. "I don't know where that last card came from, but it didn't come off the top of that deck."

Suddenly, everything got quiet. "What are you tryin' to say?" Cash asked.

"I'm sayin' you're cheatin'," Lem charged. "There ain't no way you could all of a sudden turn into the luckiest son of a gun in Texas. You're a low-down, dirty cheat, and I'll wring your neck like a chicken! Put that damn money back on the table!"

"I ain't givin' you a cent, you dumb turd. Nobody accuses me of cheatin', and if you ain't ready to get down on your knees and apologize in front of all these men who heard you call me a cheat, you better be ready to use that gun you're wearin'." He stood up and pushed his chair out of the way. Then he slipped out of his jacket and placed it on the chair. "Now, how bad do you want that piddlin' little amount of money you lost? I changed my mind. You either draw that gun or I'll shoot you down where you sit. You look like the kind of coward who would shoot a man in the back. These your friends here? Stand up and show 'em what you're made of."

Stunned like everyone else, Rudy finally thought to tell Lucy, "Go get Flint. Hurry!" She immediately ran out the door. Cash caught her exit out of the corner of his eye and grinned to himself. *Everything according to plan*, he thought.

CHAPTER 20

Lucy burst into the door of the sheriff's office, startling Ralph. "Where's Flint?" she blurted out. "There's gonna be a killin' at the saloon!"

"He's outside on the street!" Ralph blurted. "Makin' his rounds!" He ran outside with her, looking up and down the street. "He musta walked up toward the hotel first!"

Lucy took off running up toward the hotel, yelling, "Sheriff! Sheriff!"

Flint heard her and ran out of the alley beside Harper's Feed & Supply. "Lucy!" he called when he saw her running toward him. "I'm here! What is it?"

"That fellow, that Cash Kelly, is fixin' to shoot somebody in Jake's!"

Flint ran straight to the saloon. Ralph was still out in front of the office when he ran past, so he yelled at him, "Go wake up Buck! Tell him what's goin' on." Ralph grimaced, always reluctant to wake Buck after he had retired to his room for the night. But Flint sounded like he meant business, so Ralph did as he was told. Flint knew Buck would want to be notified for something of this nature.

Inside the saloon, the confrontation had come to a head. Aware there was no out for him, Lem Dixon got to his feet, choosing to die on his feet rather than as a craven coward, balled up in his chair. Cash held up his hands, even with his shoulders, palms facing Lem. "I'm going to let you get a start on me. I'm gonna count to ten. Pull your weapon when you feel ready anytime you want. But if you don't shoot before I count ten, I'll cut you down."

Flint heard the shot just as he stepped on the porch of the saloon and knew he was too late. He pushed through the door, gun in hand, to find Cash Kelly standing in the middle of the room, his gun in hand. "Put the gun away, Cash," Flint told him.

"When you put yours away," Cash returned.

Realizing he was at a standoff, Flint said, "All right, we'll both holster 'em." They did so then, each man watching the other carefully until both weapons were in the holsters. "Now, you wanna tell me what happened, and remember, you've got a room full of witnesses."

"It was out-and-out murder," Jack Spade yelled. "That damn gunslinger tricked Lem into a gunfight, just so he could show everybody how fast he is!" There were a lot of voices grumbling in agreement with Spade.

"Just hold your horses," Flint said, trying to keep the witnesses calm and maybe avoid a lynching. "You'll all get a chance to have your say." Back to Cash then, he asked, "Is that the way it happened?"

"Not entirely," Cash answered. "I was sittin' here at this table, mindin' my own business. And this saddle tramp came over to me and wanted to play poker. I said why not, and started playin'. He was all right when he won a few hands, but when his luck turned, he blamed it on me and accused me of cheatin'. I told him I wasn't cheatin', but he said I was and threatened to wring my neck like a chicken, I believe was the way he put it. I don't stand for any man to call me a cheater, and I told him so. I gave him a chance to apologize. He wouldn't do it. He wasn't gonna have it any other way than to let our six-guns settle it. I knew I was faster, so I put my hands in the air and let him draw first, which he did. But like I said, I was faster."

"Even when I hear you tell your side of it," Flint told him, "it sounds like you set that poor fellow up so you could carve another notch on your gun handle. I'm gonna have to lock you up for participatin' in a duel, and that's against the law in this town." Several voices around him were saying it resembled a murder more than a duel. "I'll see you get a fair trial, and you can tell the judge your side of it."

"Fightin' duels ain't against the law in the state of Texas," Cash replied calmly. "That man called me a cheat, and he threatened to wring my neck. I called him out on it, and he stood up against me. It ain't against the law to defend yourself against a man that's spreadin' lies about you, and he called me a cheat. So I ain't goin' to no jail for protecting myself against trash like him."

"You're just makin' it harder on yourself by addin' resistin' arrest charges on top of duelin'," Flint said. "So I'm askin' you to come peacefully and we'll make this as easy as we can."

Cash continued to stand firm, a trace of a smile on his face. "You must be havin' a little trouble hearin', Moran. I said I ain't goin' to no jailhouse. There ain't but one way to take me, so you'd best make up your mind how bad you want me." There was no sound in the busy saloon now but the voices of the two men standing facing each other.

"I'm the sheriff of this town," Flint said. "I don't participate in quick-draw contests to carry out the laws of this town. So you might as well forget about showin' off your fast draw. You're under arrest." He started to take a step toward him, but Cash quickly assumed a ready position, his knees slightly flexed like a hawk about to take flight.

It was enough to cause Flint to pause. "I told you, Cash, I'm not drawing against you, so if you pull your weapon on me, you'll hang for murder. Unless I manage to put a shot in you as well. Either way, you lose."

"Would it make any difference if I told you my name is Billy Crowe?" he said softly, so no one but Flint could hear him. Then he waited to witness Flint's reaction. He was pleased to see his confession had definitely struck home, and the sheriff was momentarily in a state of confusion. Cash wanted to drive the facts home, so Flint would have full knowledge of why he was being executed. "You remember me, don't you, Moran?" he continued. "You put two bullets in me and left me for dead in the back of the barbershop. I came back from the dead, Moran, just to settle up with you for killin' my father and both of my brothers. I had to wait a while before I could come back for you. Those shots you put in my shoulder were so close together, they caused a lot of damage, and they took a long time to heal. But they're all healed up now."

Flint realized he could not expect any help from the witnesses of this confrontation, so his best chance of walking out of this saloon depended upon how hard it was for Ralph to rouse Buck out of his slumber. So he was intent upon letting Billy continue to deliver his sentence of death. "I didn't kill your father and your older brother. They were tried and hanged for the crimes they committed."

"But it was you who arrested 'em and sent 'em to stand in front of that judge, so it was you who killed 'em. And after I'm through with you, I think Cash Kelly might call on that judge."

"Cash Kelly," Flint repeated. "I reckon you musta found out you were pretty fast with those guns you're wearin'."

Billy laughed, although it was more a sneer than a chuckle. "Not just pretty fast," he replied, "the fastest in

Kansas and Nebraska territory. And now I'm ready to *show* you how fast I am. So we're done talkin', Sheriff, and make no mistake, if you turn your back and walk, I'll shoot you in the back."

"You're makin' a mistake, Billy. You shoot me down and you'll have every Ranger and U.S. Marshal in the territory lookin' for you. Is that what you want?"

"I think I can handle it," Billy responded. "Now quit stallin' and go for your gun. It ain't gonna do you no good to keep stallin'. I gave you the chance to die like a man. I'm done talkin'." With that as his last warning, he reached for the weapons on his sides. Shock seemed to sweep across the saloon floor that sounded like one loud report, as all three weapons discharged at nearly the same time. Everyone seemed frozen for a few moments while both combatants remained standing. And then, very slowly, Billy's knees started to fold, and he collapsed to the floor, dropping his pistols as he fell.

No one made a sound until Flint spoke. "Rudy, you got a bucket of water or something? You need to put that fire out." He pointed to a table against the wall with his pistol before he dropped it back in his holster.

"What?" Rudy replied. Like most of the others in the saloon, he hadn't noticed the small fire burning on the tabletop that now held the smashed remains of a lamp. He snatched up his rinse bucket and hurried over to dowse the fire.

"Are you shot?" This came from the doorway as Buck ran into the saloon.

"No," Flint answered him. "But that's probably about as close as I'll ever come without gettin' shot."

Buck went straight to the body to make sure he was dead. He looked at the bullet hole, dead center in Cash's chest. The expression of complete surprise was frozen on his face. Rudy, standing by his shoulder after putting out the fire, spoke softly, as if he didn't want anyone to hear. "That was the damnedest thing I ever saw. It happened so fast, I ain't sure anybody watchin' it knows what happened."

"Whaddaya mean?" Buck asked.

"We just saw Cash trick that fellow, Lem, into drawin' on him. And he was like greased lightning when he put Lem away." He nodded toward Lem Dixon's body, which had been dragged closer to the door.

"Yeah, I saw him when I came in the door," Buck said.

"Well, we hadn't even had time to get Lem outside before Flint ran in, and Cash is wantin' to take him on in a gunfight. Flint tells him gunfightin's against the law, and he's under arrest. But Cash says he ain't goin' to jail and stands his ground. Flint couldn't talk him out of a shoot-out. Then, all of a sudden, Cash pulls them two guns he wears, and Flint shot him before he could get one into Flint." He shook his head, amazed. "I reckon that's what happened to the lamp. With that cross-draw holster he wore, one shot went to one side and the other went to the opposite. It's a wonder nobody else got shot. I don't know where the bullet from his left-hand gun went. Flint drew and fired so fast, I didn't even see it."

"Is that a fact?" Buck replied. He was as astonished as Rudy. Was this something he didn't know—didn't even suspect—about Flint? He looked back at him then. "He's dead, all right. Refused to be arrested, huh?"

"That's right," Flint answered. "Take a close look at him."

"I did," Buck said.

"Take another look," Flint insisted. "See anything familiar about him?" Buck took another look and shook his head. "That's Billy Crowe," Flint said.

"No!" Buck said and took another look. "Are you sure?"

"He said he was and said he had come back here to kill me because I killed his pa and his brothers," Flint said. They both stared down at the body, trying to recognize a resemblance. "I reckon if you cut the hair off short and shaved the whiskers and mustache, you might see it. It's been a long time since the last time we saw him."

Buck knelt down on one knee, unbuckled the cross-draw holster, and pulled it off of him. Then he jerked his shirt open, pulled the neck of his underwear back to expose the bare skin. "Yep, there it is, that big scar where Doc had to go in on top of that other wound. I reckon he's Billy Crowe, all right." He got back up on his feet and muttered, "I reckon I'll have to apologize to Ralph for snappin' at him when he came poundin' on my door." Then to Flint, he said, "I'll go get Walt and tell him he's got a couple of bodies to pick up."

While Buck went out the door, Flint spotted the remaining three Cloverleaf cowhands, so he walked over to talk to them. He addressed Jack Spade, since he was the oldest-looking of the three. "That was bad luck for your friend. Buck's gone to get the undertaker, but I thought I'd check with you fellows to see if you'd rather take your friend back to the ranch with you and bury him there." Jack looked at Charley and Andy, and none of the three seemed to have anything to say about it. So Flint suggested, "Or you can just let the undertaker bury him along with the other fellow."

Jack looked at the other two again, and all three of them nodded their heads. "I reckon that's as good as any," Jack said to Flint. "Lem ain't got no kin anywhere close around." Flint turned to walk away, but Jack stopped him. "Sheriff?" When Flint turned back around, Jack said, "We weren't causin' no problems. We were just settin' at a table, havin' a drink. That feller set ol' Lem up. He drew him into that poker game just so he could shoot him."

"I believe you," Flint said. "The more I think about it, the more I think he forced your friend into that fight to give me a reason to try to arrest him. It was me he was after. We had a run-in a couple of years ago, and he figured the time had come to make me pay up for it. I'm sorry he decided to pick one of you fellows to use as bait."

"I reckon there weren't nothin' you could do about that," Jack said. "I just wanted to let you know we weren't causin' no trouble."

"No problem," Flint told him. "Sorry about your friend. You can go over there and take any of his personal things— guns, money, whatever—and take 'em back to the ranch with you." He walked back to meet Buck and Walt coming in the door then. "You need to take care of both of 'em, Walt. You might find some money on the one lyin' over there." He pointed to Billy. "I'll let you settle with the council on how much you get to keep."

"You know I'll give 'em an honest count," Walt said.

"I know you will," Flint said and laughed. "That don't come under my responsibility."

"It was in the bar," Jake Rudolph said to Flint as he and Buck walked toward the door.

"What was in the bar?" Flint replied.

"The other bullet, Cash's other bullet. It put a hole in the front of my bar."

"Lucky nobody was standin' there," Flint replied.

Outside the saloon, Flint said, "Looks like I told Ralph to wake you up for nothing. I apologize for that, but I knew you'd be mad as hell with all that goin' on and I didn't wake you up."

"I wouldn't get mad at that," Buck said. "It was that

other thing I don't understand. When were you gonna tell me about that?"

"What other thing? Tell you about what?" Flint asked.

"As long as we've been workin' together; as many scrapes and close calls as we've had, you ain't never just casually mentioned you was a fast gun."

"I reckon it never occurred to me that I was," Flint replied, honestly. "The subject never came up, I suppose." He shrugged it off, as if it were unimportant. "I'm not sure I'd be considered a fast gun in the company of the real professionals."

"Here I was, worried about you gettin' tricked into a shoot-out with one of these shootists one day, and when this turkey, Cash Kelly, comes struttin' into town, I figured Dunellen had likely hired him to come after you. Did Ralph give you that telegram I got from Corporal Ron Black at the Ranger headquarters in Tyler?"

"No, Ralph didn't give me a telegram."

"I swear," Buck exclaimed. "I told him to make sure you saw it. I wired Black yesterday and asked him if they had any information about Cash Kelly. He answered my wire and said the Rangers had been notified of a face-on killin' by Kelly in a barroom in Delano, Kansas, and another one in the same saloon the next day. They were both ruled as duels. He wasn't ever tried for either one of them. So I know damn well Dunellen sent for that piece of trash, and you was his target. I just can't understand why he took a chance with you, instead of just shootin' you in the back."

"I know why," Flint said. "He made sure I knew. He wanted me to know that he was really Billy Crowe and he was fixin' to kill me for the deaths of his pa and brothers. Turns out, he didn't have any better sense than they had. He got away from jail here in Tinhorn. He shoulda just thanked his lucky stars drinkin' that whole bottle of laudanum didn't kill him and stayed away from Tinhorn." He paused, then added, "I don't think it'd be a good idea to talk about me bein' faster than he was. I think he just wasn't as fast as he thought he was. And I don't wanna find myself in that situation again."

"Well, you sure as hell ain't gonna catch me braggin' about it," Buck assured him. "And now I'm goin' back to bed. But I might have to take a little drink to settle my nerves and help me go back to sleep."

"I understand," Flint replied. "I might need one tonight myself."

The three cowhands from the Cloverleaf Cattle Company had also lost interest in remaining any longer in Tinhorn that night. There was no open hostility toward them by the other customers in the saloon. And the sheriff gave no indication that they were unwelcome; still, there was a feeling that they were in the wrong place at the wrong time. The fact that Lem Dixon was gunned down just minutes before contributed to the lack of interest in lingering in Tinhorn.

Jack Spade was the first to announce that he was ready to return to the ranch. He was quite a few years older than Charley and Andy, and the gunfights he had just witnessed were not the entertainment he had in mind when he rode into town. The two younger men could find no reason to stay longer as well, so they said they were ready to go. All three walked slowly past the body of Lem Dixon on their way out the door. Charley Tate paused for a moment to shake his head in wonder at Lem's demise. First Drew Price, now Lem Dixon gone. There was no one for Charley to idolize any longer. They climbed on their horses, Jack took the reins for Lem's horse, and they rode back out the south road. The biggest thing that puzzled them was why this fancy, card-playing shootist, who had visited Dunellen had picked a fight with one of his cowhands and killed him.

A truth they had all seen with their own eyes was the fact that the Tinhorn sheriff was quite adept at handling the Colt handgun he wore on his side. Jack couldn't help wondering what this latest loss of another man was going to cause when Ira Dunellen was told about it. He wondered if Dunellen might reinstate his offer of two hundred dollars for the assassination of Flint Moran, somehow holding Moran to blame for Lem's death. Like most of the other hands that he talked to, he wanted no part of it. He'd signed on to tend to cattle, just as they had. He didn't envy Lucas Sawyer's task of taking the report of Lem Dixon's demise to Dunellen. It was going to be hard to explain why the young fellow who visited overnight at the ranch house forced Lem into a gunfight.

CHAPTER 21

"You boys are back early," Lucas commented when they rode back into the ranch and found him sitting in front of the cookhouse, nursing a cup of coffee and talking to Gabby Skelton. "Don't tell me it didn't take any longer than that to spend your whole month's pay." Noticing the empty saddle on the horse Jack led, he asked, "What happened to Lem? Didn't he go in with you?"

"He got set up," Charley exclaimed at once, "suckered in by a professional gunfighter."

"He's dead, Lucas," Jack said then. "Charley's right. Lem let this feller draw him into a game of cards, and Lem started losin', so he called the feller a cheat. They stood up to face each other, and that feller shot him down." He paused to let that sink in before he delivered the surprise. "The feller that shot him was that slick-lookin' dude that spent the night here last night."

That captured Lucas's attention right away. "Are you sure?" he demanded. He got up from the nail keg he had been sitting on and walked over to stand beside Jack's horse. "You sure it's the same man?"

"Cash Kelly," Jack responded. "That's the name they was callin' him by. He was the same man who came out here." He went on to tell about the ensuing face-off between

Kelly and the sheriff when Flint attempted to arrest him. "It was just like he done with Lem," Jack said. "He flat-out told Moran he weren't goin' to no jail, and he finally forced the sheriff to stand up to him. He told Moran if he didn't go for his gun, he was gonna shoot him down. Well, Moran wouldn't draw on him, so he went ahead and drew on Moran. And you know what he found out? He found out that the sheriff was as much faster than him as he was faster than Lem. Nailed him dead center in his chest." He watched Lucas's face while the quiet man digested everything he had just learned. Finally, he asked, "What in hell are you gonna tell the boss?"

"Just what you just told me," Lucas said, "but I don't think I'll ruin his night with the news. I doubt very seriously that fellow was any kin of Mr. Dunellen's, so I don't see any concern about tellin' him tonight." He didn't express it, but it sounded to him like Dunellen must have hired a professional killer to get rid of Moran. And his honest feeling about the result of his contract with the killer was that Dunellen got what he deserved.

"Any coffee left in that pot?" Spade asked.

"There may be a little bit left," Gabby said. "Better git it 'cause I'm fixin' to rinse that pot out, soon as I finish drinkin' mine." He took the coffeepot from Jack after he drained the last swallow from his cup. He smacked his lips and declared, "I swear, that coffee's just gittin' right about now, and it's all gone. It's got just the right bite. I started it out this mornin' with a handful of last night's grounds 'cause they still had a little bite left in 'em. It turned out just right."

"I see whatchu mean," Jack said when he took a swallow of the coffee dregs, then spat out some grounds that came with it. "It's got plenty of bite, all right." When Gabby turned to set the pot on the step of the cookhouse, Jack poured the remainder of his coffee on the ground. He looked over at Lucas, who was grinning at him, and winked. No one was careless enough to complain to Gabby about any of the cooking. Gabby was one who never forgot or forgave an insult, especially about his cooking. "I expect I'd best take care of the horses and throw mine and Lem's saddle in the barn. Then I'm gonna turn in for the night."

"I won't be far behind you," Lucas said. "I'll tell Mr. Dunellen the bad news after breakfast in the mornin'."

"Come in, Lucas," Ira Dunellen invited when Atha showed his foreman to the door the following morning. "Atha, get Lucas a cup of coffee." Back to Lucas then, he asked, "You want a biscuit or something to eat with it?"

"Uh, no thank you, sir," Lucas replied. "I've already had my breakfast. I will take the coffee, though, Atha." *Maybe it'll help get the taste of Gabby's coffee out of my mouth*, he thought. He was aware of Dunellen's gracious mood this morning, as if he was expecting Lucas to bring him some welcome news. But Lucas knew the meeting was not going to go well.

"Well, I guess some more of the boys went into town last night," Dunellen started. "I can't blame them if they raised a little hell. We couldn't let them leave the herd until all of the cattle were moved to this part of the county. So I guess they had a hot time coming to them." He paused, giving Lucas an opening to jump in and tell him how the men took over the town. But Lucas just nodded and sipped his coffee until Dunellen became impatient with his lack of response and asked him outright, "Was there any trouble in town?"

"Yes, sir, some," Lucas answered. "We lost Lem Dixon last night."

Dunellen exploded at once. "Flint Moran! What did he do?"

"It weren't Flint Moran," Lucas said. "It was that fellow that came to see you here at the ranch yesterday. Cash Kelly, I think his name is. Him and Lem got into it over a card game, and Kelly shot Lem down."

Dunellen was rendered speechless for a long moment, thinking surely he had heard wrong. When he could speak, he sputtered almost incoherently at first. "Shot Lem Dixon? How did—? Why did he shoot Lem Dixon?"

"Lem accused him of cheatin'," Lucas said.

"What the hell was he doing playing cards with Dixon anyway?" Dunellen roared. "I sent him there to . . ." He caught himself before finishing his statement. "What happened after the shooting? Didn't the sheriff respond to it?"

"Oh, yes, sir, the sheriff responded all right," Lucas replied. "He tried to arrest Kelly, but Kelly challenged him to a gunfight. Said he weren't goin' to jail, so him and the sheriff went at it."

"And?" Dunellen pressed.

"And the sheriff cut him down," Lucas answered. "Jack Spade said Moran put a round in the center of Kelly's chest before he got his guns halfway out." Lucas was about to discuss the fact that they were going to have to hire some more men to replace those recently lost. But one look at Dunellen's face told him his boss was no longer hearing anything he said. The expression on his face was like that of a man just struck by lightning. Lucas hesitated for several moments then before asking, "Am I keepin' you from something important? Would it be better to talk about hirin' new men later?"

There was still a delay of a dozen seconds before Dunellen answered him. When he did, he spoke in a calm, steady voice that gave no sign of the fire raging inside him.

"Yes," he said, "we'll talk about that later." He got up from his chair, signaling that Lucas was dismissed.

Lucas wasted no time in leaving. Atha barely had time to get away from the study door before Lucas opened it. She slid down the hallway wall a few more feet before she whispered, "I was afraid you were gonna ruin his mood. He's been like a little kid on Christmas mornin'."

"Is that so?" Lucas replied, also whispering. "Why is that?"

"He was expectin' you to bring him some news he wanted to hear. He hired that Cash Kelly person to kill Flint Moran." By this time they had reached the kitchen, and instead of whispering, she was talking softly.

"He did?" Lucas responded, not altogether surprised to hear it but upset to hear how far Dunellen would go. "How do you know that?"

She fixed an impatient look on her face and answered, "How do you think?"

"Oh, right," he answered. "Well, his Christmas mornin' has just been blown to hell."

"Yeah, I heard," she said. "He's in there now, gittin' hisself all worked up, ready to explode. It won't be no trouble now to hear what he's thinkin', anywhere in the house. I reckon I'll be sweepin' up broken glass out of the fireplace this mornin'. When he's havin' one of his fits, he takes a drink and throws the glass at the fireplace."

Lucas had suspected as much, but he had never been certain before. Atha had never confessed so much until now. He wondered if the little old lady, who never seemed worried about anything, had finally witnessed enough to make her fear her employer. He knew that she and her husband were totally dependent upon their jobs at Cloverleaf Ranch. At their advanced ages, he doubted there were many places they could go if they were to lose employment here.

Lucas had never had any clue that Dunellen had ever abused the feisty little woman, but he felt the need to ask her now. "Atha, when Mr. Dunellen gets in one of these rages you're talkin' about, has he ever threatened you?"

"No, Lord, no," she replied. "He knows if he did, I'd take my big iron skillet and beat him to death with it." It occurred to her then that Lucas was sincerely concerned about her and Henry. She had recently felt that she, her husband, and Lucas were all three of a like mind. They suspected that they worked for the devil, so they tried not to do anything that would bring down his wrath upon them. "I appreciate your concern, Lucas, but you don't have to worry about me. Without me, Henry can't boil an egg, and without Henry, Mr. Dunellen would have to empty his own chamber pot. So he needs both of us."

"I guess you're right," Lucas said as he opened the back door and stepped outside.

"You've got enough to worry about," she said and closed the door behind him. When she went back into the kitchen, she found Dunellen standing in the doorway to the hall. "Are you ready for your breakfast now, Mr. Dunellen?"

"Yes," was all he said, then he turned around and went into the dining room, across the hall from the kitchen.

"I've got fresh coffee made. I'll bring you a cup to get you started. The biscuits are done, and I'll put a couple of eggs in the pan, and it won't take but a minute." She poured his coffee and took it into the dining room for him. She could tell by the intense frown on his face that he was on the verge of exploding, so she tried to talk him out of it, much like she used to talk to her son when he was just a tad and things weren't going to suit him. "Henry said it looks like the chickens are finally gittin' used to the new barn and they're startin' to lay. So I've got some nice ones to fry up for you this mornin'."

"They're not likely to get fried while you're standing in here telling me about it, are they?" Dunellen responded.

She tried to remain cheerful when she answered. "No, sir, I don't reckon they are. I'll get right on it." Her smile fixed firmly in place, she hurried back to the kitchen. *The damned old sourpuss, I ought to put gunpowder in his eggs*, she thought. As she promised, in just a few minutes she brought his breakfast in on a tray and placed it before him on the dining-room table. "You just call out when you want more coffee," she said, "and I'll be right in with it."

Am I going to have to go into that pitiful excuse for a town and blow that damn sheriff's brains out, myself? Eight hundred dollars can't buy a competent assassin? This is the man that Judge Franklyn Grant recommends when I ask for his endorsement? These questions continued to spin around and around in his brain until he clenched his fists so tightly that he drew blood with his fingernails. He looked down at the palms of his still-powerful hands as if he didn't know where the blood came from. Then he looked down at his plate and the two fried eggs, the yolks staring back at him, mocking him. He grabbed the plate and threw it against the wall. "I will not be denied!" he roared.

In the kitchen, Atha heard the crash of the plate and his roar of frustration. She waited for his call. It was a couple of minutes in coming as he fought to calm himself. "Atha, I dropped my plate."

Yeah, I heard it, she thought as she went at once to the dining room to discover most of his eggs stuck to the wall. Struggling now to maintain her cheerful calm, she commented, "My, you sure dropped your plate sideways. How did you do that?"

He hesitated, then said, "I shoulda said I accidentally

knocked it off. It doesn't matter how I did it, just clean it up." He stood, glaring at her. "Maybe you think I oughta clean it up myself. It seems like anything else I pay to have done never *gets* done."

She had to bite her lip to keep from saying what she wanted to tell him to do with the mess he'd made on the wall. Instead, she asked, "Do you want me to fry some more eggs for you first?"

"Damnit! Did I say I wanted eggs?" he spat back at her. "Where's Henry?"

"I think he just came in the back door," she said, having heard the door open and close in the kitchen.

"Get him in here," Dunellen ordered.

"Yes, sir," she responded and went to the kitchen at once. When she saw her husband about to pour a cup of coffee for himself, she stopped him. "Go in the dinin' room. Mr. Dunellen wants to see you. And be careful what you say. He's actin' like he's lost his mind."

That wasn't news Henry wanted to hear, so he put down his cup and went at once. "You wanted to see me, Mr. Dunellen?"

"Go down to the barn and tell somebody to saddle my horse," Dunellen ordered. "And tell them I said right now. The money I'm paying those no-good saddle tramps ought to get me better service."

"Yes, sir," Henry replied. "I'll tell 'em." He hustled back out of the room. When he went through the kitchen, he whispered to Atha, "He wants his horse saddled. Where's he going?"

"Hell, I don't know. Just go do what he says. He ain't said nothin' about goin' anywhere this mornin'." She walked to the door with him and closed it behind him. Then she went back to the dining room, but Dunellen was gone. She walked out into the hall to listen, and in a few seconds, she heard him bumping around in his bedroom. *Maybe he'll go to his study*, she thought and decided she'd best get a bucket of water and some rags and see if she could clean his breakfast off the dining-room wall. *It ain't like I ain't got nothin' to do*, she thought.

Henry saw Andy Hatcher coming out of the barn, so he told him that Dunellen wanted his horse saddled. That being an unusual request from Dunellen, Andy thought it best to relay the order to Lucas Sawyer. They found Lucas in the back of the stable. "Where's he goin'?" Lucas asked. Andy shrugged and looked at Henry, who also shrugged. "I just talked to him this mornin'," Lucas said. "He didn't say anything about goin' anywhere."

"Should I saddle his horse?" Andy asked.

"Of course," Lucas replied, "if that's what he said."

"That's what he said," Henry insisted. "But to tell you the truth, he's actin' kinda crazy this mornin'," he told Lucas when Andy hurried off to saddle Dunellen's horse. He told him then about Dunellen throwing his breakfast against the dining-room wall. It was enough to cause Lucas great concern. After Atha had confirmed Dunellen's attempt to assassinate Flint Moran, Lucas was afraid he might be planning to take matters into his own hands. Just as a precaution, he decided to saddle his own horse, so he could keep an eye on his boss and maybe keep him out of trouble.

Lucas led his horse out of the corral and saddled him, but he left the horse there by the barn when Andy led Dunellen's Morgan gelding out of the barn. "I'll take him up to the house," Lucas said and took the reins from Andy.

Up at the house, Atha was startled when Dunellen suddenly appeared in the dining room, where she was busy cleaning the wall. She had hoped he would go to his study, which was his usual routine, and forget about his request for his horse. But he was dressed in his riding clothes. "Is my horse ready?" he asked.

"I'll go see," she said and dropped her rag in the bucket. Then she hurried through the kitchen to the back door. "Here comes Lucas with your horse right now," she called back to him. So he came through the kitchen and went out on the back steps.

"Here's your horse, sir. Where you headin'?" Lucas asked, noticing that his boss was wearing his gunbelt.

"I'm gonna take a little ride," Dunellen answered.

"You want me to get my horse and ride along with you?"

Dunellen didn't answer right away. Instead, he studied Lucas with a steady gaze for a few moments. Then he said, "No, I want you to stay here and look after the ranch. That's what you're good at, looking after the ranch."

"Yes, sir," Lucas said and held the Morgan still while Dunellen mounted. Then he handed him the reins and stepped back while Dunellen wheeled the horse away from the kitchen steps and rode across the front yard at a lope, heading for the main gate. Lucas and Atha watched him go through the gate before Lucas said, "He's goin' into town. I'd better follow him and try to keep him out of trouble." He ran back to get his horse. In the saddle, he waited to let Dunellen get a good lead on him. He didn't want to take the chance that his boss would discover he was being followed.

To Lucas's knowledge, Dunellen had never ridden into Tinhorn, never having wanted to have anything to do with the town. But there was an established trail now from the Cloverleaf gate to the south end of town. It was an easy trail to follow, and it appeared that Tinhorn was where Dunellen was going. So Lucas stayed well back of him, only closing the distance once in a while until catching sight of him, then dropping back again. When he passed by the sawmill, he increased the pace until he was now close enough to keep his eyes on Dunellen. The town was not busy, but Lucas decided it was unlikely Dunellen would notice him following. Had he known the state of mind Dunellen was in, he probably would have figured his boss could have looked right at him and not realized who he was.

Dunellen rode past the saloon, then, seeing the sheriff's office and jail diagonally across the street from it, pointed his horse straight to the sheriff's office. Lucas, in a near panic because he was not close enough to prevent him from going in, could only ride up beside the jail and wait.

Inside the office, Ralph looked up from the desk when Dunellen walked in. With no idea who the man was, Ralph asked, "Can I help you?"

"I want to see the sheriff," Dunellen stated simply. "Is he in the back?"

"Ah, no, sir," Ralph answered. "Sheriff Moran ain't here right now."

"Where is he?" Dunellen asked.

"I ain't sure. He was just makin' his rounds. I think he might be in Jake's Place. Last time I looked out the door, I saw him headed that way." When the stranger looked confused, Ralph said, "The saloon across the street."

Without another word, Dunellen turned and walked back out the door. With one thing in mind, he headed straight for the saloon, taking no notice of Lucas standing at the corner of the building.

Up the street, Buck interrupted his conversation with John Harper in front of his store when he happened to catch sight of Ira Dunellen leaving the sheriff's office and heading to Jake's Place. Knowing something had to be wrong for that man to be in town, Buck said, "I gotta go!" He left Harper in midsentence and started running toward the saloon.

Inside the saloon, Flint was standing at the far end of the

bar, talking to Jake Rudolph, his back to the front door. Jake paid little attention to the stranger who walked in, then stood scanning the customers until his gaze stopped on Flint. Then, when he headed straight for them, Jake started to alert Flint that a stranger was charging at them. But suddenly the stranger pulled a Colt .45 Peacemaker from his holster and aimed it at the back of Flint's head. "Flint!" Jake cried out. Flint started to turn, but before he could, the noisy saloon was shocked by the sudden pop of a .44 six-gun, followed almost immediately by the snap of a .45. Able to react then, Flint turned around to see Ira Dunellen double up and drop to the floor, his pistol dropping from his hand. About ten feet behind him, Lucas Sawyer stood, his six-gun still extended toward the fallen man.

The eerie quiet that suddenly descended upon the noisy barroom was broken then by the commanding voice of Buck Jackson. "Drop it, Lucas, or you'll get the next one." Seeming not to care, Lucas put his weapon back in his holster instead. "Flint, you all right?" Buck asked, confused by Lucas's lack of response.

Flint was not quite sure what had just taken place, but Jake was. He had witnessed the whole scene and before Flint could answer, he interrupted. "Buck, you've got no call to arrest Lucas. He just saved Flint's life. I don't know who that fellow is, but he was fixin' to shoot Flint in the back of the head, but Lucas shot him before he could get his shot off." Several voices in the handful of spectators called out to back Jake's version of the incident.

"Well, I'll be . . ." Buck started, then asked, "Is that true, Lucas?"

Lucas, still in a mild case of shock due to what he had just done, could not put words together to defend his actions. He just stood there, shaking his head in disbelief. When words finally came, he had great difficulty putting a statement together. "I never thought—I mean, I couldn't let him—I didn't think he'd go that far—I just wanted to keep him from gettin' into trouble." He looked straight at Flint then. "When I saw him aimin' that gun at you, I thought I would try to stop him. But when I saw him cock it, I knew I couldn't get to him in time. I couldn't let him pull the trigger. So I shot him." There followed another eerie silence. Then he said, "If I'm under arrest, I'll go peacefully."

"Under arrest?" Buck exclaimed. "Hell, I say we give you a medal for savin' Flint's life." His suggestion was greeted with a roar of approval from everyone in the saloon.

Flint could see that although he had the crowd's approval, Lucas was not at all at peace with himself for what he had just done. He guessed Lucas was heavily burdened with the thought that he had killed the man who hired him as his foreman and paid his wages and therefore expected his loyalty. All the spectators had gathered around the body lying in front of the bar. Most of them had heard about Ira Dunellen, the man whose cattle were wandering the streets of Tinhorn. But none of them had ever seen him.

While that was going on, Flint pulled Lucas aside to talk to him. "First off, I wanna thank you for savin' my life," he said. "Then I want you to know that I know what a hard thing that was for you to do. I'm guessin' that Mr. Dunellen must have been a little out of his mind, and I reckon I'm to blame for a lot of it. But it still don't make what he was fixin' to do excusable. You realized that, and bein' an honest man, you did what you figured was the right thing to do. You damn sure earned my respect in addition to my thanks. But I think you'll find you earned the respect of a helluva lot of people in Tinhorn."

"I don't know, Sheriff," Lucas replied. "I think it got to be too much for Mr. Dunellen to keep straight in his head. But nobody at the ranch knew he was gettin' this crazy until this mornin', when I had to tell him about that thing last night with Lem Dixon and Cash Kelly." He paused then before saying, "And I don't know whether it makes any difference to you or not, but we didn't know anything about him hirin' Cash Kelly till this mornin' either."

"I believe you, Lucas, so don't worry about any trouble from Tinhorn law about your part in the shooting. You've got plenty of witnesses that will testify that you shot to save my life. I'm hopin' that maybe Tinhorn and Cloverleaf can work together from now on. I'd never given it any thought, but is there anyone else involved with Cloverleaf ownership?"

"No," Lucas said. "It was all the property of Ira Dunellen. He was awful proud of that."

"Then I reckon that makes you the man in charge now, doesn't it?"

Lucas hesitated. That thought had never crossed his mind. "Well, I reckon I am the man in charge after Mr. Dunellen. I haven't ever thought about running the whole show before."

"Well, maybe you'd best start thinkin' about it, because somebody's gonna have to hold that operation together. It's too big to let it come to pieces." He looked over at Rudy behind the bar. "Rudy, I think we need a drink of likker."

"I think I need one, for sure," Lucas declared.

"Me, too," Buck said and walked up to join them.

CHAPTER 22

"You know, I just thought of something that had completely slipped my mind," Lucas declared after a second drink. "I don't know if it'll come up or not, but I shoulda thought of it sooner."

"What's that, Lucas?" Flint asked.

"What I said about Dunellen being so proud about the fact that he was the sole owner of Cloverleaf Cattle Company," Lucas began. "I don't know anything about the laws of ownership of an outfit, but maybe he just had sole ownership of the name of the company. I ain't sure he owns the cattle, because he had a partner when we started out down near Houston. As a matter of fact, his partner was the one who owned the cattle when they got started. Dunellen didn't own a cow. Come to think of it, he was Dunellen's cousin, fellow by the name of Conan Daugherty. He was a younger man than Dunellen, a right nice young fellow at that. Not at all like his cousin. But the night before we started drivin' that herd north, Dunellen and Conan—we always called him by his first name—rode home to Conan's house to eat supper. Dunellen came back to camp the next mornin' without Conan. Said his horse threw him and he broke his neck. A couple of us thought that was kinda strange, but we didn't say nothing about it. It didn't seem to bother Dunellen that his cousin suddenly got killed. He never said another word about it. Conan had a wife and two young'uns. Dunellen never said anything about them either, whether there was anybody to take care of them or not."

"I see what you're gettin' at," Flint said. "Conan's wife might legally be Dunellen's partner, not to mention the fact that her sons are his heirs."

"What did you say Conan's last name was?" Buck asked.

"Daugherty," Lucas answered.

"Ain't that the name of Louis Wheeler's daughter?" Buck asked Flint.

"It sure as hell is," Flint replied. "And Louis said her husband was killed when his horse threw him, and he broke his neck. I talked to Louis on Saturday. With his daughter just recently widowed, she and her two little boys have come to live with him in Tinhorn."

"Is her name Arleen?" Lucas asked.

"As a matter of fact," Flint said and grinned. "Helluva coincidence, ain't it?"

Flint knew that Lucas was not at all certain of his position, even though he was clearly the next in charge after Ira Dunellen. There had never been any evidence of any official partnership in Cloverleaf. Dunellen had always claimed sole ownership of the ranch and the cattle. And Lucas knew that Dunellen had a great deal of money somewhere, and that was where the payroll came from. Possibly that was from the sale of last year's cattle. Lucas wasn't sure, and he admitted that he had never given any thought to Dunellen's fortune. His responsibility had been over the crew of cowhands, so he knew where all the cattle had come from. He had directed the roundup of hundreds of cows that roamed the Texas plains, as well as commanding the raids to rustle Mexican cattle. He knew how to operate the ranch, but he needed help as far as the legality of his taking over. After another drink, he asked Flint for his help.

"I know you ain't had any time to think about this," Flint asked, "but what are you plannin' on doin'? Are you thinkin' about steppin' in and replacin' Dunellen, and things just continue like they have been?"

Lucas thought about that for a moment, then answered. "No, I don't think that would be right, especially since I shot him."

"Harvey Baxter could probably give you some guidance," Flint said. "Before we talk to Harvey, though, maybe we oughta go talk to Louis's daughter to make sure Dunellen didn't buy her husband's half of the partnership."

Lucas nodded thoughtfully, then said, "That sounds like a real good idea to me. I'd like to do more business in Tinhorn. I never have thought it was a good idea to drive wagons all the way to Tyler for supplies when Tinhorn ain't but six miles away." He paused to think about the possibility of a working friendship between the ranch and the town, where his cowhands would be welcome. "Right now, I reckon I'd best take Mr. Dunellen's body back to the ranch and explain what happened to the whole crew. We need to bury him out there somewhere. It's gonna be kinda hard tellin' 'em that I'm the one who shot him. They might not believe it happened like I said it did."

"Would you like it if I rode out there with you?" Flint volunteered. "I could tell them exactly what happened."

"I would really appreciate it if you did that, Sheriff," Lucas replied.

"No trouble a-tall. I'd be glad to do it. And I told you to call me Flint. I got a feelin' we're gonna turn out to be friends."

* * *

They arrived at the Cloverleaf ranch house just as Gabby Skelton banged his iron triangle, signaling the noontime meal was ready. Those cowhands lining up to fill a plate were distracted by the sight of the two riders approaching, one of them leading a dark horse with what appeared to be a body lying across the saddle. Not a word was said as all eyes were trained on the riders until they were closer. Then Gabby broke the silence. "It's Lucas, and that's Mr. Dunellen's horse he's leadin'." No one wanted to ask the obvious question about whose body Lucas might be leading.

"Who's the other feller?" Bob Skinner asked.

"That's Sheriff Moran," Tim Walker answered him, he with the younger eyes. That was enough to break the near silence, for there was only one apparent answer to their question. By now, they all knew that Ira Dunellen had ridden into Tinhorn. For what purpose no one of them knew, but it was easy to guess that it was of a serious nature to cause him to go to town. It was the natural reaction to assume that Dunellen had accosted Moran and the sheriff shot him. When the riders rode into the barnyard, the line at the cookhouse broke apart as the men walked out to meet them.

As they gathered around the three horses, gawking at the eerie form of Ira Dunellen lying across his saddle, Lucas spoke out. "Before any of you jump to the wrong conclusion, I wanna tell you that Flint Moran did not shoot Mr. Dunellen. In fact, he was meant to be Dunellen's victim. And Mr. Dunellen was shot down as he was aiming his pistol at Sheriff Moran's back."

"Who shot him?" Andy Hatcher asked.

"I did," Lucas answered. There was an instant silence that lasted until Lucas spoke again. "I tried to get to him to stop him, but I couldn't get there in time. I had no choice.

I couldn't let him pull the trigger and murder the sheriff. So I shot him." No one voiced any outrage, or cries of anger. They were all locked in a state of shock, unable to believe Dunellen could be killed.

Flint spoke to them then. "I came out here with Lucas to testify to you men that your foreman was faced with a decision between right and wrong. Being the man he is, he chose right when he found Dunellen about to shoot an unsuspecting victim in the back. Naturally, I'm grateful that he stepped in when he did, since I was the intended target, but I think he would have prevented the outright murder no matter who the victim was."

"Are you plannin' to arrest Lucas for shootin' him?" Jack Spade asked.

"Of course not," Flint answered. "The man stopped a murderer. I just came out here with Lucas to make sure you men got the facts of the shootin'. When you come to town again, ask anybody who was in the saloon this mornin' when it happened. They'll tell you the same as I just told you." He paused then, waiting for the uproar of protest from men loyal to their employer and benefactor. It didn't come. Instead, there was a general air of disbelief as they looked at one another in amazement.

Then one voice, and then another, asked the obvious question. "Now what's gonna happen to us?"

Since the questions were directed at Flint, he answered by directing their questions to Lucas. "As far as your daily operation, nothing has changed. Lucas is still your foreman. He'll still call the shots. You're still gonna take care of the cattle. And in case you're wonderin' about your pay, I think he should tell you that."

"One of the reasons I asked him to come with me is because I've got to go search the house for Mr. Dunellen's money," Lucas said. "He made payroll every month, so he's got money somewhere. I intend to make sure we all get paid the same as we always have."

Gabby interrupted at that point. "Well, why don't we finish talkin' about this while we eat. This food's just gonna get cold if we don't eat it."

"Hadn't we oughta do somethin' with Mr. Dunellen's body first?" Andy Hatcher asked.

"Hell, he ain't goin' nowhere," Bob Skinner answered him. "It'll give him a chance to see what it's like to eat with the men who do the work around here."

They quickly formed another line, and Gabby started dishin' out the chuck. "Grab you a plate there, Sheriff," he said. "There's plenty for everybody."

"I don't mind if I do," Flint responded and got in line. He couldn't help noticing that it seemed more a meal of celebration than one of mourning. Lucas continued the discussion while they ate, trying to give the men his plans for the continuation of the ranch operation. It was quite interesting to Flint to witness the reaction of the cowhands when the subject of Arleen Daugherty was broached. He got a feeling of general sympathy for Conan's widow and even heard a couple of remarks about the suspicious death of Dunellen's partner.

After they finished eating, Lucas announced that he and Flint were going up to the house to give the news to Atha and Henry. "I expect we'd best dig a grave before we wait much longer," Lucas said. "Any volunteers?"

"I'll volunteer," Charley Tate replied. "I'll dig Mr. Dunellen's grave." Flint had noticed that Charley had said nothing to this point and had maintained an expression close to anger.

"Thank you, Charley," Lucas said. "But Charley's gonna need some help, so we'll all take a turn at it, till we get it dug."

"We'll get it done," Andy declared. "Where do you wanna plant him?"

"I don't know," Lucas answered, "just somewhere out of the way, I reckon."

"Don't bury him anywhere near the bunkhouse," Bob Skinner spoke up. "I don't wanna wake up in the middle of the night and see his ghost lookin' at me."

Lucas and Flint left Dunellen's body and horse in the hands of the men and proceeded toward the house. For once, Lucas didn't knock, then stand at the kitchen door and wait for Atha to open it. This time, he simply walked in the kitchen door and called out for Atha. "We're in the dining room," she answered his call. Lucas led Flint through the kitchen and into the dining room across the hall. He was amazed to find Atha and Henry sitting at the table eating dinner. It was something that would never happen when Dunellen was at home. She and her husband always ate in the kitchen. He was about to say as much, but Atha spoke first. "I've got eyes," she said, which was explanation enough. "And this'll be Sheriff Flint Moran, I reckon. Never got the chance to meet you in person. Peeped through the window at you when you came with the mayor and that other feller, though. That ain't to say I ain't heard your name mentioned a thousand times, and none of it complimentary." She directed her next comment to Lucas. "I saw you and the sheriff ate with the men, but I've got plenty of food cooked, if you're still hungry."

"Not for me," Lucas said. "How 'bout you, Flint?" Flint shook his head. "I reckon you'd like to know who shot Dunellen."

"I figure the sheriff did," Atha replied at once, "and now he's brought you out here to get all of Dunellen's money." Flint couldn't suppress a smile as the feisty little woman gave him an accusing stare.

"Well, you figured wrong," Lucas told her. "I'm the one who shot Dunellen." He went on to tell her and Henry the way it all happened.

The next topic of discussion was the question of whether or not Arleen Daugherty was legally Dunellen's partner. "I wasn't hired on until after all that happened with Dunellen's partner," Atha said. "But after workin' for that man a while, I wouldn't be surprised if that ol' devil didn't have something to do with his partner's accident." She looked at Lucas for help. "Fell off his horse or something."

"Dunellen told us Conan's horse threw him and he broke his neck," Lucas said. "Left his wife a widow with two little young'uns."

"And without a penny, I'd suspect," Atha commented.

"I wouldn't be surprised," Lucas said. "He never said anything about buying Conan's share or payin' him for his half."

"That poor woman deserves something for what that devil did to her," Atha declared.

When Atha had finished her dinner, she took them into the study, where Dunellen kept his private books and a small safe. "You any good at keepin' books, Lucas?" Atha asked.

"Not much," he answered. "I can read and write, but that's about it."

"I can help you there, if you need it," she said. "I used to go over his books once in a while when he was gonna be gone for a while." She chuckled. "Just to make sure he was gonna have enough money to make my and Henry's pay." She cocked a suspicious eye in Lucas's direction. "What are you gonna do with all that money?"

"The same thing he was doing with it," Lucas answered, "run this ranch."

"Well, I reckon in that case, you'll wanna see the big

safe he's got hidden under his bed, won't you?" Atha asked with a wide smile. She motioned for them to follow her.

"I reckon you could call it hidden," Lucas said. "But I built this house, and me and about four of the men built the shelf it's settin' on under the floor. Bob Skinner and two of the other men helped me lower that big safe through the floor the day it came from Tyler."

"Too bad he didn't give you the combination to the blame safe," Atha said. "'Cause it's gonna be a tough nut to crack."

"I kept the combination we put in it while we were installin' it. We used it to lock it, then make sure it would open again. I was afraid I wouldn't remember it the next day when we finished, so I wrote it down on a little scrap of paper, folded it up, and put it in my wallet." He reached into his vest pocket and pulled out a thin leather wallet. "There it is," he said. "You reckon he ever put a new combination in that lock? He said he was goin' to." He dialed the combination he had written on the scrap of paper and tried the handle. It opened. "Well, I'll be damned. He never put a different combination on it."

"Well, put it back in your wallet," Atha said. "You're the one in charge now." She crowded in a little closer to get a better look at the contents. "I never thought there was that much money in the whole world," she gasped.

Flint was inspired to say, "Maybe you might wanna think about openin' an account at the bank, so you can sleep at night."

"Looks like I don't have to worry about the payroll for another year." Lucas was figuring out loud. "And then, if we get a decent price for the cattle, that'll cover us for another year and, hopefully, afford us a bonus, too."

"I believe you folks can run a successful cattle business,"

Flint said. "I reckon I'd best get on back to town and make sure there ain't no stray cows botherin' the storekeepers."

"I promise you, Flint, I'll fix your stray problem," Lucas said. "I wanna come into town right away and talk to Arleen Daugherty, too. Nothing should be done before that."

"Anytime you're ready," Flint told him. "Henry, Atha, it was good to meet you folks on a little friendlier ground. I'll get outta your way now. I know you've got a funeral to attend."

His comment drew a loud, "Ha," from Atha and a snort from Henry as he made his way out of the house. He stepped up into the saddle and turned Buster toward the gate. Off to his right, he saw the burial detail about fifty yards from the barn. They appeared to be working two at a time in the grave.

At the gravesite, someone commented, "There goes the sheriff."

"He's a good man," Tim Walker saw fit to say.

"He's a son of a bitch" was a comment that followed immediately after, and everyone turned to look at the snarling face of Charley Tate. "What are you gawkin' at me for? You know he's the cause of all the trouble. Lucas said he shot Mr. Dunellen, but it was Moran that killed him."

"Moran didn't shoot Dunellen," Jack said.

"Maybe not, but he went after Mr. Dunellen so bad that he drove him crazy enough to go after him. That's the same as shootin' him."

"That's one way of lookin' at it," Jack allowed. "It's a crazy way, but it's a way."

"You callin' me crazy?" Charley demanded.

"No, I'm just callin' a spade a spade. That's why they named me Jack Spade." His answer drew a laugh from the others waiting their turn with a shovel or pick.

"You think you're so damn funny. Let's see how funny

you are with a gun in your hand. I'll face you right now and we'll see who's crazy."

Realizing he had let the japing of Charley get out of hand, Jack retreated. "Take it ease, Charley, I was just pickin' at you a little bit. I'm not gonna fight you. Ain't none of us gunslingers, so we ain't gonna be killin' each other. I'm sorry if I riled you. I was just funnin' around with you." Some of the other men witnessing the little spat realized that Charley might be wound a little too tight with Dunellen getting killed. They recognized him as a simple soul who picked gunfighters as his heroes. The high point of his life was being able to tag along behind Drew Price. And when Drew was shot down, Lem Dixon was the closest Charley could find to idolize. And then Lem was shot down, leaving Charley like a lost orphan. And his simple mind just naturally laid all the blame on Flint Moran.

The digging of Ira Dunellen's final resting place was a swift and somewhat casual endeavor on the part of his crew of cowhands. The grave was plenty deep, and there was an attempt to lower his body gently into it. But the two men lowering him could not reach the bottom of the grave, so they lowered him as far as they could reach, then dropped him. Before they filled the grave, Bob Skinner asked if anyone wanted to say a few words before they covered him up. No one did. He thought some sort of eulogy should be offered, so he made an attempt. "We never saw much of you, but the pay was good. That'll do it." He signaled for the dirt to be filled in.

CHAPTER 23

Flint couldn't say if it was just his imagination or not, but there seemed to be a more peaceful feeling in the town when he guided Buster toward Lon Blake's stable. Seeing him approach, Lon walked out to meet him. "Well, I see you got back all right," Lon said in greeting.

"Why wouldn't I?" Flint replied.

Lon shrugged. "Well, you know, ridin' out to Cloverleaf with the owner's dead body. That mighta been a little risky when you think about it. Weren't no doubt he came into town to kill you. Mighta been some of his men woulda tried to finish the job for him."

"You'd be surprised," Flint told him. "I think you're gonna find out that Tinhorn has a much better relationship with Cloverleaf now that Dunellen's gone." Preferring not to go over everything that happened, since he was going to have to go over it with Buck as soon as he got to the jail, he cut it short. "You ain't gonna be seein' so many stray cows in the street."

As he expected, he found Buck and Ralph anxiously waiting to hear what happened when he and Lucas showed up at the ranch with Dunellen's body. So he took them through the whole meeting with the cowhands and the couple who took care of the house. "Sounds like they might make a go of it," Buck commented. "Lucas is a good man,'cause most likely he coulda just took over for Dunellen and got away with it. Are you gonna go talk to Louis Wheeler's daughter?"

"I'm gonna wait till Lucas comes in to see her," Flint said. "He said he'll most likely come in tomorrow to do that, and I said I'd go with him."

"What about the damn stray cows?" Buck asked. "Is he gonna take care of that?"

"He said there wasn't anything you could do about that. Cows are just gonna stray. . . ." Flint didn't get any further than that before he saw Buck working up into a rant. "I'm just japin' ya. He said he would move the main herd south of the creek that runs by the ranch, and that oughta take care of the problem."

Buck laughed with him, but warned him, "You better watch how you jape with a man my age. I might go Dunellen on you." His warning confused Ralph, so Flint explained that Buck meant he might go crazy.

"Good morning, gentlemen," Clara Rakestraw welcomed Flint and Buck when she opened the door for them.

"Gentlemen?" Buck repeated, then both he and Flint stepped to the side, as if they thought there was someone coming in behind them.

She laughed at their antics and replied, "My mistake, I thought you were someone else. Come on in. We'll feed you anyway." Flint couldn't help thinking that everybody seemed to be in a joking mood since the demise of Ira Dunellen. He saw Mindy then, ready with two freshly poured cups of coffee, and that was a sight that never failed to improve his morning.

"You fellows are bright and early this morning," Mindy said. "Something important going on?"

"We're early," Buck answered her right-away. "I don't know about the bright part of it."

Answering her question, Flint said, "Lucas Sawyer is comin' in this mornin', and he and I are going to talk to Arleen Daugherty, Louis Wheeler's daughter. Her husband was Dunellen's partner."

"We've met her," Mindy said. "Mr. Wheeler brought her and her two little boys in here for supper the day they arrived in Tinhorn. She's so young to be a widow."

"Yes, she is," Flint agreed, "and it's a doggone shame the way she became one."

"She's a pretty young lady," Mindy said.

"I suppose so. I've only seen her on the street a time or two."

"She's very attractive," Mindy commented. "Even with two young children, she won't stay single very long."

"I reckon not," Flint replied. "There's plenty of single men lookin' for a wife."

"I believe we've got that all figured out," Buck interrupted. "Now, let's get started on some breakfast."

Mindy went at once to the kitchen. When she walked in, she met Bonnie coming out with two breakfast plates. "Here," she said and handed Mindy the plates. "Do you think you got Flint interested in Arleen Daugherty?"

"What are you talking about, Bonnie?"

"Couldn't help hearing your sales talk on the woman— she's so pretty, she's so attractive. If he hasn't noticed her before, he's sure to take a closer look at her now." Bonnie turned her eyes up toward the ceiling and shook her head.

"Sometimes I hate you, Bonnie," Mindy said as she spun around toward the dining room. "Thanks for filling their plates."

They didn't linger long over their breakfast, since Flint wanted to be available whenever Lucas showed up. Mindy walked them to the door and asked Flint if he would be back at dinnertime. "Far as I know," he told her. "I'll see you then."

"Be careful," she said as he went out the door. It struck him as kind of odd that she would say that. She never said that before. *More like something your mother would tell you*, he thought.

Their timing turned out to be perfect, for they saw Lucas riding past the stable when they got to the office door. Buck took Ralph's breakfast inside to him while Flint waited on the steps. "Mornin', Flint," Lucas greeted him when he pulled up in front of the jail.

"Mornin', Lucas. It ain't far to Wheeler's house, but it'll be quicker on a horse, so I'll go get mine. You need a cup of coffee? I'm sure Ralph's got a pot goin'."

"No, thanks," Lucas said. "I'll just go along with you." He walked his horse along beside Flint as he made his way to the stable. It was just a matter of a few minutes before Flint was in the saddle and they were on their way down the little street beside the hotel.

Flint had ridden by Louis Wheeler's house before, but he had never paid a lot of attention to it. This morning, when he and Lucas pulled their horses up to the front porch, he was struck by the smallness of the house. As he and Lucas dismounted, a little boy appeared in the open front doorway. He watched them for a few seconds before yelling, "Ma!"

They heard her answer in the back part of the house, "What is it, Angus?"

"Somebody here," Angus answered.

In a couple of minutes, Arleen appeared in the doorway. She placed her hands on Angus's shoulders and said,

"If you're looking for my father, he's at the post office. Sheriff," she added when she saw Flint's badge. But her curiosity was drawn to the other rider. She thought she might have seen him somewhere before, but she couldn't place him.

"Mornin', ma'am," Flint said. "Actually, it's you we came to see. I told your father we wanted to talk to you, and he said it was all right to come by the house. Is this a good time for you?"

"Well, yes, it's as good a time as any, I guess. What is it you want?"

Before he answered her, Flint looked at Lucas and he nodded, so he knew she was who they thought she was. "Just wanna talk to you about your husband, and his partnership with Ira Dunellen."

"I don't want anything to do with Ira Dunellen," she said at once. "So I expect we have nothing to talk about. If I had known he was anywhere near this town, I would not have come here."

"Please bear with me, ma'am," Flint said. "Maybe you ain't heard yet, but Ira Dunellen is dead. He was shot by this man right here."

It suddenly came to her where she had seen Lucas before and she pointed her finger at him. "He works for Dunellen. He came to my house one night to bring my husband a message from Ira, Conan said his name was Lucas."

"That's right, ma'am," Flint said. "And I understand your husband entered into a partnership with Dunellen. Is that right?"

"Ha!" Arleen spat. "Some partnership! We owned the cows they started the business with. I should say, Dunellen started the business with. He never gave us a penny for the cows, or anything else. He just took whatever he wanted. Then he wanted to move all the cattle they had stolen, and my husband didn't want to leave our home. The day he was gonna tell Dunellen he wanted to quit the partnership and let him take half of everything and just leave us be was the day Ira Dunellen brought my husband home lying across the saddle of his horse. He said Conan's horse threw him and broke his neck, and the only marks on Conan were the bruises around his neck where he had been strangled. Ira Dunellen killed my husband."

"But he surely arranged some payment for you to buy out your share of the partnership," Flint suggested. "Some kind of deal to compensate you for your loss."

"The only deal he offered me was to come with him as his concubine, forcing me to flee in the middle of the night with my two children," she fumed. "Now I think we have discussed the situation you asked about."

"Yes, ma'am, I think we have." He looked at Lucas then and asked, "You heard enough to satisfy you?"

"Indeed, I have," Lucas replied, and took over the interview. "Mrs. Daugherty, I came to see you today to see if we couldn't make up for some of your loss. I'm sorry I can't do anything to bring your husband back. But I can try to make some things right since Dunellen is dead." He looked at Flint then and declared, "I'm thinkin' for sure that she's the new owner, since she was Dunellen's partner's wife."

She was shocked. She didn't know what to think, or what to say, so she just looked at Flint and exclaimed, "Sheriff?"

"He's tellin' you the truth, ma'am," Flint told her.

"I know nothing about running a cattle ranch!" she exclaimed.

"Don't worry," Lucas told her. "You have some good folks at the ranch that do know how to run one."

"Oh my Lord," she gasped, unable to believe it. She took hold of the doorframe when she felt her knees about to fail her. "I need to sit down. Please come in. I'll make you some coffee or something. Please forgive my rudeness. Come in." She turned and went inside, afraid she was going to fall down if she didn't find a chair right away.

Flint and Lucas dismounted and dropped their reins, then followed her inside. They found her sitting in the one stuffed chair in the tiny parlor. "Just give me a minute to catch my breath and I'll put on a pot of coffee," she said. "I declare, I don't know what's wrong with me."

"You just sit there," Flint said. "I'll make the coffee." He went into the kitchen and spotted the coffeepot on the table. There was a fire going in the kitchen stove, so the whole kitchen was like an oven due to its small size. It occurred to him that the house was closer to a dollhouse than a real one. He couldn't spot the pump, so he walked out the back door to a tiny porch and found it. He dumped out the cold coffee and the grounds and filled the pot with fresh water. As he pumped, he was thinking it wouldn't be many more weeks before she'd have to get the water she needed inside every day before the pump froze.

He looked around the packed cupboard until he found the coffee beans and the grinder. In a short time he had the pot on the stove, so he went in the parlor to report on his progress. She noticed that he took a second look at the two makeshift beds in the crowded little parlor, so she apologized for the smallness of the house. "It's not my father's fault. All he needed was a place for him and my brother, Jimmy, to sleep. He didn't know I was gonna move in on him with two more kids. Papa's been talking about building another house or building onto this one, but I don't think he can afford it anytime soon."

Flint got back up and went to check on the coffee. It was ready, but by this time, she felt she was able to stand again, so she insisted on serving it. While they paused to test the quality of Flint's coffee, he noticed a faraway look on Lucas's face. He was prompted to ask, "You look like you left us there for a minute. Is the coffee that bad or is it that good?"

"I'm thinkin' about that huge house out at Cloverleaf with nobody in it but Atha and Henry Cheney. And a cattle ranch is a heckuvalot better place to raise two rambunctious little boys than a town."

"I don't know," she said, hesitating.

Thinking he might know what was bothering her, he sought to ease her fears. "I know what you might be worried about, and I don't blame you. But I think I can put your fears to rest a little bit. When Dunellen started hirin' men, he went after some real bad characters to do his dirty work. That was one of the things he and your husband disagreed on. I was just lucky he had enough sense to know he was goin' to need some honest, hardworkin' cowhands to take care of his cattle. Those gunslingers are all gone now, and the cowhands workin' the Cloverleaf brand are honest, everyday hands." There was one exception, but he didn't mention Charley Tate because he was convinced Charley was all wind. He had to have someone to lead him into trouble, and now there was no one to fill that role.

Sipping his coffee and watching Lucas making his pitch, Flint decided he was winning the lady over. She was literally beaming by the time Lucas asked her again if she'd like to bring her two boys out to visit the ranch. She said she thought that would be a wonderful day for her children. "You'll do it, then?" She said yes. "Good. I'll send a young man into town one mornin' with a wagon to bring you and the boys back to the ranch. His name will be Tim Walker. Sheriff Moran will tell you that Tim is a well-mannered and trustworthy young man. Matter of fact, he's a good friend of the sheriff." Aside to Flint, Lucas said, "He confessed to me the other day." Back to Arleen, he said, "Just tell me what day you want to come visit."

Finding it hard to control her excitement over this unexpected blessing of good fortune, she tried to think which was best. "I need to talk about all of this with my father," she said. "So why don't we say day after tomorrow?"

"Fine," Lucas responded. "Day after tomorrow it is. I guess we can get out of your way now, but I wanna say it was a pleasure to finally get to meet you. And I should tell you that your husband was a well-liked man by all the workin' cowhands."

"Thank you, Lucas, I appreciate your saying that," she responded. "And I should tell you that Conan always spoke of you as a good man in a pit of evil vipers."

Flint led them out the front door then, wondering to himself if he had just witnessed the earliest stage of a courtship. He felt like it would be a good match.

He and Lucas rode back to the sheriff's office, where Buck walked outside to meet them. "How'd it go?" Buck asked. "I don't care, myself, but Ralph wants to know," he joked.

"I'm gonna send Tim Walker in to pick her up day after tomorrow," Lucas answered him. "She's gonna come out to the ranch and see if she'd like to join us out there."

"That's a helluvan idea," Buck replied. "Whose idea was that?"

"I guess it was mine," Lucas said. "So you can tell Ralph the meetin' went pretty well, considerin' I worked for the man who killed her husband."

"You gonna hang around long enough to get some dinner at Clara's?" Buck asked.

"No. Like I told Flint, I need to get back to the ranch and get the boys started on moving the main part of the herd

away from your little town here. It's come to my attention
that our cows aren't welcome here anymore."

Flint chuckled in response to Lucas's attempt at humor.
"That might put you in the runnin' for the Tinhorn Good
Neighbor Award."

He took his leave then, and as Lucas had promised
Arleen, Tim Walker showed up at the sheriff's office two
mornings later, driving a team of horses pulling a wagon.
Sitting in his customary seat by the window, Ralph saw him
pull up, and he alerted Flint. Flint went outside to say good
morning to the young cowhand. "You come to get Arleen
Daugherty?"

"Mornin', Sheriff. Yes, sir. Lucas sent me in to get her,
but I don't rightly know where Mr. Wheeler's house is. So
I thought maybe you would tell me how to find it."

"I'll go with you," Flint said, and climbed up to sit
beside him. "Just drive right on up to the hotel and take that
street that takes off to the right beside it. Then I'll show you
which house is Louis Wheeler's."

When they pulled up to the house Flint pointed out, they
heard Angus, who was standing in the doorway, yell out,
"Mama, they're here!"

Within a couple of minutes, Arleen came out with Brendan, locked the door, and asked, "Sheriff Moran, are you
going with us?"

"No, ma'am," Flint said and stepped down from the
wagon. "It was just easier to show Tim where your house
was." He helped her up into the wagon, then helped Brendan up into the wagon bed, where Angus had already
crawled. Then Flint climbed back up into the wagon to
stand behind the seat. "Tim, this is Mrs. Daugherty. Arleen,
meet Tim Walker." They exchanged nods of howdy-do, then
Tim turned his team of horses back the way he had come.

And they drove down Main Street to stop momentarily at the jail, where Flint hopped off.

"How do you see it?" Buck asked when Flint came back into the office. "You think she'll take his offer?"

"If she doesn't, she's crazy," Flint answered. "My money says she'll work out something with Lucas and the rest of the Cloverleaf crew."

"I don't know," Buck declared. "I ain't so sure she'll move into that big house where the man who killed her husband lived. And she's convinced he killed him."

"I reckon we'll just have to wait and see," Flint said. "I'm gonna take a walk around town, and by the time I get back, it oughta be about time for Clara to open up."

"Well, howdy, boys." Clara gave them a lusty welcome for no particular reason they could determine. "Boy, are we glad to see you, Flint," she added.

"Well, I'm glad to see you, too, Clara," Flint returned. "It has been a long time since breakfast."

"What about me?" Buck asked. "Are you glad to see me, too? Or just glad to see Flint?"

"Why, Buck, we're always glad to see you," Clara declared. "I just thought that goes without saying."

"All right, then," Buck continued the joking, "that makes more sense. And that means they're glad to see you just some of the time, Flint." They headed for their usual table, passing Bonnie on the way.

She was delivering a plate of food for a customer near the front door. As she swept past Flint, she said, "I'm sure glad you showed up today." And she kept going, offering no explanation for the comment.

"What's goin' on?" Flint asked Clara, who walked to the

table with them. "Have you ladies got a bottle of likker hid back there in the pantry?"

Clara laughed. "If you're as smart as I think you are, you'll figure it out."

"That ain't much help," he called after her when she turned around and went back to her post by the door. He looked at Buck for help and was met with the same puzzled expression he was wearing himself.

Mindy came to the table with their coffee as usual. "We saw you pass by on a wagon this morning," she said. "You were standing up behind the seat, and Louis Wheeler's daughter was sitting there. We wondered where you were going."

"I wasn't goin' anywhere," Flint said. "That was Tim Walker drivin' the wagon. You remember him, right?" She nodded. "He came into town to get Arleen to take her out to the Cloverleaf ranch to visit. He picked me up at the jail 'cause he didn't know where Louis Wheeler's house is."

"Oh," she replied, "so you didn't go to the ranch with her."

"No, I didn't go with 'em," he said as he reached for a hot biscuit. When he did, he happened to glance at Buck, who was grinning as if something was highly amusing. "What?" he asked, but Buck just shook his head and chuckled. Then he glanced toward the front door, where Bonnie and Clara had been standing talking. Now they weren't talking. They were both looking back at him and both smiling. Something was going on, he decided, and everybody was in on it but him. *Buck will tell me later*, he thought, and returned his concentration to his dinner.

They finished eating, then lingered over coffee for a little while, since there was nothing of any urgency to take care of. It appeared Tinhorn was presently enjoying a peaceful period. Now that the town's biggest threat had been eliminated, maybe it could look forward to the natural growth of a profitable relationship with the Cloverleaf Cattle Company. And if Lucas Sawyer was a man of his word—and Flint was sure that he was—the sight of stray cattle in the street was a thing of the past.

"I expect we'd best take Ralph his dinner," Buck finally reminded Flint. "I'll see if Margaret has it ready." He got up and stepped inside the kitchen door while Mindy walked Flint to the front door, where Clara and Bonnie were gabbing.

"Got it ready to go," Margaret said when she saw Buck. "I was just about to call one of the girls." She brought the plate to him.

"She saw him go by in the wagon," Buck said and chuckled.

"Oh my yes, she did," Margaret said. "And all morning, she talked about how attractive that young widow is, and what a catch she would be for some young man. Thank goodness he showed up here for dinner. Does he have any idea how bad she's got it for him?"

"Not a clue," Buck said.

CHAPTER 24

They stepped outside the front door of Clara's Kitchen and paused to consider what a fine day it appeared to be in Tinhorn. "You know what, I think I'll . . ." That was as far as Buck got before they both heard the snap and felt the passing of the bullet between their heads, followed a fraction of a second later by the crack of the rifle that fired it. Neither man hesitated as Flint jumped off one side of the porch and Buck jumped off the other to take cover before the next round was fired.

When it came, Flint exclaimed, "Behind the post office!" Not waiting to give their assailant time to crank in the next round, he ran at once, angling across the street to let the post office block the sniper's line of sight. Moving quickly along the side of the post office, his six-gun in hand, he prepared to shoot at once when he reached the back corner of the building. Thinking the shooter must have seen him running to get behind him, he dropped down low to the ground to reduce the size of the target. Then he popped suddenly around the corner, only to catch a glimpse of the shooter as he retreated toward the river. "Buck! He's runnin' toward the river!" Flint shouted and took off after him.

Buck came out from under the porch and hurried down

the street to try to cut the sniper off. He thought he could make better time running in the street than the sniper could running through the shoulder-high weeds and brush between the street and the river. When he got to the jail, he saw Ralph standing on the front step. "Here!" he yelled at him and handed him his dinner plate. "Enjoy!" he shouted as he ran behind the jail, heading for the river. He and Flint arrived at the empty pen where Kelly had been keeping the cattle at almost the same time. But they were both too late to stop Charley Tate as he sprang up in the saddle and flogged his horse frantically in his effort to escape. "Damnit!" Buck swore and stopped, exhausted, as Charley raced through the brush at a gallop, flailing the bay gelding with his reins.

Not ready to give up, Flint kept running after the retreating dry-gulcher, thinking he still had a chance due to the roughness of the ground they were racing on, even though he was racing a horse. He left Buck, bent over with his hands on his knees, gasping for air.

Flint's gamble paid off, for Charley had not ridden fifty yards before the bay stumbled on a deep gulley overgrown with weeds and did a somersault, throwing Charley out of the saddle. Stunned, he sat there in the weeds for a few moments before it registered in his brain that the rustling of the bushes behind him was the sound of Flint coming after him. He thought about it for a second. This was his chance, the chance that Drew Price would have taken, to wait for Flint to catch up and face him with his six-gun ready. It was only for a second, however, for he remembered how fast Flint took Cash Kelly out. He took one look back at his horse lying suffering on the ground before he got up and started running.

Behind Charley, Flint came to the suffering horse, lying helplessly with both front legs broken. Not willing to leave the horse in that condition, he cocked his .44 and put one round in the horse's brain. Then he continued his pursuit. He was tired as hell, but at least he was no longer racing a horse.

Thirty yards ahead of him and almost to the street, Charley heard the gunshot and thought Flint had shot at him. Almost in a panic to escape now, he didn't know what to do. Then he saw the stable and knew he had to get a horse, so he headed straight for it. Had they gotten a good look at him? He couldn't say. So he didn't know if he was safe in running back to the ranch or not. If only he hadn't missed when Moran was standing right there on the porch of the dining room. His shot was just a little wide and passed right between Moran and Buck Jackson.

Free of the bushes now, he ran across the street and into the stable, where he caught Lon Blake by surprise, carrying two buckets of grain. Gasping for air, Charley said, "I ain't got time to mess with you." He held his rifle on the startled owner of the stable. "Set them buckets down and throw a saddle on that horse in the stall behind you or I'm gonna let this rifle walk all over you."

"I can't do that," Lon said, still holding the two buckets. "That horse don't belong to me."

Charley walked up close to him and threatened, "You damn fool! I'm fixin' to put a hole in your belly if you don't do like I told you." Lon just stood there for a few moments, staring back at Charley. Then, suddenly, he swung one of the buckets at Charley's rifle, knocking it out of his hand. They both scrambled for the rifle, but Charley was the first to reach it. "Now, you dumb peckerhead," Charley roared, "that just cost you your life." He aimed the rifle at Lon and cocked it.

"Charley! Drop it or you're dead."

Startled, Charley turned and fired, but not soon enough

to avoid the bullet in his head. "Are you all right, Lon?" Flint asked the now-shaken stable owner.

"Yes, sir, I reckon I am, or I will be when I go find a clean pair of drawers," Lon answered.

"That was kind of a risky thing you did with that bucket of oats," Flint said.

"I couldn't let him ride outta here on that horse. That's the mayor's horse. I reckon if I'd known you were that close behind him, I woulda done what he told me to, and just took my time doin' it."

In a little while, Buck came staggering in, still trying to get his wind back. He called out for Flint before he walked in, just in case he had come in second. Flint yelled back that everything was over. Buck took a look at the body and nodded. "That is the one called Charley."

"That's right," Flint said. "Charley Tate. He was the last of that bunch with Drew Price and his pals, according to Lucas. Lucas also said Charley wasn't likely to make any trouble on his own."

"Well, that weren't no trouble, was it?" Buck joked.

The town of Tinhorn enjoyed a peaceful afternoon after the final act in Charley Tate's life. If Flint and Buck had known how the full drama of Charley's life had played, they might have felt a sliver of compassion for the miserable little man. His role in life had been that of the idolizer of the really wicked men who preyed on honest folks, never to reach the status of the fast guns he so admired.

The two men who comprised the sheriff's department of Tinhorn were at the door of Clara's Kitchen as usual when she opened the door for supper. After a good meal of some Cloverleaf beef and a casual visit with the ladies who served it, they walked out of the dining room in time to see a team of horses pulling a wagon coming toward them. "That's Tim Walker bringin' Arleen and her young'uns home," Buck said.

Seeing the two lawmen, Tim pulled the wagon to a stop. "Well, I see you got back safe and sound," Flint greeted them. "Did you have a good visit?" he asked Arleen.

She favored him with a great big smile. "I guess you would have to say we did," Arleen answered him, but offered little more.

Flint was a little disappointed by her brief response because he had an idea that Lucas was really hoping she might like it enough to make it permanent. "I reckon it woulda been kinda hard to get much of a feel for a strange place after a visit that short. Maybe you might want to take a couple more visits to really get to know the folks out there."

She laughed and shook her head. "I'm not planning any more visits. Tim is coming back for me day after tomorrow, when we'll load all my stuff in the wagon."

"Well, I'll be . . ." Buck started. "Did you meet that couple that live in the house?"

"I sure did. That's the reason I have to move in right away. Atha insisted that I had to come help her run that big house. I told her I had to tell my father, and that's the only reason we're waiting until day after tomorrow."

"You think your dad will be upset to see you move out there?" Flint asked,

"Are you joking?" Arleen replied. "He'll be delighted to have his little house back. And we'll only be six miles away. That's a lot better than when Conan and I lived near Houston."

"Well, that sure is good news," Flint said. "It'll sure be a better place for you boys," he said to Angus. Then back to her, he said, "We won't hold you up any longer, so Tim can get back home."

Flint noticed that Tim kept a big grin on his face while Arleen gave the news to Flint and Buck. When it appeared the conversation was finished, he spoke up. "Lucas said we'd better get used to callin' Miz Arleen Boss Lady."

"Is that so?" Buck asked.

"Not entirely true," a smiling Arleen explained. "Lucas decided I was the legal owner of the ranch, but I said we should all own it. They all insisted that I should at least be half owner, and they would all split the other half."

"That sure sounds like the right thing to do," Flint commented. "I hope you appreciate what a good man you've got to run that ranch for you."

"I do, indeed," she said.

"I swear," Buck said as the wagon pulled away, "ain't it strange sometimes when things work out like a body would hope they would?"

"I reckon," Flint said. "You gonna take a drink of likker before you go to bed?"

"Yessir," Buck replied. "I think this thing today calls for one."

"Good," Flint said. "'Cause I think I'll have one with you."

WILLIAM W. JOHNSTONE
and J. A. Johnstone

BRANNIGAN'S LAND
MEAN AND EVIL

**Ex-lawman turned cattle rancher
Ty Brannigan loves his wife and children.
And may Lord have mercy on those
who would harm them—
because Ty Brannigan will show none.**

No one knows their way around a faro table, bank vault,
or six-shooter more than Smilin' Doc Ford.
When he's not gambling or thieving,
he's throwing lead—or, if he's feeling especially vicious,
slitting throats with his Arkansas toothpick.
Roaming the West with Doc is a band of wild outlaws
including a pair of hate-filled ex-cons and the voluptuous
Zenobia "Zee" Swallow, Doc's kill-crazy lady.

The gang have been on a killing spree, leaving a trail
of bodies near Ty Brannigan's Powderhorn spread
in Wyoming's Bear Paw Mountains. U.S. Marshals want
Ty to help them track down Smilin' Doc's bunch.
But when the hunt puts the Brannigan clan in the outlaws'
sights, Ty and his kin take justice into their own hands—
and deliver it with a furious, final vengeance.

CHAPTER 1

"I declare it's darker'n the inside of a dead man's boot out here!" exclaimed Dad Clawson.

"It ain't dark over here by the fire," countered Dad's younger cow-punching partner, Pete Driscoll.

"No, but it sure is dark out here." Dad—a short, bandy-legged, gray-bearded man in a bullet-crowned cream Stetson that had seen far better days a good twenty years ago—stood at the edge of the firelight, holding back a pine branch as he surveyed the night-cloaked Bear Paw Mountain rangeland beyond him.

"If you've become afraid of the dark in your old age, Dad, why don't you come on over here by the fire, take a load off, and pour a cup of coffee? I made a fresh pot. Thick as day-old cow plop, just like you like it. I'll even pour some of my who-hit-John in it if you promise to stop caterwaulin' like you're about to be set upon by wolves."

Dad stood silently scowling off into the star-capped distance. Turning his head a little to one side, he asked quietly in a raspy voice, "Did you hear that?"

"Hear what?"

"That." Dad turned his head a little more to one side. "There it was again."

Driscoll—a tall, lean man in his mid-thirties and with a

thick, dark-red mustache mantling his upper lip—stared across the steaming tin cup he held in both hands before him, pricking his ears, listening. A sharpened matchstick drooped from one corner of his mouth. "I didn't hear a thing."

Dad turned his craggy, bearded face toward the younger man, frowning. "You didn't?"

"Not a dadgum thing, Dad." Driscoll glowered at his partner from beneath the broad brim of his black Stetson.

He'd been paired with Clawson for over five years, since they'd both started working at the Stevens' Kitchen Sink Ranch on Owlhoot Creek. In that time, they'd become as close as some old married couples, which meant they fought as much as some old married couples.

"What's gotten into you? I've never known you to be afraid of the dark before."

"I don't know." Dad gave his head a quick shake. "Somethin's got my blood up."

"What is it?"

Dad glowered over his shoulder at Driscoll. "If I knew that, my blood wouldn't be up—now, would it?"

Driscoll blew ripples on his coffee and sipped. "I think you got old-timer's disease. That's what I think." He sipped again, swallowed. "Hearin' things out in the dark, gettin' your drawers in a twist."

Dad stood listening, staring out into the night. The stars shone brightly, guttering like candles in distant windows in small houses across the arching vault of the firmament. Finally, he released the pine bough; it danced back into place. He turned and, scowling and shaking his head, ambled back over to the fire. His spurs chinged softly. On a flat, pale rock near the dancing orange flames, his speckled tin coffeepot, which owned the dent of a bullet fired long ago by some cow-thieving Comanche bushwhacker in the Texas Panhandle, gurgled and steamed.

"Somethin's out there—I'm tellin' ya. Someone or some*thing* is movin' around out there." Dad grabbed his old Spencer repeating rifle from where it leaned against a tree then walked back around the fire to stand about six feet away from it, gazing out through the pines and into the night, holding the Spencer down low across his skinny thighs clad in ancient denims and brush-scarred, bull-hide chaps.

Driscoll glanced over his shoulder at where his and Dad's hobbled horses contentedly cropped grass several yards back in the pines. "Horses ain't nervy."

Dad eased his ancient, leathery frame onto a pine log, still keeping his gaze away from the fire, not wanting to compromise his night vision. "Yeah, well, this old coot is savvier than any broomtail cayuse. Been out on the range longer than both of them and you put together, workin' spreads from Old Mexico to Calgary in Alberta." He shook his head slowly. "Coldest damn country I ever visited. Still got frostbite on my tired old behind from the two winters I spent up there workin' for an ornery old widder."

"Maybe you got frostbite on the brain, too, Dad." Driscoll grinned.

"Sure, sure. Make fun. That's the problem with you, Pete. You got no respect for your elders."

"Ah, hell, Dad. Lighten up." Driscoll set his cup down and rummaged around in his saddlebags. "Come on over here an' let's plays us some two-handed—" He cut himself off abruptly, sitting up, gazing out into the night, his eyes wider than they'd been two seconds ago.

Dad shot a cockeyed grin over his shoulder. "See?"

"What was that?"

Dad cast his gaze through the pines again, to the right of where he'd been gazing before. "Hard to say."

"Hoot owl?"

"I don't think so."

The sound came again—very quiet but distinct in the night so quiet that Dad thought he could hear the crackling flames of the stars.

"Ah, sure," Driscoll said. "A hoot owl. That's all it was!" He chuckled. "Your nerves is right catching, Dad. You're infecting my peaceable mind. Come on, now. Get your raggedy old behind over here and—" Again, a sound cut him off.

Driscoll gave an involuntary gasp then felt the rush of blood in his cheeks as they warmed with embarrassment. The sound was unlike anything Dad or Pete Driscoll had ever heard before. A screeching wail? Sort of catlike. But it hadn't been a cat. At least, like no cat Dad had ever heard before, and he'd heard a few during his allotment. Night-hunting cats could sound pure loco and fill a man's loins with dread. But this had been no cat.

An owl, possibly. But, no. It hadn't been an owl, either.

Dad's old heart thumped against his breastbone.

It thumped harder when a laugh vaulted out of the darkness. He swung his head sharply to the left, trying to peer through the branches of two tall Ponderosa pines over whose lime-green needles the dull, yellow, watery light of the fire shimmered.

"That was a woman," Driscoll said quietly, his voice low with a building fear.

The laugh came again. Very quietly. But loudly enough for Dad to make out a woman's laugh, all right. Sort of like the laugh of a frolicking whore in some whorehouse in Cheyenne or Laramie, say. The laugh of a whore mildly drunk and engaged in a game of slap 'n' tickle with some drunken, frisky miner or track layer who'd paid downstairs and was swiping at the whore's bodice with one hand while holding a bottle by the neck with his other hand.

Dad rose from his log. Driscoll rose from where he'd been leaning back against his saddle, reached for his saddle ring Winchester, and slowly, quietly levered a round into the action. He followed Dad over to the north edge of the camp.

Dad pushed through the pine branches, holding his own rifle in one hand, his heart still thumping heavily against his breastbone. His tongue was dry, and he felt a knot in his throat. That was fear.

He was not a fearful man. Leastways, he'd never considered himself a fearful man. But that was fear, all right. Fear like he'd known it only once before and that was when he'd been alone in Montana, tending a small herd for an English rancher, and a grizzly had been prowling around in the darkness beyond his fire, occasionally edging close enough so that the flames glowed in the beast's eyes and reflected off its long, white, razor-edged teeth it had shown Dad as though a promise of imminent death and destruction.

The cows had been wailing fearfully, scattering themselves up and down the whole damn valley . . .

But the bear had seemed more intent on Dad himself.

That was a rare kind of fear. He'd never wanted to feel it again. But he felt it now, all right. Sure enough.

He stepped out away from the trees and cast his gaze down a long, gentle, sage-stippled slope and beyond a narrow creek that glistened like a snake's skin in the starlight. He jerked with a start when he heard a spur trill very softly behind him and glanced to his right to see Driscoll step up beside him, a good half a foot taller than the stoop-shouldered Dad.

Driscoll gave a dry chuckle, but Dad knew Pete was as unnerved as he was.

Both men stood in silence, listening, staring straight off down the slope and across the water, toward where they'd heard the woman laugh.

Then it came again, louder. Only, this time it came from Dad's left, beyond a bend in the stream.

Dad's heart pumped harder. He squeezed his rifle in both sweating hands, bringing it up higher and slipping his right finger through the trigger guard, lightly caressing the trigger. The woman's deep, throaty, hearty laugh echoed then faded. Then the echoes faded, as well.

"What the hell's goin' on?" Driscoll said. "I don't see no campfire over that way."

"Yeah, well, there's no campfire straight out away from us, neither, and that's where she was two minutes ago."

Driscoll clucked his tongue in agreement.

The men could hear the faint sucking sounds of the stream down the slope to the north, fifty yards away. That was the only sound. No breeze. No birds. Not even the rustling, scratching sounds little animals made as they burrowed.

Not even the soft thump of a pinecone falling out of a tree.

It was as though the entire night was collectively holding its breath, anticipating something bad about to occur.

The silence was shattered by a loud yowling wail issuing from behind Dad and Driscoll. It was a yapping, coyote-like yodeling, only it wasn't made by no coyote. No, no, no. Dad heard the voice of a man in that din. He heard the mocking laughter of a man in the cacophony as he and Driscoll turned quickly to stare back toward their fire and beyond it, their gazes cast with terror.

The crazy, mocking yodeling had come from the west, the opposite direction from the woman's first laugh.

Dad felt a shiver in Driscoll's right arm as it pressed up against Dad's left one.

"Christ almighty," his partner said. "They got us surrounded. Whoever they are!"

"Toyin' with us," Dad said, grimacing angrily.

Then the woman's voice came again, issuing from its original direction, straight off down the slope and across the darkly glinting stream. Both men grunted their exasperation as they whipped around again and stared off toward the east.

"Sure as hell, they're toyin' with us!" Driscoll said tightly, angrily, his chest expanding and contracting as he breathed. "What the hell do they want?" He didn't wait for Dad's response. He stepped forward and, holding his cocked Winchester up high across his chest, shouted, "What the hell do you want?"

"Come on out an' show yourselves!" Dad bellowed in a raspy voice brittle with terror.

Driscoll gave him a dubious look. "Sure we want 'em to do that?"

Dad only shrugged and continued turning his head this way and that, heart pounding as he looked for signs of movement in the deep, dark night around him.

"Hey, amigos," a man's deep, toneless voice said off Dad and Driscoll's left flanks. "Over here!"

Both men whipped around with more startled grunts, extending their rifles out before them, aiming into the darkness right of their fire, looking for a target but not seeing one.

"That one's close!" Driscoll said. "Damn close!"

Now the horses were stirring in the brush and trees beyond the fire, not far from where that cold, hollow voice had issued. They whickered and stumbled around, whipping their tails against their sides.

"That tears it!" Pete said. He moved forward, bulling through the pine boughs, angling toward the right of his and Dad's fire which had burned down considerably, offering only a dull, flickering, red radiance.

"Hold on, Pete!" Dad said. "Hold on!"

But then Pete was gone, leaving only the pine boughs jostling behind him.

"Where are you, dammit?" Pete yelled, his own voice echoing. "Where the hell are you? Why don't you come out an' show yourselves?"

Dad shoved his left hand out, bending a pine branch back away from him. He stepped forward, seeing the fire flickering straight ahead of him, fifteen feet away. He quartered to the right of the fire, not wanting its dull light to outline him, to make him a target. He could hear Pete's spurs ringing, his boots thudding and crackling in the pine needles ahead of him, near where the horses were whickering and prancing nervously.

"What the hell do you want?" Pete cried, his voice brittle with exasperation and fear. "Why don't you show yourselves, dammit?" His boot thuds dwindled in volume as he moved farther away from the fire, spurs ringing more softly.

Dad jerked violently when Pete's voice came again: "There you are! Stop or I'll shoot, damn you!"

A rifle barked once, twice, three times.

"Stop, dam—" Pete's voice was drowned by another rifle blast, this one issuing from farther away than Pete's had issued. And off to Dad's left.

Straight out from Dad came an anguished cry.

"Pete!" Dad said, taking one quaking footstep forward, his heart hiccupping in his chest. "*Pete!*"

Pete cried out again. Running, stumbling footsteps sounded from the direction Pete had gone. Dad aimed the rifle, gazing in terror toward the sound of the footsteps growing louder and louder. A man-shaped silhouette grew before Dad, and then, just before he was about to squeeze the Spencer's trigger, the last rays of the dying fire played across Pete's sweaty face.

He was running hatless and without his rifle, his hands clamped over his belly.

"Pete!" Dad cried again, lowering the rifle.

"Dad!" Pete stopped and dropped to his knees before him. He looked up at the older man, his hair hanging in his eyes, his eyes creased with pain. "They're comin', Dad!" Then he sagged onto his left shoulder and lay groaning and writhing.

"*Pete!*" Dad cried, staring down in horror at his partner.

His friend's name hadn't entirely cleared his lips before something hot punched into his right side. The punch was followed by the wicked, ripping report of a rifle. He saw the flash in the darkness out before him and to the right.

Dad wailed and stumbled sideways, giving his back to the direction the bullet had come from. Another bullet plowed into his back, just beneath his right shoulder, punching him forward. He fell and rolled, wailing and writhing.

He rolled onto his back, the pain of both bullets torturing him.

He spied movement in the darkness to his right.

He spied more movement all around him.

Grimacing with the agony of what the bullets had done to him, he pushed up onto his elbows. Straight out away from him, a dapper gent in a three-piece, butternut suit and bowler hat stepped up from the shadows and stood before him. He looked like a man you'd see on a city street, maybe wielding a fancy walking stick, or at a gambling layout in San Francisco or Kansas City. The dimming firelight glinted off what appeared a gold spike in his rear earlobe.

The man stared down at Dad, grinning. He was strangely handsome, clean-shaven, square-jawed. At first glance, his smiling eyes seemed warm and intelligent. He appeared the kind of man you'd want your daughter to marry.

Dad looked to his left and blinked his eyes, certain he wasn't seeing who he thought he saw—a beautiful flaxen-haired woman with long, impish blue eyes dressed all in black including a long, black duster. The duster was open to reveal that she wore only a black leather vest under it. The vest highlighted more than concealed the heavy swells of her bosoms trussed up behind the tight-fitting, form-accentuating vest.

The woman smiled down at Dad, tipped her head back, and gave a catlike laugh.

If cats laughed, that was.

More movement to Dad's right. He turned in that direction to see a giant of a man step up out of the shadows.

A giant of a full-blooded Indian. Dressed all in buck-skins and with a red bandanna tied around the top of his head, beneath his low-crowned, straw sombrero. Long, black hair hung down past his shoulders, and two big pistols jutted on his hips. He held a Yellowboy repeating rifle in both his big, red hands across his waist. He stared dully through flat, coal-black eyes down at Dad.

Dad gasped with a start when he heard crunching foot-steps behind him, as well. He turned his head to peer over his shoulder at another big man, this one a white man.

He stepped out of the shadows, holding a Winchester carbine down low by his side. He was nearly as thick as he was tall, and he had a big, ruddy, fleshy face with a thick, brown beard. His hair was long as the Indian's. On his head was a badly battered, ancient Stetson with a crown pancaked down on his head, the edges of the brim tattered in places. He grunted down at Dad then, working a wad of chaw around in his mouth, turned his head and spat to one side.

Dad turned back to the handsome man standing before him.

As he did, the handsome man lowered his head, reached up, and pulled something out from behind his neck. He held it out to show Dad.

A pearl-handled Arkansas toothpick with a six-inch, razor-edged blade.

To go along with his hammering heart, a cold stone dropped in Dad's belly.

The man smiled, his eyes darkening, the warmth and intelligence Dad had previously seen in them becoming a lie, turning dark and seedy and savage. He turned and walked over to where Pete lay writhing and groaning.

"No," Dad wheezed. "Don't you do it, you devil!"

The handsome man dropped to a knee beside Pete. He grabbed a handful of Pete's hair and jerked Pete's head back, exposing Pete's neck.

Pete screamed.

The handsome man swept the knife quickly across Pete's throat then stepped back suddenly to avoid the blood geysering out of the severed artery.

Pete choked and gurgled and flopped his arms and kicked his legs as he died.

The handsome man turned to Dad.

"Oh, God," Dad said. "Oh, God."

So this was how it was going to end. Right here. Tonight. Cut by a devil who looked like a man you'd want your daughter to marry. Aside from the eyes, that was . . .

As though reading Pete's mind, the handsome man

grinned down at him. He shuttled that demon's smile to the others around him and then stepped forward and crouched down in front of Dad.

The last thing Dad felt before the dark wing of death closed over him was a terrible fire in his throat.

CHAPTER 2

"You think those rustlers are around here, Pa?" Matt Brannigan asked his father.

Just then, Tynan Brannigan drew his coyote dun to a sudden stop, and curvetted the mount, sniffing the wind. "I just now do, yes."

"Why's that?" Matt asked, frowning.

Facing into the wind, which was from the southwest, Ty worked his broad nose beneath the brim of his high-crowned tan Stetson. "Smell that?"

"I don't smell nothin'."

"Face the wind, son," Ty said.

He was a big man in buckskins, at fifty-seven still lean and fit and broad through the shoulders, slender in the hips, long in the legs. His tan face with high cheekbones and a strawberry blond mustache to match the color of his wavy hair which hung down over the collar of his buckskin shirt, was craggily handsome. The eyes drawn up at the corners were expressive, rarely veiling the emotions swirling about in his hot Irish heart; they smiled often and owned the deeply etched lines extending out from their corners to prove it.

Ty wasn't smiling now, however. Earlier in the day, he and Matt had cut the sign of twelve missing beeves as well as the horse tracks of the men herding them. Of the long-looping *devils* herding them, rather. Rustling was no laughing matter.

Matt, who favored his father though at nineteen was not as tall and was much narrower of bone, held his crisp cream Stetson down on his head as he turned to sniff the wind, which was blowing the ends of his knotted green neckerchief as well as the glossy black mane of his blue roan gelding. He cut a sidelong look at his father and grinned. "Ah."

"Yeah," Ty said, jerking his chin up to indicate the narrow canyon opening before him in the heart of west-central Wyoming Territory's Bear Paw Mountains. "That way. They're up Three Maidens Gulch, probably fixin' to spend the night in that old trapper's cabin. The place has a corral so they'd have an easy time keeping an eye on their stolen beef."

"On *our* beef," Matt corrected his father.

"Good point." Ty put the spurs to the dun and galloped off the trail they'd been on and onto the canyon trail, the canyon's stony walls closing around him and Matt galloping just behind his father. The land was rocky so they'd lost the rustlers' sign intermittently though it was hard to entirely lose the sign of twelve beeves on the hoof and four horseback riders.

A quarter mile into the canyon, the walls drew back and a stream curved into the canyon from a secondary canyon to the east. Glistening in the high-country sunlight and sheathed in aspens turning yellow in the mountain fall, their wind-jostled leaves winking like newly minted pennies, the stream hugged the trail as it dropped and turned hard and flinty then grassy as it bisected a broad meadow then became hidden from Ty and Matt's view by heavier pines on their right.

The forest formed the shape of an arrow as it cut down

from the stream toward Ty and Matt. That arrow point crossed the trail a hundred yards ahead of them as they followed the trail through the forest fragrant with pine duff and moldering leaves.

At the edge of the trees, Ty drew the dun to a halt. Matt followed suit, the spirited roan stomping and blowing.

Ty gazed ahead at a rocky saddle rising before them a hundred yards away. Rocks and pines and stunted aspens stippled the rise and rose to the saddle's crest.

"The cabin's on the other side of that rise," he said, reaching forward with his right hand and sliding his Henry repeating rifle from its saddle sheath.

Both gun and sheath owned the marks of time and hard use. Ty had used the Henry during his town taming years in Kansas and Oklahoma, and the trusty sixteen-shot repeater had held him in good stead. So had the stag-butted Colt .44 snugged down in a black leather holster thonged on his buckskin-clad right thigh.

The thong was the mark of a man who used his hogleg often and in a hurry, but that was no longer true. Ty had been ranching and raising his family in these mountains for the past twenty years, ever since he'd met and married his four children's lovely Mexican mother, the former Beatriz Salazar, sixteen years Ty's junior.

He no longer used his weapons anywhere near as much as when he'd been the town marshal of Hayes or Abilene, Kansas or Guthrie, Oklahoma. Only at such times as now, when rustlers were trying to winnow his herd, or when old enemies came gunning for him, which had happened more times than he wanted to think about. At such times he always worried first and foremost for the safety of his family.

His family's welfare was paramount.

That's what he wanted to talk to Matt about now . . .

He turned to his son, who had just then slid his own Winchester carbine from its saddle sheath and rested it across his thighs. "Son," Ty said, "there's four of 'em."

"I know, Pa." Matt levered a round into his Winchester's action, then off-cocked the hammer. He grinned. "We can take 'em."

"If this were a year ago, I'd send you home."

Again, Matt grinned. "You'd try."

Ty laughed in spite of the gravity of the situation he found himself in—tracking four long-loopers with a son he loved more than life itself and wanted no harm to come to. "You and your sister," Ty said, ironically shaking his head. He was referring to his lovely, headstrong daughter, MacKenna, who at seventeen was two years younger than Matt but in some ways far more worldly in the ways seventeen-year-old young women can be and more worldly than boys and even men.

Especially those who were Irish mixed with Latina.

Mack, as MacKenna was known by those closest to her, was as good with a horse and a Winchester repeating rifle as Matt was, and Matt knew it. Sometimes Ty thought she was as good with the shooting irons as he himself was. Part of him almost wished she were here.

"You're nineteen now," Ty told Matt.

"Goin' on twenty," Matt quickly added.

"Out here, that makes a man." Ty jerked his head to indicate the saddle ahead of them. "They have a dozen of our cows, and they can't get away with them. They have to be taught they can't mess with Powderhorn beef. If we don't teach 'em that, if they get away with it—"

"I know, Pa. More will come. Like wolves on the blood scent."

"You got it." Ty narrowed one grave eye at his son. "I want you to be careful. Take no chances. If it comes to shootin', and we'd best assume it will because those men likely know what the penalty for rustling is out here, remember to breathe and line up your sights and don't hurry your shots or you'll pull 'em. But for God sakes when you need to pull your head down, pull it down!"

"You know what, Pa?" Matt asked, sitting up straight in his saddle, suddenly wide-eyed, his handsome face showing his own mix of Irish and Latin, with his olive skin, light brown hair which he wore long like his father, and expressive, intelligent tan eyes.

"What?"

"A few minutes ago, I wasn't one bit scared," Matt said. "In fact, I was congratulatin' myself, pattin' myself on the back, tellin' myself how proud I was that I was out here trackin' long-ropers with the great Ty Brannigan without threat of makin' water in my drawers. But now I'm afraid I'm gonna make water in my drawers! So, if you wouldn't mind, could we do what needs doin' before I lose my nerve, pee myself, an' go runnin' home to Ma?"

He kept his mock-frightened look on his father for another three full seconds. Suddenly, he grinned and winked, trying to put the old man at ease.

Ty chuckled and nudged his hat up to scratch the back of his head. "All right, son. All right. I just had to say that."

"I know you did, Pa."

Ty sidled his mount up to Matt's handsome roan, took his rifle in his left hand and reached out and cupped the back of Matt's neck in his gloved hand, pulling him slightly toward him. "I love you, kid," he said, gritting his teeth and hardening his eyes. "If anything ever happened to you . . ."

Feeling emotion swelling in him, threatening to fog his eyes, he released Matt quickly, reined the dun around, and booted it on up the trail.

Matt smiled after his father then booted the roan into the dun's sifting dust.

Ten minutes later, father and son were hunkered down behind rocks at the crest of the saddle. Their horses stood ground-reined twenty feet down the ridge behind them.

Ty was peering through his spyglass into the valley on the saddle's other side, slowly adjusting the focus. The old trapper's cabin swam into view—a two-story, brush-roofed, age-silvered log hovel hunkered in a meadow on the far side of a creek rippling through a narrow, stony bed.

The cabin was flanked by a lean-to stable and a pole corral in which all twelve of his cows stood, a few chewing hay, others mooing nervously. Five horses milled with the cattle, also eating hay or munching grass that had grown high since the place had been abandoned many years ago. That fifth horse might mean five instead of four men in the cabin. One man, possibly whoever was buying the stolen beef, might have met the others here with the cows. Ty would have to remember that.

A half-breed named Latigo He Who Rides had lived there—an odd, quiet man whom Ty had met a few times when he'd been looking for unbranded mavericks that had avoided the previous roundup. He had never known what had happened to He Who Rides.

One year on a trek over to this side of the saddle he'd simply found the cabin abandoned. It had sat mostly abandoned ever since, except when rustlers or outlaws on the run used it to overnight in. It was good and remote, and known only by folks like Ty who knew this eastern neck of the mountains well.

Rustlers had moved in again, it looked like. Ty had a

pretty good idea who they were led by, too. A no-account scoundrel named Leroy Black. His brother Luther was probably here, as well. They were known to have rustled in the area from time to time, selling the stolen beef to outlaw ranchers who doctored the brands or to packers who butchered it as soon as the cows were in their hands.

Knowing the Blacks were rustling and being able to prove it, however, were two separate things.

The Black boys were slippery, mostly moved the cattle at night. They were probably working with their cousins, Derrick and Bobby Dean Barksdale. The Blacks and Barksdales made rustling in the Bear Paws and over in the nearby Wind Rivers a family affair. That they were moving beef in the light of day meant they were getting brash and would likely get brasher.

Ty grimaced, his cheeks warming with anger. Time to put them out of business once and for all.

Ty handed the spy glass to Matt hunkered beside him, staring through a separate gap between the rocks. "Have a look, son. Take a good, careful look. Get a good sense of the layout before we start down, and note the fifth horse in the corral. The odds against us likely just went up by one more man. We'll need to remember that."

"All right, Pa." Matt took the spyglass, held it to his eye, and adjusted the focus. He studied the cabin and its surroundings for a good three or four minutes then lowered the glass and turned to his father, frowning. "They don't have anyone on watch?"

Ty shook his head. "Not that I could see. They've gotten overconfident. That works in our favor."

"We gonna wait till dark? Take 'em when they're asleep?"

Ty shook his head. "Too dangerous. I like to know who I'm shooting at." He glanced at the sun. "In about an hour, the sun will be down behind the western ridges. It'll be dusk in that canyon. That's when we'll go. Knowing both the Blacks and Barksdales like I do, they'll likely be good and drunk by then."

Matt nodded.

Ty dropped to his butt and rested back against one of the large rocks peppering the ridge crest. He doffed his hat, ran a big, gloved hand brusquely through his sweat-damp hair. "Here's the hard part."

"The hard part?"

"Waiting. Everyone thinks lawdogging is an exciting profession. Truth to tell, a good three-quarters of it is sitting around waiting for something to happen."

"Good to know," Matt said. "In case I ever start thinkin' about followin' in my old man's footsteps."

"Forget it," Ty said, smiling. "You're needed at the Powderhorn. That's where you're gonna get married and raise a whole passel of kids. We'll add another floor to the house." Suddenly, he frowned, pondering on what he'd just said. "That is what you'd like to do—isn't it, Matt?"

A thoughtful cast came to Matt's eyes as he seemed to do some pondering of his own. Finally, he shrugged, quirked a wry half-smile, and said, "Sure. Why not?"

Ty studied his oldest boy. He'd always just assumed, since Matt had been a pink-faced little baby, that the boy would follow in Ty's footsteps. His ranching footsteps. Not his lawdogging footsteps.

Now he wondered if he'd made the wrong assumption. His own father had assumed that Ty would follow in Killian Brannigan's own footsteps as a mountain fur trapper and hide hunter. That they'd continue to work together in the Rockies, living in the little cabin they shared with Ty's hard-working mother halfway up the Cache la Poudre

Canyon near La Porte in Colorado. Killian Brannigan had been hurt when Ty had decided to go off to the frontier army and fight the Indians and then, once he'd mustered out, pin a badge to his chest. One badge after another in wide-open towns up and down the great cattle trails back when Texas beef was still being herded to the railroad hubs in Kansas and Oklahoma.

Those years had been the heyday of the Old Western gunfighter, so Ty, too, had had to become good with a gun.

Despite what Ty had said to Matt about lawdogging being three-quarters boredom, it had been an exciting time in his life. While he'd visited his parents often, he'd never regretted the choice he'd made. Being a mountain man and working in tandem with his mountain woman, Ciara Brannigan, pronounced "Kee-ra," had been his father's choice. Killian and Ciara had both been loners by nature and had preferred the company of the forests and rivers to that of people. While Ty had loved his parents and enjoyed his childhood hunting and trapping and hide-tanning alongside his mother and father, he'd been ready to leave the summer he'd turned seventeen.

And leave he had.

Now he realized he should have known better than to assume that his own son would want to follow in his own ranching footsteps. It wasn't a fair assumption to make. And now Ty wondered, a little skeptically as he continued to study his son, if he'd been wrong. He hoped he wasn't, but he might be. If so, like his own father before him, he'd have to live with the choice his son made. That time was right around the corner, too, he realized with a little dread feeling like sour milk in his belly.

He just hoped Matt didn't make Ty's own first choice.

He didn't want his son to be a lawman. He wanted him to stay home and ranch with Ty and the boy's mother, Beatriz.

Time passed slowly there on the top of that saddle.

The sun angled westward. Deep purple shadows angled out from the western ridges. Bird song grew somnolent.

Ty kept watch on the cabin. While he did, two of the four men came outside, separately and at different times, to make water just off the dilapidated front stoop. Another came out to empty a wash pan. That man came out the cabin's back door a few minutes later to walk over to the corral and check on the cattle that were still mooing and grazing uneasily. That was one of the Barksdale brothers clad in a ragged broadcloth coat and floppy-brimmed felt hat. He wore two pistols on his hips and held a Winchester in his hands.

On the way back to the cabin, he took a good, long, cautious look around. Then he reentered the cabin through the back door.

While Ty kept watch, Matt rested his head back against a rock, tipped his hat down over his face, and dozed.

Finally, Ty put his spyglass away and touched his son's arm. "Time to go, son," he said. "Sun's down."

He picked up his rifle and looked at Matt, who yawned, blinking his eyes, coming awake. He wanted to tell the kid to stay here, out of harm's way, but he couldn't do it. Matt wouldn't have listened, and he shouldn't have. He wasn't a kid anymore. He was almost twenty and he was part of a ranching family. That meant he, like Ty, had to protect what was his.

Ty hoped like hell they got through this all right. If anything happened to that kid, his mother would never forgive Ty and Ty would never forgive himself.